Ian's blood seeped from the gashes in his side onto the gray, weathered floor. This time I couldn't heal him. I could only free him. Outside, in the strangely bright sunshine of a North Carolina morning, things you don't want to imagine in your worst nightmares tried to rip the building's big windows out of their aging brick sills.

Downstairs, the broad chestnut doors of the old Asheville Bible printing shop bulged inward as Pig Face slammed it again. The wood began to splinter.

I cocked the pistol. Everything inside me screamed against pointing it at Ian's heart. I hated his body; I ought to be able to kill that body without caring.

I knelt over Ian, straddling him. I put both hands on the shaking gun to steady my aim. My tears fell on his blood-stained face.

He managed a rueful smile. "Now, that's a sight I'll remember to death and back," he whispered. He clamped one bloody hand on mine. As always, we shared the choices, the pain, the passage.

We had found each other again, across centuries. Why hesitate on a single sunny day in North Carolina?

"See you later," I said hoarsely.

I pulled the trigger.

About Leigh Bridger

Leigh Bridger is the pen name for New York *Times* bestselling women's fiction author Deborah Smith (A PLACE TO CALL HOME, Bantam Books, ON BEAR MOUNTAIN, Little, Brown & Company, and A GENTLE RAIN, BelleBooks.)

As Leigh Bridger, Smith writes the Solomon's Seal miniseries and the Soul Catcher series.

Visit her at www.leighbridger.com

Soul Catcher

Book One: The Outsider Trilogy

by

Leigh Bridger

Bell Bridge Books

This is a work of fiction. Names, characters, places and incidents are either the products of the author's imagination or are used fictitiously. Any resemblance to actual persons (living or dead,) events or locations is entirely coincidental.

Bell Bridge Books
PO BOX 30921
Memphis, TN 38130
ISBN: 978-0-9821756-8-2

Bell Bridge Books is an Imprint of BelleBooks, Inc.

Printed and bound in the United States of America.

We at BelleBooks enjoy hearing from readers. You can contact us at the address above or at BelleBooks@BelleBooks.com

Visit our websites – www.BelleBooks.com and www.BellBridgeBooks.com.

10 9 8 7 6 5 4 3 2

Cover design: Debra Dixon
Interior design: Hank Smith
Photo credits: Girl - Branislav Ostojic @ Fotolia
                  City - Rolff Images @ Dreamstime
                  Flame & Texture - Rolff Images @ Dreamstime
:Le:01:

Dedication

For DD, my best friend, business partner, editor, adopted sister, and the only person who answers my emails at 2 a.m. For Myra and Myra Ann, the sisters I was fortunate enough to win in the marriage lottery. And for my husband, Hank, who has been my Soul Hunter since we started sitting beside one another on the bus in ninth grade. We didn't speak—we are, after all, natives of the Geek Tribe—so we just sat there in silence, until college. But we knew it was love.

Esse Quam Videri, "To Be, Rather Than To Seem."

— *North Carolina state motto*

1

Paint them. Trap them. Burn them.

I found those words scrawled in jagged lines on the wooden floor beside my bed one morning when I was seven years old. A jar of my white tempera paint sat open beside them, its contents reduced to a dry, lumpy dough. I was already an avid artist, smearing watercolor scenes of the Appalachian Mountains of western North Carolina and flowers and portraits of my dolls on broad sheets of cheap paper Momma bought for me.

We lived in Ludaway, a tiny town high in the mountains an hour north of Asheville, not much more than a post office, a grocery store, a gas station and two churches. The kind of town where ghosts and secrets thrive, and unspeakable acts are forgotten or turned into charming legends.

Momma loved my paintings and taped them on the fridge, the doors, and, when I painted a smiling portrait of her and Daddy and my baby brother, Alex, she taped that one on the dresser mirror in hers and Daddy's bedroom, next to Daddy's UNC Tar Heels football stickers and Momma's pictures of her cuddling me and Alex.

"My Livia sees the world in such sweet ways," she told people. "She has a special vision of beauty."

But not that morning. I stared at the strange words, then looked in shock at the crust of white tempera on my own fingertips.

I had painted the words in my sleep.

Paint who, trap what, burn why?

I ran through the house, found Momma standing very still and strange in her oversized sweater and skinny jeans, her bare feet making sweat marks on the kitchen's checkerboard linoleum floor. She stood staring at nothing outside the window over the sink. I pulled her by one hand to my bedroom.

"Paint 'em, trap 'em burn 'em, Momma. What's that *mean?* Why'd I paint this while I was asleep? I'm scared, Momma."

She recoiled as if I'd spit on her. Then she drew back a hand and slapped me so hard I careened off the Malibu Barbie sheets of my bed. I gaped up at her. Momma did not hit us. *Ever.* Her gray eyes had gone a color I'd never seen before, like rust. "*Momma?*"

Without a word she twisted a fist in my long, black hair and dragged me to the front hall. She shoved me into a coat closet of our small, clapboard house. Nearly suffocating among the overcoats and sweaters, I yelled, I begged, *What did I do wrong, Momma?*

"Conniving bitch," she said in a voice I'd never heard before.

Then she slammed the door shut.

Alex, only three years old, heard me pounding the door. He plopped down outside and jabbered at me worriedly. "Livvy, don' cry, Ize here. Mommy be back. Don't cry, Livvy. Love you, Livvy."

Daddy and his mother, Granny Belane, were off on one of their business trips, buying folk art from the secluded mountain folk, they said, which they resold to galleries throughout the South. They would never have let Momma hit me or put me in the closet, if they'd known. In fact, they couldn't have *believed* that beautiful, loving, kind, Carly Belane, who composed children's songs on an old guitar and loved to knit, quilt and sew, had suddenly turned into an abusive mother. I couldn't believe it myself. She had changed overnight, as if my words, painted on the floor, were a warning to us both.

While I continued to bang the door she scrubbed the floor in my bedroom and scraped flecks of white paint from the wood until her fingertips bled. She threw away all my paints and papers and brushes.

And then came the sounds of struggle. Of Momma's body slamming against the walls.

Alex wailed.

I bent my face to the streak of light at the bottom. "Stay here, close to me, okay, Bubba? It's okay. *Stay right here next to me.*"

He wiggled a hand under the door crack, and I stroked his fingers.

The house went stark silent. I heard Momma staggering down the hall. She collapsed outside the closet door, sobbing. "Something is happening to me," she said. "I'm sorry, Livia, I'm sorry, Alex. Babies. My babies. Something is wrong with me. Oh God. I don't know what it is. I'm trying to fight it."

I heard Alex mewl again, "Is all the bad gone, Mommy?"

"All the bad is gone, baby," she answered between heartbreaking sobs. "I'm so ashamed. Livvy, please don't tell Daddy. I swear this will never happen again."

I pressed my cheek to the door. "I won't tell him. I won't tell anyone. It's okay, Momma."

She let me out then. Her peculiar *spell* was over. She begged me to never again say or write the words I'd painted on the floor. I hugged her legs and cried and promised I would not, although I was scared *of* her and *for* her. Hard new lines carved her pretty face; she cried and hugged me back. Her hands shook as the three of us ate ice cream in our pretty little kitchen, decorated with Momma's hand-sewn curtains and my innocent artwork, which now looked like postcards from some previous life.

How could I keep myself from painting in my sleep? I tried to shove the fear and confusion deep in my brain and forget it, the way children do. I loved her dearly and wanted to please her. I would not, could not, tell Daddy or Granny what had happened. I didn't understand it myself.

*

Momma returned to normal, or pretended to, when Daddy and Granny came home.

My tall, gentle father, Tom Belane, hoisted me into his arms and danced with me each time I ran to meet him. Then he would grab Momma, and kiss her, and she laughed and hugged him and turned her beautiful, kind face up to his, and he beamed at her with the most romantic look in his eyes.

He'll stop loving me if I tell him about her. Maybe he won't even believe me.

I was intimidated by Granny Belane, but I trusted her. I sat with her at nights on the back porch of our little house, struggling to tell *her* about Momma, but never able to say the words.

Momma acted as if the closet incident had never happened. But from then on I was always nervous; I stuck close to Alex, especially when Momma was near him. Moon-faced and cheerful, Alex was incapable of recognizing any emotion other than love. What if she went crazy again? He needed protection.

Yes. Beware.

In the gray light of dawn I stared in horror at those new words, gooey and pink, on my bedroom floor. A cake of my pink bath soap lay nearby, one end scraped flat. I looked at my hands, caked in dried pink soap.

Shaking, I snatched off my Smurf night shirt, spit on the floor to wet the pink words, and used the shirt to scrub the floor clean.

Momma had given me a wonderful Cinderella clock for my birthday. From then on I set Cinderella's alarm, and she woke me every morning before dawn. And every morning I got up in the dark, took a flashlight from under my pillow, and checked the floor for words.

I even hid my school supplies in a dresser drawer at night, with my pencils and ink pens tied tight with twine, hoping I couldn't find them in my sleep.

Not that I slept much, anymore.

*

Normal didn't last long. Over the next year or so, Momma began to suffer spells when she was alone with me and Alex. She would forget to cook meals; she would disappear on long walks, even in the worst weather. She would sit at the windows for hours, saying nothing, not moving. She would turn dark, strangely gleeful gazes on us, the way cats watch birds.

Worst of all by far, there began to come times when I

overheard her *growling* at invisible people. At least, they *seemed* to be people. She talked to them as if they were listening. *You can't protect her forever*, she said. And, *I'll bide my time*.

But every time Daddy and Granny Belane came home from their latest business trip, life went back to something like happy. Every time I verged on telling them about Momma's bizarre moments, love and fear stopped me.

As long as she didn't try to hurt me or Alex, I stayed quiet. I learned how to give her a certain look when she got a savage expression on her face, and she'd leave us alone.

I chewed my fingernails to bloody nubs.

*

One day, when I was nine and Alex, five, I caught Momma trying to shove him into the hall closet, just as she'd shoved me. Alex looked bewildered, and was struggling.

I grabbed a green marker from Daddy's office, and a notepad. Daddy used markers to color-code the inventory notes for his folk-art business. I ran back to the hall, where Momma was about to slam the closet door shut with Alex inside.

I swiftly drew a creature with a knotty head and claws, a green horror with its mouth open in a snarl, rows of jagged teeth dripping green drool. I couldn't say why the image of that thing came into my head. It was as if a potent *Knowing* suddenly channeled my hands.

I thrust the drawing at Momma. "*I see you*," I yelled.

Momma stared at that drawing with her eyes going furious, then scared, then dark and sad, like mirrors were shifting inside her. She clicked back to normal. Trembling, she looked down at her own hands as if she couldn't fathom being rough with Alex. She jerked the closet door open. "Baby, come out of there."

Alex bounded out, his face pale. "It's okay, Momma," he said, weaving his gaze from her to me. He looked startled but, as always, forgiving. "You were just playing."

I grabbed him and clamped the drawing to his chest, facing outward, like a shield. I glared up at Momma. The old words rose in my brain.

Paint them, trap them, burn them.

But . . . who was *them?*

"I'll keep this drawing, Momma. Just to help you remember what you look like when you're not feeling right."

Momma sagged. "I try to tell the doctor about these . . . feelings, but I can't make the words come. It's like a hand around my throat. Oh, honey, I don't want to be taken away from my family."

"I promise you, Momma, I won't tell anyone. Not so long as you behave."

Momma clutched her head in her hands and shuffled to her bedroom, as always, secluding herself behind a closed door.

I hid the drawing of the monster.

Somehow, that drawing would keep me and Alex safe from her.

At least for awhile.

I took to carrying my drawing all the time, wrapped in a plastic clingy sheet from the kitchen. I tucked it into a pocket of my shorts or jeans or, when I wore dresses, inside my panties, even as I slept.

Her spells got worse. I was outside in the back yard with her that fall, pounding little nails into our wooden fence on which to hang Christmas lights, when she suddenly turned toward me with her hammer aimed at my head, smiling. "Happy Holidays," she said in a voice like a rock grinder.

My heart froze. I didn't know what else to try so I said very quietly, "I've got that drawing on me right now."

Her hand spasmed. The hammer fell to the ground. She looked toward something only she could see. She made that grotesque *hissing* sound I'd heard before. Her eyes narrowed. She glared down at me. She went back inside.

I sat down on the lawn with the hammer clutched to my chest, and cried.

I felt an invisible hand stroke my head, but the comforting sensation only terrified me more. *Maybe I'm turning crazy like Momma.* Maybe I would start seeing people who weren't there.

Maybe, when I was in a mood like hers, my eyes would gleam with a shimmer like red stars in the dark.

Go away, go away, go away, I told the hand.

And it did, but trailed gentle fingers over my face as it disappeared.

*

I had to reach out to Granny. I had to try.

At night, the fields and farms of our valley spread before us like a broad moat stroked with lines of growth. Behind them, the high, round peaks of the mountains scalloped the blue-black sky. I regarded it as a secret world of terror and wonder, the future, the past, life itself, an untaught Waiting. In the twilight I listened in bewilderment to the muted sounds from my parents' bedroom, the gentle murmurs and laughter.

Was I the *only* one who saw Momma's dark side?

"Granny," I said on the porch one night, "One day a couple of years ago, I, uh, got this strange notion. And I drew a . . . a kind of *monster*. You think that's weird?"

Granny Belane's hand jumped. She flicked hot, red sparks off her cigarette into the night wind. Suddenly I could imagine ghosts floating down the mountainsides and from the deepest hollows, drawn to those tiny lights. "Have you drawn any more?" she asked.

"No, just the one. But I . . . one morning, before the monster painting, I woke up and saw I'd painted some words on the floor."

More sparks shivered off her cigarette. "Tell me."

I looked furtively toward the light in Momma and Daddy's bedroom window, then dropped my voice to a whisper. "*Paint them. Trap them. Burn them.*"

Granny crushed her cigarette on the arm of her chair. She watched the glow as it faded on the wood. I could hear her breathing hard. "Is that why you threw away all your paints and brushes?"

"Maybe."

She turned to me in the darkness. Her voice low and hard, she said, "Don't tell another soul what you just told me. I'll buy you some new art supplies. You are meant to paint whatever comes . . . *through* you. You should paint a picture of it, good or bad. It's important. Hide the paintings under your mattress. Don't tear them up, don't throw them away. I'll find out what you're meant to do with them. Do not," she repeated, "tell *anyone* about this."

"W-What about the first one I drew?"

"You've kept it?"

I nodded shakily. One hand moved to the pocket of my jeans.

"Good. That one is the most . . . " she hesitated.

"The most what, Granny?"

She took my hand. Carefully she said, "It's a clue to what scares you the most."

Thoughts of telling her about Momma fled before a new and different fear. Granny added more weight to my worries. Her fears showed there was substance to them. I was too afraid to ask more questions.

She bought me the art supplies, and I set them on the desk in my bedroom, and at night I laid on the covers staring at them, trying not to sleep. But I couldn't stay awake forever.

I began to paint in my sleep every night. Grotesque things. Wicked animals. Creatures that didn't exist. Some more human than not. Cinderella woke me every morning, and I cleaned up the spilled paint, the smears on my hands, the brushes scattered on the floor. Shaking, every morning I aimed the flashlight at the newest horror on my art pad.

Then I hid it under my mattress, with the others.

Every time she visited, Granny looked at the collection, her face stone-cold grim. "Good work," she said.

At night I *felt* the paintings trying to escape from beneath me. I dreamed about them coming to life, like a horror movie I couldn't erase. My bones got tired from trying to hold the fear down.

A soft, kind voice began to soothe me in the darkness. Not really male or female, a mix of both. I stared hard into the shadows each time but no one stood there. Just the voice.

This is where it starts, again, Livia. It is meant to be.
Again?

*

The next spring my beloved Daddy stumbled off a mountain cliff. He and Momma had gone up to Ludaway Ridge for a picnic on their eleventh anniversary. While she napped on a blanket, Daddy took a walk with his camera, as he often did, snapping pictures of the waterfall up there.

Somehow, he tripped and fell. By the time the volunteer fire department found him at the bottom of the falls, he was broken beyond fixing.

Momma retreated to her bedroom, her eyes like fractured silver marbles. Her grief was real; I never doubted that. It was why I never suspected her. My own heartbreak colored my view of things. I couldn't think straight. Daddy was gone.

Granny Belane, her eyes hollow with misery, moved in with us, because Momma couldn't care for me or Alex in her grieving state. Late at night I lay on the floor beside Alex's bed, where I took up guard duty after Granny went to sleep, and I heard Momma sob and shriek and mutter in hers and Daddy's bedroom.

Often she wandered the hall up to my locked room, then stopping at the open door of Alex's room, standing there for an hour or more, staring down at me on the floor, and him. Alex remained sound asleep on the bed. I remained wide awake, holding her gaze, my eyes strained to bursting, watching her dark eyes recede into her skull. Eventually she would walk back to her room slowly, methodically, her footsteps a metronome.

Eventually, I would doze, my face turned toward the doorway.

One day she didn't get out of bed. She stayed in bed *for months*. A psychiatrist visited from Asheville, prescribing anti-depressants and other drugs. People said she was heartbroken.

Parts of her were, yes. But the rest?

Granny sent me into Momma's room carrying her lunch on a tray, and I found Momma curled in a corner with one wrist

9

tied with a rope to the leg of her heavy, cherry wood dresser. She lunged at me with her eyes on fire and her teeth showing like a dog's. The rope stopped her like a kennel chain, jerking her up short. She snarled at me, and yet her free hand shoved at the air, pushing me away.

"Go away, *run*, honey," she gasped between animal sounds. Then she collapsed in a heap. I dropped the lunch tray and ran to get Granny. She would see, she would finally see.

"Mama's having a spell!"

But when Granny rushed into the room with me on her heels, she found Momma up on her feet, wiping the mayonnaise off the floor from my spilled sandwich, gathering the potato chips.

There was no rope.

"Livia gets upset so easily these days," Momma told Granny. "I'm all right. I got out of bed. Felt a little woozy. I must've looked like I was about to faint."

I stared up at her. Was she lying or did she not remember?

Momma smiled down at me sadly. It was her, the Momma I knew. Not a lie.

The *other* Momma had disappeared again.

That's when I got worse about the drawing and painting. That's when I started cutting myself.

"What's wrong with you, child?" Granny Belane said wearily. "You need to talk to me. You need to tell me what you're feeling, and what makes you so worried all the time."

I shook my head. It was all locked inside me by then, too hard for sharing.

Granny squatted in front of me. Her eyes bored into mine. "You can't run from what you are any longer. You're old enough to hear the truth, now."

"What am I?" I whispered.

"A soul catcher," she said.

Without any more explanation than that, she loaded me into her truck, and we headed for answers on higher ground.

*

There are energy vortexes in the Appalachians powerful

enough to conjure Godzilla out of a toilet in Tokyo. The vortexes around Asheville are party central for the dispossessed.

We drove into Preacher T's yard after bouncing over at least two miles of rutted dirt road along mountain ridges only the hawks and clouds could reach. What I saw made me tremble in my jeans and Rainbow Brite t-shirt. I could feel my black braid shivering down my back.

Preacher T had giant snakes in his yard.

They crawled from the carcasses of junked cars; they slithered from the roof of his run-down cabin; they lay in sinister piles, like puppies sleeping, in the dark eye of his barn loft. Some were made of metal car parts; others were linked pieces carved from wood. All were painted in mind-blowing bands of color, the brightest house paint an old man could buy or scrounge from the county dump. All had wide, all-seeing eyes.

And all had a white crucifix painted on their heads.

"Is he plain crazy?" I asked Granny.

"No, he's one of your spirit guides," she said. "You might as well know. He's up here hiding. Or else they'd have killed him by now."

They? My head whirled. They *who?*

Preacher T wasn't your regular North Carolina fire-and-brimstone preacher; he wasn't a preacher at all. He painted primitive art, folk art, outsider art, some called it. Outsider art bewilders most people, and some seem convinced it's a kind of devil worship.

It offers up a double-dose of doom and weirdness, and some of the artists who create it come off like homeless schizophrenics talking to invisible beings on street corners, preaching the soul's apocalypse. For sure, Granny's folk art cronies painted some bizarre-ass demons and unholy, weeping angels and devil-things. Plus they scrawled incoherent messages on their paintings and sculptures, like warnings encrypted in rambling Bible references.

"Warnings and illumination," Granny said. "That's what

this art is about." Postcards from a war zone. *Most Wanted* mug shots off the post office wall. Illustrations from the programming manual at GoodVersusEvil.com.

That's what I am, I thought. *An Outsider artist. Way, way outside.*

She locked the door of her big pickup truck and tucked a pistol in her macramé tote bag. "He's not crazy. But he's got the sight. And that makes people *think* he's crazy. Come on, Livia." She dragged me by the hand through that yard of huge, watchful snakes. "Don't be scared of the beast in its hard form; these hold the spirits of guardians. You can call them *angels* if that makes you feel better."

I didn't want to call them *anything.* I wanted to leave.

A huge old black man in paint-smeared overalls rose from a circle of large dogs and green-eyed cats on the cabin porch. Dark tattoos covered his arms and forehead, merging with his dark skin in places. Religious symbols and images from his art hung from every rail and rafter. I stared at spiked creatures with angel wings. They didn't look angelic to me.

The cats perched on old kitchen cabinets like the ripped-out kind you buy at salvage stores. Preacher T had painted them with symbols and strange animals. The disembodied cabinets made a fort around him. Behind him, an open screen door let me peek into a dark room crammed to the ceilings with paint cans, brushes, bolts of canvas, and tools.

"I've been waiting to meet this child a long, long time," Preacher T announced in a voice like a bear. I squinted at him. For just one moment he grew a black-bear snout and fur. "I see the light around her, Jeannie. Maybe this time she'll live long enough to become . . . "

Granny cut him off with a slash of her hand.

Live long enough to . . . live to . . . maybe this time I'd live? My head swam.

"She doesn't know what she is?" Preacher T growled.

"Godssake, Preacher, she's only ten. She needs help. I thought she had more time to grow up, but the spirit is already upon her. *She's painting them,* Preacher. Already. And now the girl has taken to cutting herself. Even when she's got paint on hand, she uses her own blood. She's done lots more paintings since Tom died. The other realms are already afraid of her, Preacher. I can feel them nosin' around."

"Have you got an inkling for the whereabouts of her soul hunter?"

Granny's face darkened. "No, he's lost, and I hope he *stays* lost. You know what it means when such as her doesn't want her soul hunter to come home. It means he betrayed her some how."

"Well, she gonna need him sooner or later."

Granny snorted.

Soul Hunter tucked itself in a distant corner of my brain, alongside Soul Catcher, not quite forgotten, but hidden under layers of worry.

Preacher T took my arm in a huge hand etched with words on the backs of every finger. PRAY. WATCH. GUARD. RESIST. He touched the fine cut marks in the cusp of my elbow. He studied me and my scabs a long time. Then he reached behind him, into a pile of whittled amulets, and pulled out an ankh on a leather thong. "This'll do for a start," he said, and slipped it around my neck.

Granny took the necklace off and handed it back. "She wears a cross, see here?" Granny lifted the small gold emblem that dangled from a chain near Rainbow Brite's cartoon face. "Here momma might be upset at un-Christian symbols. Poor Carly's got some mental . . . well, she's not feeling too good since Tom died. She gets upset easy. She's always been too gentle for her own good."

Preacher T scowled. "You better find another way then. This ain't no game. The good spirits are drawn to peaceful symbols. This child needs to lure all the help she can."

"What are y'all talking about?" I asked in a low, horrified voice.

Preacher T squatted in front of me. "Livia Belane, you're special. It's a gift or a curse, but you got it, either way. I know you don't understand now, but you will, child, I'm sorry but you will. You got to be strong. There are trials and tribulations for the holy, that's what the Bible and all the other good books tell us. You remember that, whatever happens, it's the spirits trying to push you this way or that. Try to think for yourself and whatever you do, don't stop your painting. What do you see when you paint pictures, child?"

"They're monsters. I've never seen anything like them in movies or comic books. Not even in Star Wars. I'm scared to sleep. I can almost hear them. And when I do fall asleep . . . that's when I paint them."

"Those are demons, child. Demons and their helpers. When you're grown up and powerful enough, you'll be able to see them outright. And not just demons. But angels, too. You'll know the difference."

"The things I paint are *real?*"

"Yes, baby. I'm afraid so."

Did this mean the drawing I'd made of Momma might be a demon?

I backed away. "I don't want to see them!"

Granny grabbed me and stroked my hair.

Preacher T made a soothing sound. "I know, child, but your soul chose this job for you, and it knows best." He looked at Granny. "Has she gotten any messages about her *way*, yet?"

Granny nodded. "She's been told to burn the paintings."

"Good." He smiled at me. "Now here's what you do, Livia. When you wake up and find that you've painted a demon during the night, you take that picture outside right quick! And you burn it."

He jerked his head toward Granny. "Your grandma'll help you with the chore. But you do it every single time, all right? 'Cause that's your way to send a demon out of this life forever. It's a banishment."

"We'll burn the paintings she's made already and all the ones from now on," Granny assured him.

"Good. What's happening, child, is that you're snaring demons in your art. Like you've set a rabbit trap in the woods, you understand? And once you catch one, don't you set it free again! No, ma'am. You got to banish it while it's trapped in your painting. Right quick."

He was telling a ten-year-old that the light behind the very air we breathe really does hold horrors. And that the green marker *thing* I'd drawn when I caught Momma pushing Alex into the closet might actually *live* inside Momma. But . . . if I'd trapped her demon already, how come it was still inside her? "Are they always trapped when I paint them? They can't hurt anybody anymore?"

"*If* you've seen them clear enough. You just a baby, it's amazin' that you even dream 'em clear enough to catch 'em, yet."

"You mean, if my painting isn't good enough then the demon is still runnin' around loose?"

"Well, yeah, but it's like you've put a ol' chain-gang ball on its leg. It ain't able to create as much trouble. It's held back. That don't mean it can't hurt nobody, just that it can't do as much damage as it would if it weren't hobbled by your painting. But I promise you, Livia, as you get older and your vision gets stronger, you'll see 'em better than you ever wish to, and you won't just slow 'em down, you'll trap 'em permanent, and then you'll send 'em to Nothingness. If you don't, they'll kill all who you love, and lots more besides."

Nausea boiled in my throat. *Momma had been the last person to see Daddy alive.* I gagged. "Did demons kill my daddy?"

"Yes, baby. Your daddy is one of your spirit guides. Demons always try to pick off the spirit guides first."

I exploded. "How come he didn't see the demons?"

"Spirit guides can't see 'em the way you can. They can get a *feel* for 'em, but smart demons can fool a spirit guide."

"He'd fight! My daddy wasn't tricked! He fell off the high falls at Ludaway Ridge. He tripped and fell!"

Granny turned me to face her. "No, Livia," she said in a low, sad voice. "While your sweet Momma was napping, demons lured him to the cliff, and they *pushed him.*"

I stared at her until I thought my brain would melt. *No, that demon inside Momma pushed him. It's tricking you, too.*

"Can a person have a demon inside them and still be a

person?" I whispered.

"Sometimes. Demons can take over fully, or they can take charge just part of the time. Depends on how strong the soul is that's wrestlin' with them."

"How do you get the demon out of a person?"

Preacher T and Granny traded a dark look. Preacher T patted me on the back. "Child, you ain't no demon."

They didn't suspect my point. Good.

Granny grasped my hand. "Do you understand, Livia? Don't be thinking there's something wrong with you. You're on the side of right and good. Okay?"

I nodded. "But if somebody *else* has a demon inside them, how would I get it out?"

They went quiet for a minute, then Granny said bluntly, "You have to kill the person's body, and then, when the demon shows its true form, you have to see it well enough to paint it quick and then burn the picture before the demon rips you apart. It's a hard trick to master."

"That's why the child needs to find her soul hunter to stand guard for her," Preacher T said grimly.

Granny glared at him and shushed him. "I'm tellin' you, there's got to be a good reason she's alone in this. You can't trust soul hunters all the time, you know that, Preacher."

"That's not how I see it."

My heart sank. I wasn't listening to them anymore. I stood there thinking, *I can't kill Momma. I can't. What if I'm wrong about her? What if she's just sick?* I gulped for air. "What if . . . I paint a drawing of a demon that might live inside a person? What if I burn the drawing? Doesn't that work?"

Preacher T shook his head. "No, baby. You can't banish a soul that's taken up haven in a living body of this world."

Granny stared hard in my eyes. "Don't you worry. We're gonna protect you until you're fully vested in your powers."

My breath shuddered. "Something touched me on the head last year. Something invisible. It . . . patted me. Like it was trying to make me feel better. And I've heard a voice at night. Telling me it's time to begin again. It sounds like a *nice* . . .

voice."

Preacher T grunted. "Good. You got some friends out yon, child. You can't see 'em yet, but they are fightin' for you in the other realms."

I looked at Granny for confirmation. She nodded. "You don't need to ask a lot of hard questions right now, baby. Just know that you're safe, I swear to you."

No, you don't see what's inside Momma, and I do.

If Momma had a demon in her, I just better hope my drawing of it was good enough to keep that demon on a chain. When I was grown and my powers got strong enough, I'd rescue her from the demon. Somehow.

Still, the thought that Momma might be *possessed* was too terrible. My brain sucked it deep and hid it in scar tissue. I pulled away then stumbled across the yard, halting in the middle of Preacher T's junk-art snakes. I looked at one of them, banded in white and purple with the white cross gleaming between its black eyes, and my vision blurred, and it seemed to me, it seemed at the time, *that the snake pulled back its lips and smiled at me.*

I screamed.

Granny grabbed me up, cooing. I went nearly limp in her arms. I felt as if my eyes would roll back in my head.

"The child's heard enough," Granny told Preacher T. She nuzzled my black hair with her cheek. "All you need to do for now is learn and grow," she whispered. "And don't stop painting."

Preacher T came down from his ramshackle front porch, his animals around him. "Jeannie Belane, you protect that child with every spirit symbol you can," he boomed. "I tell you, you do it now. This world is filling up with demons and they're getting worse every day. She's got a job to do and this time, by God, she better live to do it."

"I'll find a way," Granny promised. I was staring at the purple snake again. The one who'd smiled. It smiled again. Wider.

Preacher T looked from the purple snake to me. "She's

found her a friend, Jeannie. Good."

He went back inside, and when he returned he pressed a whittled miniature of the tiny purple snake into my sweating hand. At the center of its back was a bored hole with a small metal ring through it. "This little totem's name is Nahjee. That's how you say it. You spell it n-a-g-i. It's Hindu for 'snake.' Those Hindus, they say snakes are wise and know all about rebirth. Snakes shed their skins and start over. Snakes got *ancient* wisdom. Little Nahjee here won't steer you wrong."

Granny took off one of the many gold chains she wore, stuck its carved quartz pendant in her pocket, then threaded Nahjee onto the chain and clasped it around my neck.

The tiny wooden amulet instantly warmed the skin at the base of my throat.

"You talk to Nahjee," Preacher T said. "She'll listen. And she'll tell you things you need to know."

The snake charm seemed to move against my skin. So warm. Comforting. Strange, for a snake.

Hello, Livia, Nahjee whispered in my brain. *I will help you recognize danger, I promise. Because yes, your mother is battling a demon that wants to kill you.*

I vomited on myself, Preacher T, and Granny.

*

Granny drove me straight to Asheville from Preacher T's home. We bounced along narrow roads that wound around mountainsides like snakes. Everything was a snake, to me. I lay against the truck's passenger door with my face against the cool glass, unmoving. I didn't tell Granny what Nahjee had said.

Granny patted my leg. "Livia, hon, try to cheer up. Souls are like a diamond you can crack open and turn into lots of smaller diamonds, but then merge it back together. We're all pieces and parts of other souls attached to the core of our own. All that matters, Livia, is how much of you is the diamond, and how much of you is a chunk of coal, only fit for burning. I promise you, you have a good mission in life. Your Daddy wants you to do what you're doing. I promise. And your poor, sweet Momma doesn't know anything about all this, and she doesn't *ever* need to know. So don't you worry about upsetting her."

Pieces. Parts. Diamonds. Coal. *What parts of Momma are only fit for burning?* My head swam.

*

Asheville is necklaced by the French Broad and Swannanoa Rivers. Its back streets are narrow and filled with deep shadows. Its massive and gothic downtown buildings sink their foundations into ancient trails and the lost dreams of Cherokee Indians. Many gilded and violent lives have passed through the streets and the mists along the rivers. And many of those souls were still there.

The city was just starting to recover from decades of genteel poverty, beginning in the Depression. Many shops stood empty; boarded over, many streets were wind tunnels haunted by pigeons and trash.

Granny carried me into an alley where moss clung to damp drain pipes. I looked down woozily at stepping stones set with weird patterns of beads and colored glass. We ducked into a doorway beneath the stained glass symbol of a bleeding moon.

A young woman with long blonde dreadlocks and gold lame' leggings frowned at us over her tattoo machine. She was etching a marijuana leaf on her own forearm. Granny handed her money and they talked in long, hushed words. I didn't want to hear. My eyes drifted over walls of strange designs, fascinated. Nahjee curled tight over the fast pulse in my throat.

Don't look at those, Livia, Nahjee whispered. *Some of them draw banes.*

I didn't know what a bane was then, but I averted my eyes anyhow. If Nahjee kept talking to me. I'd better listen. Which seemed all right, considering. The blonde woman gestured. I curled on my side atop a softly woven rug on the floor, and Granny undid my long black braid and parted it vertically down the side of my skull, just above my left ear. She plucked the hair one strand at a time. Later, when I had the courage to lift my hair and look in a mirror, I saw a naked strip two inches long and an inch wide.

My brain hummed as the tattoo needle buzzed in my ear. Tiny symbols embedded themselves in me. A cross, a Star of David, an ankh, and other symbols, some so odd that Granny drew them on paper for the tattoo artist to copy.

I was marked now, or protected, or scarred, depending on your point of view.

When I got home I slipped into Momma's room and watched her sleep. Even drugged on psychiatric meds she looked uneasy and sad. But she was Momma, not some other creature, no matter what came and went inside her.

I don't know if you can ever save her, Nahjee whispered.

I laid a hand on Momma's arm gently.

One day, when I'm strong enough, I'll try.

*

We muddled along for the next few years. Momma remained sedated and distant, but except for a few worrisome moments she didn't scare me. Maybe because I could feel my own power growing; every night I painted in my sleep, and then Granny whisked the paintings away and burned them. I began to sense other spirits around me, good ones, their shapes forming in soft shadows. Still, I couldn't yet see the spirit world the way Preacher T and Granny said I would.

I was happy enough just keeping Momma's dark side under surveillance, waiting for the day when somehow I'd understand how to rescue her. Alex continued to be happy, comforting, my best friend. He began to turn handsome, like Daddy.

Then, when I was sixteen, a hiker found Preacher T beaten to death in his high-mountain yard, with all his snakes and his art in pieces around him. A month later, Granny Belane was shot in the head as she filled her truck's gas tank at a convenience store near Asheville.

The sheriff said it was robbery, but nothing was stolen.

They were gone. Both of my spirit guides, wiped out a month apart.

Was I strong enough to survive without them? Was I ready?

On the cold January night after Granny's funeral, I sat at

the kitchen table watching Momma wander the room. My skin prickled. From the den came the laser-gun sounds of *Street Blaster*, a video game Alex and I often played. Even Alex was subdued, now. He sat in the den in his coat and dark, dressy church suit, randomly firing the controls.

"Set your blasters on 'High,' morons," a voice called with a certain mechanical sarcasm. One of the many scripted commands uttered by the game's star character, a smug, sci-fi commando named *Leonidas*. "Get ready to attack the tri-level dungeon through the portal."

I kept my eyes trained on Momma. "How are you feeling?" I asked, trying to stay calm. Something was definitely not right with her.

She kept her back turned. My stomach twisted as her hands roamed over the thick handles of carving knives protruding from a wooden storage block. My heart raced. I slowly pulled a notepad and a pencil from the pocket of the overcoat I hadn't yet removed.

I laid the pad on the table.

I picked up the pencil.

Don't make me draw your demon, Momma.

Suddenly the air filled with shadowy forms, electrified.

"Kittycat," a voice shouted. It was Leonidas, the video game character. *Kittycat* was my screen name.

A video game character was yelling my video game name at me from the computer.

"What the heck?" Alex called. "Okay, Sis, how did you manage to program Leo to say your name?"

"Livia," Leonidas shouted. "Your mother has lost the game. The demon has taken over. *Kittycat, your mother is gone forever. Get ready to fight.*"

The thing inside Momma's body turned to face me, a knife in her hand. An ice-cold breeze froze my skin.

Then the demon hissed and leapt at me.

*

I came to a quarter of a mile away, in a neighbor's rural yard, with my hair in singed hunks around my face and the skin peeling off my burned feet. My feet were bare and blistered. I swayed and hugged myself, kneeling, sobbing, broken, ruined, dazed.

Paint them, trap them, burn them, kill them. Alex, Momma. I'm so sorry.

That's what I was chanting when the sheriff and the paramedics found me.

*

Firemen dug Momma's charred body out of the kitchen, along with Alex's. I couldn't tell anyone the truth; they wouldn't have believed me. That an unspeakably obscene creature had emerged from my mother's physical body, that I had dodged into my bedroom just barely ahead of its lethal grasp. That it had ripped my brother's chest open as he'd tried to defend me, and that the creature vaporized after I pulled a childhood drawing from my pocket and set it on fire with a cigarette lighter.

Nope. Not a believable defense.

Even I began to think I'd only dreamed seeing a demon, that I must be psychotic, though Nahjee kept telling me otherwise. I wouldn't listen, couldn't think straight. The authorities decided I was mentally ill and therefore, innocent of criminal charges. The forensics seemed to back up my claim that our mother stabbed Alex, but also indicated the fire was all *my* doing.

So they sent me to a psychiatric institution way over in the flatlands of Chapel Hill, where researchers from the university gave me heavy doses of anti-psychotics that still didn't keep me from painting demons with my own blood at night. I willed myself to *never* see another one in the flesh. Nahjee whispered to me from time to time, her tone sad. *Even if you do not allow yourself to see them, they are still there.*

"I paint them when I sleep. That's crazy enough," I told her.

Finally, after a couple of years, the doctors gave up, judged me harmless to anyone but myself, and let me out.

They were right. I could only harm myself.

*

I wandered to Asheville and lived on the streets, selling my hand-painted postcards of local scenes. It wasn't so bad being diagnosed as completely, totally delusional. I was used to it now. A highly functional schizophrenic. Possibly homicidal, but innocent by reason of insanity.

Better to explain my weird shit in those terms than to think the things I saw and did were rational reactions to my terrible memories, the questions that would never be answered, the everyday reality. Otherwise I'd end up gumming my oatmeal in a padded room again or dead under a bridge near a homeless shelter. No biggie.

I could handle self-destruction, either way. I tried to kill myself about a dozen times, but my hallucinations kept interfering. Angels, right. Hands that tugged and pulled me away from the gutter. Nahjee soothing, *Time will tell. You will find your way again.* I just didn't have the guts to off myself in a competent way. I'd have to keep practicing.

In the meantime, I collected tattoos like a squirrel collects nuts. I wanted to disappear under protective symbols so my imaginary friends and enemies couldn't see me hiding.

Soon images covered both my arms from shoulders to wrists. Cherubs, skulls. Momma and Alex's names, and Daddy's, Preacher T's and Granny Belane's. Celtic eternity knots, and Hindu symbols for protection. Barbed wire and daggers. Snakes, lots of snakes. And my favorite line from the 23rd Psalm. *Though I walk through the valley of the shadow of death . . .*

Many of the tattoos hid scars. Slash marks. A streak of burned skin inside my right wrist, from the fire.

And then there were the piercings: five in the right ear, six in the left. I mostly filled the holes with simple little gold studs. Hey, a girl has to be conservative to keep her professional look, right? Especially at night, when the demons still came.

Over the years I'd tried the obvious solution to stop painting demons in my sleep. I locked myself into bathrooms. Handcuffed myself to beds. Handcuffed myself to men I fucked so I wouldn't have to sleep alone. I sat on park benches all night, playing checkers with the street people, beating African drums, me and the homeless and the stoners and the other lost souls.

It never worked. When I was in a trance I used whatever made a mark. Ketchup, barbecue sauce, mud, soap. Or, deprived of all else, my own blood. Old childhood habits are hard to break. When you're in a trance the surface of your skin parts under your teeth and fingernails like a fine seam. I never felt the pain until I woke up the next morning with a new gash in my arm and something awful and bloody staring at me from the nearest paintable surface.

But I hadn't suffered any more wide-awake hallucinations like the night of the fire. Just the dream-paintings. Nothing came shuffling after me and tried to squeeze between the molecules of my bedroom door.

Nope. I was cured of all that.

But I knew in my heart that the darkness, filled with demons, would continue closing in.

2

Six years later

Through some lucky quirks of fate, I carved out a warped but survivable life for myself. First, Charles and Sarah Ablehorn took a fancy to my art and invited me to work at their gallery. My big, abstract landscapes began to sell. The Ablehorns rented me an old building they owned, where I set up a studio and a living space.

Next they introduced me to one of their patrons, a local nightclub owner, Dante. He offered me a part-time job as a bartender. Extra money, working late nights, perfect.

I almost felt . . . *settled.*

Then one night, not long after my twenty-fifth birthday, I made the mistake of sleeping alone, sober, and soundly.

I jerked awake in the bleary light just before dawn. My arms and body were smeared with paint. Open tubes of acrylics seeped bright colors all over my blanket. Unwashed brushes lay along the gooey trail my footprints made across the loft's scarred plank floors. My fingers were so sore I could barely bend them. I staggered out of my bed, gasping. My gaze followed the brush and paint trail to a canvas standing starkly against a brick wall between my tall windows.

The pig-demon *thing* looked straight back at me. It had the basic shape of a man, but its legs were short and scaly. It squatted, grinning at me, with its massive arms draped over its obscenely spread knees. Jutting from between its thighs was a major boner.

Stay focused, be calm, Nahjee counseled. I'd worn her to a faded luster over the years. My sweaty fingerprints were practically embedded in the wood. *Speak your prayers,* she instructed. *Take a deep breath.*

I moved my dry lips silently. *Though I walk through the valley of the shadow of death I will fear no evil . . .*

Fuck me. Because I did fear evil. I seriously did.

Squatting by Pig Face's cloven hooves was some other creepy thing, like a pet. This one had a long, sharp nose and his fur was striped red on a chalk-gray hide; he or she or it had the fanged grin of a rabid wolverine and the long tail of a monkey. Its feet looked agile and vicious. Each paw had eight long toes, with claws, and the heel of each paw had a spur. Eight Toes watched me with opalescent eyes that gleamed a cold, bluish white. It was laughing at me.

Burn them. Burn them both right away, Nahjee urged. *Don't wait for full light. These two are really dangerous.*

I threw on some leggings and a long sweater, shoved my scarred feet into mud-colored earth sandals, strapped a long Bowie knife to my waist, grabbed the painting, and rushed downstairs. The lower level of the building acted as my garage. I never parked the truck outside, even though getting ripped off by prowlers of the ordinary variety was the least of my worries.

I elbowed a lever on the brick wall. Gears whirred in the room's ceiling. A massive warehouse door slid sideways on its tracks. I stepped out slowly, looking both ways. I lived in an abandoned industrial area in the flood plain of the Swannanoa. It was a world of urban forest, weeds, junk and isolation.

Further down, approaching the highway, the road was going upscale. Big-box retailers, fancy landscaping, even a riverside park. But not here. My nearest neighbors were a family of raccoons who lived in a boarded-up ice plant. I put out dry dog food for them. They climbed up my building's outer walls to perch on its deep window sills at night, where they fought, fucked, and pawed at the glass.

No problem. I liked waking up in a cold sweat to discover it was just them. Reality is one big mofo thrill ride. Scream then laugh. Yeah, just raccoons. *This time.*

Shivering in the early March chill, I sliced the painting to pieces. Eight Toes, the grinning little parasite with the fucked up feet, occupied a small piece of canvas by himself. He'd go into the fire first. *Hurry*, Nahjee whispered. *Something's happening.*

My hands trembled as I dumped charcoal into a rusty metal drum. The world felt empty, and the morning light over the tall buildings of Asheville seemed to glow a weird yellow-green. Car traffic and freight trains rumbled in the distance.

Above me, a faded angel mural looked down from the bricks, her face weeping through the mortar. Beneath her bare feet the painted ghost of the building's logo still showed.

HARKEN BIBLE PRINTERS, INC.
THE GOOD WORD SHALL ABIDE

I squirted lighter fluid into the metal drum, stepped back, tossed a match, and watched the plume of orange flames shoot up. Good and hot. "Back to hell, motherfucker," I said loudly. It never hurts to talk some serious kick-ass movie dialogue to a hallucination

I bent and grabbed an armful of canvas. I held the jagged pieces face down. I didn't want to see Eight Toes and his big friend, the one with those bloody, lecherous eyes and the moldering, pig-like face. I especially didn't want to look at the thing's erection again.

I tossed Eight Toes at the flames. He didn't go.

A gust of wind caught the piece of canvas. I grabbed but the wind flung it just ahead of me, like a taunt. I dropped the rest of the canvas and leapt after that scrap. Picture my long black hair flying like an electrified flag over my tattoos and studded ears. I chased the windswept canvas through woods strewn with junked washing machines, old tires and moldering liquor bottles.

You can't run fast enough, bitch, a guttural voice said from nowhere. I slid to a stop in the cold muck atop the Swannanoa's steep bank. Eight Toes settled gently on the dark water. He smiled his monkey-wolverine smile at me as he floated downstream, disappearing around a curve in the woods. The river would carry him under a small bridge and then into the highway culverts, where I'd never be able to reach him.

I hugged myself, bent over and vomited into the soggy muck.

Go back to the fire, Nahjee said urgently. *Run back and burn the rest!*

Oh, my God. I raced back through the woods, my heart tearing itself against my ribs.

The rest of the canvas was gone.

Eight Toes had faked me out. He'd distracted me, moved me away from the fire, away from his master. Did that mean the lecherous, bloody-eyed thing, which I'd snared, was now free again, gaining strength and pissed off at me for trying to burn him?

Slowly I lowered my gaze.

Tracks. *I saw tracks.*

Tracks. In my studio's backyard. Tracks no living animal could make. Nothing known to man has eight finger-like toes on its paws, long claws, and a heel hook like the spur on a rooster's foot.

Not inside the city limits of Asheville, anyhow.

I stumbled inside the bottom floor of Harken Bible and lowered the warehouse door as quickly as I could. Gasping, I leaned against my battered pick-up truck. My mind went blank. I was heaving, numb, terrified. I blinked. My mind cleared. I stared at the truck's dusty passenger window, and then lifted my dusty forefinger to the words I'd written on the glass during that quick little trance.

> *Beware my love. He's found you, but so have I.*
> *- Ian*

My legs headed south. I sat down limply on the cold brick floor. Who the fuck was Ian?

*

Someone stuck a bumper sticker on my truck once, outside Dante's club. *Keep Asheville Weird*, it said. You see that everywhere around town. It's a state of mind. Freak capital of the south. More Wiccans and New Agers per capita than anywhere else. The big-little city sitting on a mountain of quartz bedrock that channels electromagnetic fields like a quartz watch spinning in every direction. So the spiritual gurus say.

That night, after the canvas disappeared and I saw the tracks in my yard, then found the message from the stranger Ian, I needed to feel weird. Weird was good. Weird was familiar. I headed for the club early.

The owner, Dante Fusion—probably a fake name, but no one would dare ask him about it—was a big, black, lean, mean, Zen-gentle kickboxer and martial arts master. He let me take classes for free at the studio he owned. He'd taught me to throw the knife. He seemed to know I might need to kill something.

I smoked an herbal, hand-rolled cig as I drove up shady streets lined with old Victorians interspersed with modern high rises and turn-of-the-century office buildings. A collision of accidents and money and fate and heartbreaking dreams made Asheville such a seductive old city, bohemian and counterculture and filthy rich and *Oh, that's just another prophet singing on the sidewalk* tolerant, a place of ghosts and memories and homebrew and weed and unexplained energies that could fuck up a person who didn't have a solid identity to fall back on first. Me, I was solidly weird, so it worked.

I flipped a page on the calendar lying beside me on the truck's cracked vinyl seat. I wrote down strange thoughts and dates of infamy, sort of a personal almanac and journal, my own whacked horoscope of coincidental events. The calendar had cute kitties on it. I never let anyone see my kitty calendar. They would have laughed. Me. With cute kitties. Fuck 'em.

I scanned the calendar page just to see what synchronicity I had going on for the night. A nasty little prickle went through my head. I pulled into the parking lot of the warehouse-cum-concert-club and lifted the calendar to the steering wheel for a second round of study.

Asheville has plenty of dead notables. O. Henry. Thomas

Wolfe. Various Vanderbilts. But I identified with one in particular. Zelda Fitzgerald.

Zelda burned to death in an Asheville psych hospital in 1948. She was a seriously long-time schizophrenic—at least that's what they diagnosed back then. I think her mind got fucked up by being F. Scott's wife and for a lot of other reasons. Had she mourned for Scott and their gilded Gatsby age? Had she seen things in the shadows nobody believed but her? When the fire came, it went up the shaft of a dumbwaiter in the hospital's main building. Nine women didn't get out of the top floors. Zelda was one of them.

I laid the calendar down slowly. *Why do I collect this morbid shit?* I said out loud, but my voice shook. I don't know why the calendar notation creeped me out so badly.

It's not weird; it's Asheville.

In Asheville, you could find, do or be anything you wanted.

But, in return, anything could find, do or be *you.*

*

"Are you bouncing or mixing tonight, Livia? And put that out. What's wrong with you, sweetheart? You want to die young?"

Ensconced in a dark corner of the club's empty bar, I looked up at Dante over the glowing tip of my cigarette. I found his *die young* comment so very amusing. "It's herbal," I said.

"Still bad for your lungs." He reached over and pinched the cigarette from my fingertips. I stuck my hands in my lap. Now what would keep them from shaking? Dante doused my smoke in a glass of water then bent across the tiny table, scrutinizing me in the purple light of a lion's head wall sconce. He was maybe forty years old or a thousand, his face timeless, his hair in short dreads. He favored black pullovers and black parachute pants. The muscles in his arms looked like steel cords. Whenever he wanted to he disappeared into the shadows.

Occasionally, a brave soul joked about him. *Dude thinks he's in charge of the Matrix.*

Maybe he was.

A pale white line slashed his throat from ear to ear. He said it was a birthmark. I stared at that ominous line. He stared back. "Livvie, why weren't you at class today, girl? You don't miss class. No one misses my classes, not if they want to stay."

I shrugged. "I was busy."

"You never miss class. What's wrong?"

"Look, I'm here on time for my shift, and that's all that counts. So which is it—do you want me to work the back room or the front room tonight?"

He frowned and straightened. "Work the front." He pivoted and started away, then halted and looked back. "You know, if you need help, just tell me."

He was one of the few men who didn't say pretty things just to get laid. I'd worked at his club for three years, and he'd never once hit on me. I wouldn't call him a friend, because that might doom him. People tended to die around me. But I did think highly of him.

"I'm fine. I just like being a mystery," I said.

He shook his head and went upstairs to an office that overlooked the club floor.

I got up wearily and walked behind the bar. The skin of my hands glowed amber in the light reflecting off the bourbon bottles. My family name, Belane sounds vaguely French but it's actually a Celtic surname. I was very white, my hair very black. Granny Belane had said we were part Cherokee, like a lot of mountain southerners. And Scots-Irish, which is also a standard mix. At any rate, I looked like the living dead. Yeah, that's how I felt.

It was only seven p.m.; barely wake-up time for the denizens of the dark. Dante's Room was still empty except for a couple of early-shift waitresses flipping through their order pads and adjusting their fishnets.

I twirled a long paring knife, stabbed a lemon with it, and began carving wedges. The club was Goth with a side order of bondage-and-discipline types. Lots of black. Lots of tattoos and piercings. Music that sounded like a funeral dirge on uppers and steroids. I spent every night until at least three a.m., closing time.

"Hey, Livia," Ronnie Bowden said as he loped past, earrings jangling. "You're whiter than usual."

"Eh," I answered.

Ronnie, who worked as the club's sound man when he wasn't hustling tips on the street as a fire eater, began testing the system. The soft hiss of reverb made me jump.

"I won't go easy," I said to the darkness.

*

Gigi, the pink witch, arrived by nine. A few months back I'd rescued her from some boozed-up rednecks who stole her tip jar and tried to pull her clothes off while she posed on a sidewalk as a Goth-Wiccan 1880's saloon girl. She'd been my personal pet puddy-tat ever since.

She pirouetted up to the crowded bar and grinned at me under a wide-brimmed black hat adorned with pink feathers and pink faux fur, also anchored with streamers of glass beads and silver charms. She claimed her last name was Dumond, but word on the street said she'd made that up.

Gigi lived in a tiny house outside town with six other student witches, all of them more students than witches, since they were undergrads at UNC's Asheville campus. By day she worked at a New Age shop called Mystic Road. She spent her nights at the club charging a couple of dollars a head for tarot card readings. The shit she told people about themselves freaked them out. She also performed as a street mime, sold handmade jewelry, cast love spells and mixed healing charms, and advised on herbal fragrances to improve one's mood.

Just your average Asheville Wiccan. Cute like my calendar kittens.

"I have another necklace for you to try, Livia."

"I told you, I'm not buying."

"It's a gift." She offered it, hidden inside a small, pale hand decked out in fingerless pink lace gloves. Weird-shit little Wiccan. Wiccans wear black, as a rule. Gigi dutifully wore black leggings and long, belted blouses she bought at Goodwill then dyed black. But somehow, their original bright colors still winked through.

I ignored her as I mixed a martini. "I don't take gifts." She sighed. She huffed. Gigi was short and pudgy, with a scruff of lanky brown hair she tinted pink around her face. She drank herbal tea and secretly listened to Celine Dion on her Nano. That kind of music would get you jeered out of Dante's. People would throw their Cure CDs at her. Gigi was no Goth. She was the tag-along kid sister I'd never had and couldn't afford to encourage. Especially now. Like I said, the people in my life didn't last long.

Her good-hearted innocence rammed icicles into my brain. She reminded me of Alex.

"I owe you a gift," she insisted. "Come on, Livia. *I keep trying to give you a gift.* I'm learning to mold glass pendants."

I stabbed a paring knife into a lemon. "What part of 'Fuck off,' do you not understand? I don't want your gratitude and your cheesy gifts, all right? Stay away from me."

Her face crumpled. "You don't understand," she said in a small voice, which made me feel like the mean bitch of all time. She laid a tiny crystal snake on the bar. Purple striped, with pink dots of molten glass for eyes. "This isn't just about you. You need all the help you can get. Here's a friend for Nahjee. She needs a little sister. This one is named Tabitha." She hesitated, looking a little awkward. "After Samantha and Darren's daughter in *Bewitched*."

By the time I'd finished staring at the pendant, she'd disappeared. How did she know Nahjee's name? I'd never told anyone, anywhere. Ever.

Nahjee said gently, *Gigi's friendship is no accident, and we do need her help. She and Tabitha are no strangers to your soul and mine._*

My hands shook as I put the necklace on. The tiny glass snake snuggled close to Nahjee.

Long time no see, Tabitha said.

Welcome back, Nahjee answered.

*

By midnight I was filling drink orders on autopilot.

Numbness had set in. The lost canvas. Demon tracks. The message from Ian. Gigi's psychic divining of Nahjee's name. The reunion of snake charms.

Once or twice I almost laughed. A sick, tight, terrified tickle kept crawling up my throat. My self-defense mechanism, I guess. It was one way I coped.

Beware, my love. Beware. He's found you, but so have I.

That chant kept circling my brain. Ian. Had I ever known an Ian? Never.

I'd spend tonight up here in town. Hang in a coffee shop, sleep in my truck. I didn't want to be alone at the studio.

"You look as tired as I feel," the stranger said in a deep, pleasant voice. He sat by himself at one end of the bar, steeped in shadows. I didn't remember noticing him walk in. But then, I'd been off in my own world all evening. From the main room came the thick *thump* of drums and the abrasive chords of amped-up guitars. It was hard to hold a conversation. And yet I heard his voice clearly. It was not southern. It seemed to flow with the sensual roll of the music.

My radar said he was clean. Nothing dark around him.

I swiped a bar towel near his hands. Big hands, strong, no rings. "Sorry. Didn't notice you. What would you like?"

"Just a beer. Something local, please. I hear you have some nice microbreweries around here."

"Yeah. Do you want a lager or . . . "

"That would be nice, thanks. You pick it out. I'm not much of a drinker. I don't do the dark ales."

I filled a cold mug from the taps, set it on a napkin in front of him, and inhaled his scent. My God, what kind of cologne did he use? He smelled good. Warm and fresh, like a memory . . . the high mountain balds in springtime, when the rhododendron blooms. Like sky and granite and sunshine and earth; a view across endless blue mountain ridges. Daddy, Momma, Alex and I had picnicked in one of those high mountain meadows one spring. That painfully sweet memory, long hidden, suddenly seemed as vivid as my own breath.

"You have a wonderful smile," the stranger said.

I blinked. His outstretched hand lay near the mug. I'd let my hand settle near his on the bar top when I placed his drink there. The heat off his fingertips seemed to enter mine and flow through my body. Comfort. Friendship. Safety. Affection. Sex.

I stepped back, put my hand by my side, and stared at him. I didn't roll over for seductive men. I'd never had what you'd call a positive sexual experience. When you get popped at eighteen by a fellow nutcase in the psych ward you tend to develop some warped attitudes about intimacy, not that my other attitudes were cozy-sweet. Lust, like fear, was something to be controlled. Women make stupid choices when they let their bodies do all the thinking.

And yet . . . who was this guy? I looked him over seriously. He wasn't a Dante's type, to say the least. Too tanned, for one thing. Not a night crawler. And older than our average, at least thirty. And way more conservative. No piercings, no obvious tattoos. He wore a beautiful leather bomber jacket over a golf shirt. I walked out from behind the bar to deliver a drink and noted his creased tan slacks. Slacks. A golf shirt. Jesus. Had he wandered in from a Young Republicans Convention? Bodybuilders for Jesus?

His shoulders and arms were huge, and his neck bulged with muscle. He must be six-four, six-five. Even sitting on a bar stool he loomed above the scrawny drinkers standing at the bar's other end. His face was strong-jawed, almost Dudley Do-rightish in its angles; he had short, glossy brown hair, a dimple beside the left corner of his mouth, and riveting gray eyes.

He smiled. His teeth were even and white. His smile was mesmerizing. "I don't fit in here, no," he said.

I caught my breath. "You're a little too bronzed, that's all. You could use some white foundation and some eyeliner. And a lip stud. But we'll let you drink here anyway."

"Thank you." His smile simmered. Sadness seeped into it. "It's a cold winter night. I walked down here from my hotel. Asheville's covered in fog and so is Atlanta, where my flight was headed. So we landed here, and I'm stuck for the night. No offense. I'm sure this is a great town. But I'm trying to get to Miami to see my mom. She's sick."

I have a sharp ear for bullshit, especially the kind designed to get in my pants, but this guy radiated nothing but wistful honesty. In a world full of geeks, Goths, come-ons, put downs, loneliness, terror and demonic hallucinations, he was a big, hot slice of apple pie with a sickly mama on top. Talking to him pushed the morning's fear further into a corner where I could pretend it was all just my imagination.

"Would you like something from the kitchen?" I asked. "This is Asheville, where we have more vegetarians than you can shake an organic carrot at. How about an avocado sandwich on multi-grain bread with a side of Indian *dal*, hummus dip and raw mango rice?"

He laughed. "Whatever you said, okay." He held out a broad, handsome hand. "My name's Greg Lindholm. I'm from Minnesota. Land of the Swedes and Lutherans."

"Livia Belane," I answered, and clasped his hand. "I'm from wherever." He squeezed my fingers so gently. The heat. My God. He made me feel I'd never be cold again.

*

I wasn't stupid, all right? Just lonely and scared shitless. Just desperate for the hope that every night of my life didn't have to be bleak. I wanted to believe I deserved a Barbie Doll romance with someone nice, someone I could trust.

After the club closed Greg said, "I'm not sleepy. That's not a come-on. How about coffee and donuts at that all-night diner down the hill? My treat."

"Yeah, sure." I shrugged into a black leather jacket. "I'll drive us. Hope you don't mind an ancient pick-up truck with no heater."

"I don't mind at all, Livvie. I'm just glad to have more time with you. Believe it or not, I'm not much of a talker, usually. But you make me feel comfortable."

"I stunned you. You probably don't meet many starving artists with five studs in each ear."

"I've never met anyone like you before, and I mean that as compliment."

Oh, he was good. I decided to see where the rest of the night took us. If we ended up at his hotel room, fine by me. After we fucked I'd get to sleep, really sleep, in a comfortable bed with his thick, hot, serenity inducing arms wrapped around me. No demons could get past that much Midwestern weight-lifting muscle.

I drove us a couple of blocks down the hilly, empty city street past a string of little buildings that housed small businesses and shops. Asheville doesn't tear down much of the old, so the downtown streets are a nice hodgepodge of styles, most of them built before the nineteen sixties, some going back to the eighteen hundreds. There are lots of trees just off the main drags, and the hills sink down into dark, forested valleys before rising again with the lights and lawns of in town neighborhoods. That night, everything was shrouded in a pearl-white mist of fog. The streetlamps pooled their auras in the soft glow.

I parked in the misty lot of a tiny diner where a retro coffee cup beamed its white neon outline to the night. The lot sloped off to a crumbling curb behind the old building, and behind that, the land dropped steeply into woods and shrubs.

"I warn you," I said to Greg Lindholm, as I opened my creaking driver's side door, "the donuts here are made from grains you probably never heard of, and the gourmet coffee is imported from countries whose names are full of strange vowel combinations."

He smiled. His heat and his large, powerful body seemed to take up all my air. "Sounds good, Livvie."

As we stepped out of the truck a bedraggled, half-starved puppy appeared from the darkness. It limped badly, and shivered. The puppy gobbled up a few crumbs of donuts beside a dumpster then whined and looked our way, wagging its tail.

"Oh, no, I'm a sucker for a homeless puppy," Greg said. He headed for the animal. The puppy tucked tail and scooted toward the woods. "Don't be afraid, little guy," Greg called. He disappeared into the fog.

I frowned. The darkness made me nervous. I cupped my hands around my mouth. "If you can catch him I'll take him to the humane society tomorrow." Gigi volunteered there. Maybe she'd put a charm on the puppy. Make sure it got a good home. Somewhere in the fog at the lot's back edge, the puppy whined with heartbreaking need. "Come here, little guy," I heard Greg coaxing. "Sorry, Livvie. He seems to be afraid of men. Give me just a second."

Afraid of men? Men were the least of the unknowns that lived in the dark. I sighed. "I'm good with dogs. I can probably catch him."

I reached behind me, under my jacket, and touched my fingers to the knife tucked into a small scabbard sewn into the lining. I stroked the knife handle, pulled the knife free, and headed into the fog. *Always try to stay on the safe side of paranoia.* That was my motto. I could barely see. I heard Greg shuffling in the edge of the woods. The puppy whined nearby.

"Here, puppy," I called. "Come on, little guy, come on—"

Greg Lindholm slammed his thick fist into my face.

I sprawled backwards. My head nearly snapped off my neck. My brain short-circuited for a few seconds. I heard the slurpy, panting sound as something else, not a puppy, it had never been a homeless puppy, joined us. It swatted me across one arm. Its claws felt like razors.

Greg Lindholm grabbed me by my long black hair and dragged me down the hill into the woods. His scent rose up, a stinking, rotting smell, like a corpse. The thing inside a stranger's body laughed deep in its throat. Then it spoke to me with guttural contempt.

"Time to die again, bitch."

3

I woke up or regained consciousness. Hard to say which. Somehow I'd driven myself back to the studio last night. I didn't remember how. I lay naked on the hard plank floor upstairs, shivering. When I managed to lift my head, the last trickle of vomit trailed away from my bleeding lower lip. My skin was sticky with blood and semen. Everywhere. All the strategic spots and then some. All raw, torn. My right eye was swollen shut. My right arm was ripped; dried blood covered it. I had bruises on my breasts in the shape of Lindholm's fingers. I hurt all over.

Time to die again, bitch. Time to die again. Again.

Greg Lindholm had tried very hard to kill me with his dick and his fists, but something, or someone, had stopped him. I'd managed to stab him in the leg before he slung me against a tree, but that only slowed him down. He'd beaten me until I was limp, fucked me as painfully as possible, and then he'd wrapped his hands around my neck and begun to squeeze. As my mind went black I felt a *swoosh* of energy and saw a flare of light. I heard Eight Toes scream and make a gargling sound, then go totally silent. Lindholm jerked his hands away from my throat and got to his feet. Another *swoosh* sliced the air and then the deep thud as an object struck the tree only inches away.

Lindholm muttered something about "waiting" and "patience." And he left me laying there.

I had had help from someone. Or, like I said, some *thing*.

Now I squinted in the morning light. My head whirled. Slowly, trembling, I pushed myself upright. I stared at the canvas leaning against a post less than two feet from me.

I had painted a new picture.

This time there was no unspeakable creature in it, or like other paintings, no malevolent faces of people I'd just as soon didn't really exist somewhere.

This time, there was a pioneer. A fucking pioneer, like the

corny paintings in kids' history texts or a stalwart young frontiersman in some cheesy 'Old Mountain Times' mural. He was the kind of realistic, traditional art I never painted, asleep or awake. I stared up at him through my pain, with one good eye. I'd painted him life-sized, on one of my largest canvases.

He was tall and lean. He looked older than me, but still young. He wore leather leggings, coarse knee boots, and a rough cloth coat. He had long black hair and eyes too blue to be anything other than a drugged mistake dabbed in place with the wrong shade of cerulean blue acrylics. He stood in the woods, a blur of green I'd only slapped around him, some vague mountain world. He was vivid. His world was not.

In one hand he clasped a long, bloody hatchet with some kind of native markings. He held out the other hand to me. Reeling, I looked down at my hands. The smear of blood on his fingertips matched a smear of flesh-colored paint on mine. Apparently, we'd tried to do a little hand holding.

He looked down at me, straight down at where I huddled on the floor, and he kept his hand out as if offering help, and in his eyes, there was fury. And there were tears.

A message was scrawled across the floor in front of the canvas. A puddle of blood showed where I'd dragged my fingers through it to ink them.

Call my name. I won't let him near you again. Swear to call my name. 'Tis Ian.

My teeth chattered. The light in my brain faded in and out. I stared at the painting, at the tender, outraged eyes, the bloody tomahawk. My rescuer? Or just another demon smart enough to trick me?

I managed to get up and stagger to the canvas.

Right before I passed out again I turned Ian, or whoever the fuck this new demon might call himself, to the wall.

*

Nahjee was gone. Judging by the raw ribbon of skin on the back of my neck, Greg Lindholm had ripped the pendant off by its gold chain. Only Tabitha remained, smeared with my blood. But she didn't talk. She radiated alarm. Yeah, Tabitha was freaked out. I understood. She huddled against my feverish skin

Stop imagining things. You probably just dropped Nahjee when you crawled out of the truck last night.

Hope springs eternal when your grip on reality is sinking into quicksand. I staggered outdoors and sank down on the cold, littered March ground, dressed in nothing but a thin geisha robe. I pushed my bruised hands through the scruff of brown weeds and trash. "Naaaah shee?" I slurred. "Please be here. I need you. Naaah shee?" Every movement seemed to tear more of my muscles loose from my bones. I was dimly aware of fresh blood seeping down my thighs. Sweat stung my raw eye.

Pebbles and bits of metal dug into my elbows. My hands were frantic. I had to have Nahjee back. "Talk to me. Why don't you talk to me, Nahjee? I need you. That thing is going to come back for me. That thing in a man's body. Oh, God. Someone tell me what to do."

"Livia, we're here," a sweet female voice said. "Ssssh. Livia. Livia? Oh, honey. Nahjee managed to send us a message before he put a spell on her. You aren't alone in this battle."

I hugged myself and sat up slowly, dizzy, gasping for air. The light came and went. "What?"

"Livia? Can you hear me?" The soft female voice drawled again, right beside me. "Charles, here she is."

A plump, middle-aged woman knelt by me among the weeds and debris, cooing. The smooth cotton of her long peasant skirt spread out like a fan, brushing my bare heels. Her strong hands stroked my shoulders.

The Ablehorns, Sarah and Charles. My landlords. Their gallery was in the river district of the French Broad. They tried to treat me like a daughter, but I kept them at a distance, like everyone else. "Livia, oh, Livia. Charles, get my medicine kit."

"I'm coming, hon," he called. "Just chatting with Sheba. She tells me the little bane was banished in the fight. Sheba got a look at his master, the one that was in Livia's painting. Yes, it's Pig Face. He's loose, and he's commandeered some poor bastard's body. Guy's name was Greg Lindholm. Oh, and Sheba says Livia painted another canvas just before dawn. Someone named Ian. A soul hunter, Sheba suspects."

"A soul hunter?" Sarah echoed. Even to my dizzy brain Sarah's voice came through loud and worried.

"They're not all lost, wandering souls, Sarah."

"I'd rather not deal with one, regardless. They're rough men."

"They're not exactly peaceniks, but they get the job done. Chill out. We'll talk about it later. By the way, Livia's heat is off, Sheba says. And the back gutter needs mending."

"All in good time. Help me with Livia."

"Coming, hon."

I swayed. Sheba? Who or what the fuck was *Sheba?* And how did she know what I did inside my own home? And if this Ian was some kind of tough-ass ghost, that didn't sound too reassuring either. Their conversation fluttered through my mind and disappeared around a bend. Too much to consider. How had the Ablehorns known to communicate with Nahjee?

I pawed at Sarah's examining hands. "Leave me alone, leave me . . . go away. Something's after me . . . it's not safe . . . "

"I know, Livia. I know. But we're here to help you fight back. Charles, we'll move her upstairs. The two of us can manage."

"You don't understand," I slurred. Violent chills came over me. "I'm psychotic. There's no demon. Some guy tried to kill me. He'll get you too."

She bent her head close to mine. I smelled jasmine and kindness. "No, sweetie, you're not psychotic. You never have been. Demons are real, and Pig Face is one of the most vicious ones, and he's been looking for you a long time."

"Oh, *fuck.*"

She stroked my sweaty hair. "For now, just understand that we're your friends. Old friends."

She and Charles lifted me into their arms. It was like floating.

My feverish brain swore I felt the soft tickle of feathers.

*

I wished I could stay inside the cocoon of Sarah Ablehorn's hand-stitched quilt forever. The heirloom quilt transformed my bed, which was just a twin mattress and box-springs I'd set on concrete blocks in one corner of the studio, next to an aged metal sink, a small fridge, and my toaster oven. Now it became a soft nest.

Sarah dosed me with antibiotics. She rubbed me with ice and alcohol to help the fever. She stitched up the ripped flesh of my arm, and also between my legs.

"Didn't know you were a doc," I whispered groggily when I finally could.

She rubbed cinnamon-scented liniment on the bruises and claw marks along my bare back. "Oh? Didn't I ever mention that I used to be a nurse practitioner?"

"No . . . you said . . . you and Charles used to be teachers. In Cincinnati. High school teachers. Then you moved to Asheville to follow your dreams."

"I see you've paid attention to our chitchat much more than you've ever let on. You secretly adore us. Thank you. We adore you too."

"You don't really understand what happened, what I've done, what I see . . . "

"There, there, Livia." Her hands were as soft as down pillows, smoothing away the pain in my spine. "We'll talk about that when you're feeling better. There, there. Chill out."

She gently palpated my bruised belly and, speaking as if her psychic pee test could not be doubted—pronounced me *not pregnant*. The horror of that idea nearly undid me. Pregnant with *what?* What kind of being, exactly, had raped me? Was Greg Lindholm a human being or the pig-faced demon or both?

"Pig Face took the man's body," Sarah said. "He's a very powerful demon. That's why he was able to trick you. He's afraid of you. He needs to eliminate you. He always tries the obvious ways first."

Oh, *that* was helpful news. "So what stopped him?"

"The Soul Hunter—if that's what this *Ian* really is—took a swing at that little bane and killed it."

"That thing . . . clawed me."

"Yes, and it's a nasty bane wound, one that's backed with the passions of a major demon. If you were rested and strong you could probably heal it, but not in your current vulnerable state. Bane wounds are illusions, but they're such powerful illusions that our bodies can't resist believing in them."

"I was . . . clawed . . . once before. The night my mother . . . "

I stopped. Old secrets die hard.

Sarah patted my shoulder. "We know about the demon who infiltrated your family. Your mother fought a brave battle against that creature. You can be proud of her."

I stared up at her, gasping. After years of torment, confirmation had come. "You . . . believe me?"

"Absolutely. *Pig Face* sent that demon to destroy your family. But he underestimated your power, even when you were a child. And he underestimated the forces that had massed to protect you. Your sweet Alex. I believe Alex saw the family's fate very early, on a soul level. He had to stay there for you. He's always been your sweetest spirit guide. He and your mother will show up in your life again, eventually."

"Where . . . when . . ."

Sssh. She stroked my face. "Your mother is a good soul, and she'll find you again. Mothers always do. Livia, take comfort. You banished the demon who killed your entire family. An amazing feat for a teenager. We knew then that you would become the most amazing soul catcher of your generation."

The drugging effect of her fingers, her magic, stilled every shocked and painful thought. *Soul catcher, best of my generation. Soul catcher.*

I cried without tears.

Momma.

Then came the rage.

Pig Face murdered my family. He's responsible.

"How do I catch him again? Pig Face? I've got to banish the bastard . . ."

"Yes, but not until you're stronger." Sarah stroked my forehead. "Pig Face is regrouping. He won't be so careless next time. Sssh. Rest. You're safe here. Sheba is on duty twenty-four seven. Not even a demon can get past a house pog in its own digs. Sheba was with you in your childhood. She gained power from your rage and grief. She won't let you down again."

"A pog, a what?"

Sarah's hand drugged me. A sweet fog filled my brain. "Sssh."

I curled on my side in a tight ball under the quilt.

"There, there," Sarah sang softly, as I tossed and turned. "There, there. It will all make sense when you're well again. Just sleep. You're safe inside this building. You always have been. That's why we rented it to you. And why Dante offered you a job. And why Gigi has watched the shadows on your behalf. We are imperfect assistants, Livia, which is why Pig Face found you before we realized it was him. But we're here now, closing ranks against him."

Sarah's quilt had small songbirds on it, embroidered in the finest detail. They came out of the material, perched on my shoulders, and nuzzled my cheeks. *There, there*, they sang.

I slept, despite myself.

*

April shoved March out of its body and took over, like a demon. Or like a soul hunter. Ian, whoever he was, didn't leave another message, or put in another appearance. Regardless, I was never going to trust any man again. Even one who was just some kind of ghost.

Soft afternoon light poured in through the windows of my studio one afternoon, sifting dust motes through the air. They seemed to sparkle. I lifted my head from my pillow, squinting in the light.

Across the room, seated in the sunshine at a work table I'd never seen before, Doris Harken bent her pretty head over a

Bible that still lay in sections, unfinished. Her brunette hair was short, in pin curls. A long apron covered her dungarees, which were rolled up to reveal sweet little ankle socks. Her plaid shirt had an embroidered cowgirl on the chest. She tapped the toes of her saddle oxfords to a big band beat only she heard. Her face was peaceful. Her agile hands worked a curved needle strung with thick thread. She was sewing the spine of the Good Book. Piecing Deuteronomy to Joshua and Luke to John.

Except for the fact, of course, that she'd been murdered nearly seventy fucking years ago.

In its heyday Harken Bible Printing had been a neatly whitewashed brick two-story fronted by a pretty magnolia tree and a row of well-tended zinnias. In the photos I'd found at the Asheville library the Harkens—who liked theological puns, you can tell—posed proudly in front of their business. A good-looking young couple, smiling and hugging. He had a handsome mustache and a cool fedora. She wore the lapels of her tweed suit turned back to show an extra inch of sexy throat, and her nifty little hat was decorated with white lace. The Harkens, Caleb and Doris, reminded me of Gable and Lombard in a romantic old movie.

Their mission in life was to spread the good word one handmade Bible at a time. They didn't get much chance to do that, though. Caleb and Doris were robbed and murdered in 1940. Workers from a nearby garage found their bodies under their magnolia. They'd been stabbed to death.

No. Get real. *Hacked* was the word the newspaper used. Hacked.

The killer was never caught.

Not long after I moved in I found sections of a Harken Bible stuffed behind the plaster board in an upstairs wall. What beautiful fonts Doris and Caleb had used, what fine, smooth paper, strangely un-yellowed. I stitched the sections together into a makeshift spine then carefully glued a soft rectangle of leather in place as a cover. I latched that cover with a piece of thong attached to a slender spire of quartz and a chunk of tin I found outside in the trash. Tin was elemental and friendly, in my opinion. Nobody ever got hacked to death with a tin ax.

Now my folk-art Harken Bible sat in the midst of a little shrine of crucifixes, menorahs, Buddha's, vintage old-time southern Bible fans and nature what-nots on a table I'd bought at the flea market up the road. That shrine was pieces of a Bible in particular and faith in general. Good versus evil. It was as if the Harkens had bequeathed me hopeful parts of the New Testament but also some fairly worrisome sections of the Old Testament, pertaining to demons.

A warning? Or a field guide?

I shut my eyes. When I dared open them again, Doris was gone and Sarah sat in her place on a plain metal chair I'd bought at a yard sale. She bent her head over a lap full of quilting pieces. Her graying brown hair was a cap of chunky layers; she'd gotten stuck, style-wise, in a seventies Dorothy Hamill 'do. But it was pretty. It was Sarah. Her fingers deftly wove a needle in and out, stitching silk to cotton, brocade to wool. She liked all the textures. I liked all the textures of Sarah. And of Charles. Mostly, that feathery one.

I had just seen Doris Harken and Sarah in the same patch of sunlight.

Did Pig Face kill the Harkens, too?

Oh, my God.

There, there, the quilt birds sang. *Rest.*

Under their spell, I slept again.

*

"She's so beautiful. Such pretty black hair. Her eyes are deep green, you know. Like well-fertilized catnip. She tries not to get close enough for people to notice, but they're really, really green. Hello, Tabitha, how is she doing?"

Better, my amulet said. *But she misses Nahjee. And she's afraid to leave this building. She won't admit it though.*

I kept my eyes shut. *Tabitha, you outted me. I should smash you on a rock.*

Oh, my, Tabitha said. *I'm sure you don't mean that.*

Try me.

Dante's deep voice said, "Show me the tats her

grandmother put on her head when she was a girl."

"All right. I'll just part her hair a tiny little bit, right . . . here. See? I told you. Her grandmother had her tattooed with faith symbols when she was ten. Not much protection, but at least it got her this far."

"When she sleeps she looks almost happy. I've never seen her like that at the club or in my classes. She's a fighter. And scared. She barely trusts *me*."

"Join the crowd. She thinks *I'm* a pest. Well, okay, I am a little pink pest. Hmmm. I think she looks like Cher. A young Cher."

"Cher? Please, Gigi. Show some taste. I'm thinking of Tomyris."

"The one who led the army against Cyrus, the Persian? Oh, come on. No way. Tomyris was too short. Livia is nearly six feet tall."

"Then Zenobia, the Syrian."

"Bad vibes. The Romans eventually whacked her."

"Dante, you're missing the point."

"All right. Boudicca, the Celt. Not that I liked her all that much. And the Romans, again . . . I'm thinking Majiji."

"Dante, Dante, Dante! The Romans eventually whacked Majiji, too. Don't fixate on losers."

"I'm talking spirit, you know. Not form."

"Okay, then what's wrong with Cher?"

"I give up."

"Shush. She's opening an eye."

I opened *both* eyes. When I looked up I saw Gigi's sincere, pink-framed little face surrounded by a floppy velveteen hat covered with pink feathers and faux pink fur and beads. She held a small brocade amulet bag to her denim heart. Witches who dye their overalls black to fit the Wiccan dress code are, somehow, hard to take seriously.

She stood there alone. Where was Dante? I looked across the room. He nodded at me from a casual pose, leaning against a window. He'd opened the bottom of the big industrial panes. "I like the air," he said. "Maybe I used to be a bird. A hawk.

An eagle. You never know."

You never know. I looked back at Gigi. Her eyes, which already looked tender, glistened like wet marbles. "I'm so sorry about what happened, Livvy. You have to understand, it's not like we looked the other way. You're the turning point. The portal. The link. Oh, I'm no good at metaphors." She wrung the amulet bag. "You're the YouTube channel. We're the videos. You have to upload your spirit guides willingly."

My sluggish brain sorted the weird play list she'd just handed me. "I . . . choose . . . funny cat videos . . . instead."

Her mouth popped open. She arched a thinly plucked brown brow, decorated with just the tiniest ankh tattoo at one corner. The Egyptian hieroglyph for life. Her teary eyes widened. She began to laugh. She bent double, chortling. Her feathers and faux fur jiggled. "You have a sense of humor! This is a good sign! A brightness I never expected!"

"Thanks. I'm so glad to entertain you." I pushed myself up on the pillows, wincing. Some days I still felt like I'd been gutted.

Her laughter faded. My tank top showed the healing slashes on my arm. Eight thin rows of stitches. Eight Toes. Eight claws. They bisected my honor roll of family names. Momma, Daddy, Alex, Granny, Preacher T. Their names would have scars across them from now on. Sarah had not repeated that point about me being able to heal a bane wound. I guess it was clear I was too much of a rookie.

Gigi studied the slashes. "Oh, Livia. That bane was an awfully powerful one. Sheba was right about him."

"Whatever."

Gigi pulled up a folding metal chair—one of my other pieces of fine furniture—and sat beside me. "You don't really want to believe anything we say yet. That's okay. It's a lot to take in. Let me try to explain just a little."

She twiddled a long feather that drooped off her hat, sighed, then launched into a spiel. "There are many worlds. You can call them 'heavens and hells' or Elysian Fields or dimensions or universes or whatever. I like to think of them as a layer cake."

"Sure. Why not."

"When you eat a piece of layer cake, you can sample the chocolate icing, the cream cheese center, the chopped pecans and the layer of jelly all at the same time. Or you can take a bite of the icing, then move your spoon down and scoop out a bite of the cream cheese. Or you can only eat the rum pudding layer. I think of this world right here—" she whirled her finger, indicating our planet, dimension, whatever—"as the rum pudding layer. But just because you spend your whole life nibbling the rum pudding doesn't mean you're not part of a much bigger dessert. Which you *can* taste, if you try."

I adjusted my thin tank top for semi-modesty then folded my arms under my breasts. "I'll stick with lemon cookies."

"Cynicism is blindness. Free your mind."

"Thank you for that motto, Morpheus."

"Livia, I'm just saying that all these layers exist at the same time, they're all going on, all around us, all the time. The past, the present, and even the future. Time means nothing. It's not a straight line from here to there, like, duh. Time is like a soup. And we're in the middle of it."

"What kind of soup? A cream soup or a broth? Can I be a dumpling? I don't want to be a carrot or a Brussels sprout."

"Livia, please. I'm telling you: There are many worlds, and many, many souls in all those worlds, and this particular world is very tempting to some of them. This world is vulnerable and young. They see it as an unclaimed frontier. They want to carve out territories. Grab some action."

I settled back on my pillows. "So . . . it's like we're living in *Casablanca* and bad-asses from other dimensions drop by Rick's nightclub for a drink and a chance at the roulette table. What do they want with me? Of all the gin joints in the world . . . "

"You're the bouncer," Dante put in. "You decide who gets kicked out of the club for bad behavior."

"Oh? Then I quit. It's a lousy job. I didn't apply for it."

"Your soul did. Your soul knows best. This is what your soul chose to do."

"Excuse me while I text message my soul. 'OMG. WTF?'"

"You have a gift. There aren't many like you."

"Go figure. Nobody wants this job. No perks, no pension plan, no health insurance . . . "

"No perks?" He spread his dark, muscular hands in supplication. "Livia, how about first-hand proof that the soul is everlasting and death is just a door to another life?"

"I'd rather have a 401K and a company car. Make that a Vespa. I've always wanted a scooter."

Gigi patted my quilted leg. "Livvie, we know you've been through a lot . . . "

"Look, I plan to track Pig Face down and banish him. I'll find a way to send that fucker to Hell. But that doesn't mean I'm interested in a permanent soul-catching job."

Dante sighed and walked over. He stopped at the foot of my bed. "This isn't about your personal revenge. Demons are a threat to all living beings. They can't be allowed to stay here."

"I've seen one demon up close, guys. In its real form. I fought it. I banished it. But ever since then, I've tried my best to cut that memory out of my brain." I dug the heel of one hand into my forehead. "I see my brother dying. I see my mother . . . her body, her face, even if wasn't really her anymore . . . I see her morphing into . . ."

"Livia, that will get easier, I promise." Gigi sighed. "Take a break. We'll talk more about your mission, later."

"Do you have any clue what happened to Nahjee? Has Pig Face hurt her?"

Dante shook his head. "No, I think he plans to use her in some way. To cause trouble for you."

Great.

"How about my knife? Did anyone find it?"

"Not yet, sweetheart."

Gigi sighed again and stood up. A long strand of beads and charms trailed from her overalls' chest pocket to a tiny pocket on her hip, meant to hold a watch or lighter. Gigi pulled the strand free then stooped and tucked it between my mattress and box springs. "This little fellow will help you sleep." She opened the brocade amulet bag and laid its contents on the chair's seat. A crystal. "This will help clear your mind." A dried rose. "This will help your wounds heal faster." And finally, she laid an enameled lapel pin on her palm and held it out for me to peruse.

I stared at a Starfleet insignia. "This will help me get into a Trekkie convention?"

"It's not the form of the talisman that's important, Livia, it's the spirit. This will help you smile. And it's already working. Yes, that twitch at the corner of your mouth? That's called a teensy, tiny *smile*."

"Amazing," Dante added. "Maybe one day we'll see her teeth."

Gigi placed the lapel pin on the chair, arranged it and the other low-rent talismans on the velveteen bag, then dusted her hands with a ceremonial flutter of pink fingernails, as if casting pixie powder. "We'll be back to visit tomorrow. Buh bye."

They headed toward the loft stairs. I wrestled with pride for a second, then called, "Thank you, guys. I'm sorry I'm such a bitch. But the people I care about . . . they always die because of me."

Gigi pirouetted and smiled. Dante turned slower, his expression gentle "No need to thank us," Gigi chirped.

Dante nodded. "We sacrifice our bodies for the sake of decent souls everywhere. Just as you do. It's an honor."

Ta-dah. They went down the heavy factory steps, their feet echoing off the beamed ceilings and high, tin roof.

I lay there feeling as if I'd just wandered down a new path in *The Twilight Zone.*

The sound of large wings outside the windows made my blood freeze.

I shoved the bedcovers back and struggled to move my weak legs to the side of the bed. The wings grew louder. Big wings. I started to yell for help from Charles and Sarah.

No. If Pig Face is here, I have to face him alone.

I grabbed a drawing pad and charcoal pencil.

A hawk settled on the wide wood. The largest hawk I'd

ever seen. Not gray or red, like ordinary mountain hawks, but a deep, burnished black, like a crow, only with fine stripes of silvery gray. A two-foot-tall tabby-cat hued hawk? What the fuck? Somebody call *National Geographic.*

It carried something in its talons. The hawk unfurled its claws, studied me with its glossy black head cocked to one side, and then simply flew away.

When I could breathe again I inched one bare foot ahead of the other until I reached the window sill. My knife lay there. Greg Lindholm's dried blood was caked the blade. Words were scratched into the blood's crusty surface.

Found it, love. From Ian.

Sweat ran down my clammy skin. I crawled back to bed.

I dreamed of layer cakes and giant hawks and the soul hunter named Ian.

*

"I need to show you what you did last night," Sarah said gently. "For the record, Charles didn't wake up and see you. Only I did. Your dignity is safe with me. He's a very gallant and fatherly man, so I promise he won't look if it happens again."

She sat in a chair across from my bed. She didn't seem upset, but she did seem concerned. I sat on the side of the bed with a plate of wheat toast going cold on my lap. I tugged my geisha robe tighter around me. "Just when I thought it was safe to go back in the water."

Sarah held up her cell phone. "This happened about two a.m."

I squinted as the tiny video screen filled with a shadowy image. Okay, that was me. Getting out of bed, my eyes locked in a thousand-mile stare, night-of-the-living-dead me, okay. Dressed in nothing but my tank top and panties, I limped slowly across the studio, following a familiar trail between paint cabinets, a rack that held big rolls of canvas, and a large work table I'd made from two big pieces of plywood. I went straight to the far wall, where dozens of half-finished landscapes leaned, face-forward against the aged bricks. I shuffled them aside, latched my hands onto the biggest one, and turned it around.

Black-haired pioneer Ian, yes. Him and his bloody hatchet and his outstretched hand and his angry tears on my behalf.

I propped that painting against a post.

And then I made out with it.

I stepped as close as I could get to the fabric, pressed my whole body to his, raised my hands to his hair and face, kissed him, stroked his hair, his face, his clean-shaven jaw and his shoulders then slid my hands to his thighs. I stroked them slowly, up and down, inside and out, then angled my pelvis against his and rotated, gently grinding my wounded parts to his painted ones. Finally I pulled my hands back up to his shoulders and curled my fingers along their broad tops, as if holding on. I turned my cheek to his painted neck.

And I rested happily.

Sarah clicked her phone shut. "You stood there for about an hour, then you turned the painting back to the wall, and you went back to bed. Do you remember anything at all?"

"No." I didn't mention the erotic Ian dreams that flooded me around dawn.

"Livia, let me tell you what I know about soul hunters. Well, first off, let me tell you this about soul *jumpers*, because it's related. Charles, Gigi and Dante and I, we've been around a long time. We've been part of your life going back through a *lot* of lives. We know how to jump from life to life. We find . . . uhmmm, willing bodies to use."

"You evict them," I said wearily, drained of surprise. "Like what happened to my mother."

"Oh, no. God. No. *No.*"

"Then where do the souls go when you ditch them?"

"Think of it this way, Livia. A body is just the container for the soul. Bodies die, souls don't. They move on. Not that it's a good thing to leave your body. It does some damage to give up a body you're attached to. We don't recommend it." She frowned at me knowingly. "Generally speaking, when you deliberately kill the body you live in, it's like you're kicking your soul out of its house with no warning."

I looked away, clenching my teeth. She knew I'd tried to off myself about a dozen times. "So where *do* you get a body to use? Is there a 'Bodies R Us' store?"

She arched a brow at my humor. "Nooo. We look for souls who are ready to move on. They've learned all they want to learn from their life's experience. Their bodies—and all the associated faults and personality bugaboos and all that fleshy identity stuff that overlays a soul—are in a mess. These are people in despair, people who've ruined their lives and can't picture a happy future. We give them a chance to . . . to move to a new neighborhood a little earlier than a natural death would allow. It's voluntary. It's a mutual agreement."

"So, you and Charles, and Gigi and Dante . . . you took over these bodies I see, and they have some bad history."

"Yes, they do, thanks to their former owners."

"Like what? I can't imagine you being anything but a wonderful . . . " Too intimate. I shrugged. "A nice person."

She smiled. "Thank you. I *am* a nice person. So are the others. We're good souls, if I do say so myself. Let's leave it at that."

"I remember you saying something to Charles about soul hunters being lost souls. You didn't sound happy about Ian."

She nodded. "Soul hunters tend to be tormented. They have unsettled business. They aren't at peace. They soul-jump too much, looking for trouble, looking for a fight. Looking for old, old enemies. They're kind of obsessed with revenge." She studied me intently. "Or they're looking for their lost soul mate. But . . . soul mates are only lost because they want to be."

"So you're saying I might be on the run from him?"

She nodded. "For some reason only your soul knows."

"I've got a demon after me *and* a stalker ex-boyfriend?"

She sighed as she got to her feet, lifting both hands in a prayer-like posture, palms up. She gazed heavenward. "God only knows." Then she looked at me again, gently. "But I'd say, judging from what I saw last night, that you're ready for him to find you."

4

Looking up Greg Lindholm on the Internet seemed like such a good idea. Okay, maybe not *good*, but unavoidable. If I thought of him as a man, maybe just a man, albeit a sadistic fucker, I could deal with the fear better.

But what did I expect? That he had a Facebook page? That I'd find out his favorite hobbies were collecting Bob Dylan vinyls and blogging about his pet ferret?

As things turned out, it wasn't what I found online that scared the piss out of me.

It was what found me.

I could move around the studio at will, though I winced and held onto furniture. It was May, now, and warm. Outside the loft's big windows I heard Charles and Sarah at ground level below, singing Woody Guthrie songs off-key as they tilled the building's weedy front yards. They were planting zinnias, just like they'd done when they were Caleb and Doris.

This land is your land . . . this land is our land, from the demon-infested suburbs to the soul-hopping high lands . . .

I glanced out the window at them. Songbirds swarmed around them every time they walked outside . . .

My heart raced. Barefoot, I eased my way across the studio floor, binding my robe tighter around me and clutching my knife. It went wherever I went, even to the tiny, drafty bathroom near my makeshift kitchen. I showered with the knife tied around my waist in a plastic bag.

I never claimed to be coping well.

The corner of the loft I called my office was nothing fancy. A desk, computer, wall shelves crammed with art books, a file cabinet. The computer was my only connection to the outside world. Here sat reality in a familiar package. Here I good inhale the reassuring high of information. *Just the facts, ma'am.*

If there was a Greg Lindholm out there in cyberspace, I'd find his salon-tanned ass.

I sat down gingerly on the chair in front of my funky desk. I slid my bare, burn-scarred feet onto a cozy carpet scrap. I placed my shaking hands on the five-point star inlaid in the wood. I'd built the desk from the top of an Art Deco dresser I'd found by a dumpster. Looked like it'd spent years in a leaky garage or barn. I sanded the walnut and mahogany star, detailed it with fresh wood stain, shellacked it, and now it gleamed in hypnotic brown and red tones from the center of the weathered gray veneer.

Profound beauty lives inside even the lost and abused souls. Outsider artists live by that motto.

I turned on the computer, waited for it to boot up, practiced some yoga breathing, gave up, tried to meditate on the rows of art books crammed into makeshift wall shelves, gave up then turned to one side and vomited bile into an old nail keg I'd painted bright yellow and used as a trash can. I wiped my mouth and hands with the tail of my robe.

My fingers trembled. I pecked Lindhom's name with the tip of my forefinger. Maybe Google had a special category for demons in human form.

Greg. Lindholm.

Ready. My right hand froze on the mouse.

I put my left hand over my right and forced my finger to click the mouse.

My skin crawled when a long list of Greg Lindholms popped onto my screen. A chiropractor in Oklahoma, a real estate broker in Oregon, a bar owner in Illinois. How many Swedish-American Lindholms *were* there? I went through the entries with my eyes half-shut against what might show up. But it didn't matter. He could be the chiropractor, the broker, the barkeep or a dozen other Greg Lindholms. There weren't enough details, and most entries didn't include photos of their specific Greg Lindholm. But okay, wait. Further down, there were a few. A photo of a middle-aged plumber with a beer gut. No, not him. A photo of a gayish wedding designer with long blonde hair and pale eyes. No, not him.

But then, suddenly, there he was, smiling that handsome,

deceptive smile at me from a picture in a Minnesota newspaper. The article was dated six months ago.

Tragedy Strikes Local Lawyer
Community Football Coach and Gridiron Star Mourns Loss

Well-known Tinsdale attorney Greg Patrick Lindholm, 34, is shown here at a chamber of commerce fundraiser with his beautiful wife Tracy, in happier times. Tracy Cherice Lindholm, 30, died last Thursday when she lost control of her SUV on Foltrane Highway. Also killed was the Lindholms' four year old son, Jeremy.

"It's a heartbreaking situation," said a family spokesman. "Greg is devastated. He and Tracy were high school sweethearts. They married during college and never spent a day apart since. Jeremy was the light of their lives. Greg is absolutely lost without Tracy and Jeremy."

Lindholm, a junior partner in the law firm of Cardon, Alton and Bartlett, played quarterback for the state champion Tinsdale Rams and was a star player at the university.

In recent years he's become a beloved coach in the Tri-County Youth Football League. "Just the other day he was saying how much he looked forward to coaching Jeremy in a few years," the spokesman said.

I slumped in my chair, gazing numbly at the computer. Just because a man is swank, successful, a doting daddy and married to the sorority girl of his dreams doesn't mean he's not harboring a nasty Mr. Hyde inside his golf shirt.

Demons pick the weak people, Sarah had said. I guess Lindholm was the right guy at the right time. Full of grief? Despair? Rage over the shitty hand fate had dealt his wife and child?

Had Momma been too naïve, so gentle and trusting that she was a pushover?

I leaned closer, frowning as I studied Lindholm's square-jawed face, his smiling gray eyes. Clean-cut jocks weren't my type. I mean *really* weren't. I couldn't figure out what had made him so irresistible to me in person.

Time to die again, bitch.

I bookmarked the Greg Lindholm entry then turned the computer off.

The screensaver—one of my gothic landscapes, and I was proud of it—blipped to black and the hard drive whirred to a stop. I reached over to shut the computer's top.

But then . . . words rose on the screen. On the turned-off, dead-black face of my computer. Stark, bone-white letters. They slowly intensified, like a sinister smile taking its time, enjoying the shock value. As the words reached a radioactive glow I pushed so far back in my chair that I turned it over and hit the floor, scooting back from the computer as if something might squeeze through the screen.

You won't get away next time, bitch. You can't hide much longer. You'll see.

*

I woke up to find Sarah and Charles sitting beside my bed, frowning at me. Gigi and Dante stood across the studio, arms crossed, grimly studying my new painting. I shoved myself upright in bed. My t-shirt was splattered with acrylics. Tubes and jars were scattered all over the bed. Brushes lay where I'd dropped them on the studio floor.

Across the way was a giant post-it note. I'd painted one of my bigger canvases in a nice rainbow of colors. In the center I'd painted a message. Its script was old-fashioned, flowing and beautiful, yet from a strong masculine hand, with thick loops and brusque jabs. Not my choppy way of writing.

I know you're scared, love. Not feeling too grand,

*that's for sure. But you can't pretend the bloody langer
didn't speak at you t'other day from inside that metal
book or whatever 'tis. Do not be thinking about offing
yourself because of him. 'Tis never as simple as taking a
walk next door, you ken? If he gets to you, speak of me.
Speak my name. I'm beating my fists on the wall
between us. He's coming after you, and there's no bloody
thing I can much do about it until you're willing to see
me again.*
    Ian

Around me, the disappointed silence was not exactly
golden.

"You should have told us the demon spoke to you again,
sweetie," Sarah said.

Charles nodded. "We're on your side, and you can't keep
secrets from us."

Gigi sighed. "What is going to take for you to believe what
we're telling you?"

Dante frowned. "Livia, we're all in danger here. Not just
you. And not just us. The rest of the city, too. If this demon
gets rid of you, he'll be able to hurt a lot of people."

Wrapped in Sarah's bird quilt, I shuffled miserably to the
canvas, searching the words for tricks, for hidden meanings. "I
don't want you guys or anyone else to suffer because of me. I'll
go away. I'll pack up and hit the road . . . "

"That's what the demon wants you to do, sweetie," Sarah
said gently.

"He wants you to be all alone again," Gigi agreed.
"Vulnerable."

Charles nodded. "He knows you're gathering your own
forces, just like he's gathering his. We're in this together. We
always have been."

I shuddered. I continued to rake the painted words for
clues. "*Who are you, Ian?*"

Dante stepped up beside me. He touched a dark finger to
the word *langer*. "We know one thing about him. This is Irish

slang." He touched the word *grand.* "This, too."

Gigi popped forward and tapped a pink fingernail to *ken.* "But this is old school mountain dialect. *You ken?* Is like saying, 'Okay? You get it, babe? You understand?'"

"What is he, a hillbilly leprechaun? So what does langer mean? Is that an Irish word for demon?"

Dante worked his mouth and cleared his throat awkwardly. "No, it's Irish for *penis.*"

"Prick," Gigi amended, blinking.

I stepped back from the canvas. "How do we know this is a good guy named Ian talking and not . . . Greg Lindholm in disguise?"

Charles patted my back. "I can tell you this much about your Ian—whoever he is, the boons are fond of him. We've been asking around. A few of them have heard of him. They say he is ethical, for a soul hunter. They vouch for him."

Asking around. Asking the boons? And what precisely, was a boon? I pivoted like an arthritic old woman. "If you guys can see all the shit that goes bump in the night, why do you need *me?*"

Sarah shook her head. "We don't see the demons and their little banes clearly. We hear them, we sense them, they communicate with us, they often help us, the boons, do, that is. The banes of course, are nothing but trouble, and the major demons, like Pig Face, are deadly. But we don't have your gift. You can see them *clearly,* the banes, the boons, the demons, the good souls, the bad, big and small, if you want to. You are the only one who can capture the banes and the demons. You can send them away—and not just temporarily. Permanently."

Dante put a hand on my shoulder. "You're a soul catcher, Livia. You really are."

Suddenly, dozens of songbirds lit on the windowsills. Shrieking. Sarah and Charles closed in on me protectively. "Get dressed," Sarah ordered. Gigi dragged me toward the old armoire I used as a closet. Dante ran to the window, thrusting a hand inside his long, black jacket. Seventy-five degrees in May and he dressed like a gunslinger. He pulled out a pistol.

Gigi stood guard as I shoved my legs into jeans and pulled a shirt over my tank top. She tossed a pair of paint-spattered tennis shoes at me then reached inside her pink-trimmed black overalls. "Here. This is a helpful charm." She opened a tiny vial. A sickly sweet fragrance filled my nose. She dabbed the oil on my forehead, chin, and throat. She grabbed my hands and smeared oil on my scarred, tattooed wrists.

I drew back. "I smell like over-ripe coconuts."

"Boons love this scent. It will help draw them to you. They can't stop a demon but they'll certainly toss some tricks his way and slow him down. But you have to ask them, Livia. They don't butt into people's lives. You have to want them there."

Not likely. I rammed my feet into the tennis shoes. Across the way, Sarah, Charles and Dante gazed grimly out my windows. Dante's shoulders sagged. He slowly put his gun away.

Sarah pivoted wearily. "The police are here. I expect the demon has something to do with this."

I froze. Once I was outside this sanctuary . . . Silence. Grim looks were traded. *Oh, shit,* I thought. *Oh, shit.*

Hundreds of songbirds now occupied the sill. A pair of flies zipped past them. They lit on the armoire's open door and gazed down at me.

"There, see?" Gigi smiled gamely. "You've already caught the attention of a couple of sweet little boons. They'll go with you to the police."

House flies? Cold sweat slithered down between my breasts. Police. The Man. The System. The Authority. Or to put it in old-time southern lingo, The Law.

I doubted a pair of flies would be much help against demons and The Law.

*

A few hours earlier, The Flame Master, aka Ronnie Bowden, the likable geek-freaky sound man at Dante's Room who also worked as a street performer spewing fire out of his mouth, had walked into Asheville's prettiest downtown green space, Pritchard Park. He stood in the middle of its pleasant little sunken plaza.

As the morning's usual audience of street people and business folk watched in horror, Ronnie yelled, "I love you, Livia Belane, even if you don't love me," then soaked himself in gasoline. Next he chopped off the fingers of his left hand with a brand-new hatchet he'd bought at Asheville's westside Home Depot. Then, as his blood spurted on a bed of freshly planted pansies, he flicked the ornamental dragon lighter he'd bought at the big fantasy and comic con down in Atlanta.

And, ta-dah, *he roasted himself alive.*

The good citizens of Asheville were reeling. Pritchard Park, a haunted triangle of artistically landscaped boulders and stone checker tables in the heart of the downtown shopping district, already had its share of infamy, but nothing like this. There were the unexplainable lights at night, the ghost of a Confederate soldier from the old Civil War staging grounds that lay beneath the modern pavement, and plenty of Wiccan holiday rituals by the local covens, which, in Asheville, didn't draw that many odd looks.

Ordinarily the park was home to stuff as unremarkable as drum circles, music jams, protest rallies, street mimes, hellfire preachers, homeless men muttering to invisible friends, stoned college students fucking behind the shrubbery, and white bread tourists strolling through on their way to bars, restaurants and art galleries. Until that morning the friendliest public park in Asheville had not been the site of self-amputation and self-immolation, all in one bloody, chargrilled package.

Ronnie left behind a note. He also left behind Nahjee.

You gave me this pendant. You gave me your heart, he wrote. *You told me to prove I loved you.*

Nahjee was now stuck in a plastic bag somewhere in a police evidence locker. I could feel her struggling to communicate, but Pig Face's spell still imprisoned her.

The Asheville P.D. were curious about me. An understatement.

"All right, Olivia, just tell me if you knew Ronnie was going to barbecue himself. If maybe, hmmm, you encouraged him?

Maybe you were teasing the boy? Maybe he took a flirtation the wrong way? Excuse me. These pair of flies just won't stop buzzing around my head."

I watched numbly as Detective Sam Lee Beaumont swatted at my two boon-flies., Sam Lee was Asian American and looked like a cross between Jackie Chan and Larry the Cable Guy. He had the Larry drawl, too.

My lungs wouldn't expand. The tiny, windowless room at the Asheville Police Department felt like a coffin. They couldn't accuse me of anything; Ronnie had killed himself in front of many witnesses; so, at worst, people might believe I was a skank who provoked his suicide. That's despicable, but not a crime.

Still, my hands sweated on the metal table. The overhead fluorescents flickered. My eyes darted toward every shadow. Detective Beaumont glared at the escaping flies then sighed heavily as he looked my way again. "Now. Livia. Tell me again. Just as honestly as you can, hon. I just want to fill out the forms and close this case. What was your relationship with Ronnie Bowden?"

"We didn't have a relationship. He was the club sound man. Dante let him perform in front of the club on weekend nights. He'd worked up a decent fire breathing routine. Some nights he made fifty to a hundred bucks in tips. When the bar was slow I'd take him sandwiches and Cokes. I do that for all the street performers. Dante okayed it."

"So any romantic relationship between you-all was just in Ronnie's mind?"

"Yes, sir."

"How many times did you-all hook up?"

"I said we had no relationship. That means no fu . . . no sex, in any form."

"Come on, now. You know what I'm talking about. Was he a 'friend with benefits?'"

There's no benefit to being my friend, mister.

"No, sir. He wasn't a friend. He was just a sweet guy who liked to wear eye liner and run the club's sound booth and juggle torches and spew fire out of his mouth. Like I said, I took him sandwiches."

"So you're sure this romance was all in his mind?"

"I don't know what was in his mind, sir. He was shy. We didn't talk."

Detective Beaumont gestured at the last, fading yellow speckles from the bruise around my eye. "Livia, who beat you up? I asked around at the Inferno. You haven't been to work in two months."

"That has nothing to do with Ronnie Bowden. Sir."

"Oh? Then tell me who it does have to do with? Who's your abusive boyfriend, Livia?"

Oh, just a demon from another dimension. Who may be closing in on me even as we speak. Bile rose in my throat. I swallowed hard. "I can't discuss that, sir. But I swear it has nothing to do with Ronnie."

Detective Beaumont scowled. When his face compressed he looked like a jowly Pekingese. "Livia, let me paint a little clearer picture for you. This mornin', a young man mutilated himself in a city park, and then he burned himself alive. Not only did his suicide note implicate you in his decision-makin' process, but he had a weird snake pendant in his possession that belongs to you. Now here you are lookin' like you're recoverin' from a major butt-whuppin' by *someone*. In your art studio you've got a great big painting of a fierce-looking back-to-nature honcho who's holdin' a bloody hatchet. Ronnie Bowden used a hatchet on himself. You like hatchets, Livia?"

"No sir. I just . . . it's just a painting. A coincidence. "Look, you can't charge me with anything. I have a right to leave."

"Livia, hon. Ronnie Bowden is the son of the CEO of Mid-States Mountain Bank. His folks were none too happy when he rebelled and turned into a club rat, but he was still their sweet baby boy. They're never gonna accept that he was just a messed-up little geek who offed himself. They're lookin' for a villain. And they're none too picky about who they blame."

"I thought rich people had no more clout than the rest of

us, under the law."

He smiled. "You're an idealistic girl, I can tell."

"I . . . Detective, I swear to you, I don't know a thing . . . "

He slapped a hand on the table. "Livia, do you see my face? See me gettin' angry? Do you think I haven't looked into your records? Holy crazy creepiness, girl. Nine years ago you set a fire that killed your mama and baby bubba, then you spent court-ordered time in a psych lock-up. What is it with you and fire?"

"Coincidence?"

He thumped a folder on his desk. "And the bunch you hang out with? Dante and that little pink-haired gal and those two old hippies? Every one of 'em has a criminal record. Every single one of 'em."

My skin prickled.

He went on, "Livia, gal, give me a reason I can convince the Bowden's lawyers not to crawl up your drainpipes and peer in your windows for the rest of your life, hon. Tell me you weren't a bad influence on their son. Tell me his tox report is going to come back clean. Tell me I'm not gonna find out you deal drugs and he was your customer. Tell me!"

The flies zoomed at his open mouth. He leaned back, waving at them. "Damn. I'm getting' a fly swatter. I'll be right back." He stomped out of the room.

The flies lit on the table by my fingertips. I stared at them. They stared back. I glanced up at the room's security camera. I looked back at the flies, and shut my eyes. *Thank you for helping me.*

One of the flies flicked its wings. A tiny voice, trilling and sweet, went through my mind. *No problem. We're trying to stall him until your lawyer gets here.*

The flies buzzed away. They settled high on the wall, in a corner.

Sparkles crowded my vision. My stomach churned. I was talking to flies.

And they were answering.

Someone knocked on the door. An officer popped her

head in. "Your lawyer's walking up the hall."

Relief. Sarah and Charles had called a lawyer they knew. Lucille Hanson. Now I'd get out of this death chamber pronto.

Greg Lindholm walked in.

Wrong one, the flies said urgently.

My chair hit the floor. I backed up until a wall stopped me. Oh my God. Oh my God. He smiled at me, then at the guard. "Thank you so much."

She smiled back, batting her eyelashes. "No problem."

I darted forward. "Don't leave me here. He's not—"

The guard shut the door. Greg Lindholm's eyes gleamed. "She sees what I want her to see. They all do. She doesn't hear you, bitch." He nodded at the overhead camera. "And nobody sees anything unusual now." He cracked his knuckles. "And they won't realize anything's wrong until they find your body."

He threw the table against the hall and came at me with his hands rising toward my throat. He was fast, he was strong, and the room was too small for maneuvers. I grabbed my chair and held it in front of me like a barricade. He laughed as his hands latched onto the leg braces. When he threw the chair I held on and got thrown with it. I slammed the adjacent wall, hard. He ripped the chair out of my hands and slung it out of the way.

Gasping, I tried to jam a knee into his stomach but he pushed me tight against the wall with his body. A rancid odor rose from his skin. His breath was hot and greasy. His thick fingers sank into my throat.

"Die slowly, bitch," he whispered. "I always like to watch you go."

I gagged and struggled, flailing. I'm not small, I'm not delicate, but he held me by the neck as if I were nothing. In another few seconds I *would* be nothing.

Was it better to die with one demon smiling as he strangled me rather than risk inviting a second demon to help him? I'd be dead, either way.

Ian. I need you. Please. You said you'd come if I asked.

The air contracted and expanded as if a tornado had sucked the room into its vortex. Weird pressures squeezed me hard then let me go. I was free. Oxygen swirled down my throat. White energy—that's the only way I can describe it, a pulse of whiteness—filled my mind. For a few seconds I couldn't see or hear. I slid down the wall, dragging my fingers over my aching neck, feasting on the revival of life inside my lungs.

Sound and sight rushed back. I stared at Greg Lindholm. He lay on the floor across from me, convulsing. His eyes rolled back, he flailed, he jerked. The sharp heels of his polished loafers rattled in an electrocution rhythm, making a grotesque staccato on the hard linoleum floor. His hands squeezed into white-knuckled fists. He grunted. A deep, enraged rumble came from his throat.

And then he went limp.

Good work, soul catcher, the flies chorused.

I got to my feet, swaying. My chest heaved. I flattened myself against the wall and inched into a corner. I was afraid to take my eyes off Greg Lindholm's unconscious body, but I stole quick glances around me.

"Ian?" I whispered. As if he could be hiding beside me in a ten-foot-square room.

Nothing. No answer.

The security camera whirred back to life. My knees buckled. I grabbed a chair for support. The door burst open. Detective Beaumont rushed in. He knelt beside Lindholm, checked his pulse, poked a finger in his mouth to see if his tongue was choking him then looked at me. "Does he have a history of seizures? Is he epileptic?"

I shook my head. "Don't . . . know."

"What's his name?"

"Greg Lindholm."

"Don't worry, we got a couple of EMT's hangin' out in the lobby, flirtin' with the dispatchers. You should have yelled for help when he started havin' the seizure."

I stared at him. Maybe I'd appreciate the irony some day.

The paramedics strode in. I remained flattened in the corner, my skull pressed into the hard angle, my eyes straining in my head. It was hard to see Greg Lindholm through the crowd of people squatting around him. My gaze shifted to the open door. I edged toward it. I'd rather be chased by the police than a demon.

"Greg Lindholm? Mr. Lindholm?" one of the paramedics said loudly. He lightly slapped Greg Lindholm's face. "Can you hear me, Mr. Lindholm?"

"There he comes," the detective said. "He's blinking. He's okay."

My blood turned to ice. *The open door. Go for it. Now.*

I lurched forward just as the other paramedic stood up. We collided. He grabbed me by one arm. "You all right? You don't look so good. Here, sit down. Sit. I'll give you a whiff of oxygen and check your blood pressure." He guided me into a chair. "Be right back with the oxygen tank."

He walked out and shut the door behind him. The lock clicked loudly. I stared at the huddled backs of the detective and first paramedic, still blocking my view of Greg Lindholm. One of his legs flexed and shifted, then slowly rose to a bent position.

I stood. "Don't let him up. *Do not let him get up.* You have no idea . . . "

"Calm down, hon," Detective Beaumont said over one shoulder. "He seems fine now. Don't you worry." He looked back down at Lindholm. My pet flies dive-bombed Beaumont's face. He swatted at them while peering closer at Lindholm. "Mr. Lindholm? Hi, there."

Both flies lit on the detective's forehead. He slapped a hand there. They zoomed away a split-second ahead of it. "Goddamn flies," he exploded. His face turned pink. "Sorry, hon."

"No problem." I couldn't see Lindholm's face behind the detective and the paramedic.

Detective Beaumont slapped Lindholm's shoulder. "Awright, awright. Comeon, Mr. Lindholm, let's get you out of this fly-infested jungle. If you want to go to the hospital for a quick check-up, say so. Otherwise, we'll call it a day. I'll have somebody drive you and Livia to your office."

I gagged. I was being handed over to the demon who'd smiled at the idea of watching me smother slowly inside the grip of his hands. I knotted my fist tighter and raised it. Lindholm would have to drag me out of there in a bloody heap.

"She's mine, then?" a deep voice said, lifting the sentence upward at its end. "That's grand. I feel all the better now, thank you indeed. I'll be having a look at her, please."

"Sure, buddy," the paramedic said.

Beaumont nodded. "Yeah, let's help you sit up. Let Livia get a look at you, too. So she can see that you're back to normal."

I couldn't move, couldn't breathe. The voice that wanted a look at me wasn't Greg Lindholm's. Was I the only one hearing a stranger's Irish-inflected baritone?

Slowly, the man on the floor sat up. Beaumont clapped him on the shoulders again then scooted back so I could be reassured that my attorney was in the pink.

Greg Lindholm's gray eyes met mine. It was still him in the flesh—his body, his face, every physical feature that reminded me that he'd rammed himself into every hole of my body and twice tried to kill me.

But in his eyes was a new expression, pained and urgent, studying me as if he'd waited a long time to see me again. The look in his eyes belonged to a different man. His throat worked. "'Tis good to be with you again, my . . . Livia."

I slowly lowered my fist.

Some souls you recognize by sight. Others by instinct.

And some, whether you admit it or not, come to you by deep and endless and tormented love.

Ian was here.

5

The new stranger in Greg Lindholm's body stood in the middle of the shabby-chic, old-hippy atmosphere of the Ablehorn Art Gallery. The massive building had been a weaving factory in the early 1900's. The windows were enormous, built to let in light for the workers at their looms. The floor and walls were made of heavy beams, to hold the weight. Downstairs was Charles' pottery studio and a large apartment where he and Sarah lived. It was a sanctuary, like the Harken Bible building.

But now this stranger stood in the middle of that sacred place like a large, caged wolf impatiently waiting for us to flip the cage latch and let him taste our throats. Sarah, Charles, Gigi and Dante surrounded him, mainly to keep me away from him. I sat on a small couch in a corner, suspicious and wounded, nursing my bruised neck with an ice pack.

"Livia," he asked again. "How's the neck? Better?"

I stared at him, still not willing or able to form words. Fate? Destiny? Recognition? Soul mates? Lovers?

Temporary Delusion. He's a stranger. Now I look at him and only see Lindholm. And Pig Face.

When I gave no answer, he shifted and shrugged his big shoulders against the tailored material of Lindholm's dark, three-piece suit. He looked down at his polished loafers as if they felt funny, then frowned at the silk tie he clutched in one big hand. "Will I be needing to wear this leash?" he asked me.

His eyes seemed more silver than gray now, with an unnerving edge of sadness in them. He turned his intense scrutiny on me at every chance. He kept ruffling a hand over Lindholm's styled brown hair; which now swirled in uneven prongs. Somehow that salon haircut looked shaggy already, like a mink morphing into a wolverine. When I returned nothing but another locked-down stare, he patted his suit jacket until he found the pockets, then stuffed the tie in one of them.

"Stick to the questions at hand," Charlie told him.

"Tell us what we want to know," Dante added, one hand casually cupping a pistol.

Ian nodded. "Ay, I ken."

"You set the demon loose?"

"Ay. I evicted the bastard from Lindholm's carcass. Being kicked out of a fine home weakens a demon considerable. It'll take him some time to find such a brawny self as this one to use, but he will. And then there'll be no way out but to kill the body and nab the soul." He looked at me again. "That's what you must be ready for. To see him as his real self, and capture him with your magic, and banish him. You have the way. But you have to be willing to fight. And you'll need my help. A soul catcher must have a bodyguard to track demons and fend them off while the catcher goes about the banishing spell."

"We're not a team," I rasped.

"Then you *are* a soul hunter?" Sarah asked, frowning.

"Call it what you will, mum. I know it's a wee bit notorious. Mainly, I'm here for Livia." He looked over at me once more. Damn, he had such sad eyes. "You needed me. You asked me here. I've been looking for you forever it seems. You've been good at hiding yourself. You never wanted to need me again. I'm sorry I didn't find you afore himself did. I'm sorry, love."

I worked my throat and finally rasped, "Don't call me that."

"I'm sorry, Livia."

"Why shouldn't I believe you're not a demon, too?"

"If I were, I'd have killed you where you stood. He *meant* to kill you for certain this time. I stopped him the only way I could. I took his body. Willing bodies are not so easy to procure. Perk up, Livia. Isn't this one handsome?"

I threw the ice pack at him. He caught it with one hand then let it fall to the gallery's whitewashed floor. His eyes never left me. I got to my feet and started towards him. Gigi tried to block me. "Livia! We may not know exactly what this guy is here for, but the boons say he's not a demon. I know it's hard to look past Greg Lindholm's face and body, but remember, it's the soul that counts. Hey, this is like *Terminator 2*, right? Sarah Conner had to wrap her mind around Arnold turning into the good guy."

"Arnold wasn't programmed to use rape as a weapon." I shoved past her and got into the stranger's all-too-familiar face. He didn't move, didn't even blink. Just looked down at me with that quiet misery of his. "Why did you pick Lindholm's body? You could have taken the detective's, or a police officer's. You had plenty of choices. If you'd chosen one of the other men, you'd have been armed with their guns. Then you could have killed this . . . this . . . " my throat worked as I raked his body with disgust . . . "this piece of garbage. Then the demon would have been freed, and I'd have gotten a detailed look at him again, and I could have drawn . . . "

"That's a lot of 'coulds,' Livia."

"Why did you pick this body?" I repeated. My voice rose. *"Unless you like what this body is capable of doing to me?"*

He flinched as if I'd slapped him. "Livia, I'd as soon cut off my hands as do—"

"You were there, that night. You, not just him. You watched him rape me. You killed his . . . his eight-toed *pimp* with your hatchet, didn't you? Then why couldn't you help me or warn me or stop Pig Face from what he did?"

"I could not see anything clear from where I was, Livia. No more than you can see everything clear in other heavens, no more than you can make out more'n just shapes on a misty night. Being out there—" he waved a big hand toward the ether, then froze when I flinched at the aggressive gesture —"Out in the *yon*, Livia, it's not like here, not like you're thinkin' in the same way as a flesh and blood body, makin' choices from this place—"he pointed carefully at his head —"but from *yon*—" he made a large circle with his arms, watching me carefully in case I spooked.

"Stop." I shook my head.

His arms sank. "I'm no good with words."

"Excuse me," Sarah put in gently. "What he's saying, Livia,

it that our souls make their decisions based on a purity of purpose we cannot comprehend. When we're in that realm, our souls know *precisely* what's best for us. What they do, how they decide our future, is a mystery we're not capable of understanding. They choose our way with the infinite grace and purpose of the Holy Spirit. They are listening to God."

"Or to His opposite," I countered.

The melancholy deepened in Ian's eyes. I knew I was being a bitch, but he, or his body, had tried to kill me *again*, just a few hours ago. I wanted to rip his skin off and find the Ian I'd painted. That soul was trapped behind Greg Lindholm's face, and God help me, but I would always see the hatred and lust in Lindholm's eyes. And worse—I would see the grotesque creature from my painting.

"Do no' look at me that way," Ian rasped. "Tell me what I can do to convince you I'm a fair and able and decent man, not a beast of Hell."

I shook my head again, backing away from him. "Nothing. Just keep your distance from me. I'm sorry, but just stay away."

"*Livia*. My ken of this body is naught. It's a cipher to me. I haven't even yet taken a look. I've got no pretty words to heal you, Livia; it was always you with the education, not myself. So I can only put it so: Your jabs, your arse, your gee and all the giblets from minge to hoop are like my own flesh to me, and I will protect them against all who'd try to hurt you."

"I have no idea what you just said."

"All your tender parts are like my own. You want to have a look at me? Well, then. Have at it." He nodded to the others. "All of you." Then, to me: "Let's you and me both see what reeking monster I've brought into your midst."

He kicked off his shoes. His feet were bare. He shrugged out of his jacket then dropped it in a heap. The air off his body was clean and warm. He fumbled with the small buttons of his vest, flung it aside, then worked at the buttons of his shirt. My mind reeled. The shirt came off in rustle of fine cloth. Suddenly I was gazing at the center of his bare chest.

He flexed his thickly muscled arms and scowled down at

himself. He prodded the spot where his tanned belly disappeared into his pants without the softness of a single body hair. Lindholm had been a waxer and a tanning bed enthusiast. "Hah. What's this bare pelt? This man has no more fur than a babe. But 'tis clear he's spent time working hard under a hot sun, so that's good."

He pulled a slender leather belt free then struggled with the pants' button and snap fastener. Finally he tore the snap off. The rip of the cloth made my spine twitch. He shoved his pants down and kicked them off. He stood still, grimacing down at himself.

No underwear. I believe he was as surprised as the rest of us.

In the tense silence I heard my own sharp breath and the muffled sounds of Gigi's shocked snort plus a gasp from Sarah. Charles and Dante struggled manfully to show no emotion. Why should I feel shy? Why should I care? But I kept my eyes on his chest, refusing to look down after my first startled glance.

He raised his intense eyes to mine. "Here I am, Livia. I ken to your pain and I'll do my best to off any demon and kill any flesh and blood fecker who lays a hand on you. But I need a good strong body for the work at hand, and that's not easy to come by, like I've said, so I have to make do with this hateful one, and you do, too. It's a man's flesh, Livia. It's hung with a big stick and clackers the size of apples and a mind for horning up every time it's near you. Don't take that as a threat or a sign of evil lingering under the skin. All that you'll find inside this skin is love."

Silence. A challenge. I looked down at his crotch. The long, thick penis that had torn me up now gently pointed my way. A dick is just a dick, yeah. It's only a weapon if it falls into the wrong hands. But my stomach rolled at the thought of that penis ever sliding inside me again. The body carries memories of its own. And mine rejected Ian's.

I gagged and put a hand to my mouth. I backed further away from him, and turned my gaze aside.

His big shoulders sagged. He stood there with his hands hanging helplessly, the palms open, his bare feet braced apart. His bawdy hard-on instantly faded.

Sarah stepped past me. "Charles, get my kit. That wound has to be treated. It's infected."

My eyes darted to Ian's left thigh. My stab wound. Pus seeped from under a large bandage on the meaty outer muscle. Several sinister red streaks already radiated from the wound.

Dante straightened ominously. "Sorry, Ian, but I put a small bane lure on her knife."

Ian nodded to him. "A smart thing, man. No apology needed."

Gigi *eeeked*. "Oh, yes, that looks like a bane at work. I'll get some fresh herbs and make a poultice. The farmer's market just got in some fresh cilantro. The healing boons love it."

"You're not going outside alone," Dante put in. I'll take you."

"Do you think it's safe to leave him unguarded?"

"Yes, I do. Besides, Sheba's here. She'll keep an eye on him."

As they hurried outside Sarah dropped to her heels beside Ian's leg. She was earthy and practical. She didn't seem to notice the naked man-junk twitching just inches from her face. "This may hurt when I pull it off." She plucked at the bandage's corner.

Ian stared dully at me. "Go ahead, mum. I'm not in a mood to care."

I dragged my hand across my mouth and took a deep breath. "All right. You're not a demon. I'll keep telling myself that your name is Ian, that you saved my life, that you haven't said or done anything to deserve being hated by me, and that I should give you a fair chance to do what you say you've come here to do. All right. But just . . . stop talking as if you've known me before. I don't remember you, not in this life or any other. Why do you think I should?"

The bandage made a wet, slurping sound as Sarah peeled it from the gooey flesh of his thigh. The puncture made by my knife had swollen on the edges. The wound resembled an obscenely pursed mouth. Pus and blood dribbled down to his bare knee. My stomach lurched again. I bent over, forced the bile back into my stomach, then straightened wearily.

All he saw was more revulsion. He slowly furled and unfurled his hands. "I didn't expect you to remember me, but I wish to God's heaven you did. You'd at least remember that I belonged to you, heart and soul, and that you did not hate me, though you were heartbroken with me the last I held you, and you're the same now. I suppose 'tis something to be said for more'n two hundred years of a woman's unchanging bad mood."

"Why do you think you know me?" I repeated hoarsely. "Who was I?"

A long breath shuddered out of him. "My wife," he said.

*

Shadows flitted across my mind that night, half-formed and mysterious, then vanishing. Ronnie Bowden disappeared in a grisly plume of fire and spurting blood. Every time I jerked awake I thought I saw creatures and human faces in the air around me. And I thought *they* saw *me.*

And always, always, a chant went through my mind: *His wife.* The soul hunter's wife. No, Greg Lindholm's wife. Pig Face's "wife."

No, Ian's wife.

Ian Thornton. That was his full name. His brogue pronounced it *Tornton.*

"When you're ready to know the whys and wherefores . . . " he had said grimly.

I wasn't ready. Not even remotely.

So now I slept badly in a deep, pillow-filled window seat in the second story of Sarah and Charles' gallery. The window overlooked the gallery's gravel parking lot. I hugged my knees to my chest, wrapped in one of Sarah's protective bird quilts. Each time I woke up I craned my head to check a pair of massive industrial doors that led in and out of the big room. I'd rolled them shut and locked their thick iron latches. I checked the doors again. Ian slept on a futon Sarah and Charles set up for him on the floor of another room. My skin crawled.

This part of the gallery was big and airy, the ceilings twenty feet high. It had good vibes. It featured my Bible-verse infused mountain landscapes. I felt safe with my scenes around me. Sometimes I meditated on them, trying to absorb myself inside their blue-green mountains and deep creek coves. Imaginary places. Imaginary happiness. When I dozed I could hear the distant rhythm of the looms, and the mountain songs of weaving women.

I tilted my head against a cool window pane. A full moon glowed over the woods across a narrow paved road and the French Broad curled in wide, lazy darkness beyond those woods.

Asheville was built on a high plateau surrounded by three Appalachian ranges, all of them bedrock towers of earth, stone and sky. At the bottom of the plateau the river district's deep, flat cove was home to factory buildings, most of them more than a century old and abandoned. A few had been renovated by artists with a need for large loft spaces. They squatted like dark-eyed sentinels guarding the waterway.

Guarding. That's how it felt, yes. Because there really *were* demons everywhere, large and small. A fucking infestation of boogie men and ghouls and things that went bump in the night. I'd been happier when I thought I was just crazy. But there were angels, too. Some so small they didn't mind working in disguise as houseflies.

That bizarre thought did me in. Exhaustion loosened every muscle. My neck throbbed with Ian's fingerprints. I mean, Ian's *body's* fingerprints. I wanted to forget the feel of his hands on my throat.

I slept. I dreamed.

*

I walked down a steep path pocked with deer tracks and something larger. I stopped and studied the marks. Buffalo. Somehow I recognized buffalo tracks. I was in a time when small bison still lived in the Appalachians. I looked around in wonder. Tall mountains rose on either side, and through the vast green umbrellas of majestic chestnut trees—long before a blight killed every single one of them in the 1930's—I glimpsed blue vistas. Feeling a little bewildered by my time traveling, but not scared, I kept walking down the path, moving deeper into fairytale woodland scented with earth and water.

I came to a boulder as big as a house. I could hear water gurgling. I clambered over thick tree roots that twined around the base of the enormous rock. A rotting tree trunk lay in the way, a remnant of a chestnut tree so big my head barely crested the trunk's side. I dug my fingers into the soft bark, braced a foot on the boulder, and climbed up on the tree trunk.

Now I could see in front of the rock. At its base was a deep mountain spring. Water trickled from that beautiful pool into a rocky creek bed, frothing and giggling as it slipped along a fissure down the mountainside. I studied the rock in awe. Carved on the rock's smooth face were symbols. Stars, circles, and strange lines that intersected each other in no obvious pattern. I didn't know what the carvings meant. They were even older than the Cherokees who lived nearby. I knew this much, somehow: *This is the Talking Rock.*

Very ancient and very wise. It drew beings from the other worlds.

Ahah. Now I knew where I was. A portal. I let out a breath of relief.

"Hello, soul catcher," a voice said in Cherokee. "It is good to see you again."

I looked up to my right and there, on top of the rock, lay a huge version of Nahjee—a purple, striped snake as thick as a man's body and at least thirty feet long. Its head was V-shaped and fierce but its eyes had a soft lavender glow, like a sunset sky at the rim of the mountains. Ahah. An *uktena*. One of the spirit animals.

Standing beside the uktena was a perfectly shaped miniature Cherokee woman, no more than knee-high to me, with beautiful white hair that hung to the ground. Her clothing was old-school: a deer leather shawl that would flash her bare boobs when she lifted her arms, a wrap-around leather skirt, and moccasins. Her hair was decorated with rows of small songbird feathers.

She smiled at me. "Hello again, Mele. Or are you always *Mary* now?"

"I go by either name, thank you, Bird Mother." I knew her. One of the Little People. A fairy. No introductions needed.

"You're looking happy, Mele. It's not easy for a soul catcher to be happy. So many battles to fight."

"Yes, that's true. But I'm doing well these days, thank you."

I looked down at my reflection in the pool. My skin was a light golden brown. My eyes were still green, but now my face had Cherokee features. My hair was inky black. It hung to my hips and was braided with colored ribbon. My ears were pierced. I wore thick gold hoop earrings so heavy they pulled my lobes down. My long calico shirt was belted with a woven leather sash, and the sash was decorated with rough crystals, some clear, some green, some blue. I wore a long leather skirt rubbed soft and faded at the thighs and knees.

And I wore handsome, black boots.

"Very pretty boots," the snake said.

"They're from my father's trading post. Brought by ox wagon all the way from the Carolina coast, and before that they had traveled on a ship all the way from Philadelphia, where they'd been made by the finest boot smith, especially for me."

"A gift?"

I smiled. "Yes. My husband gave them to me."

"Is he one of the People?"

"No, he was born across the big water, like my father. But he's a very good man. I love him with all my heart."

"Good in bed?" Bird Mother asked, grinning. Cherokee fairies weren't shy.

"Very good." I grinned back

The uktena tilted its head. "He must be a brave man, to marry a soul catcher."

"Yes. Very brave. I've tried to explain the spirit world to him, and he's trying hard to understand. But he doesn't realize how dangerous it is." A lie. He didn't believe me at all. But he was polite about it.

"Ah. Yes. So you've come to ask us how best to protect him?"

"Yes, thank you."

"Hmmm. Let us ponder it." Bird Mother sat down next to the snake and pulled a trio of long clay pipes from beneath her hair. Fragrant tobacco smoke rose in the air. She handed a pipe to me, then tucked one in the uktena's mouth.

The three of us smoked, watching eddies in the deep pool as minnows came up to visit. Then Bird Mother took the cold pipes and tucked them in her hair again. She and the uktena looked at me grimly.

Bird Mother said, "He does not remember, but he is a soul hunter."

I went very still and silent. My heart sank. "Are you sure?"

"Yes. There is a lot of blood on his hands, and he has not lived out a long, contented life since many ages ago. He dies in violence, every time."

"Because of me?" I asked sadly.

"Yes. Always in your service, and . . . always doomed by his love for you."

"You will never be happy with this man," the uktena added. "And he will never be safe with you for long."

I stiffened proudly. "What can I do to save him?"

"You cannot. It is your path and his."

"Help me *try*."

They sighed. Bird Mother said finally, "Do not live in the village. Do not live beside your father's trading post. Build your cabin deep in these woods near here. The white light of the Talking Rock will protect you and your husband as long as you live nearby."

The uktena eyed Bird Mother. "What if she can't keep her husband from wandering? You know how soul hunters are."

Bird Mother shook her head. "Then his fate is cast in sorrow again, and so is hers." She shook a finger at me. "You should not have gotten married, you know. You have many enemies among the demons. They will separate your husband from you. You will always have to search for him. And him for you."

I stood. "I won't let him wander from here. It's as simple as that."

The uktena and Bird Mother clucked their tongues at my arrogance. "Whatever you do," the uktena said, "keep his name close to your heart. Then you will always recognize him."

I nodded politely. I wouldn't lose my husband. I'd cast spells to keep him at home, and I'd ask the good spirits to help me.

Bird Mother sighed. "What is the name of this fine, doomed husband?"

I lifted my head. "Ian," I said.

*

I woke up sweating. The air of the gallery felt heavy on my chest. I was hyperventilating. I fumbled for a window lever. At the bottom of each towering window were sections that could be opened with a simple hand crank. My fingers closed on the lever's cool metal.

A child said loudly, "Oh, don't do that, Miss Livia!"

My blood froze. Breathing hard, I turned my head toward the voice.

In a shaft of moonlight, just a few feet away from me, stood a red-headed little girl. She was about ten years old. She wore a simple shift dress. She had a small bow in her hair. She appeared to be as real as I was. She wrung her hands. "Miss Livia, don't dare open that window, please, don't."

I wet my lips with my tongue. "I'm sorry, but I need some fresh air."

"There's a bane outside that window, Miss Livia. It's trying to get you."

My hand convulsed on the lever. The vent popped open just an inch.

Something hissed. A wet tentacle slithered through the opening and wound around my wrist. On the other side of the glass, just inches from my face, a dark shape clawed the window.

I exploded—yelling, kicking, fumbling for the knife I'd tucked by one knee. I braced my feet against the sill and lurched backwards. The bane held on and jerked hard. My hand rammed into a window pane. The thick glass made an ominous, crackling sound.

The phantom child uttered a shriek. "He'll slam-bam you until the window busts! Then he'll pull you through the broke glass!"

The creature pulled so hard that I hit the window like a limp doll. Stars exploded in my vision. I began to slump.

Suddenly, feet thudded on the wooden floor behind me. A strong hand snared me by my free arm and dragged me off the window seat. The tentacle stretched but didn't let go. I stared woozily at it in the moonlight. It was gray with shimmering scales.

Steel flashed above my head. I saw Ian in the light. He was shirtless; his face was carved in deadly concentration. He braced his feet apart, drew back his right arm and brought an ax down. The tentacle severed with a gush of stinking fluid.

The thing outside the window shrieked and disappeared.

Everything got very quiet. All I heard was the chattering of my teeth.

Sarah, Charles, Gigi and Dante rushed into the room. Charles flipped a light switch.

I lay in the floor at Ian's feet, wearing only my t-shirt and panties. He wore nothing but his trouser pants, which hung halfway down his taut, hairless belly, since the snap was still broken at the waistband.

The window pane stood open, and the ax was embedded in the window sill. Stenciled on its handle was *AFD*, for the Asheville Fire Department, and also ONLY FOR EMERGENCY USE.

I wondered if that included attacks from tentacled demons

As my head cleared I frowned at the sill. No chopped-off tentacle, no spattered bane blood, and no other sign that anything I'd seen or felt had been real. I looked around shakily.

No little red-headed girl, either.

"The Pig Faced bastard's found himself another servant already," Ian said grimly. I looked up at his half-exposed belly, his muscled stomach, his broad chest. He looked down at my pale, bare legs, scarred feet and heavily tattooed arms, and his frown softened to a tender wince.

I wanted to crawl away. *He sees how ugly I am. I'm not the beautiful Cherokee wife in the dream.*

"Why is there no evidence of what happened just now?"

"'Twas not real, not exactly. The banes mostly work by playing with your ken of what's possible. A few are powerful enough to harm the body—like ol' Eight Toes did—but most just feck with your mind. This one would have had you throw yourself out the window and t'would look like you did it all by yourself." Ian pried the ax loose, hefted it by the handle, and tested its balance with a slow chopping motion. "I'll need better than this the next time."

"The *next* time?" I rasped.

Dante walked over and eyed the ax with expert scrutiny. "I can get you something more agile, or would you rather make one yourself?"

"I'd druther make it myself. Is there a forge hereabouts?"

"Up the road there's a sculptor who does metal work. You can use his equipment."

"Good, then. I'll draw more powerful boons by my own smithing." Ian looked down at me wearily. "G'night, Livia. Stay away from windows, you ken?"

"Ian, I—"

"I'm your bodyguard. Think o' me that way and nothing else. It'll be better for the both of us." He offered me a hand up, but I shook my head. He squared his shoulders and walked out of the room. Dante and Charles followed him.

"Are you hurt?" Sarah asked with a tone of motherly concern, as if I'd just fallen off my bike. She and Gigi huddled beside me. I held up my arm. A pale pink welt rose on the skin of my wrist, next to a tattoo that circled my arm like a bracelet. Stars, circles, and intersecting lines. I'd copied them from the symbols Granny Belane drew for the tattoo artist when I was a child.

Suddenly I realized what they were. My skin prickled.

The symbols from the Talking Rock, in my dream.

Gigi clamped a hand over the welt. "Livia, like Ian said, banes create illusions. That's how they manipulate people. They can make you think you're being pulled out a window, or that they've grabbed you, or you're poisoned, or wounded—anything bad you can imagine, they make you believe it, and that makes it real enough to hurt you. Now, here's what you do. Shut your eyes. Concentrate. Say something to banish the illusion. Whatever means the most to you. It's your spell, so make it personal."

I looked at Sarah. She nodded. "You're rested and strong again. Give it a try."

I shut my eyes. Twenty-five years of fear and confusion and rage and pain and grief boiled up inside me. I was a long way from being a kick-ass convert to this bizarre reality, but the blood river of revenge already flowed through me. "Paint them," I said. "Trap them. *Burn them.*"

I opened my eyes. Gigi still had her hand clamped over my wrist. Her brown brows perked like cats' ears. Her ankh tattoo quivered. "Wow," she said.

"Let's see if it worked," Sarah said impatiently.

Gigi lifted her hand. The welt was gone.

She and Sarah patted me on the back. "Your mind is opening up. You're on your way to fully using your powers."

I admitted very quietly, "I was warned about the bane by a little girl with red hair. Do you have any idea who she is?"

Judging by the ecstatic looks they gave me, I should have kept quiet.

6

The ghost-child's name was Dolly McCrane, and she had drowned in the French Broad flood of nineteen sixteen, not long after her tenth birthday.

Her parents had proudly run McCrane's Fine Floor Coverings, a small weaving factory in the building that was now Sarah and Charles' gallery. Their wool rugs, woven in geometric patterns based on Scots-Irish pioneer and Cherokee Indian basket designs, had been prized by Asheville's Victorian-era families. Several McCrane rugs had even graced the floors at Biltmore, the Vanderbilts' vast Asheville estate.

When the French Broad's waters receded, Dolly's body had been found among the ruined looms in the factory's ground floor.

Where I now stood with Sarah and Gigi.

"That's where the flood crested," Sarah said, pointing to a stain on the faded bricks high above our heads on the walls of Charles' pottery studio. The morning sunlight made jigsaw patterns on the roughly mortared surface. "No one could have predicted that the French Broad and Swannanoa would rise that high," Sarah went on. "Of course, back then, people here in the river bottoms didn't get much warning. That's why so many died. A lot of the river businesses were wiped out. Only the toughest old souls, like this one—"she knocked on the weaving factory's foot-thick walls—"survived."

Gigi pressed her cheek to the wall. "Yes you did, didn't you, booba boo?"

I stared at her. She was talking baby talk to a *wall*.

"Because you're not a quitter are you, old girl?" She listened for a moment, then nodded at Sarah and me. "Sheba says this building's happy to still be alive."

I clutched a coffee mug tighter. I was on my tenth cup, but my head still felt like a grainy photo album full of stills from a really nasty horror flick. I glanced out the lower windows for signs of Dante's aged silver Jeep. Dante and Charles had taken Ian shopping in downtown Asheville. A reincarnated North Carolina frontiersman in a Midwestern lawyer's stolen body, shopping for modern threads. The idea seemed absurdly reasonable compared to everything else.

"Livia? You paying attention?" Sarah asked. "You're got so much to remember, to re-learn. This is important information."

"I'm paying attention." I recited, "The flood wiped out half the buildings in the river district and killed people up-and-downstream for miles. That's why this valley is one of the most haunted places in Asheville. And . . . Dolly McCrane and her family have been dead and buried for just over ninety years."

Sarah wagged a finger at me. "*Dead's* not right. I know 'passed on' sounds prim and old-fashioned to you, but it really is more accurate. They're simply somewhere else."

"Except they haven't 'passed on,'" I retorted. "They're still here. At least, Dolly is."

"She's not *here*," Gigi corrected, spreading her arms as if hugging the factory. "She's *there*. Back *then*. She senses us just like we sense her. Through a glass darkly."

"Then how did she find me last night? By stepping through the looking glass?"

"Ahem. *Speaking* of mirrors," Sarah said.

She and Gigi traded a calculating look that sent shivers up my spine. I set my mug on a work table caked with the dried *slip* of Charles' pottery, layers upon layers of simple clay slurry, its minerals decomposed from millions of dead animals and humans and plants, the forgotten heritage of eons past, reduced to the essence of a material that became coffee mugs and platters for the living descendents of the dead materials.

I put a hand on the sheathed knife I'd stuck in the waist of my jeans.

They grabbed my free hand and dragged me upstairs.

*

Above the pottery studio on the old factory's ground floor and the galleries on the second floor was a long, low-roofed third floor, little more than an attic. Thick rafters lined the ceiling, and only small patches of spring sunshine crept through a row of small, shuttered windows. The attic was packed with a century's worth of stuff—big pots used for dying yarn, thick stanchions that had once been the supports for a loom, the umbrella-like frames of yarn swifts, and jumbled furniture, most of it dusty and in bad condition.

"All right, I'll bite." I said. "You brought me up here to help you organize this shit for a yard sale."

"Very funny," Gigi huffed. She and Sarah were busy pushing furniture aside on some mysterious quest I really didn't want to understand.

I frowned at them from a dim corner and noted a small iron skillet hanging from a nail. I wondered if I could club a bane with it. "How did Ian get inside my room through a locked door? How did he know I was in trouble?"

"Dolly told him," Sarah answered breezily.

"And she showed him how to open the door from his side," Gigi added. "She knows this building inside and out. She was born here."

I sat down on a small stool. I felt heavy and sad. "And she died here, along with her parents, during the flood."

"No, she *passed over*," Gigi insisted. "She's still around."

Sarah yipped. "Here it is." They pushed the tall headboard of a bed frame to one side. Behind it, leaning against a wall, was a large, rectangular shape draped in a dusty canvas. The mystery shape scraped its slow way toward me. They leaned it against a wooden pillar that supported the ceiling. Sarah dusted her hands. "There. All ready."

Gigi came over and squatted in front of me, rocking on her pink crocs. "Now, Livia, listen carefully. This is so you can practice. You saw Dolly once; you can see her again. You're in training now, like we agreed."

I stiffened. "I don't even know what I'm looking for."

"Advice. Clues. Help. Dolly's a good soul. A regular, garden-variety ghost. They're the easiest souls to see in the spirit world and the most likely to *want* you to see them. We're their tribe. People, that is. Not like the banes and the boons and the rest of the souls, who have their own little soul-cliques going."

"Just what I wanted to hear. The soul world is full of gangs and sororities."

"Be serious."

"You can't imagine how serious I am. If I ever feel like laughing again, I'll let you know."

"I'm sorry for everything that's happened to you. But peace of mind will come with self-confidence and acceptance. Now, let's give this a try—"

We heard chimes. The security system sounded whenever anyone opened a door. Sarah trotted to the stairwell. "It's the menfolk." She called down cheerfully, "We're up here."

I stood. My hands sweated. Being around Ian produced a mix of ingrained terror and miserable regret. I wanted to believe in him. I wanted to forget he looked like Greg Lindholm. I wanted to, but that didn't make it easy.

I shivered as his, Charles and Dante's heavy footsteps echoed up three flights of wooden stairs. Gigi studied my stark expression and yipped. "You'll get used to him, Livia. He'll remind you less of *you know who* every day. I could give you a charm or two to help erase the—"

I shook my head. "I'm hardcore. I like my reality in real doses. What's left of it."

I turned my back to the stairs. Sweat collected in my palms. The footsteps reached the attic and walked up behind me. I could feel Ian looking at me. "Ian, you make a handsome hunk of modern man," Sarah said.

His deep, lilting voice chorused through my brain. "Would that be a good thing? A hunk of what, are you saying?"

"Being a hunk is a very good thing," she promised, chortling. "Nice work on the shopping spree, boys."

"We didn't have to lift a finger," Charles noted drolly.

Dante grunted. "Every female salesclerk in Asheville wanted to help him get dressed." Dante held out a hand to Gigi. He helped her from her squat then looked at me kindly.

"How's our soul catcher this morning?"

"Just dandy," I lied.

Ian said quietly, "Livia, would you do me the courtesy of giving an opinion on my new lugs? It's not my vanity speaking. I'm wanting to make sure you see less of t'other owner of this hide, and more of *me*."

I pivoted as casually I could and looked up at him. His worried gray eyes watched me from a face where dark-brown beard stubble was quickly taking root. A soft gray pullover hugged the big muscles of his chest and arms. His new jeans needed a few hard washings to relax the denim around his long legs and lean hips, but they were already gilding those lilies pretty well. His feet looked rugged in tall, laced work boots.

Amazing—how the inner soul changes the outer being. It wasn't just superficial. The set of his face, his eyes, the way he stood. A different man. But still in Greg Lindholm's body.

"You look like an urban lumberjack," I said.

He frowned. "Whatever that is, I'm guessing 'tis not so bad, the way you say it."

"You'll do," I said dully.

His expression fell. "At least you should be happy knowing I've now got my man bits bound up safe in . . . " He looked at Charles and Dante " . . . what's that you called them?

Charles coughed. "Tighty whities."

"Enough chitchat, y'all," Gigi ordered. She and Sarah pulled the dusty canvas off the mystery rectangle. A large antique mirror emerged, reflecting dust motes floating in streamers of sunlight. The mirror was so old its silvering had begun to flake, and only a few specks of faded green paint clung to its simply carved frame. "This belonged to Dolly's family," Gigi explained. "Mirrors are strong portals between ours and the other worlds."

"Look deeply into your own eyes," Sarah added, "and you might see everyone you've ever been."

I froze. "Why this mirror and not others?"

"Mirrors remember what they've seen. This mirror has seen Dolly. And more."

Gigi shooed everyone with a pink-nailed hand. "Stand back. Livia's about to practice some good old-fashioned *scrying*. Livia, pull that stool a little closer and have a seat while I explain what—"

"I know what scrying is. No offense, but I'm not really up for peering into an antique mirror to see what peers back. I'd like to take a little vacation from terror this morning."

Sarah patted my shoulder. "Just try to talk to Dolly. You'll be making a conscious decision to see only her, just her. You're in control. That means no banes or demons can sneak through the mirror and attack you. And we'll all be right here, backing you up."

I scanned the resolute faces around me. Sarah nodded gently. Charles and Dante didn't appear worried. But when I met Ian's eyes, I saw uncertainty.

I pivoted, pulled the stool closer to the mirror, and sat down. I wiped my sweaty hands on my jeans. I looked up at Sarah. "Will you be able to see what I see and hear what I hear?"

"No. Just hints and shadowy forms. You're a soul catcher, so you have an innate ability to see through the veil between worlds far more clearly than the rest of us."

"All right. So what do I do first?"

Gigi sat down cross-legged beside the mirror. "It's very easy. Close your eyes and concentrate on relaxing."

"Is there a second option?"

"Eyes shut, Livia."

I gave up and shut them.

"Now, take deep yoga breaths. In through the nose, out through the mouth. That's right. Good. And while you're breathing, picture Dolly, or even just imagine her name, Dolly, in your mind. And tell her you'd like to visit with her."

The deep breathing ritual took all my effort. My lungs were used to hyperventilating. My oxygen preferred to hang out in the upper lobes, like a cat afraid to come down off a safe shelf. In through the nose, out through the mouth. Concentrate.

Dolly. Sweet, dead Dolly.

Thank you for warning me last night, Dolly. I'd like to know more about you. What the fuck am I saying I don't want to meet any more ghosts or banes or demons . . . breathe . . . Sorry about that, Dolly.

"Breathe in, breathe out," Gigi chanted. "And when you feel that the time is right, open your eyes and look at the mirror."

Behind my eyelids, the darkness deepened. *Dolly, I'm trying to stay calm. I've never called up a spirit on purpose before. You're not one of those Beetlejuice ghosts who like to scare people for fun, are you?*

"Your eyelids are twitching," Gigi whispered hotly. "You're thinking too hard."

Sarah shushed her. "Livia's breathing has slowed remarkably. Look at her. She's a natural. That's a soul catcher at work, right there."

Their voices seemed distant. The world inside my closed eyes began to expand. *Dolly, I hope you're not afraid of me. Am I as much a ghost to you as you are to me?*

"Miss Livia," Dolly said happily. "Hello. I'm not supposed to talk to strangers in Amabeth's mirror, but since we've already met, you're not really a stranger anymore."

I opened my eyes.

There, standing across from me in the mirror, was Dolly.

"Hello," I said. "Thank you for warning me last night."

"That was one mighty bad haint."

"Yes, it was."

Behind her, in her world, the attic was a cozy, sunny space with pleasant wooden furniture. A vase of flowers decorated a nightstand beside an iron bedstead, which was prettily made up in quilts. There was a potbellied stove, a wash basin on a dresser, and an oil lamp with an amber glass shade. On the floor was a beautiful McCrane rug in rich earth tones. A triangular pattern marched diagonally across its finely woven surface. I tilted my head, listening. There were background sounds.

"What are those noises?"

"Oh, those are just the looms downstairs. Aren't they pure fun to listen to?"

"Yes." The sound was a soothing rumble, a gentle *clackety clack*, like large wooden animals on the march. I nodded. Her eyes followed the movement, which freaked me out a little. "Can you see where I am?" I asked her.

"No, it's dark behind you. I see *you* real well, though. I hope it's not dark and cloudy where you are all the time."

"Is this your bedroom? Up here in the attic?"

"Oh, no, I just come up here to play. Amabeth is teaching me how to draw. I can draw apples and pumpkins and oak trees, now. Last week she helped me draw Papa's automobile. Isn't that exciting? We finally have an automobile! One Sunday soon we're going to visit Mama and Papa's friends who work at the Vanderbilts' dairy, and Amabeth has promised to teach me how to draw cows."

"Who is Amabeth?"

A shadowy figure walked into Dolly's background. Dolly bit her lip and looked over her shoulder. "There she is. Oh, I hope she's not upset with me. She can get right fussy about this mirror."

Unlike Dolly, who was crystal clear, all I could see of Amabeth was a glimpse of a hand clutching sheets of coarse paper, the hem of a long skirt, the flash of a foot buttoned inside an ankle-high shoe. The half-formed shadow went to a desk against one wall.

Dolly leaned toward me and whispered, "Amabeth works for us, and Mama and Papa rent her the attic to live in. She's all alone. People say she's s crazy, but I don't think so. She's always drawing strange pictures and burning them. She won't let me see them. But she weaves the most beautiful rugs. And she watches out for me. Like a big sister." She grinned as if Amabeth's sketch-burning habits were just interesting.

I took a few seconds to breathe deeply and clear the light flecks from my vision. *Paint them. Trap them. Burn them.* Was Amabeth a soul catcher, too? The shadow turned around, suddenly noticing Dolly and the mirror. It spoke to Dolly, rushing toward her. Dolly swiveled its way and looked sheepish. I heard the muted, urgent sounds of the shadow's voice, but couldn't make out the words.

Dolly shook her head. "Amabeth, it's all right. Look and see. She's very nice. Her name's Livia. She has funny drawings on her arms. She must like to draw, just like you do." The shadow dropped to its heels beside Dolly. I caught the quickest flicker of a pale, worried, thin face, with short brown hair crimped into snug waves. The Amabeth shadow spoke again, but I still couldn't make out the words.

Dolly's expression fell. "Amabeth says I have to go downstairs now, Miss Livia. See you later."

"Bye, Dolly."

"Bye."

She walked out of the frame. I stared at the shadow. The shadow stared back. I took a deep breath. "I'm not a demon," I told it. "I paint pictures of demons though, and I burn them. Am I right in guessing that you and I have a lot in common?"

The shadow began to grow more detailed, like an old TV tuning in from gray static. It flickered, it faded, it returned, and, as details segued into place, it changed. At first it was the crimped-hair stranger in a floppy work dress and button shoes who gazed back at me. But then, slowly, that image segued into a different one. Me.

Not my reflection. *Me.* Only different.

"Who er you?" the other me whispered in a heavy mountain accent. "If you ain't a demon, *what* then er you? You tryin' to fool me by takin' on my image?"

"No. I . . . see you. I mean, I see myself. But in your attic room."

"Liar."

"Don't get testy. I'm telling you the truth."

"I'm one spit away from drawin' your picture and burnin' it."

"I'm not a demon. Don't threaten me. I'll get a pencil and draw *you.*"

Stalemate. Talk about arguing with yourself. I was a stubborn pain in the ass. Me, too.

She took a deep breath and clutched her hands in front of

her. I looked down at my hands. No, I was sitting still. Only my reflection had another life. "What I do look like to you?" I asked.

"You tell me first, and be right quick about it."

"You have long black hair, you're wearing jeans . . . I mean, pants made of blue denim cloth . . . and a T-shirt . . . that's a short-sleeved white shirt . . . and tennis shoes. Tennis shoes are shoes made of cloth and rubber. And you have tatt . . . ink drawings on the skin of your arms."

She grunted. "That's a pack o' lies. Pictures on my *skin?* You take me for a fool?"

"Only if you won't listen to me. Tell me what *you* see."

She chewed her lip. "*You* have short brown hair, you're wearing a work jumper and a apron, and you got no drawings on you, because you look just like me and *I ain't got nothing etched on my arms.*"

"Trust me, I'm looking at you and you look just like *me.* I live in the twenty-first century. About ninety years from your time."

"Jesus loving god," she whispered hoarsely. "Are you really me?"

She crept forward. I got down on the floor, trembling, and crawled closer to the mirror too. My knees gave way and I curled my legs under me. I reached a hand up and touched the glass. Amabeth's green eyes—my eyes—followed my movement. She lifted a hand. Her fingertips met mine, separated only by a thin membrane of molten sand and the infinity of parallel lives. Tears rose in her eyes. And in mine.

I was looking at myself, my soul image, a good ninety years ago, in a different life. One that was already doomed. "Yes, I think I am you," I whispered.

She moaned. "Godawmighty." She jerked her hand down and glanced around her attic frantically. "If we're able to talk like this it means something's changed. The evil one must be up to something. My guides were trying to warn me. They musta sent you."

I heard a soft moan behind me. Gigi or Sarah, listening. My

heart thudded faster. "Tell me about your guides, please."

"Lilah and Dew Parsons. Kimmy Oldwater. Frank Turtle. The Parsons wuz school teachers and gospel singers; Kimmy sold tonic waters and elixirs from a little donkey wagon she drove around town, and Frank was a gunsmith. Half-Cherokee." Her voice cracked, and she scrubbed a tattooed forearm across her damp eyes. "Lilah and Dew was found on a back road with their throats slit, and Kimmy wuz strangled by a customer, and Frank got lynched. They said he forced hisself on a white girl, but that's a damn lie."

I knew instinctively these were Sarah and Charles. Gigi. And Dante. My spirit guides. And hers.

My versions were still alive. I clenched my fists. I intended to keep them that way.

"Er they there?" Amabeth asked hoarsely, looking past me. "Your guides? I cain't make 'em out."

"Yes, they're here." I cleared the tightness in my throat. "Safe and sound. I promise you."

"They ain't *never* gonna be safe and sound around you. Me. Us."

"Then help me protect them. Can you answer some questions for me?"

"I was sure nuff hoping you could answer some for *me*. 'Cause I ain't got a whole lot of answers so far. Sssh." She looked around again. "I feel trouble nearby. They's always sneakin' around now, watchin'. Damned banes. I got to go." Her mouth flattened. "I got some drawin' and some burnin' to do."

She leapt up, ran to the desk, and came back with a piece of paper and the whittled stub of pencil. She knelt in front of the mirror again, laid the paper on her knees, and began writing. "I'll send you this here private message. The boons'll keep it safe and Sheba'll tell you where to look for it."

Amabeth and everything around her began to fade. "Don't go," I said hoarsely.

"Got to. If they see us talkin', they'll come after you, too. Hoppin' across ninety years is easy for these devils." Her voice faded. "You and me, us, we always end up alone. That's just the way it's meant to be. I'm leavin' this place soon cause I'm feared that I'll get little Dolly and the rest of the McCranes kilt. You stay strong, you hear? And keep to yourself. You're a danger to every soul who cares about you." She faded even more. "I know Lilah and Dew and Kimmy and Frank ain't gonna let you go it alone, but I swear to you, *they gonna die again.*"

I pounded the mirror. "Amabeth, listen to me. There's a flood coming. When the waters rise, you and Dolly stay up here in the attic. This building is solid; it won't collapse. You'll be safe, I promise . . . "

The mirror faded to black before I finished. Slowly its reflection reverted to normal. I stared at myself, this me, not Amabeth. Behind me was the stored junk of the modern attic. Slowly I sat back on my heels. Gigi cried softly from her cross-legged position on the floor, but gave me a thumbs up. "I had lovely brunette curls when I was Kimmy," she moaned. "And I was skinnier."

Sarah and Charles smiled at me somberly, acknowledging their Parsons past. When I looked at Dante, he gave a little bow with his head. I asked quietly, "Do you always choose to be different from the majority? Racially, I mean."

"My soul makes the choice, sweetheart. I assume I need to be a little bit of an outsider to do the work my soul is destined to do. On the soul level, differences in race and gender mean nothing."

I avoided glancing at Ian. But I could feel his gaze, always on me.

"Livia, you've proved you have the power to reach through worlds," Sarah said softly. "You found one of your old selves. That is a great step forward."

Ian finally spoke. "Good on you, Liv. I knew you could do it."

I looked away. How could they be so calm? I'd just discovered that the old me was about to die in a flood along with an innocent little girl. I'd been doomed then and was probably doomed now, and so were all of them. Every brave soul who befriended me. Including Ian.

I got to my feet. "All right, so where's my message from Amabeth?" I scanned the air, the ceiling, the walls. "Sheba, whatever or whoever you are, could you help me the fuck out here?"

Everyone scowled at me. Charles shook his head. "Always speak respectfully to your boons."

"Ay," Ian added. "Do not be pissing off a home pog. They can turn sour."

"Okay, what, exactly, is a *pog?*"

"It's Irish slang for a type of boon." Dante explained. "A term of endearment."

"Ay, a pog is a tribe of boons." Ian went on. "A race or a tribe or a clan—whatever you like to say. Each tribe of boons, like tree pogs or cave pogs, have their special ways, and you'll be needing to get clear on what those are. Home pogs are a wee bit possessive and temperamental."

I gritted my teeth. "I just want that note I left myself before I drowned."

"Try speaking to Sheba again," Sarah counseled. "Nicely."

I took a deep breath. "Sheba? I apologize for talking to you that way. May I please have the note Amabeth wrote to me?" Silence stretched out. A full minute went by. My forehead felt like a tight zipper. Why did I have to deal with a pouting home pog?

A fist-sized chunk of plaster fell off one wall. It left a small hole edged in frayed layers of paint.

"Say thank you," Gigi whispered, as I rushed forward.

"Thanks, Sheba. I owe you." I shoved aside dusty, cane-backed chairs and a yellowing dress mannequin. I put a trembling hand to the open space and slid my fingers inside it. They clothes-pinned a square of folded paper. I slowly drew it out. Dust poofed from the coarse yellow surface. I unfolded it gently.

Amabeth's handwriting, full of pretty, old-fashioned swirls, leapt out at me. She was far better educated than our conversation had revealed. Maybe she used the poverty of style as a disguise.

The pig-faced demon will kill every living body who tries to help you. I can't figure how to get rid of him for good so it may be that all I can ever do is knock him back a step or two. If he comes after you remember this: You're the only one who's got the power to send him away from this world forever, and so you have to fight him alone.

The handwriting grew jagged and emotional. My skin prickled with goosebumps.

Don't ever let Ian find you. He can't save you, and you can't save him. He's a good man but he'll only break your heart again. I haven't seen him in this life but I know he's out there looking for me. If he does find you, tell him you've loved him in every life you've ever lived and you'll love him forever. Because trust me, you have and you will.
Then get away from him as fast as you can.
Love,
From you to me to us.
Amabeth

I folded the note and put in my jeans' pocket.
Gigi crossed her arms. "Not sharing?"
"She didn't tell me anything I don't already know."
Ian said quietly, "She told you to go it alone. But you were wrong then and you'll be wrong this time too, if you listen to such faithless advice."
I stared at him resolutely then shifted my gaze to include the whole group. "Just answer one question for me," I asked quietly. "In the past, have all of you *always* died because of me?"
The looks on their faces were priceless. Like it was no big

deal.

"Passed on," Gigi corrected.

7

Not long after midnight I crept downstairs in the dark, with a backpack over one shoulder. The cold scent of old bricks seeped into my skin. I stood in front of a thick metal door at one end of Charles' pottery studio.

I knew there was very little chance I'd get far without being killed by Pig Face or one of his minions, but I had to try. How many innocent people had to die just so I had a shot at fighting demons I couldn't kill?

Maybe I could go out in a blaze of glory this time. That way I'd free Ian and the others from their duties as my spiritual posse—in this life, at least. Maybe they could hook up with another soul catcher. One with a better track record.

"Sheba," I whispered, trying hard to sound calm and friendly. "If it wouldn't be too much trouble, I'd like for you to unlock this door without setting off the alarm system. You and I both know that the only way to save the others is for me to disappear. For their sakes, please, help me get out of this building without them knowing it."

Nothing. Silence. I heard only the hiss of a gas furnace and the creaks and pops of any massive building of advancing years. No rustles or flutters or slithers that might indicate a home pog was hustling to my aid. A home pog. "Fuck," I said under my breath. "This is crazy."

"Just when I thought your manners had improved," a low voice said. It gurgled the words.

I clamped a sweaty fist around the backpack's strap. The voice from the darkness of my childhood bedroom. *Please let this be Sheba.* "I apologize. I thought you weren't listening. Are you Sheba?"

"Yes. And I'm *always* listening." Her words became slow, watery, smug. The voice surrounded me like a claustrophobic tide. Sheba.

"Ian calls you a home pog. Is that all right? I don't want to piss . . . offend you."

"You don't offend me. I know you mean no harm. You can't help feeling angry and defensive. You've been that way for more lives than I can count. Perhaps some day you'll improve your attitude."

"I doubt it. Look, I need to get out of here. Will you help me?"

"Of course. I always have, sometimes despite my better judgment." Her watery voice made the air around me feel moldy. My spine shivered. Maybe she had a second career as a cave pog.

Something moved on the brick wall above my head. Something clasped a foot or a paw or a webbed talon to a wooden rafter. The rafter creaked. Then came a series of soft *mmm-wok* sounds, like suction cups moving across the bricks.

Heading down the wall. Heading toward me.

"Are you trying to scare the shit out me?" I asked softly. "Because it's working. That's not funny."

"You imagine me to be some horrible creature. But you adored me, as a child."

"Well, frankly, I'm getting a mental image of a large, wet lizard. I hope I'm wrong."

"You can see me, you know. The others can't; they don't have the talent. But you do."

"Will I see you the way you are, or some illusion?"

"You'll see me the way you want to see me, based on what you know to be true about me, on a soul level. If you think you have the courage, give it a try. Shut your eyes, tell yourself you want to see me, then open your eyes, and there I'll be." She uttered a sound like a fountain trickling over rocks. Her idea of a laugh, I think. "I won't bite you," she said.

"I'm more afraid you'll *slime* me."

I heard the trickling sound again. "Have a look. I'm not so bad."

I shut my eyes. My heart raced. I had a feeling she wouldn't help me unless I played this hide-and-seek game. Fuck. All right. Another step down the Surreal Highway. *I want to see*

Sheba, I told myself, hoping I didn't catch on that I was lying. A soft golden glow hit my eyelids. I opened them.

Sheba clung to the wall just above the door. Her long, slender, golden neck was craned outward so she could tilt her golden, horse-like head at an awkward angle and look straight down at me with golden eyes. Her golden tail, which ended in a fluke like a dolphin's, curled lazily around a rafter a good twenty feet above her head. Her scales shimmered. Her webbed feet ended in gleaming white nails with a glittery disco sheen to them. Her half-folded wings cast rainbow shadows on the walls.

I let out a long, astonished breath. When I was about six years old Daddy gave me a stuffed toy dragon for my birthday. It was covered in gold lame' fabric and had iridescent wings. I thought it was the most beautiful imaginary creature in the world. For years, as the dark nightmares and their ugly creatures took over my life, I slept with the shimmering gold dragon in my arms. I fantasized about it coming to life.

And now it had.

"*Now* do you like looking at me?" Sheba asked. Her pink, forked tongue flicked between her even, white teeth. After all, she was a child's toy. No fangs.

"Were you there when I was little? Really? That was you? The invisible hand, or . . . paw . . . that stroked my head, the voice that spoke to me?"

"Yes. I kept you safe as best I could, or the demon inside your mother would have done far, far worse to you. I was driven away by powerful banes after the fire."

Silence stretched out. A thousand shocked memories whirled inside me. "Did you help me, that night?"

"Yes. Sorry for throwing you out the window so roughly. Banes were attacking me. I was . . . distracted."

"Thank you for saving my life."

She gave a golden shrug. "I knew you'd need me here, eventually. I protected you here before, when you were Amabeth. She saw me as a dragon, too. From a painting she found in a Catholic text. Something from the Renaissance.

Flemish. St. Margaret of Antioch. St. Margaret had a way with dragons, you know."

I looked up at Sheba in heady wonder. Amabeth had some classy references for a backwoods mountain girl. Mine were cheesier, more on a *Puff the Magic Dragon* level.

Suddenly I had a deep, childlike urge to hug Sheba and fall asleep with my face hidden under one of her wings. It would be so easy to just curl up on the dusty studio floor with my big pet dragon snuggling me. To sleep. To dream of golden pet dragons, not demons.

"You're trying to hypnotize me," I said abruptly. I shook my head.

Sheba sighed. The air sparkled with her alluring breath. "Oh, well. It worked when you were younger. I helped you sleep as best I could. Worth a try."

"Please, just open the door for me."

She sighed again, producing a golden plume of exhaled air. "All right. Stubborn girl."

The door clicked softly. It even swung outward an inch. She looked down at me, her golden eyes blinking slowly under opalescent brows. "Speak to the boon outside. He'll make sure nothing bothers you, at least for a little ways. He'll drive you to town. You'll recognize him."

"Thank you." I eased toward the door, then halted. "What was the deal with your creepy water effects and sticky feet?"

"Remember the time you put me in the washing machine? And the time you glued my feet to your headboard so I looked as if I were flying over your pillow at night? Don't fault me for wanting a little payback."

My guardian spirits had a warped sense of humor. I reached a hand up. I had to know. She lowered her head. I stroked her flared nose. "You feel so real," I whispered.

"What you see is what you get, Livia."

"You were always my favorite stuffed animal. You still are, even if you do like to mess with my head."

She exhaled another golden plume. It cast a soft glow on my face. "I'll pray for you to come back here safely. If you don't, I'll see you again in another life. Perhaps I'll be a stuffed toy monkey next time. I'm fond of things that climb. Stay safe, soul catcher."

She vanished into the wall.

I could have done without that last comment about other lives. Trembling, I slipped outside uneasily under the sparse light of a half moon. The spring air was chilly. Beyond the parking lot stood a sagging chain-link fence with a gate Charles and Sarah rarely locked, and beyond that was a narrow, pockmarked road. On the other side of the road lay a weedy open area, and then a deep fringe of trees that marked the river banks. A freight train grumbled in the distance.

It was a lonely place, and a lonely night. I crept down a short set of concrete steps and gave one wistful look back at the large, dark windows and sturdy brick walls towering over me. *Goodbye, everyone. Goodbye, Ian. Again.*

"Pick up the pace, Kittycat," a slick male voice said. "I've got aliens to kill."

I froze. *Kittycat.*

A sports car was parked in the weeds at the side of the road. A slender shadow leaned hipshot against its hood. The shadow straightened. "That's right, Kittycat. I'm your ride. Leonidas. Move it."

I took a few steps toward him then stopped. "As stupid as this is going to sound...despite the fact that Sheba vouched for you, I have my doubts." He sighed and lit a cigarette. The tiny flame of his lighter illuminated his face like a torch. The slanted eyes, the high cheekbones, the whole Keanu Reeves-in-need-of-a-tan look. He smiled at my reaction, which he could apparently see even in the dark. "Yeah, Kittycat, you know it's me."

"Leonidas."

"Well . . . not exactly. I chose his form. I'm far more important than a video game character."

My skin prickled at the memory of his voice coming out of the computer, warning me when the demon finally took full control of Momma's body. "Thank you for what you did that night."

He shrugged. "You had a crush on me. I was flattered."

His tone rankled. "So you think you're too hot for me to resist?"

"You were a fan."

"When I was a kid, yeah. When I thought *Street Blaster* was the coolest video game in the world."

"You were into it, Kittycat. Scoring those alien duels. Practicing for real life, pretending you could kill demons with a click of your thumb, just like your idol, me, Leonidas, killed the ten-armed sloths on Level Four." He tossed his smoke into the gravel. "Climb into the Leo mobile, Kittycat. I'll drop you off on the mean streets. Not that I approve. But your wish is my command."

I moved cautiously to the car's passenger side. "Is there a tribe of boons who hang out around video games? Is that what you are? A Play Station pog?"

He snorted as he opened the driver's door. "I like technology. You could say I'm a techno pog. I can only protect you as far as town. Once I let you out there, you're on your own."

"I'm going to catch a ride to the interstate, and then see how far I can hitchhike."

"Whatever, Kittycat. Your fate is your choice. Free will and all that."

I got into the car, fitting my feet between piles of computer components on the passenger side floor. The dash was crowded with gadgets. Wires and plug-ins dangled from the ceiling. "You're not real, but this car is. Right?"

He snorted. "You think I'm made of ectoplasm or something? Touch the goods, Kittycat."

I prodded his arm. Flesh and blood, or a great substitute. After all, Sheba had substance, too. I had touched her. "Why don't pogs and boons nab human bodies, the way spirit guides do?"

Another snort. "Who wants to be stuck in a container that gets fat and sick and wrinkled?"

"Look, I'm just trying to understand the physics of all this."

"You can't. You think inside the box. You believe in the reality you know best. It's a dimensional issue, Kittycat. You're stuck in one boring lane on the highway of parallel universes. Me? I'm able to accelerate, back up, or take the off ramps at will."

"So, Techno Pog, where were you and your big dimensional ego when Amabeth and Dolly drowned? Getting your freak on with one of those fancy new hand-cranked phonographs?"

Leonidas popped another cigarette in his mouth and lit it with a lighter shaped like a Nano. "I tried to warn you that day, Kittycat." The cigarette bobbed on his lip. "But you always play solo. I told you to call Ian for help, but you wouldn't. So Pig Face took over Daddy McCrane's body, tricked Mama McCrane and their kid Dolly and even *you*, Amabeth, into thinking he had a rowboat downstairs, and he convinced you chicks that all you three had to do was follow him downstairs from the nice, safe attic, swim out the front door, and get in the boat." He halted, arching a brow at me, almost jaunty.

"There was no boat," I said wearily.

"Bingo, Kittycat. So after mama and her chicklet waded into the water downstairs ol' Piggy Dude shoved them under. You crouched on a dry top step with a soggy pencil, trying to scribble Pig Dude's picture on the stairwell's wall before it was too late. But he grabbed you by the ankle and pulled you down, too."

I clutched my stomach at the mental image. Leonidas grinned. A sickly glow appeared on his aquiline face as if spotlighted by an invisible map light. His skin went blue-gray. Water drooled from one corner of his gaping mouth. He mimed drowning. Then he looked at me with slitted eyes. "Blub blub blub, Kittycat," he said sarcastically. "Game over. You lost. All because you wouldn't ask for help. *Again.*"

I thumped a button on the door's armrest and sucked in some fresh air as soon as the window whirred down. "Somehow I doubt you'd have been worth calling on, Street

Blaster. You and your unpredictable sense of honor."

"Yeah, well." He started the car's engine with a flick of one hand. "You're no high scorer yourself."

*

There wasn't much evidence left that Ronnie Bowden had mutilated and burned himself in Asheville's pristine downtown park. The bricks of the small amphitheater that stair stepped down from College Street were hosed clean. The city's grounds crew had clipped the charred branches off nearby shrubs. The crime-scene tape was gone.

I kept to the deep shadows under the park's single large shade tree. I wanted to offer Ronnie a mea culpa before I left town. Or before Pig Face killed me. Whichever came first. I didn't want to die with Ronnie on my conscience, too. It seemed pretty obvious that Pig Face had manipulated him to commit suicide.

I looked down a street in the general direction of the downtown police station. Nahjee was there, boxed in an evidence locker. I didn't want to leave her behind. I fumbled with Tabitha at the base of my throat. The amulet hadn't said a word in days.

"Tabby, can you help me get Nahjee out of jail so I can take her with us?"

Nothing. Not a peep. I tried again. "Can't you two move around, change forms, take up new homes, the way Sheba and Leonidas do? Hmmm? Comeon, Tabby, just answer that for me."

With a sound like an annoyed huff, the amulet's fragile little voice said, "We are boons, not pogs."

"Sorry, I'm not up the subtleties yet."

"Our kind has as many varieties as fish in the sea and birds in the sky. All with different habits and habitats." Tabby's tone became smug, as if I were too ignorant to tolerate. "Nahjee and I must be attached to our host soul before we can function as our kind intends."

I couldn't stop myself. "Oh? So you're like a *leech*."

There was a long, brittle silence this time. "Shit," I said

under my breath. "All right, I apologize."

"Livia, Nahjee is safe for the moment. But you are most certainly *not*. Go about your business and do not annoy me further."

Angry click. Dial tone.

That's how it felt, anyway.

White light filtered through the tree's spreading branches from the antiseptic glow of the downtown streetlamps. The checker tables and benches were empty. The park wasn't a particularly private place; it could be strolled from end to end in an easy minute or two, and it was surrounded by the watchful window fronts of ground floor shops and cafes. But late at night it became a deserted island in the sea of the sleeping city.

I shut my eyes. "Ronnie, are you here? I just want to tell you I'm sorry that something in the . . . underworld . . . connected you to me. I'm the reason the demon went after you. I'm sorry. I hope you rest in peace. Or that your soul goes some place wonderful, wherever it wants to go next."

"Quit yer whining and stop yer conniption fits, gal," a heavy drawl said behind me, thick with sarcasm. "Souls don't keer to hear yer balderdash. Git on to yer battle! There's lives at stake!"

I whirled around. A skinny, bearded Confederate soldier stood there, glaring at me over wire glasses perched on the tip of his nose. We weren't in Pritchard Park anymore, and it wasn't nighttime. We stood on a muddy wagon road in the blue-silver light of early morning. Around us was open pasture rimmed in forest. The rutted road disappeared into hills covered in trees. Beyond them rose mountains. Everything was shrouded in a silver mist.

My hand went to the hilt of my knife. The soldier hooted. "Save your pig sticker fer demons. Ain't no need to go pokin' ghosts with it."

"Are you the soldier who haunts Pritchard Park?" My voice shook. I kept my hand on the knife.

He spat tobacco juice on the soggy ground. "Ain't no sech

thing as hauntin'. Ghosts don't haunt places. They on a mission, gal. Waitin' for something or somebody they ain't yet been able to see. I'm just bivouacin' here 'til my wife finds me. She said her goodbyes to me right here—" he swung a uniformed arm at the open field—"'cause this here's where the local infantry mustered up."

He spat again. "I died at Antietam. Then a pack of goddamn Yanks come through these mountains and looted our farm and shot her dead. Left our kids to starve. The kids have done come along and gimme a hug to say they's fine, but she's a mite confused, I think. Woman never did come to town but that onct. Skeered of townsfolk. I reckon she's still hiding from the Yanks." He spat. "Burn in hell, the ones who done it to us. Demons wuz involved, you bet."

Okay, I'd heard enough. I wanted out of his alternate realty. I backed away a few steps and pivoted in a quick circle, hoping I'd rotate through time to downtown Asheville *circa*, like, *now*, please. I'd have given anything for the sight of the ATM at the Bank of America building or the awning-covered patio of Tupelo Honey. But all I saw were more woods, the wagon road, and among the trees some chimneys and a distant steeple.

I slowly faced the soldier again. He shook his head and sighed. "You're seein' me fer a reason, gal. I'm supposed to introduce you to some folks." He waved a hand toward the road. "Well, come on. Soon's you git it over with you can skeedaddle back to yer doom."

I stared at him. "How can I resist when you put it like that?"

He hunched the strap of his rifle higher on one thin shoulder and headed across the field. I followed on shaking legs. Around me, shadows began to form. Horses and men, lots of men, their gear clanking, their drawling voices bawdy and hopeful and scared. I heard women and children too, coaxing, praising, crying, saying goodbye. None of the troops or their families appeared to notice me. Only the landscape and my soldier-guide remained vivid.

When we reached the edge of the woods he threw out an arm to halt me. "No need to intrude on their privacy anymore'n we got to. They can't see or hear us no-how, but we can see and hear them. Just cock your ear and listen, gal."

He waved a hand. A tall, handsome man in an officer's uniform materialized in front of us. His hair and beard were dark blonde; his bearing was aristocratic. His plumed hat lay on the ground. He held a woman in his arms, one hand around her waist, the other cupping her head. His eyes were closed and tears streaked his face.

Her face was turned to his shoulder and her arms were wound tightly around his neck. Her hair, pulled back in a large knot at the nape of her neck, was a soft reddish-brown. A blue bonnet tumbled from its ties down her back. Her dress was blue as well, nothing fancy but definitely upscale. The bodice had puffy sleeves with lace trim, and the skirt belled out. Whoever she was, she could afford lace trim and steel hoops.

Her shoulders shook. She sobbed. Then she pulled back from him abruptly, planted both light-brown hands on his chest, and tilted her beautiful, light-brown face with its African features up to him. "I'll hate you the rest of my life," she said, crying. "I'm glad I won't live long without you."

"I refuse to believe in your prophecies," he said hoarsely. "I *will* return for you, Maratile. And we *will* find a way to live as husband and wife. I swear to you on every ounce of honor in my soul."

"What does your honor count for, Paxton? There's no honor in fighting for this cause."

"I'm fighting for my family and my homeland, not for any man's cause other than that."

She knotted her fists into the fine braid of his coat. "You are riding to your death. And you are leaving me to mine."

"If I thought I was condemning you to a premature death or a life of misery, I'd cut my heart out on this spot. But I believe this fight will end as quick as it's begun, and gentleman of both sides will come to agreements, and there will be a new world of freedom and opportunity for all, with as little bloodshed as possible. Your people and my people will be free of the past. Can't you pretend even a little hope and faith in my vision of the future?"

She shook her head. "We can leave *now*. Go West. Or North. To the great frontier of California or to Mexico or Canada. I have no fear of what we'll find in those unseen lands. But I have great fear of what we'll find inside the unseen lands of this war."

"My love, I *will* come home to you."

I watched Maratile and Paxton trade a look of sheer tenderness and despair. He swept her up and they kissed wildly. There was nothing demure or courtly about it. It was hot, ferocious, desperate. She pushed away from him again, swaying, crying. More tears slid down his face.

She pulled her bonnet up, tied it with shaking hands, then hid those brown hands in the pockets of her skirt. She rushed past me, her head bowed, her shoulders shaking.

And he stood where he was, looking after her tragically, as if his life would end the second he couldn't see her anymore. I strained my eyes but he slowly faded to nothing.

The soldier and I stood at the edge of the woods, alone again.

He studied me shrewdly and seemed a little amused by my stunned silence. "Cat got your tongue, soul catcher?"

"Was that me and Ian?"

"Ohhh, you're a smart one."

"What happened to us?"

"Paxton got shot to pieces at Bull Run. And Maritile got beat to death in a race riot up in New York."

My breath shuddered. "No, really. Go ahead and be blunt."

He guffawed darkly. "You asked."

"So Ian *was* able to track me down in that life. Does he remember?"

"Nope. 'Cause you don't want him to, and you don't want *you* to, neither. You cain't erase what he recollects of the misery that *started* this here cycle, back in seventeen such-and-such, but you *can* keep the jump on him about the lives since then."

"What I just witnessed makes me *less* likely to change my mind about our fate. So why did you show it to me?"

He shrugged. "Some o' the boons asked me to give you this tour. They didn't say why, but boons generally know best. Now, if you want *my* opinion, it's to let you know that there ain't no value in you hidin' from your man. A soul catcher needs a soul hunter beside her. Maybe if you own up to whatever happened to start this, your fate could change."

"I have my doubts. Especially since I've got no clue what happened to Ian and me in the seventeen such-and-suches."

He leaned closer to me, his eyes accusing, sympathetic, demanding. "Whatever happened don't matter no more. You gonna let it be so easy for the demon to git rid of you and your man and all your spirit guides *this* time?"

Suddenly the air began to feel hot. The shadows, the scene, him, began to fade. "Time fer me to move along," he added. "If'n you see my wife, tell her where to find me."

"I will. But wait—"

"If you get kilt aforehand, send your ghost back by for a chat. Sometimes it gets right lonely here on the muster grounds."

And then he was gone, and I was alone in Pritchard Park.

Before I could re-orient myself, Tabby spoke urgently.

"The griffins are coming. *Run.*"

I looked around wildly. Griffins? What the fuck did she mean by *that*? I grabbed my backpack, pulled the knife out, and ran up College Street to Haywood, a main drag that heads straight for I-240. Haywood Street is lined with grand old department stores and shops; it's like a walk through the 1930's. Most of the buildings are apartments, restaurants and art galleries now.

At two in the morning all I saw was the shadows of the street lamps, and all I heard was the quick, rough hiss of my breath. I kept close to the shop windows, my knife carefully in front me as I slipped from one awning covered door to the next. I scrutinized planters and benches as if they might come alive. I turned left down a side street. I'd take Battery Park to

Page, a short cut past the Grove Arcade, then reconnect with Haywood.

The Grove Arcade. *Wait a minute.*

The arcade is a vast marble building from the 1920's, several stories tall, and it takes up a whole block. Inside and out it's opulent and lined with nice shops and cafes; the top floors have been turned into luxury condos. There are dozens of gargoyles on the façade and . . . I slowed down even more. The heat was sweaty for an early spring night. The air shimmered.

The Grove Arcade is decorated with dozens of gargoyles, yes. But flanking its grand entry way are not more gargoyles, instead . . . there are a pair of . . . giant, growling, winged lions.

Some people call them *griffins*.

I heard wings. *Big* fucking wings. I whirled around and bolted back toward Haywood. Behind me the wings grew louder, and with the sound came low, echoing growls. I careened back onto Haywood's wide mercantile lanes then ducked inside the darkness of a doorway alcove.

My drawing pad. I opened the backpack then grabbed the pad and the thick stub of a charcoal pencil. But as I flipped the pad open, two slimy, lizard-like hands appeared out of thin air near my knees. They reached up like a child grabbing for a treat. I squinted in horror at a small, shadowy form with a rooster-like comb, snake eyes, and the slobbering grin of a deranged Cheshire Cat.

"Gimme," the bane gurgled.

It snatched for my pad and pencil as I frantically jerked them back. The little fucker sprang upwards like a kangaroo, flashing thick thighs and powerful feet. He ripped my pad and pencil from my hands.

The bane chortled as it leapt away, carrying my only defense.

Swoosh.

The sound of wings right overhead. *Huge* ones. Large enough to carry a Volkswagen.

I flattened my back to the cold glass of a shop door. The alcove was deep and narrow. Good hiding, but I couldn't see what was happening on the street. The wings settled to earth with a fluttering noise. After that, just a tingling silence.

I strained my ears.

Click. Ka-click. Ka-click.

Large claws clicking softly on concrete.

Sweating in the spring darkness, I stared at the windows across the street. They reflected the streetlights; they reflected my dark doorway.

And then they reflected the emerging twin profiles, the stalking crouch, the glittering yellow eyes and flaring, sniffing nostrils of two lion-like monsters. Hunting me. Hunting *me.*

I couldn't see them clearly. Just glimmers and shadows. But it was enough to make my guts shrivel.

I lifted the knife and looked at it. Ten razor-sharp inches of ridiculously hopeless steel. No drawing pad, just this. If I really *was* a soul catcher—something special—why didn't the job come with a learning curve that gave me a fighting chance to fight hell like hell?

I stepped out of the alcove. I felt the heavy weight of loneliness on my chest. Everybody said I just needed to ask for help; all right, I'd test that theory. I tilted my head back and called loudly, "My name is Livia Belane. I'm a . . . soul catcher. If there are any good spirits around who'd like to cover my back, I'd really appreciate it."

No answer. No flashing sirens, no spiritual cavalry riding to the rescue.

The giant bird-cats instantly swiveled their malevolent heads my way. I squinted at them, trying to make out more details. Soul catchers have a gift for seeing banes and demons, boons and pogs and angels, too, in perfect, living detail, or so everyone kept telling me. Obviously I still wasn't up to par; my shivering mind backed away.

I braced my feet apart and balanced for action. Slowly, with all the menace Dante had taught me in one of his combat classes, I swirled the knife through the air in front of me. "Here, kitty, kitty," I called in a shaking voice.

They leapt. I dodged behind a lamp post as a massive paw

swiped at me. Metal cracked. Sparks spewed. The light crashed to the pavement. I lunged forward. I stabbed the knife into the griffin's paw. Blood spurted.

Okay, so I could wound them just as they could wound me. Even if it was only an illusion. My encounter with the tentacled bane at the gallery had shown how the illusion worked: The bane would trick me into hurting myself. So the griffins were hoping for . . . what? That I'd run blindly into a storm drain, plunge headfirst through a shop window, or my heart would explode from the overwhelming terror and effort of the fight?

The thing drew back, howling, but its companion opened its fanged mouth and uttered a shriek that hurt my ears. The sound was a cross between an enraged roar and the scream of a hawk.

And then it pounced. The tip of its huge muzzle rammed me in the stomach. I hit the pavement with my lungs knocked empty and no time to breathe. I managed to hold onto the knife and swing it quickly enough to slash the thing's open mouth. Its gray tongue split from the tip to the root. Blood gushed over me.

See them, I commanded myself. *Dammit, use your skills. Don't let these sorry-ass predators punk you. Man up.*

See them.

I shut my eyes then opened them.

I looked up at vivid white fangs as long as my forearm. They were closing over me, coming down . . .

"Up, up, Livvie get up with you now!" Ian shouted. He snared me by one arm and pulled. I scrambled as he half-lifted, half-dragged me up the sidewalk. The hawk rose in the air, dodging the first griffin's enraged swipes.

The second one advanced on us, crouching. Its slit tongue had suddenly healed. The red handle of Ian's fire ax flashed in the corner of my vision as he lifted it. The griffin's yellow eyes tracked the movement, and his pace slowed. We backed up the sidewalk. The griffin took one careful step forward for every step we took backwards.

Dante ran up, an elegantly lethal figure wielding a sword, of all things. "I'll hold them off. Run."

A prim male voice spoke out of nowhere. "Well, honestly, I've opened a door for you people. Are you waiting for an engraved invitation?"

I looked around wildly. Across the street, below the colorful art deco façade of the old Woolworth's department store, now an arts and crafts gallery, a pair of double glass doors stood open among the gleaming windows of the ground floor.

Ian swung me toward the store. "Run. I'll be right behind you."

I bolted. Dante and Ian's heavy footsteps echoed on my heels, along with the rhythm of the griffin's claws.

When I burst inside the open doors of what had once been Asheville's most gloriously elegant five-and-dime, I whirled around with my knife ready. A griffin planted one paw on one of the doors, blocking it. Ian got between him and the doorway, his ax posed over his head, both big hands wrapped tightly around the end of its long handle. Dante shouldered up beside him, the sword raised.

Both griffins crouched, ready to jump.

"Banish the bastards, Livia," Ian yelled over his shoulder. "If you can see them full and clear, all you have to do is speak the words. They're banes, not as powerful as demons! You can draw pictures of 'em if you're a mind to but you do no' have to do it that way. Just banish 'em with words!"

"*What* words?"

"Whatever you believe in! If you've got the faith in yourself, you can do it! When I fling the ax, you shout to the beasties! Tell them to scat!"

Ian's broad back—Greg Lindholm's well-muscled, bodybuilding back—flexed then surged. The ax flew end over end.

I flung out my hands as if waving dual wands. "Go the fuck away!"

The ax sank between the griffin's eyes.

Both griffins vaporized. They literally *exploded* in a gush of dark, sparkling energy. But as they went, the one nearest us swung a paw. It slapped Ian across the chest. The impact knocked him inside the doorway. He slammed into a massive metal sculpture and slumped to the marble floor at the top of the old department store's wide terrazzo staircase.

Dante ducked inside. The glass doors closed graciously behind him. The dead bolt slid into place. It was over.

The only other sound was the three of us dragging air into our lungs. Outside, the streetlamp stood back in place, Ian's ax lay where it had fallen on the pavement, my knife lay just outside the doors, and no ethereal griffin blood stained the sidewalks.

Inside, however, I realized that my hands, clutching Ian's shirtfront, were growing wet and sticky. Ian made a wheezing sound.

I scrambled around in front of him. "Turn on a light, please," I yelled.

"Give me a moment, will you?" the Woolworth pog answered. "I only have two hands." The pog spoke in an arch, uptown drawl, the voice of the perfectly unflappable manager of a white-glove world where ladies had once sipped cherry cokes at the soda fountain and the sales clerks suggested just the right face powder at the cosmetics counter. He stepped down from a tall, abstract painting, a geometric collision of brilliantly colored shapes, not human in form, but somehow giving the distinct impression that he looked at us down an aquiline nose.

A section of the overhead lights flickered to life.

"We've got a problem," Dante said.

Ian's shirt was ripped and bloody. He looked at me through eyes slitted with pain. He managed a sardonic smile. "I believe the bastard nicked me just a wee bit."

My hands shook as I jerked at the shirt buttons. Dante squatted beside me. "This is bad, Livia. He's been hurt by a large bane. Like the welt you got the other night. He doesn't have the power to ignore it or heal it instantly. Not without your help."

I opened the shirt. A trio of deep gashes ran from Ian's left collarbone diagonally to his right ribcage. Blood poured from them. I could see the red meat of his chest muscles. I flattened my hands on the wounds. Blood trickled between my fingers. I straddled him with one foot down on the wide surface of the stairs' first descending step and the other leg curled under me along his hip. I met his eyes. "Do you believe I can do this?"

"Ay, love," he whispered. "I've always believed in you."

I bent my head and shut my eyes. *Paint them, trap them, burn them. Banish the wounds they make.*

"You might give me a kiss," Ian whispered hoarsely. "It could help."

Without opening my eyes I pressed my lips to his. Greg Lindholm's lips were about the only part of his body that hadn't hurt me. Ian, not Greg, kissed me back. It was sweet, tender. No tongue.

"Good work, Livia," Dante shouted. "You did it."

I opened my eyes. Ian was fine. His shirt lay open on his chest, but not torn and not bloody. His chest and belly had returned to the sleek, six-packed icon of man-muscle they'd been before. "Livia," he said softly. "I've waited more'n two centuries for you to kiss me again. It was worth gettin' slashed open."

I climbed off him, stood up, and backed away. I gave Dante a hard glare. "Were his wounds gone *before* he asked me to kiss him?"

Dante looked away innocently. I swiveled my gaze to Ian. "You cheated."

His face hardened. "You want to complain about me weaseling you for a simple kiss after you nearly got us all killed?"

"I didn't ask you to come after me. I wanted to leave. I knew I'd probably die. I tried to do what's best for you and everyone else. *I'm a death sentence for all of you.*"

He got to his feet. Anger pulsed in the air. "Can you not understand that this isn't just about you? Do you not ken that soul catchers are God's own fighters in a war between the good and the evil of this world and others? Do you not ken that a soul catcher such as you and a soul hunter such as me *have to work together*, along with other fine souls—" he swung a hand at Dante—"who've devoted themselves to the battle? When you go it alone, you put us all in more danger, not less."

"From everything I've been able to learn so far, *you* keep deserting *me*."

Ian began forcefully buttoning his shirt. "I do no' make that choice. My soul does. As does yours."

"Bullshit. I don't believe you. I don't believe I've *made* you forget me in life after life. I suspect you've been *trying* to forget *me*. Otherwise, you'd remember more than just that one life in the seventeen hundreds."

Dante got between us. "The life you had together back then was obviously a crucial one. Nothing's been the same since then. You'll have to find out why. It's important to know."

Ian thrust a finger at me. "Ay, it's been since then that you've *run* from me like a coward. Ever since."

"People, people, *enough*," the Woolworth pog interjected, shuffling its gaudy jumble of colors. "I have a store to open in a few hours. I don't have time to officiate over marital feuds. Good night." The doors opened slowly. "I've asked someone to escort you all to your car. Have a nice evening. Please shop with us again soon."

Outside the open doors, a large, shadowy figure began to form, towering higher than the door frames. As it deepened from a shimmering mist into a pale blue image with glowing white edges it fluffed and folded its magnificent wings. It landed gently on the sidewalk.

"Come with me," it called in a soft, feminine voice. "You'll be safe on the walk to your car."

"Who is she?" Dante asked me. "I can just glimpse the wings."

"She's a big class o' boon, that's for sure," Ian added, sounding grim and tired. "At least you've made *one* friend, Livia. Speak to her."

I stepped outside slowly. The shadowy form looked down at me. "Do you really want to see me, Livia?"

"Yes."

"Then you shall."

She came to life. I stared up at her calm, classic face, her robes, her wings. She wore a whimsical little star on the crown of her head, as if it were a Christmas tree topper. I gasped. "You're the bronze angel in front of the city art museum."

"Yes," she said, with a beatific smile. "Thank you for the lovely drawings you made of me when you first came to Asheville, Livia. The cards you drew for tourists to buy? I *like* being drawn in bright pastel colors. I feel that colorful. You see me the way I feel. I do so like being blue with white trim, instead of plain bronze."

Even angels have their vanities. Go figure. "You're much prettier in person," I assured her.

She escorted us to Dante's Jeep. Ian and I kept our distance from each other. Between the city's tall buildings, a quiet, starlit night looked down on us. Under the soft glow of street lamps, Asheville's many architectural beings watched us pass. Gargoyles and carved faces, bestiaries on marble posts. I studied them shrewdly, looking for movement. Several times, I'm sure I saw heads nod, as if bowing to me. "We're being watched," I announced. "But it seems friendly."

"The word is spreading," the angel confirmed. "A soul catcher and soul hunter are on duty."

I'd never look at the city the same way, again.

8

The walls of the artist's forge were made of scrapped tin and rusty metal billboards. An electric bellows kept the coals glowing. Outside the forge's screened door was a fenced yard filled with junked cars and piles of useful metal widgets. The work area shared space with mechanized tools and welding gear. Hanging, finished, on long steel shanks, were the artist's modern craft creations: curlicued towel hooks, ornamental door knockers, goose-necked hangers for kitchen pots.

Ian, dressed in jeans, a faded football jersey and an asbestos-lined welding apron, tapped a hammer on an ax blade. We stood around him, enthralled.

"And so," he continued in the cheerful tone of a born storyteller, "there I stood in the smithy shed, me and little Squirrel, and every time that boy-o would chirp and twitter, the birds would come about like pieces of candy with wings. I'd never seen such a sight! Now, aye, comin' across on the ship from the old country I'd seen a tame bird called a *parrot* sit on the captain's shoulder, but I n'er expected to see little parrots in these Carolina mountains, not coming down to chat with Squirrel that way."

I swayed, suddenly a little dizzy from the smoke and the heady effect of Ian's sweaty blacksmithing. I shut my eyes.

When I opened them, sparks flew against the dark walls of the forge and floated through the cracks between the massive logs, open to daylight. Their firefly light shimmered on the glaze of sweat along Ian's bare arms. Errant sparks spewed outward through a wide log doorway, where dozens of small, parakeet-sized birds, unbelievably colorful and exotic, chattered on the limbs of a massive oak tree. I had never seen anything like those birds in the Appalachians.

Ian's lean and sunburned arm, flecked with old burn scars and also the evidence of childhood pox marks, flashed up and down, wielding a thick hammer. The hammer clanged on a glowing ax head, which Ian held with tongs atop a crude stump of iron. A small boy with Cherokee features and shaggy black hair, naked except for a buckskin loin cloth, grinned as he pumped the bellows that fed a bed of glowing coals in a large iron pot.

Ian grinned back at him. "Steady, Squirrel lad, that's the way. Good work."

Squirrel peered outside the cracks in the shed and uttered a long trill. The birds chattered happily, in return.

Clang tap. Clang tap. Ian hammered the red-hot ax head each time then bounced the hammer onto the anvil. A hypnotic rhythm, the heave and thrust. My eyes watered from the smoke and the charred scent of the coals, but I strained not to miss a single move he made.

He was irresistibly masculine. He wore no shirt, only thin, sweat-stained britches and a heavy leather apron that protected him from chest to knees. The britches clung to his hips and thighs and outlined the muscles and the crack of his ass, and a very fine ass it was. He brushed a fight-scarred knuckle over his thick, dark brows and flung sweat into the coals, where it sizzled. A spark settled on his hair, and he laughed and shook his head like a tall dog. The musky stink of singed fur wafted into the air. His hair, long and brown-black, was tied back with a dirty piece of string. Soot smeared his skin.

He had been a helluva blacksmith. And the most handsome, compelling, desirable man I had ever seen in this life or, I felt sure, any other.

I blinked and the image snapped back to now.

"You all right?" Gigi asked, putting a cool little hand on my forearm. "You're pink and sweaty."

"It's just the heat," I said, and took a deep breath, smoke and all. "Ian, those . . . birds you remember. Does anyone know what they were?"

"Carolina parakeets," Sarah said wistfully. "The only parrot species found in this part of the country. Beautiful little budgies with green bodies and yellow heads. They were prized for their feathers, unfortunately."

My heart sank. "They're extinct?"

Charles nodded. "Yes. The last ones died in the early 1900's."

Ian looked at me, frowning. "*Extinct?*" He rolled the word on his tongue. "That does no' sound good."

I nodded. "It means people slaughtered all of them."

His frown deepened. "Demons and banes were behind such waste, I'll guarantee it."

"What about human choice?" I asked. "Don't we have free will?"

"Aye, Livia. Free to be evil or good. Do not go around thinkin' demons are outside of us. I myself believe they are part of us, like the shadow we cast in the sun."

He sighed and went back to his hammering.

I looked at the others, depressed. "You agree?"

They nodded. "But we're also part-angel," Gigi said. "It's all a matter of percentages."

I shoved my fists into my jeans' back pockets. The Cherokee boy, Squirrel, was long dead, his descendents driven onto reservations, and the Carolina parakeets had been hunted to extinction because of human vanity and greed.

Friends of a feather die together.

I tried not to look at Gigi, Dante, Sarah and Charles. They'd forgiven me for trying to hit the highway on my own, but made me swear never to do it again. Not that they had to worry. I was under surveillance. Sheba had awakened Ian up and told him I'd gone. She'd snitched on me, and she'd promised to do it again.

"That should finish the job," Ian announced. Using a pair of tongs, he rammed the ax head into a bucket of water. Steam hissed upward and vanished in the suck of an exhaust fan. Ian laid the dripping ax head on a low iron ledge, next to four others just like it. "I'll do the polishin' and the sharpenin', then add strong oak handles. But first . . . " His grim eyes rose to mine. "Let's have the calling for them, Livia, if you please."

The calling, as he termed it, was a kind of spell only a soul catcher could perform

"If you please," Ian said again, frowning at me gently.

I unzipped a small leather portfolio and pulled out a sheet of heavy art paper. I'd printed the words the others had instructed me to use. Then I had written in flowing script, using a black calligraphy pen, *I, Livia Belane, soul catcher, call all who are good of spirit to guide these weapons against all who are evil of spirit. May peace and kindness reign over chaos and cruelty.*

Sarah nodded. "That's perfect. Place the paper on the axes." I did as she said. "Charles, as the eldest among us, you go first."

He arched a jaunty brow at her as he stepped forward, then flicked ashes from his balding head. Ian handed him a pair of tongs. Charles picked up a glowing coal and laid it atop the papers and the ax heads. "Patience," he said. He handed the tongs to Sarah.

"Hope," she said, and placed a second coal on the paper.

I stared as the paper remained completely unscorched. The hot coals should have turned it into charred specks by now.

Dante took the tongs next. "Courage," he said.

Gigi smiled as she laid a coal on the papers. "Faith."

She handed the tongs to Ian. He looked at me. "Love," he said, and dropped a coal atop the others.

He handed the tongs to me. I lifted a coal slowly. "Trust," I said. Like a challenge.

When my coal touched the pile, the papers ignited in a startling *swoosh* of blue-orange flame. Not even a wisp remained. The coals tumbled around the ax heads.

The ax heads now bore engraved symbols.

We gathered around to study them. From the looks the others traded I knew this was amazing, even to them. "I've never seen anything like this before," Sarah whispered.

"It's not just a blessing, it's a message," Charles said.

"Ay, but what message is there in these squiggles and lines?" Ian asked, scowling.

Gigi and Dante traced them with their fingertips. They shook their heads.

Dazed, I recovered enough to lift my arm. Everyone stared

at the symbols tattooed on my wrist. The encryptions from the Talking Rock.

*

Ian and I sat cross-legged on the floor of an upstairs room of Sarah and Charles' art gallery, looking at high walls filled with my quirky landscape paintings. They resembled the setting of my dream. We'd spent hours staring at the paintings, trying to connect any fragments of instinct or buried memories to the mysterious Talking Rock. Friendship had eased into the spaces between us, though still quiet and fragile.

"When I visited the Talking Rock in my dream, the spirits there asked me if I was Mary or a name that sounded like this: May-lee. What does May-lee mean?"

Ian looked at me carefully. "Your papa was an Ulsterman, like me, and so he gave you a good solid Presbyterian name, you ken? But your mam's people couldn't speak it; they didn't have the right sounds. They said it like so: *May-lee*. And your papa wrote it like so." Ian drew invisible letters on the floor. "*Mele*. So, Mary-Mele-Livia, that's the name you dreamed of when you walked inside these pictures?"

I nodded. "That's what the giant snake and the midget fairy called me." I didn't mean any disrespect, I just wasn't sure how else to describe them.

"You're sure they lived at the Talking Rock?"

"Yes. But that place name means nothing at all to me. To you?"

"No ken of it. I remember parts of our life, but other parts are lost. Tell me more about your dream."

"I felt I'd known the snake and the little woman a long time, and that I'd been to the Talking Rock many times before. They asked me about you. They said you must be a brave man to marry a woman like me—a soul catcher. I said you didn't really understand what the spirit world was all about. That you didn't really believe there were demons among us."

"Hmmm. Sorry. I had a lot to learn back then."

"But I told them . . . " I halted. *I told them I loved you dearly anyway*, I almost added.

He bent his head closer to mine, studying me with soulful eyes. It helped that a three-day beard stubble now covered his lower face. "Speak on," he coaxed.

I shrugged. "They said we should build our home near the Talking Rock. That a powerful spirit lived there and we'd be safe as long as we were under its protection." I held up both hands. "That's all I know. Then I woke up and Dolly was standing beside me—" I gestured—"over there by the window, warning me that a bane was trying to get in."

He looked disappointed. "You've got no more ken of our life together than that one dream?"

"No. I'm sorry." I tilted my face up to his, searching his eyes and wishing I could see deeper inside him. How could I believe we were soul mates, lovers in multiple lives, plus husband and wife in at least one of those lives, yet cringe at the thought of him touching me in *this* life? "Was Mary a good wife?" I asked gruffly.

His face lit up. The tenderness, the pleasure of my small question made him happier than I'd ever seen before. I had so much power over him. It shook me up. I'd never let a man be responsible for my happiness and I'd sure never tried to be make a man happy just because I liked seeing him smile.

"You were full of great ponderings and smart notions and laughs and lust, good sweet lust, that is, oh, Mary, when we . . . when you reached for me, when I laid myself on you at your calling, it was, Mary, Livia . . . "

He reached out, I flinched, and he quickly lowered his arms. He took a second to subdue himself, then exhaled and said simply, "Ay. I could happily live a lifetime in every day and every night we spent together."

"Do you think we died in some really fucked up, horrible way? You definitely believe Pig Face was responsible?"

His throat worked. He tapped his chest. "Here, in my heart, I know this much: the pain was so great I've n'er forgotten it and you've n'er forgiven it. So what we went through must have been terrible. And ay, I believe the pig-faced fecker was there."

I groaned. "It's my fault he's here again. He came through my painting. He found us all again that way."

"You've been under powerful protection from the boons and angels and such, or he'd have found you long before now, Livia. That demon that took over your mam's body was linked to Pig Face, you betcha, but your guards kept her from doin' his full bidding. Or him finding you hisself."

"Were you one of my guardians?"

"I dunno. What happens in the other realm is a fog, and once a soul comes back here, the memories fade right away." He paused. "But I do myself believe that I was out yon, workin' to protect you. I know it's what I've always done, not that it appears with much success, I'm sorry to say."

"I don't look at it that way." I glanced away from him to hide my emotions. "I'm betting you're one of the main reasons I've survived this long."

"We'll make it this time, Mary-Livia. I promise you."

"I've been sucked in by Pig Face's tricks in every life I've lived . . . "

"Now, now, don't be hard on yourself. He and his ilk have been dueling for control of this world since forever began, dueling with the angels and their tribes—the boons and the pogs. You're still able to kick their arses straight back to whatever hell that spawned them." He looked at me earnestly. "I'm proud of you."

Goosebumps frosted my arms. "Why was I given this . . . talent . . . if I'm not very good at it?"

"You're a very fine soul catcher, who's just had a run of bad luck for the past couple hundred years."

On that note, I looked up at him with the breath tight in my throat. "When Ian and Mary were together . . . can you remember any specific events in their lives?"

His eyes softened. "I remember one day like my own name. We were married in the springtime, under the open sky near your papa's trading post. Words were spoken by an old shaman, and then your papa read from his Bible. Your mam's people put a blanket around our shoulders. One blanket shared by two souls. Your papa wrote the date in his Bible. The third of June, seventeen and seventy-five."

Seventeen seventy-five. He said it so calmly. Over two hundred and thirty years ago. If the twenty-fifth anniversary gift is silver and fiftieth is gold, what would our number two thirty be—a keepsake photo of Ben Franklin and Thomas Jefferson downing brandy shooters at our wedding reception?

Ian straightened grimly. "No need to look as though you've been bogged by a kick to the head. 'Tis not as if you were sentenced to eternity in debtor's prison." He got to his feet and headed toward a door.

"You're telling me we lived during the Revolutionary War," I called.

"What's that?" he asked, not looking back.

"The war between the colonial settlers and the British. Do you remember whether or not you enlisted in the colonial army?" An unspoken accusation simmered under those words, then boiled out. "Did you disregard the haven we were given at the Talking Rock? Did you leave me knowing it would doom us?"

He whirled about. "I probably did, Mary-Livia. I've never let other men fight my fight for me. And like most any soul born in the Irish lands, I was none too fond of the fecking English. So go ahead and have a say at me. Ay, I probably went off to war . . . I probably left you to some terrible fate, and thus brought us to misery and ruin." He curled a fist to his stomach. "It boils my guts to wonder how many times you've died hating me."

"I didn't die hating you, I'm sure of that."

I blurted out those words as if I knew them for a fact.

Ian's eyes widened. "Mary-Livia, do you ken of a sudden?"

I shook my head. "I just . . . I don't believe I hated you."

We gazed at each other sadly. His throat worked. "Mary-Livia, we are *meant* to be married, be it for two hundred and thirty-some years or yesterday."

"Only until death do us part," I said hoarsely. "We've done a lot of dying since then."

He scowled. "Oh, so you think? Dead's just a state of mind, but married is a sacred bond. Do I look dead? Do you? We're standing here plain as day, alive and together. And so I pronounce us *still* married." His voice tightened. "Even if you n'er love me again."

Before I could tell him that it wasn't a matter of loving him again, but of never *sacrificing* him again, we heard a commotion downstairs.

"Livia, Ian," Charles called. "Come down quick. There's trouble."

*

Leonidas's lean, jaunty face filled the screen on Charles' office computer. Leo was, after all, a techie boon who loved the camera. "Hello, Kittycat. It's time for you and Ian to exit through the third-level escape portal. The ogres are headed your way."

I hunched close to the screen. Charles, Sarah, Gigi, Dante and Ian closed in behind me, their eyes riveted to his not-quite-real-looking face. "Don't be coy, Leo. What the fuck are you talking about?"

"Detective Beaumont is coming for Ian, Kittycat. Well, not for Ian, but for Greg Lindholm. I like to browse the computers at the Asheville police department. It's like listening to police radio calls, only way heavier. They've pegged Lindholm as a suspect in his wife and kid's deaths."

"Wait a minute. They died in a car wreck."

"Not so fast, Kittycat. The wife's family says Mr. All American Good Guy liked to slap his wife around. She was planning to leave him. Her family's found evidence he rigged the brakes on the family SUV. That's kickin' it old school. Beaumont's gonna pick Lindholm up today then cart him back to Minnesota."

"Where would this 'Minnesota' be?" Ian asked grimly.

"Frontier territory," Dante explained. "West of the Mississippi."

Leonidas went on, gazing straight at me. "And they really, *really* want to know what *you* have to do with all this, Kittycat.

Like, you know, how come Greg Lindholm left Minnesota six months after his wife and kid died and showed up here as your lawyer."

"Oh my god," I whispered.

Leonidas shook his head and tsk-tsked. "I'll see what I do to help on my end, but next time, Ian, do a better background check before you pull a transformer routine on a new I.D, all right?"

Leo's image began to fade, then brightened again. "Oh by the way, Kittycat, I convinced the APD pog—she's one stern butch dyke, if you ask me—to pinch something of yours out of the police evidence lockers. I had a little birdie drop it off. It's in Sarah's big clay flower pot by the main door. Good luck to you and Ian. Play to win this time, Kittycat."

The screen went blank.

I ran outside, with everyone close behind me.

Nahjee lay atop the flowers, a squiggle of purple wooden happiness against the red blooms of impatiens.

Oh, I missed you, she said, as I grabbed her in grateful hands.

Right back atcha. I cuddled the amulet, and its tiny boon, to my heart.

*

Dante held out a set of keys. "You can take one of my cycles. Head into the mountains. See what you can find out about the Talking Rock. We know Ian and Mary lived among the Cherokee. Go to the reservation and see what kind of vibes you pick up. Stay at campsites. Don't use your cell phone. Beaumont can track it."

"How are we going to fix these charges against Ian's body?"

"I don't know. But we'll think of something."

"I'm worried about leaving you guys here alone. What if Pig—"

"We've got your back, Livia. That's our job." He put a hand on my shoulder.

I'd worked as his bartender for several years; wrestled him over knives and nunchucks in his classes, and come to depend on him more than I ever realized. I brushed a hand over my eyes.

He shoved me lightly, a gentle gesture of rebuke. "You're not going to get all soft and girly on me, are you?"

I shook my head. "Fuck, no."

"Good girl. Now go."

Ian stepped up behind us. Dante held out a hand. "Take care of her, soul hunter. She's not as tough as she sounds."

"Ay, she's a pearl in an oyster shell."

Wise-ass. They shook hands.

"One second," Gigi said. She pulled a wad of beaded necklace from her overalls. "Extra protection. Boons love shiny beads." She handed one to Ian as well.

He nodded gently then scowled as he looked down at the delicate jewelry in his thick hands. "What kind o' man was Lindholm? To beat and kill his wife with these hands, to kill her along with their own son! How much meanness is in this body?" He pivoted toward me. Anguish radiated from him.

I shook my head. "For all we know, these charges are a scam to find you quicker. I'd bet money Pig Face is behind this.,"

"What if he's not? I'll be a marked man as long as I'm in this shell o' Greg Lindholm's, and the more I learn about him—" his eyes rested on me—"I cannot blame you for seeing naught but him, instead of me, who I was."

"I saw you. That day at the forge. For just a minute, I saw you as you were in the old life."

His face lit up. "You did, gal? So you can say how handsome and fine I was?"

"If I liked sweat and soot, maybe."

He smiled at my effort to avoid confession. I slipped the necklace over my head, and he placed his over his own head.

Sarah and Charles scurried off to collect camping gear. Dante put a pistol and a box of bullets into a backpack. Gigi dabbed me with protective herbal oils and told me how to identify helpful boons, pogs and angels. Ian slid his finished axes head-down into a second backpack, leaving only the

132

handles to protrude. We said our goodbyes. I tried not to hyperventilate, since the others looked perfectly calm.

I made them promise to stay safe.

"Let go of your fear," Sarah counseled gently. "The more you trust yourself, the more you'll see what you need to see, and you'll understand how you and Ian can fight back."

"Couldn't I just text-message the demons?"

She sighed at my joke.

Suddenly, Sheba's soft, hissing voice filled my mind. "I will give you directions to a safe place for tonight. The pog there is an old friend. Take care, little girl."

"Hugs," I told her. "Hugs to my gold lame' dragon."

"Hugs," Sheba hissed gently, in return.

A few minutes later Ian and I left the haven of the gallery, the familiar isolation of the haunted river valley below the spirit-filled city on the hill, and the comfort of the friends we had known and died alongside in every other lifetime.

We were armed, alone, and on the run.

9

Other bikers looked at us and laughed, especially the hard-ass dudes who wore do-rags instead of helmets—the type who leaned back fearlessly on their vintage hogs, sans mufflers, zooming past us at ninety mph with their tiny balls hidden inside their jeans and their caveman brains set on permanent *sneer.*

"What are those feckers gaggling about?" Ian asked over the audio system in our helmets. His voice boomed in my ears. His big hands felt like warm clamps on my hips. His inner knees pressed against my outer thighs. He leaned when I leaned. He seemed comfortable riding on Dante's big black touring cycle at high speeds on a mountain back road. We'd only had time for a quick lesson after I wheeled the bike out of Dante's garage, near the club.

"Men usually drive," I told him. "Women usually ride on the backseat. It's just stupid tradition. Don't pay any attention to those macho assholes."

"So they think I'm not a full man?" He sounded amused. "Is there a name in this world for that?"

"Among bikers? *Back warmer* is one of the politer ones."

"Back warmer." His disembodied brogue made a deep hum in my head. His broad chest warmed my spine even through the quilted jacket he wore and the leather jacket I wore. His hands tightened, palms and fingers, holding my ass firmly between his spraddled legs. My body was in a permanent state of *cringe.* "I'll tell you, Mary-Livia," Ian went on, cluelessly happy, his voice echoing inside my skull, "I do no' mind being your back warmer. Those front seat feckers don't know what they're missing."

*

Yonah Creek Camp Ground. Yonah means *bear* in Cherokee. Native American place names crowd the maps in the Appalachian mountains of North Carolina. There are memories hidden in them, old markers of villages and hunting trails and spirit worlds.

"You're a quiet one," Ian said as we sprang a tiny, two-person tent beside a rock-rimmed fire pit with a small cooking grill laid across it. Campsite number seven. Assigned to us by a sweet old couple who ran the place. Other old couples camped there, most in RV's or pop-up camping trailers. They smiled at us and waved from their grills and lawn chairs. A small creek gurgled past us. Huge mountains rose above our heads. The spring air was ripe with angels and demons. A whole layer of beings operated invisibly alongside everything we saw, heard, touched and smelled.

Or in my case, not so invisibly.

"Just wondering where the local pog hangs out," I grumbled. "And *what* the pog is."

Ian tossed a pair of insulated blankets in the tents. Talk about primitive. We didn't even have sleeping bags. I frowned. I was not a camp-outdoors kind of woman. "The pog'll visit in its own fair time, Mary-Livia. Pogs are temperamental beasties, but they have a soft spot for we humans. As long as we respect their places. Pogs are keen on their homes, you see. Be it a building, a bit of land, a grandmotherly old tree—tread kindly in a pog's home, and he or she will welcome you."

"Whatever you say." I squatted beside our small fire ring, prodding a pile of dried branches with a lit match. No luck. "That's the last match," I said dully.

Ian knelt beside me, holding one of his axes. "Mary-Livia, do it like so." He piled dried leaves and grass next to one of the fire-rim rocks, raised his ax with the head turned backward, and brought it down at an angle on the rock's granite surface. Sparks flew. A small flame bloomed in the leaves and grass. He scooped them up then tucked them under the branches. The flame grew and spread. Ian blew gently on it. Soon we had a campfire.

"Good work, Daniel Boone," I said with testy thanks.

Ian smiled. "Ol' Daniel claimed he could make a fire just by whistling. I n'er quite believed him."

*

Late night. How could I sleep? I hunkered by the slow-burning campfire, thinking about Pig Face, Detective Beaumont, Greg Lindholm, Ian, and our future or lack thereof. I kept staring into the shadows while Ian walked the campground's perimeter. I worried about him. I kept one hand on the hilt of my knife.

Hello, Yonah Creek campground pog, I kept saying in my mind. *I like your campground. I respect it. I do. If you're around, could you speak up? And don't scare the shit out of me in the process, please.*

No answer.

At the other campsites, the lingering glow of banked campfires made soft red mounds. The RV's and trailers were dark. A security light cast a small circle near the creek. Frogs sang. Deer shuffled through the forest. I jumped at every sound.

"Mary-Livia," Ian said.

I nearly fell off my laced-up-boot heels.

Ian sat down beside me. "'Tis a pleasant bit of forest and creek about us. I don't have your ken for seeing the spirits, but I have a nose for sniffing out their trouble. I neither felt nor smelled any sign of a bane or a demon. They'll not toy much with a powerful pog. I think we're safe enough for the night."

"I hope you're right. So far, the pog is ignoring us." I poked the last hotdog on our low-rent grill. "Still hungry? Nothing like a charred weenie for dessert."

He filched the blackened frank with quick fingers, blew on it, then held it out. It pointed at me like a little grilled dick. "You barely ate. Let's go halves."

A shrewd once-over convinced me his phallic symbolism was innocent. My stomach, however, made a closed fist. I shook my head. He downed the hotdog in two quick bites.

I frowned at him. "How can you eat like that? We have no clue what to do next. The police are looking for us and Pig Face is probably lurking around the next corner. Aren't you worried?"

He frowned back at me. "If I thought we didn't stand a

chance I'd be pissing my britches. But I try not to think about all the worry at once." He looked up at the sky, his face pensive. "'Tis a beautiful, starry spring night. The earth is turning green for a new year. The farmers are planting their crops and the animals are making their babies." He lowered his gaze to me. "And I'm sittin' here with you, wonders of wonders. We're not done for, Mary-Livia. We've come back to life again and again. We'll beat the pig-faced bastard yet."

"And if we don't?"

His eyes went dark. "Then I'll find you in the next life, and the one after that, and all the lives forever."

Goosebumps rose on my arms. I scooted a little farther from him and hugged my knees to my chest. To me, everything in life was about self-defense, putting a physical and emotional wall between me and everyone else. Even now. "I've hidden for *your* sake, not mine."

"Ah, now, I do like that you're so worried about my flesh and hide." He spread his arms to the night, a broad gesture that encompassed me too, if I'd let him. "But no matter what happens, I'm the happiest man who ever lived or ever will live."

"*Why?*"

He curled his arms to his knees and studied me as if I were dense. "Because I finally found my soul mate again."

He dug tears out of me that wouldn't have fallen for anyone else. I didn't squint, grimace, sob, no. I just sat there with hot streams spreading down my disciplined face. When he reached out to wipe my cheeks with the back of one finger I flinched but let him.

He could tell this intimacy was about to go a bridge too far. "Get some sleep, Mary-Livia," he said gently. "Roll up in a blanket inside the tent. I'll sit out here and guard the night for us."

I retreated to the tiny tent behind us, where I wrapped myself like a human burrito and lay facing the open door flap, so I could watch him watch the fire.

Guarding the night. For us.

I slept. Amazing.

*

No wonder I dreamed of mushroom soup. Another blast of hot air gushed into my nose with a musky scent like smoked shitakes. I opened my eyes. I stared up in the dim gray light just before dawn, nose to snout, into the black eyes of an enormous white bear.

"I think we've got the pog here," Ian said in a low voice. "I sense him more than see him. He's just a big shadow to me." Ian paused. "A very, very big shadow."

The other breaking news was that Ian lay beside me in the tent, though wrapped chastely in his own blanket, and on a side note, I'd been sleeping contentedly with my head on his shoulder.

"I guess this is why the campground's named after a bear," I finally said. My voice shook. "Hello, Yonah."

Yonah touched his cool, mushroomy snout to my forehead, sniffing me. Then he placidly sniffed Ian's face, blowing softly on him. Finally he looked at me again. *Hello, soul catcher. I hear that you and this soul hunter banished the pair of winged lions who terrorize Asheville. Nasty banes, those two. Though I have nothing against winged cats in general. There are some about who are quite trustworthy.*

None of that was said with anthropomorphic lips moving on an ursine face. Instead, he *thought* the words at me.

"Can you hear what he's saying, too?" I asked Ian.

"Ay. It's a whisper, but I can make it out."

Ian and I sat up slowly. Yonah's huge head, which he'd poked through the tent's open flap, crowded the space. I lifted a hand. "Would it be okay if I touched your fur?"

Of course. It would be an honor, soul catcher.

I put one hand on his forehead. The fur was pure white and as soft as feathers. I drew my fingers through it. "You're beautiful."

So are you, soul catcher. What can Yonah do for you today?

"We don't know which way to turn next. We're looking for a place called Talking Rock. Have you heard of it?"

Hmmm. There are several such place names in the mountains here and yon, but you're looking for a certain special one, I take it?

"Yes."

Come with me. I'll introduce you to a pog who lives nearby. As I always say, if you want to know about a rock, ask a rock pog. He withdrew his head majestically. Ian and I clambered out of our blankets. Ian reached for the backpack he'd tucked nearby. As he hooked the strap over one big shoulder the ax handles clicked with soft wooden sounds, deceptively harmless.

"I hope we won't need those," I said, while making sure my knife was strapped to my right hip.

"Ay." He ducked out of the tent then stood and stretched. I scrambled out on all fours and took his hand-up without hesitation. That small concession brought a light to his face. "Did you sleep well, Mary-Livia?" His lilt turned my name up at the end and gave the question just a hint of spice. "Not crowded or anything?"

I grunted. "My pillow had beard stubble and smelled like burned hotdogs."

He grinned as we hurried after a spirit bear the size of an elephant.

*

I was having a *Last of the Mohicans* moment—that terrifying scene at the end of the movie, with all the fighting and the throat-slashing atop rocky ledges overlooking a panorama of green mountains. It was filmed in North Carolina for a reason.

Cliffs. High-ass, shit-yourself-and-don't-look-down cliffs.

"This rock pog must not be afraid of heights," I muttered as a gust of wind made me sway.

She calls herself Promontoria, Yonah said.

Ian studied the jumbles of lichen-flecked boulders and plunging escarpments around us. "And what would that name be meaning?"

"Big-ass *cliff*," I explained dryly.

Yonah nodded. He blew softly on the rocky ground. *Dear Promontoria, are you listening? Come out and speak with us, if you please.*

139

Nothing. A chilly wind *swooshed* through the silence. More than a dozen turkey buzzards wheeled in the pink dawn sky high above us, their wings making shadows.

Suddenly Nahjee whispered to me. *I don't like the spirit of those birds.*

Indeed, Tabby whispered. *They are not of this world.*

Not what I needed to hear while we were perched on a cliff face like a target. I looked at Ian. "Nahjee and Tabby say the buzzards may be banes."

He stiffened as he looked up at the circling birds. "Ay, it's not right for turkey buzzards to be hunting this early in the morn. But then again, it's not impossible."

Yonah spoke quietly. *I'm afraid your dear little boons are correct. Those birds are in service to a demon. They are banes.*

I took two trembling steps backward and my shoulders hit the cliff face. "Last soul catcher down's a rotten egg," I said. "I'll lead the way."

Yonah blocked me. *Now, now. They're surely not eager to tangle with me. Only a very powerful demon would challenge a pog as old as I.*

Ian said quietly, "No offense, Master Yonah, but I fear this demon is able and willing."

Yonah studied me with his head tilted. His great, dark eyes seemed puzzled. *You're afraid of these banes?*

I gave a jerky nod. "Shouldn't I be?"

No. A soul catcher powerful enough to banish the griffins of Asheville can surely banish mere banes with a flick of her hand.

"That's good to know, but I haven't tested that theory yet. I'm still a rookie."

Yonah frowned. *Oh, dear.*

Ian slowly pulled an ax from his backpack. "Just in case you need some time to practice your banishin' skills, Mary-Livia, I'll get ready to chop these flying feckers. See if you can rouse madam rock pog. We came here for help. Let's not run from a fight."

Ah, Yonah said, arched a white brow at him. *He truly is a soul hunter. In love with the challenges of battle.*

I stared at the rocky surface around my feet. My mouth was

so dry my tongue stuck to my teeth. "Hello, Promontoria. we need your help to locate a large rock that has special meaning to us. I've seen it in my dreams. The Talking Rock. It's not on any maps of these particular mountains or mentioned in any histories around here. Can you help us find it?" *Before we're pecked to death by giant buzzard banes,* I added to myself.

The wind whistled. The banes spiraled in a sudden descent.

Yonah stepped in front of us. *Guard your soul catcher,* he said to Ian. he said. *I'll take care of these fellows.* He rose on his tremendous hind legs.

Ian stepped in front of me, facing the banes, his ax raised. "Stay behind me, Mary-Livia. And don't stab me accidental-like with that toothpick of yours." I raised my knife and balanced on the balls of my feet. The average *real* turkey buzzard is big and ugly, but no threat to anyone or anything that's still breathing. They eat carrion. They don't sing or squawk; they only grunt and hiss. Their heads are naked and purplish red. Their beaks are white and hooked. That's what the *real* ones are like.

I squinted at the banes, trying to see them through a mist that clouded each one. Yonah roared. *The demon's trying to hide them from you, soul catcher! Concentrate!*

"You can do it, Mary-Livia!" Ian yelled.

"No! Too fast! Too many!"

They dive-bombed us.

Yonah took out three banes with one swipe of a huge white paw and two more with the other. *How dare you invade my territory,* he roared. When he hit them they exploded in streamers of dark light, like inverse fireworks. But the streamers reversed themselves, and I watched in shock as the banes re-formed.

Yonah rumbled loudly, *Only you can banish them forever, soul catcher.*

A group swarmed him, dodging his claws and teeth, distracting him so others could swoop past, headed for Ian and me.

Ian took out one with a swing of his ax and fended off

more with wide arcs of the deadly blade. Dark sparkles lit the air then sucked back together like a film in reverse. I swung my knife into the heart of one reconstituted bane as it swooped past Ian. Its shimmering fog parted long enough for me to stare up at glowing red eyes and a head like a cobra's, only bearing a forked beak long enough to pierce a human from chest to spine.

"Shit! Beat it," I gasped.

The bane vaporized.

That one did *not* re-form.

"Good on you, Mary-Livia," Ian yelled, bashing another to temporary bits with his ax.

I gaped at the empty air. *I really can do it! Just like the griffins!*

A bane lunged past Ian. He slashed it in half with his ax. A wing of its inky energy slammed into me as it re-formed. I staggered.

And stepped off the edge of the world.

Ian leapt after me, catching me by one arm. We slammed against craggy rocks, him spread-eagled on the ground above me and me grasping for a hold on the face. My fingers curled over a small hummock of stone; I dug the toes of my hiking boots into crevices.

The banes closed in on him, shrieking, their forked beaks open, their long talons arched to rip into him.

I shouted to the ether. *I want to see them.*

My vision cleared. The mist was gone. Their wingspan was vast. They were covered in scales, not feathers. Their puke-yellow feet had claws that curved like scimitars.

And they *knew* I saw them. Their huge wings tilted vertically, like the flaps on a jet, trying to slow their approach. Their shrieks changed from fierce to frightened. I flung out one hand at them.

"Paint them! Trap them! Burn them!"

And they did burn. Oh, how they burned.

The air shattered with their flames. It sounded like a sonic boom. The morning light gleamed with black diamonds. And then they were gone. Incinerated.

Pink-blue sky replaced them. Peace and quiet returned.

Ian, dusty and gasping for air, looked down at me with awe. "You banished the bastards, Mary-Livia. All of them at once!"

He lost his grip and began to slide. I yelled. The rocky surface lurched and flexed as if powered by underlying muscles. Suddenly, gnarled arms—I counted five of them, each with a gray, nubbled, mitten-shaped paw—enfolded him. I yelled again as sets of the same rock-gray arms lifted me too.

The many-armed Promontoria hoisted us to the ledge and shoved us safely against the cliff wall. Yonah blew out a long breath of relief. *Well done, Promontoria. Well done, Ian and Livia.* Yonah bowed his head to me. *Miss Soul Catcher, you are too modest. Clearly, you are no rookie.*

Ian and I dragged fresh air into our lungs. He looked at his ax. The blade had been ripped up its center. The encryptions glittered like broken mirrors.

Then the steel healed itself.

The encryptions joined, settled, glowed. He laid the ax aside, and patted it. "Many thanks, friend."

My, my, a deep female voice said. Promontoria had the husky rasp of an old cheerleader who's smoked one too many cigarettes. *What have we here? A handsome soul hunter and an intrepid soul catcher. My, my. I wasn't sure they were worthy. But now . . . oh, my.*

Impressive, aren't they? Yonah replied.

A face emerged from a boulder like clay being pushed from inside. Granite-silver eyes with heavy brows peered at us. Promontoria's eyes might be rocky, but they were all-girl. She had thick, flirty, lichen-green lashes.

She aimed those rocky eyes at Ian. *Soul hunter. I see you as you are, not in that body you're using. You remind me of Daniel Day Lewis. He stood right here when they filmed the movie, you know. Oh, I liked the look of him, I tell you.*

Okay, at least we were back in the land of *normal* Strange Shit.

Ian and I staggered to our feet. Ian said gallantly, "'Tis a great honor you're paying us, Promontoria."

Hmmm, a good, rock-hard man. My, My.

A rock pog was getting her rocks off on Ian. I bit back a smile. An extraordinary man, a seducer of granite. I looked at him with a growing warmth.

"Well, madam," Ian said gallantly, "I'd be blushing if it weren't all true. And from such a lovely lady."

Her lichen-lashes fluttered.

Yonah cleared his throat. *Dear girl, Livia and Ian are in a hurry and in a good deal of danger, as you've seen. They have a question for you.*

I know, I know, I heard it already. The gnarled gray eyes swiveled their lichen lashes at me. *Soul catcher, do you realize that the source of your greatest strength comes from the source of your greatest pain?*

"Yes, I'm beginning to understand that."

Do you realize that the life memories you seek at the Talking Rock formed a crucible which nearly destroyed you and your very handsome soul hunter? That it changed your future forever?

"I feel that possibility, yes."

Are you willing to risk despair to find out more?

"We don't have any other choices, Promontoria. If we don't find out who we were, we'll never know how to fight the pig-face demon."

So be it.

If granite and bedrock can sigh, she did. *Wonaneya,* she intoned. She said the strange name again, her voice and face fading back into the rock. *Look for Wonaneya in the ancient rock places you call the Smokies. Take care of your partner, soul catcher. He is so fine.*

And then she was gone.

Ian and I traded a bewildered look then gazed up at Yonah. "Wonaneya?" I said.

The great, ursine head drooped. *I had no idea you were searching for that sad place.* He turned and began to shuffle in his huge way back down the path to the campsite. *I will give you directions, but then I'll say no more about it. This is a matter for your souls to engage. Not for pogs to counsel.*

We hurried after him. "Can you at least be telling us what the name means in English?" Ian asked.

Yonah stopped. He turned his majestic white head and looked back at us over one shoulder. His eyes were sad. *Once upon a time in the old days, Wonaneya was a Cherokee peace town. A place of refuge. The word means Talking Rock, at least as modern people have written it from the old language. Wonaneya's fate has been hidden by time and the lies of history.* He looked at us sympathetically. *The demon destroyed all who lived there.*

*

Boom. The ground shivered with another round of thunder. A swirling, muddy creek gushed past our wet boots. We huddled, heads bent, our mood clubbed into dull silence. Yonah's morbid hints about our history in the long-gone Cherokee town named Wonaneya weighed heavily on us both. Even Ian couldn't manage any jaunty shrugs. Around us, the oldest mountains in the world drained their tears our way.

Land of the blue smoke. That's what the Cherokees called the Great Smokies that straddle North Carolina's western border with Tennessee. Ancient mountains, cloaked in all-natural organic blue mist, some standing over a mile high. Climb to their craggy, bald-rock tops under a full moon and you can imagine all sorts of other worlds connected to the same sky.

The Smokies are an even stranger blue stew of unexplainable boogie men than Asheville: vanished villages and towns, forgotten tribes, ghost choirs, odd lights, UFO's, mysterious writings on trailside rocks, rumors of Atlantis and glimpses of beasts and beings that couldn't possibly exist, right? Plus *twenty-four* active energy vortexes, according to the New Age swamis. A major power point on the power grid of the planet. Big-time mojo. Shit happens there.

But for Ian and me, squatting under a narrow rock bridge on a lonely back road alongside the motorcycle, while rain sluiced down, lightning cracked our eardrums and thunder made earthquakes under our feet, the vast mountain range west of Asheville had taken on darker shadows than we'd ever expected.

I prodded a wilting map from a guidebook we'd bought at a convenience store. "This big green blob is the Great Smoky Mountains National Park," I told Ian. "Over eight hundred square miles. Ninety five percent in wild forest, and a big chunk of that is old-growth. That means it's never been cut for timber and it's like taking a walk back in time. There are some old pioneer settlements like Cade's Cove—no one lives in them, they're just preserved as part of the National Forest— but nothing on this park map shows the name *Wonaneya*. I have no clue how we're going to find the site of a Cherokee town that was . . . " my voice trailed off. I didn't want to finish that sentence. *Destroyed by Pig Face more than two hundred years ago.*

Ian scrubbed a hand across his jaw. His beard was now a thick brown mat, not just stubble. "There was a trading post there too, you ken? Your father's place. It was right beside your mam's Cherokee town."

"Do you remember what my father's last name was?"

He shook his head wearily, then pounded a fist on one knee. "Why won't these things come to me? Why would such memories go hiding from me? I know we don't always remember the lives we've shared, but the happy parts of *that* life, with you, are clear as fresh water to me."

We traded an agonized look. "Only the happy parts," I said hoarsely. "Maybe because the rest was too horrible."

"Oh, come on, you know better than that," a trilling female voice said.

We stared at the creek. A small, blue-green, woman-like creature stepped gracefully from the rain-swollen water. She was no more than a foot tall, hairless and chubby and naked. Raised patterns—swirls and stars—decorated her skin. She looked like a cross between a fertility totem and *Mystique* from the X-Men movies. She braced his legs apart defiantly and plopped her hands on her round hips.

She sure wasn't shy. The only part that wasn't blue were her pink nipples and the bright pink crevice between her hairless blue thighs.

Ian regarded her with amusement. "I do wish I could see you better, Miss Spirit."

"Oh, you sweet talker." She gazed at me with firm blue eyes. "Hello, soul catcher. No need to fear me. I'm a boon." She plopped down on the damp, grassy earth in front of us and curled her arms around one up-drawn knee. "My name's Crescendo. Don't ask why. It's a family thing."

"Nice to meet you, Crescendo. I'm Livia and this is Ian . . . "

"Like I don't know? Why, you two are big news. Fought off the winged lions in Asheville and banished a whole flock of banes just this morning. Everyone's excited. We've been waiting a long time for you two to get your act back together. Two centuries."

Ian put a warning hand on my arm. "Boons don't visit just to have a chat and a cup of tea, Mary-Livia. She's got news to tell."

Crescendo smiled, nodded and got to her stubby blue feet. "I came here to tell you that if you want to find Wonaneya, go to the Cherokee reservation and ask for Crow Walker. Got that? Ask for Crow Walker on the Qualla Boundary reservation. At the casino."

At the casino?

She glanced up the creek. Another clap of thunder rattled us. Rain gusted beneath the bridge. When her eyes settled back on us the whites had merged into the blue and she began to fade. "And I came here to tell you a head-high wall of floodwater is coming down this creek gully right now. The demon sent it." She disappeared.

Ian and I leapt up. He pushed the bike while I grabbed our backpacks. We struggled up the steep bank in a downpour of cold spring rain. No more than five seconds after our feet touched the pavement of the narrow mountain road, a roar came from upstream. A boiling, muddy, limb-filled cascade filled the creek bed, cresting only a few inches from where we stood.

As the mountain storm drenched us we watched Pig Face's

killer flood filter away. The rain eased to a trickle. The little creek returned to normal. Cold steam rose off the paved road.

When we turned to mount the bike Ian looked at me with an arched brow. "That was a bit close for comfort."

"Ay," I said.

He laughed loudly as he threw one soggy, bluejeaned leg over the bike and settled contentedly onto the girly back seat.

10

The Cherokee Indians of North Carolina are stuck on a hundred square miles of isolated mountains and wild forest at the entrance of the national forest, whose unbroken arms close like a defensive hug around the tribe's to-cringe-at tourist district full of cheap, insulting knickknack crap, low-rent diners and shabby motels.

On the other hand, the boons and angels have never deserted the tribe. There's also a high-tech museum, a cultural center, and other proud and authentic testaments to the tribe. Plus a good hospital, social programs, and schools. Every summer, at an outdoor amphitheater, the tribe stages an epic, fuck-the-white-man historical play that guilty white people pay to watch.

Still, it's a weird world. Picture upwards of ten thousand Cherokees tucked away on narrow back roads and ridges and deep hollows, living in everything from house trailers to suburban ranches, spending their tribal annuity checks and suiting up every day to work for the area's two biggest employers: the tribal government or the tribe's small casino.

Welcome to the Native American reality, where you're probably either a civil servant or a blackjack dealer. I had no clue where to look for this Crow Walker, unless he played the slots. I had no access to Google, a cell phone, or any other way to look him up.

I gazed at the casino's entrance morosely. My rain-soaked clothes had dried stiff and coarse. Fear crawled through me like a trickle of acid.

Ian stood peacefully beside me, looking up at the casino with his mouth open. "What the feck kind of place is *this*?" he asked. "I've never seen so many old folks heading in the same direction."

I chuckled hoarsely. The casino front bore lots of rustic stonework, faux native atmosphere, bright lights even in daylight, and yellow pansies in the landscaping. "It's the tribe's gaming hall," I explained. People come from all over this part of the country to gamble here."

Ian shook his head. "I've n'er said anything against cards and dice, nor on betting on a fight or a race, but this is . . . God's balls, look there, Mary-Livia. Another pack of sweet old granmam's walkin' into a gambling hall, proud as you please."

"They travel in herds." I pointed as a big bus rumbled past us.

He sighed. "Is this a good thing or a bad thing?"

"Both. It's making a fortune for the tribe. They put it to good use. They can earn a living they couldn't earn before."

"Even in our time, Mary-Livia, you told me you could hear the banshee singing for your mam's people."

"Oh, did she?" a Santa Claus-sized voice boomed. "Did you hear *me* coming, soul catcher?"

We jumped.

The question was followed by a hearty laugh. Ian pushed me behind him as a massive shape began to gather in front of the casino's main doors. The creature lumbered toward us. The ground shook with each of his steps. I heard a loud jingling sound, like thousands of coins shimmying. The viscous shape was several stories tall.

"I can see naught but a lot of twinkles," Ian warned. He reached for one of the axes in his backpack.

I grabbed his arm. "Wait. He's grinning. I think he's the casino pog."

"Why, soul catcher, you're a sweet, smart girl," the thing boomed. "Yes, I'm a pog. I'm the big-ace pog of this casino! And I've heard plenty about *you*, soul catcher! And your soul hunter too! Come, let me give you a hug!"

I could now see the pog clearly, though I had to tilt my head back to look up at him. He was cheerfully obese, and his green head was bald except for a tall, money-green mohawk. His features were somewhat Cherokee but generic enough to include any race. His face and head were entirely tattooed—the only way to describe the effect—with symbols from a dollar bill.

George Washington's face covered the right side of his skull and the Great Seal covered the left side. On his left cheek was the dollar's pyramid. I could clearly see the Latin inscriptions. They seemed almost luminous. *Annuit Coeptis.* God has favored our undertaking. And *Novus ordo seclorum.* A new order for the ages.

The rest of his corpulent, jingling body was layered with silver and gold coins, like scales on a fish. He tinkled like a thousand wind chimes. He gleamed in the sunshine. He shoved Ian aside with his car-sized foot, reached down, grabbed me in a gentle hug, and lifted me off my feet. I dangled high in the air, nervous.

What passersby saw, I don't know. Probably just Ian and me standing, dumbstruck, in front of the casino. But what I saw was the up-close pearly whites of a jolly, overfed, casino pog. His fleshy curves enveloped me. He smelled like money— that crisp, earth-green ink scent that fresh bills give off.

He set me down carefully. Ian quickly re-stationed himself by my side, scowling. His hand flexed on the handle of an ax. "Do not be hoisting her again, if you please."

The pog grinned down at him. "A trusty soul hunter! Always on guard! Good boy!" The pog squatted in front of us with the huge grace of an elephant perching on a stool.

He propped his gold and silver arms on his spraddled knees. "It's been a long time since I've seen a soul catcher," he said. "I was afraid this part of the world might have to do without a good soul catcher for a while yet. But here you are! With an ornery, ax-wielding soul hunter as a partner. I'm so pleased. Do you plan to start rounding up demons and banes right away?"

I couldn't decide how to answer that, so Ian took up the slack. "We're on a bit of a personal hunt first, but we'll get to the soul-catching business anon. You have our word."

"Very good! It's high time for you two to clean up this neck of the woods. This neighborhood is going to Hell. Pun intended." He guffawed. "But seriously. The demons around here have gotten awfully powerful over the years. And the bolder they get, the more banes they recruit. And then they start turf wars with each other. It's all we pogs and boons can do to keep them from hurting more souls than they do."

Recruiting? Starting turf wars? I pictured demons in skewed baseball caps and baggy lowriders, spray-painting dumpsters. Worse, I imagined Pig Face as the godfather of an entire mafia family of demons and banes, all of them determined to make sure Ian and I ended up sleeping with the fishes.

"Have you ever seen a pig-faced demon?" I asked.

"Well, now, soul catcher, that's a strange question. What a demon looks like is all in how you look at it. What a demon looks like to me isn't necessarily what a demon looks like to *you*. Demons are tricky that way. Which is why it's important that you soul catchers have a special talent for seeing straight to the . . . well, straight to the demon's soul."

"So you haven't met a pig-faced demon, but that doesn't mean he's not around here. You just wouldn't recognize him as pig-faced."

"Correct. And if he's taken over a human body it's nearly impossible to recognize him at all. That's when demons are the most dangerous. In disguise. That's why the world could use more soul catchers."

"How many soul catchers *are* there?"

He flopped his hands. "I have no idea. My expertise is just money. Happy money. The joy of owning money. You know, they call it *filthy lucre*, but as the Bible says, it's greed that's bad, not money itself. Of course, people's greed is what lures the demons and banes." He sighed. "I'm here to protect people from the influences of their darker nature." He pointed a gleaming finger at us. "Good fighting evil. The old eternal battle for souls. Just another days' work for we soul warriors, right?"

I looked up at him defiantly. "If you're on the job, why do you need me?"

The money pog slapped his coined hands on his knees.

"You think you ought take no responsibility for the fate of your fellow living flesh? That's what you're saying? Why, who *better* to fight for the survival of the human spirit than living mortal humans? Souls are not static, Miss Soul Catcher! They are enhanced or weakened by each life they live. Someone of their own kind has to fight for them. It's a representative government, you see! And it's not just the human world at stake."

He leaned forward squinting at me, making George Washington hunch an eyebrow. "Soul catcher, you *do* understand that people aren't the only ones with souls? That souls take up residence wherever they please. A demon, a bane, a cat, a dog, a being as small as a spider or less, a house, a tree, a mountain, a casino? When you defend one good spirit, you defend them all!"

Ian angled in front of me. "You'll not be talking down to her. She's proved herself worthy of better than such. We're seeking answers to a few questions, that's all."

"Crow Walker," I said. "We have to find him."

"And what do you promise me in return, Soul Catcher?"

Since this pog liked drama, I put a hand over my heart. The fast pulse under my palm said I believed in the lecture he'd given us.

"The demon I seek has killed or threatened my family more than once. My family includes souls of many kinds. I pledge my mission to all the souls who depend on me for help in this and other worlds."

He applauded. "Well done, Soul Catcher."

Ian nudged me. "I'm proud of you."

"Go a few miles up one road, Soul Catcher, then down another then up one, then down. Only an hour or two on your bike."

Ian frowned. "Does this certainty of yours mean Crow Walker has word we're coming to visit and will signal us?"

"Oh, yes, old Crow Walker is hard to surprise. He's been expecting you for over two hundred years."

A bead of sweat crept down my face. "What kind of spirit

is he? An ordinary man? Sorry, I don't really know how to ask this question politely."

"Old Crow Walker? An ordinary man?" The pog threw back his dollar-bill head and laughed so hard my eardrums vibrated. "No, he's a memory keeper."

"What's a—"

"Oh, you'll see. Sorry, but it's time for me to get back inside my home." He stood up slowly, heavily. The air shimmered with his reflective metallic light and his money music. Money, after all, is irresistible. "I feel naked without my treasures around me."

He touched a golden fingertip to my head. *"Ka-ching."* then gave Ian the same petting touch. *"Ka-ching."* A slot-machine blessing.

He faded away.

A little shaken, I looked at Ian. "I wish just once a pog would say, 'Have a nice day,' and leave it at that."

Ian nodded grimly.

*

Grotesque masks stared down at us from the deep shadows of log walls blackened by endless campfires. Their eyes were empty, their mouths open in shrieks. They leered, they howled, they laughed obscenely. Some were made from large gourds, others from carved pieces of wood. One wore a turban made from a hornet's nest.

"Booger masks," Crow Walker drawled, gazing at us over the red-orange flames of his fire pit. The flames seemed to run up the crags of his cheeks. "Faces. Our Enemies. Worn in tha dances. Don't be' fraid of 'em. We all wear masks. Our bodies er jist that. Jist to wear an' throw 'way. Only the soul behind the mask is e-ternal."

He returned to smoking his pipe. Long silences punctuated what little conversation we had with him. For all I knew, we had stepped back through time the moment we got off the bike and walked up the hill to his log shanty. Or we'd entered a different dimension. Or we were hallucinating from some secret ingredient in the old-school tobacco he'd tamped into our clay pipes.

His shanty was three-sided; the night outside was so dark it might be part of the moonless sky. We might be floating in an astral plane, or lost in the middle of deepest space.

Or fuck, just heading down a mystical rabbit hole with a stoned old man. His skin was leathery, his cheekbones high and gaunt; his nose long and hawked. His head was wrapped in a red turban anchored by a long pin made of bone. *Not human bone*, I hoped. Small gold hoops pierced his ears from the lobes to the tops. He wore buckskin britches, moccasins, and a long red shirt tied with a beaded belt. He wrapped himself in a plaid blanket that seemed vaguely Celtic.

We wrapped ourselves in our camping blankets.

I looked at Ian over my long pipe, for a clue to his opinion of the situation. He cupped the bowl of his own pipe in the crook of one forefinger, drew on it expertly, then gestured with a flick of his eyes toward the white smoke that trickled lazily upward. It joined the smoke of the campfire, wafting toward a small hole in the shanty's roof. The Zen of air currents, or something.

Be one with the smoke? All right. I'd chill. Relax. *Chilax.* Sure.

"Yo'soul keeps even tha mem'ries you try t'forget," Crow Walker said. He gestured at the flames, and they died down as if turned low on a gas burner. He passed his hand, palm down, over them, and a silver-gray pool of water took their place.

I looked at my startled reflection and Ian's worried one. Our faces were lit by invisible firelight.

"What d'ya wanta re-member?" Crow Walker drawled.

I said warily, "We want to know what happened to us when we were known as Ian and Mary Thornton. How did we die? Why? What are we supposed to learn from it, so that our new lives won't always be doomed?"

Crow Walker looked at Ian. "That what you wanta 'member, you sure?"

Ian nodded.

"Then you'll live yo' mem'ries ta-gether."

The booger masks shimmered, coming to life. My head

swelled with the smoke, the narcotic fear. Ian put a hand on mine, and after a stiff moment I wound my fingers through his. He was the alpha and omega, everything I was or had ever been. Just as I was the beginning and end for him too. Ian said quietly, his voice hoarse with arousal, "Mary-Livia, I also wish for you to remember why you loved me."

I bowed my head, wanting him, wishing he were free of the body I hated. I couldn't see beyond that yet. But we had to know who we were. And why we were drawn back to one crucial, turning-point life.

Crow Walker pointed at the watery mirror.

We looked into the past.

11

Liver Eater. That's what I named her. That's what she was, this deadly demon in a woman's form who called herself *Susannah St. John.*

It was she who brought the pox to Wonaneya town.

I crouched in the shadows beyond the log house and outbuildings of my father's trading post. Ian slept soundly in our room there. We hadn't been married long, and we'd just begun building our cabin near the Talking Rock, on the site the uktena and Bird Woman had counseled me to choose. I'd put Ian under a charm, so he wouldn't notice me going out alone in the night.

He didn't understand my work as a soul catcher. He assumed it was just one more part of my Cherokee religion, and he considered religion a whimsy. *Any* religion, from either his world or mine. It was hard to convince a man that demons existed when he only looked into shadows to search for *me.*

It was a moonless night high in the Cherokee lands of the Appalachians, long before the end of the great Cherokee empire that controlled the southern highlands. In the broad creek valley nearby, campfires burned outside dozens of low huts. Shamans chanted to the spirits to save the sick. People mourned the dead. Ghosts, shocked and grieving at their untimely passage, wandered everywhere I turned. I spent many hours gently urging them to let the wind carry them to the middle realms, where souls consider who to become next.

A tall, blond woman stepped from one of the small cabins my father offered to visiting traders, especially those bringing wives and children with them. She wore fine silk and petticoats, even here in the wilderness.

She traveled alone, strangely unafraid of men or beasts. Several weeks ago she had arrived at my father's trading post with a wagon full of goods to trade for the rubies, sapphires and other stones the people of Wonaneya dug from our secret mountain caves. She wanted to see the caves for herself. She wanted to see the Talking Rock. Everyone told her it was a ghost-rock, a hidden being, but she just laughed.

My father, a burly Celt who had become as much Cherokee by nature as Irish over the decades among my mother's clan, would not reveal the gemstone's locations but agreed to barter with her on behalf of the village. This aloof white woman with her high-pitched British voice might be greedy and ingratiating, but she'd brought many useful things the people wanted—fancy knives and metal pots, brass buttons and glass beads.

I was wary of her from the start but she charmed everyone else, including Ian. He'd traded her some blacksmithing work on her wagons to get me a beautiful silver gorget. That pretty silver pendant had tricked even me.

Now I realized a bane was attached, and that bane had pulled a mist over my eyes that kept me from seeing the demon behind Susannah St. John's smile.

Until it was almost too late.

Liver Eater headed up a path that led to the high ridges. She walked fast and with sure feet, as if she could see in the dark. *Help me track her,* I said to Owl and Fox, two of my most helpful boons. Owl glided from a high tree limb without a sound. Fox led my way up the trail, his bushy tail giving off a soft red glow only I could see. Small hands slipped into mine. "We are here," an old man's voice said in Cherokee. "You should not track a demon without all of us going along to keep you invisible."

I looked down. Dozens of little people surrounded me. Men and women, old and young. Miniature Cherokees in appearance, only knee-high to me. Bird Woman, my guide and teacher, had sent them.

I nodded a silent thanks.

We followed Liver Eater up the mountain.

*

Standing atop a craggy granite bald with only the stars above her, she stripped off her white woman's bodice, her skirt, her petticoats, her chemise, her shoes, even her jewelry.

She unfastened her blonde hair. It curled down her body like yellow tongues, stroking her bare breasts and naked back, licking her skin. She arched her spine and raised her arms to the sky. A harsh purple light slowly grew from the massive rock beneath her feet. It swirled around her, illuminating her and everything around her for a dozen strides in all directions.

She is calling her banes, Fox said. I squatted with my small troop of boons in the forest, watching through the trees. Fox gestured with his head. *See their eyes burn red at the edge of the shadows?*

My stomach twisted. Slowly, dozens of ugly and frightening banes crept or slithered or flew from the darkness. Most were so strange I couldn't compare them to any living animal; not even in parts. Some reminded me of insects, some of lizards, some of birds, and some of grossly misshapen animals with shaggy fur. Most had dangerous claws and fangs or long, agile tails with sharp tips. Some oozed putrid oils from their skin, dripping and drooling as they moved forward. And some had sexual parts similar to human men and women. Those parts were engorged, ready.

They gathered around her with eager, upturned red eyes. They shivered and wiggled with anticipation. She lowered her arms to a wide embrace, welcoming them all. The banes wrapped themselves around her legs. They crawled up her body. The entire pulsing, wiggling crowd climbed over each other to reach every inch of her. They sucked and kissed her skin, they licked her breasts, they slid the tips of their tails between her legs, front and back. She parted her lips to let their long, flicking tongues slide inside her mouth. Their spines flexed in quick humping motions.

She smiled. With her eyes shut and her head drooping back, she let the mass of lecherous, orgasmic beings lower her to the rock with them beneath her, around her, on top of her, inside her. They spread her legs as if her inner body was a feast. Two, three, four five banes burrowed between them at the same time, licking and thrusting. Her body flexed and spasmed. She cried out again and again until she went limp and sighed.

The creatures licked her clean of their filth and her own juices. They dressed her as she slept, exhausted. Then they crept and slithered and flew back into the shadows. I crouched lower as several swooshed by above my head. I knew how to banish the usual banes; I'd been doing so since childhood. But for once I was glad to be invisible and let them go.

I shook all over.

Liver Eater was a major demon, commanding a large, loyal troop of banes. She had stolen a human form to work her evil in the human world.

And she had come to Wonaneya for no good purpose.

*

When the terrible, oozing sores began to speckle my younger sister's skin I knew Liver Eater was behind it. I blamed myself. If only I hadn't been fooled by the demon for so long. If only I had come up with a plan to fight back before now.

Now Cera lay dying. Her face and body were covered in festering sores. The breath rattled in her throat. She lay on a sweat-soaked straw mattress in our father's log house, clutching her favorite flower, a wild pink orchid. Her golden hands shook with fever. Her long hair, which had always had the prettiest hint of Father's red Irish in its black Cherokee strands, trailed off the mattress in damp ropes.

"Would I have made a good witch, *Mele?*" she asked.

"A very good one," I whispered, tears streaking my cheeks.

"Maybe next time," she moaned.

When she died, the pink orchid wilted instantly.

Our father cried alongside me as we wrapped Cera's body in a blanket. His name was Hagan MacMahon. I was Mary MacMahon Thornton, known as *Mele* by the people of Wonaneya. My Cherokee mother was long-dead by then. I had a deep instinct that I lost my mother young in nearly every life. Wherever she was, she must have some reason for leaving me each time, I hoped.

Ian helped Father carry Cera's body outside and gently laid it under a tree. Ian held my hand as Father and I sat beside her corpse. My Aunt Red Bird and Uncle Turtle sat with us. "Don't cry too long for her," Red Bird soothed. "She'll be with us again in another life." Uncle Turtle nodded sagely.

"Maybe sooner than we wish," Ian said under his breath. I turned to stare at him. His strong, weathered face had a slight pallor that scared me. Cera wasn't the only person sick with pox in Wonaneya. The fever and the sores were spreading. What if I lost Ian too? "Don't you believe we come back in new lives?"

"Mary," he said sadly, "'tis not for me to say."

"You *don't* believe."

"Love, I'm not much for religion of any kind. I see naught but the here and now."

Father shook his head. "Well, Ian, I believe 'tis true that we return. Though God Himself only knows why. He will no' allow us to remember who we were before, at least not always. I suppose because there are new lessons to be learned each time, and 'tis up to our hearts to recognize the people we have lost before."

Ian loved my father and always treated him with respect. So now he hid his own thoughts and just nodded. I knew what Ian's silent nods meant. I gripped Ian's hand harder. "If you ever die, you must try to come back to me. Whether you believe this talk or not. Promise."

His face softened. He put an arm around me. "Love, you know I'll come huntin' for you. I promise. Will you swear you'll always be waitin' for *me?*"

"I swear it."

Such an easy oath to take.

I turned my tear-streaked face toward Father, Red Bird and Turtle. A strange sensation came over me, a kind of trance, and in that moment I saw them all differently; I glimpsed faces they had worn in other lives or might wear in lives to come. Faces I didn't recognize; sometimes the faces of children, meaning they had died very young in those lives.

I pulled down the blanket that covered Cera just enough to let me see her face. It faded into the image of a pale white woman with pink hair, and then again into a young white girl. When I turned my eyes up to Red Bird and Turtle again I saw an aged white man in a gray uniform, and a weeping white woman; a moment later those images were replaced by a white couple carrying Bibles. Their clothes were so odd—the woman's dress stopped at her knees, and the man's coat and trousers were dark with fine gray stripes—that I decided they must be from a distant future.

But it was my father's face that made me gasp. His raw-boned, red-bearded Celtic self faded and shifted. I looked at him and saw an African smiling kindly at me. Then the African segued into a pale, strong-jawed white man with thinning brown hair, cut very short. He wore a shirt with a strange emblem over the heart. As I looked closer I realized it was the letter N laid over the letter C. And under the emblem were these mysteries words. TAR HEELS.

The stranger's kind face faded away, and once again I saw only burly, redheaded Hagan MacMahon, my father. He gently covered Cera's face with the blanket again, leaving just the crown of her head exposed. He stroked one big, ruddy hand along her dark, burnished hair.

"Haste ye back," he whispered in a heavy Scots brogue.

Fear crawled through me. It took all my courage to look at Ian again. What faces would I see? Who had he been, and who would he be, and what if none of his many faces meant anything to me?

But when I looked at Ian, nothing changed.

Nothing. I saw no other face but the raw-boned Irishman's I loved right now, heart and soul.

Why couldn't I see his history or future? Why didn't I want to remember him as he had been before this particular life, or glimpse who he would become next?

*

"Why can't I see my husband in other lives?" I asked miserably.

I sat beside the Talking Rock. Bird Woman and the uktena looked down at me from atop it, as always. My pipe lay unsmoked in my hands. "Because your soul has chosen to hide him from you, the uktena hissed. Or you from him. We warned you. He's a soul hunter."

"How can that be? He doesn't know it . . . "

"He has rejected the calling. He senses its doom. He wishes it were not so. And so, he has made himself forget during this life. But his soul *never* forgets. Whatever happens next is his soul's fate. And yours."

"Does this have something to do with Liver Eater?"

"Yes. You must kill Liver Eater's human body," the uktena said.

"And banish the demon inside her," Bird Woman added.

"I've never fought a demon this powerful before."

"It will take more than you alone, soul catcher," the uktena said, its tongue flickering in the shadowy forest air. "You will need your husband's help."

"But Ian doesn't . . . believe. He isn't drawn to the spirits. He doesn't *see*."

"He is a soul hunter, nonetheless. You must show him how to help you. Together you can send this demon away forever."

I bowed my head. "He has the pox. I'm so afraid he'll die. I'm trying every charm I know to keep him alive. But he's getting sicker."

"There is a way to save him—this time. And to fight the demon."

The light began to change. The air sparkled and turned white. "What is this?" I asked, afraid.

"It's the spirit of the Talking Rock," Bird Woman explained. "It's very ancient and very loving. It has known you and your soul hunter through many lives."

My skin warmed as the light closed around me and its namesake boulder. Symbols began to glow on the rock. It was covered in them, line atop line of some ancient language. "There are secrets in this writing that only the being of light remembers," Bird Woman said.

The light tickled my skin, caressed my face, and smiled inside me—that's how it felt. It *spoke* inside me. "Soul catcher," it whispered. "You still have much to learn, and so does your soul hunter. I will show you a trick. Chip off a piece of my stone. Grind it into powder and mix it into a drink. Give it to your soul hunter before you go to fight the demon. He will be able to go with you and help you, even if he is sick."

"Will he live?" I whispered back.

The light kissed me inside. "For now," it answered.

*

I hoped Ian would forgive me for turning him into a panther.

I could see only a few feet beyond our shanty, into the deep mountain darkness. My knife was ready. I couldn't risk the rustle of my deer hide skirt against the forest underbrush, so I wore only my belted muslin blouse, a loin cloth, and soft, silent moccasins. My hip-length hair was bound in a tight braid.

Ian's soft growl rumbled against my bare thigh. *Be patient, husband.* He remained ill, even in this form. His fur was damp with fever, his breathing harsh. The Talking Rock's potion had turned him into this powerful animal because the pox couldn't weaken a panther as much as it weakened a man.

A log door creaked open.

Bile rose in my throat. The panther hunched lower. We watched Liver Eater sling a dark cape around the shoulders of her dress. She headed up the path to her nightly rendezvous with the banes.

"Now," I whispered to Ian. We slipped forward, keeping low.

Like most demons, she had one major weakness: she thought she was invincible. She had never suspected that I was a soul catcher. My own magic was strong enough to hide that fact.

I attacked her before she realized it was an ambush. She only had time to pivot and throw up her hands before I sank my knife into her throat. The panther slammed her to the ground. Her blood sprayed us. She flailed and gurgled, fighting death. As Ian held her down I dropped to my heels beside her. Her furious eyes were already going blank. "Come out and let me see you," I ordered.

She strangled on her blood and slowly went limp.

I stood and stepped back, stroking Ian's panther form. *Move aside, husband. Her human body is no threat to us anymore.*

The panther, his black sides heaving, slunk away. It prowled the perimeter of a circle I drew in the forest loam with my knife blade. I dropped to my knees and brushed the leaves aside, making a clear spot. My hand hovered over that spot. The cat and I waited just outside the circle as the thing that had called itself Susannah St. Johns drew its last human breath.

The moment that body died, Liver Eater emerged.

A vaporish green glow radiated from her, fiercely lighting our small pocket of the forest. Liver Eater was a tall, thick, mottled creature, twice the size of a bear, with long arms and short legs. Her skin was covered in black warts that oozed a pale slime. Her head was small and sharp, like a dog's; two long fangs protruded from her upper jowls. Her eyes were large, unlidded, and entirely black. She flicked an agile, sharp-tipped tail.

She drew back her lips in a fanged smile. "You're no match for me and mine. If you harm me, my Other will come." Her voice was high-pitched and crackled; it made me think of small bones snapping. "Stupid witch, you should not risk the wrath of my Other."

I pointed up at her. "You brought the pox to my people. To my family. To my husband. I am no ordinary conjurer, stupid or otherwise. You were foolish to bring your evil to my doorstep." Still squatting over the cleared spot I'd made, I swirled my hand in the dirt. "*I see your face. I capture your face.*"

She went very still. Suddenly she understood. I was a soul catcher.

I made another symbolic swirl, as if painting her image into the soil. "I see your teeth. I capture your teeth." I slashed fang marks in the dirt.

She charged me.

The panther broadsided her. They went down inside the circle, clawing, snarling. Her powerful hands had short, thick nails. She raked the panther's back. It sank its teeth into her shoulder and held on. She shrieked.

"I see your arms," I yelled. "I capture your arms." My hands flew over the dirt. "I see your breasts. I capture your breasts! I see your belly. I capture your belly!"

On and on, the trapping ritual. She fought the panther wildly. His fur grew wet with blood. I hurried. "I see your sex. I capture your sex. I see your legs. I capture your legs." And finally. "I see your feet. I capture your feet. *I am done.*"

I raised my dirt-streaked hands into the weirdly lit air. She slung the panther aside and huddled, staring at me. "Grant me mercy," she begged. "If you let me go I swear to you that I will leave this place and never return. I promise you that you and your husband and your loved ones will live long, happy lives and no demon will ever enter this town again. This place will be protected forever. Your children and your children's children and so on forever will be safe and happy here."

"I don't believe the word of a demon. There is only one sure way to keep a demon from returning."

"No. I swear to you. I beg you!"

I pointed at her. "I banish you from this world forever."

She fell forward, writhing in pain. Demons took longer to go than banes. She howled. "Fool! Now my Other will come for you and yours! He will punish you and everyone you love for a thousand lives!"

The sickly green light reversed its glow as if sucked down a narrow hole at the center of her forehead. She absorbed it and it absorbed her. With one last grisly crackle of bones crunching, she withered to nothing, and vanished.

I ran to the panther. It lay on its side, breathing hard, flecking the ground with its blood. I quickly scratched some wood together and lit a fire with a spark from my flint. I knelt over the cat, flattened both bloody hands on him, and shut my eyes. "Liver Eater is gone forever," I told him. "These wounds of hers are not real. Let them be gone, too."

His texture changed under my hands. Fur turned to skin. When I looked at him he was Ian again. He lay there, naked and whole, stretched out on his side, his eyes shut as if sleeping. I pushed his long black hair away from his handsome face. The seeping pox sores had already begun to heal. And there was no sign of the wounds Liver Eater had given him.

"Ian," I whispered hoarsely. "Ian." I pronounced it with Cherokee inflections. *E-on-a.*

His dark lashes moved. He inhaled sharply and turned onto his back. I curled my bare legs under me and sat close beside him. I held one of his big hands to my heart. I stroked my other hand down the center of his darkly haired chest. He made a sound of pleasure, low in his heart, but then frowned. His eyes opened. His throat worked. "Aw, Mary, how did I get out here?"

He didn't remember anything. I helped him sit up a little and cradled his head on my lap. "You wandered. The fever had hold of you. But I've found you now."

He shifted his legs and arms. "Hmmmph. The fever's broken. I feel like a new man. Like I've shed my skin or something."

I swallowed hard but said nothing. Best to leave the truth a secret.

He smiled up at me. "Your potions and notions are working, my girl!" His cock sprang to life. He raised his head and looked down at it. "Ay, now there's a fine sight! Let's take him inside and see what he does next."

Relieved, I curled around him and lowered my head to his thick hard-on. "I'll give it a few kisses for good luck."

I closed my lips around the tip, and he sighed deep in his chest as I sucked him. I charmed him that way, while my boons removed the gore-covered body of Susannah St. Johns.

No one in Wonaneya would ever find her body.

Victory was sweet. Were not Ian and I more than a match for any demon?

Like a demon, I thought we were invincible.

Like a demon, I was wrong.

12

"Ay, this is the finest cabin in all these mountains," Ian proclaimed, as we stood in our secluded yard among the rubble of wood shavings and cast-off logs. I shook dried mud off my leather skirt and nodded. He wrapped a sweaty arm around me. "Are you sure you'll not wish we were closer to the trading post and the village?"

They're just a quick walk through the gap. "I like being alone here with you."

I had not told him that the uktena and Bird Woman counseled me to build our home here, near the sacred rock. He wouldn't have believed me. Transforming into a panther had done nothing to awaken his memories as a soul hunter.

He looked down at me somberly. "You've been moping about since the pox. Missing Cera. Don't be worrying, Mary. There'll be no more miseries. You know, I think that St. Johns woman was bad luck somehow. Since she's been gone, everything's better."

Ian, like everyone else in Wonaneya, thought the strange white woman had just packed up and disappeared into the night. Ian went on cheerfully. "Look at my fine self." He thumped his broad chest. "Healthy as a horse, now." He gestured at the tent forming in his britches. "A very stiff horse."

I smiled up at him with tears in my eyes. "Come along, Hung-like-a horse Husband. What's the point of having a fine bedstead and a feather mattress *inside* if we're always *out here* in the yard?"

He laughed, gently hoisted me and slung me over his shoulder, and carried me inside.

We had three large rooms, connected by dog-trot hallways to let in fresh air. We had split log floors instead of dirt. There were two creek-stone fireplaces with fancy iron spits and pot hooks Ian had made at his forge. Ian's handmade iron hinges held the heavy log doors. To the curious amazement of all who visited, sunlight poured into our cabin through a pair of glass windows on the front walls, one in each of the two front rooms. Father had given them to us. They'd traveled all the way from the Carolina coast, by ox cart.

The forest surrounded us; we were in a small valley near the creek, and protective ridges rose all around us. In a small clearing we'd built a low log barn. We had two horses, a milk cow, and chickens.

We were rich. We had each other. We had proven we could fight off demons together, even if soul catching remained a secret I never shared with Ian. We were safe.

I pulled him, smiling, into our bedroom. The walls were strung with protective amulets covered in swirling symbols from the Talking Rock, symbols I'd etched on bits of wood or turtle shells. We stripped naked, then rinsed each other with water from a wash basin in one corner. I took his hard cock in my hand and rubbed the tip against my belly. His back arched; he face flushed and his eyes narrowed with pleasure.

It worried me that we had no baby yet; we'd been married for two years by then. Soul catchers have a need to be solitary; we are peculiar and suffer obvious risks. I had never dearly wanted a husband and children until Ian made his way to my life. Some men would have commented on a wife who didn't conceive, but Ian always said 'The wee folk will come along when they're good and ready,' as if our children were outside playing chase and would not come when called.

On the bed, among jumbled blankets and pillows, he spread my legs and burrowed his face between them. The first time he did that to me I thought a mischievous bane had possessed him. We Cherokees fucked without much shyness, but I'd never seen or heard of such a thing—licking your lover down there.

His tongue had quickly convinced me that a wonderful boon, not a bane, had control of him.

I stretched backwards and moaned. The world between my legs was wet and alive, soft and aching. He held my knees apart with his big hands and pressed his tongue deeper inside me. As I writhed I became aware of the light changing around us. It began to whiten and sparkle, as if a million fireflies had filled the late afternoon air. I felt it on my skin, rubbing softly. That magic light sucked my breasts, stroked my belly, and even flickered like hot rum along the curve of Ian's tongue, making me swell even more. I realized there was some being in the room with us. That it was energized by our lust, some essence of our tenderness. I didn't feel invaded; I felt included. We had built our home in the territory of a powerful, protective pog, and now we channeled the pog's own passion for eternal renewals, the thrust and suck of sex.

I orgasmed into that hot white light, groaning Ian's name, and felt the light pulse contentedly in return. When I pulled Ian up my body and wrapped my legs around him his face was hot and damp, his slight smile the hardcore promise of a quick, rocking fuck about to happen. I gently bit the hard sinews of his neck as he slid his cock deep inside me. The sensation threw my head back. I came a second time.

"Ay, that's a girl," he praised, then slipped a hand between us and squeezed one of my nipples as he rode me fast.

The light surrounded him too, it was part of him, even if he couldn't see it, couldn't recognize the spirit of the Talking Rock joining us in that bawdy, loving act. When he came he pulled up from me to lever his cock deeper inside for the final thrust. I moaned as I felt the fluid white light spurt into my womb. We had given ourselves to the spirit, and the spirit had mated with us both.

The room remained alive with the light for several hours. We nuzzled, we slept, then we fucked again, him behind me that time. I came once, twice, and Ian gasped happily as his belly slapped a wet, sodden rhythm on my ass. He spurted every last bit of his juice inside me.

We collapsed on the bed as the sun went down. The sky outside was deep lavender. Brightly colored birds, doomed to disappear from the earth, still sang in the woods; impossibly large herds of deer and flocks of wild turkeys still scratched in the loam. Bear, panther, wolves and even a few bison lingered in the last wilderness of the undiscovered valleys and high ridges. The spirits of the huge forest, the giant oaks and chestnuts and others still living, untouched since any human could remember, chanted a mourning song for what the future showed them.

Songs unsung, a melancholy beyond words, seeped inside me. Suddenly I was cold to the bone, despairing.

Words came to me as if I were reading a letter.

It is the beginning of the end for these Cherokee people and this charmed place.

Shadows pooled in the corners of the sparse little log room. The pog glowed brighter, chasing my mood back into the light.

Eternity is filled with hope. Look past the brief span of a single life.

Ian, unaware of my thoughts or our visitor, cupped my back to his front, with his relaxed cock tucked contentedly into the hollow at the bottom of my hips. "My love, I declare this house fully fecking well fekked," he whispered against my ear with an exhausted sigh.

I laughed. We kissed and I turned on my back, wrapping my arms around him. He fell asleep with his head on my shoulder, one big, rough hand curled gently around my breast. I stroked his long, dark hair and watched the shimmering spirit that had no face and form around us.

Will you protect him? That's all I ask. He's a good man. I was told we would be safe so long as we live right in this spot.

That is true. But you won't be able to stay here for very long.

My blood chilled. My hand stopped moving on Ian's hair. *Why not?*

War is coming.

War? It can't be. We're at peace with the Creeks and the other tribes. And at peace with the whites.

But the whites are not at peace with each other. I will send you dreams. I will tell you all I can. But my power is here. Only here. And there are yet more demons about.

The breath froze in my throat. *Should I have traded revenge for a bargain with Liver Eater?*

No, Talking Rock answered. *You are a soul catcher. You are called to protect others, not yourself.*

A pog's coy answer. My thoughts whirled. I held Ian tighter. *Did I doom us?*

The pog's voice grew softer; the light began to fade. *There is no doom. Only balance. Good must always balance evil. All the realms of the spirit must remain in balance, and sacrifices happen for the greater good. That is one of the lessons you had to learn in this life. And so it is done.*

I didn't want to sacrifice Ian. I'll keep Ian here. We will stay together, here, and be safe in your blessing.

Not in this life, the voice whispered, as the last of the glorious light turned back into ordinary air.

*

A light winter snow covered the mountains around Wonaneya town, hiding the red pall of fate. More than two-hundred unsuspecting people gathered in the warm heart of the council house, a huge, seven-sided structure of wooden poles and mud-thatched reed walls. The number seven was sacred to the People because the seven walls of a town's council house represented each of the seven clans. A sacred fire burned in the center, its smoke rising to a small round hole in the roof. The tobacco of our clay pipes rose along with it. Important women and men made up the primary circle, closest to the fire.

I was very young to have a place of honor in that inner circle. I kept my head bowed out of respect and hugged my blanket around me. Ian and my father sat behind me, supportive. Aunt Red Bird and Uncle Turtle were nearby. I darted glances at the esteemed town leaders. The men were tattooed, pierced and plucked. Hawk and eagle feathers dangled from the mohawk pigtails of their hair. The esteemed women also wore bird feathers and beads in their long braids. Both men and women were adorned with amulets of beads, bronze, and crudely polished sapphires and rubies from the hidden mountain mines.

The ceremonies of a council meeting were formal. Each clan was acknowledged, including mine. When they came to me our chief said, "We welcome the paint clan, in charge of sacred paints for ceremonies."

I nodded. "I am Mele, the daughter of Standing Snake. And I am the daughter of Snake's husband, Hagen, known as Fire Hair."

"You may speak."

I drew deeply on my pipe. "I know there are many who do not believe me. But I tell you what my dreams show me, anyway. Our people fought the white settlers when I was a little girl. We withdrew to the mountains and gave them the land near the big waters, and made our peace with them. And so it continues. This new war, between the whites and their English king, doesn't win either way for us. We should stay out of it."

A man from the deer clan said, "You are wrong. The chief of the English will win this war. We have allied with him just as we did when the English drove out the French. The great council of the People has decided it. It is done."

I cupped my pipe in my trembling hands. "I have seen the truth in dreams. The great chief of England will *not* win this time. This is not like the war with the French. The white settlers will never forgive us for taking sides against them. We will be destroyed if we side with the English this time."

Our peace chief raised his pipe, Feathers fluttered from the long stem. "I tell you again. The great council has decided. Our People are allied with the English. We will help them push the others out. We will secure our lands and our power as friends of the English from now on. If we fight this war well, we will never have to fight the whites again. Maybe we can even make peace with them. That is that."

Ian prodded my shoulder from behind. I tried to ignore him. We had argued politics for days. He was making me furious and breaking my heart. He poked my shoulder again. Father, who sat next to me, leaned over and said, "Are ye not ken to playing fair, Daughter? Your husband has something to say. Let him speak."

Everyone heard Father's words. There were nods and craned heads. Young girls twittered at the hope that handsome, exotic Ian, with his white skin and blue eyes, would address the town. Boys and young men looked over at Ian eagerly, wanting to hear his wisdom. Ian was a favorite of the People. He could play the stickball game as wildly as any Cherokee man. He could throw a tomahawk as if born to it. Unlike me, he laughed and joked; he believed the world was a very good place, overall. I preached doom and gloom and saw demons, great and small, everywhere. I was always on guard.

Ian, on the other hand, was inspirational. Our chief waved his pipe, granting Ian some floor time. "*Eonah* may speak," he said.

"Go ahead and have your say," I said to him coldly, over my shoulder.

Ian whispered, "Will you be talking the language for me or is your heart too hard?" Ian's Cherokee was acceptable but hardly nuanced enough for a speech at the council meeting.

"You can trust me to repeat your words fairly, Husband," I vowed without pleasure.

He stood. "Like my wife's father, Fire Hair, I was born in a place where the English rule. When I was a boy they drove my people out of the place called Ulster—my parents starved because of them, and so my parents put me on a boat to save me, they put me into a big canoe to cross the big river between my home and here. I came here all alone, when I was no bigger than Squirrel—" he pointed to the grinning little boy who helped him at the forge—"and I was a servant to an Englishman in the big town of Philadelphia. That bastard . . . that Englishman . . . *owned* me. I was no better than a slave. If I ran away, he had me tracked down. I have whip scars on my back because of that bastard . . . that Englishman.

"I learned to make iron into tools; I became a blacksmith; people respected me. But I was still owned by the Englishman. When I finally earned my freedom from him I decided I would never be any Englishman's slave again. I traveled here to the mountains of the People to see what a man could become outside the white towns ruled by the English. I found good people—he swept a hand at the faces around us—and I found a good family—" he pointed to Red Bird, Turtle, and my father—"and I found my heart."

He put a hand on my shoulder, a gesture that made tears rise behind my eyes and caused my voice to break for a moment. "I am not Ian Thornton anymore," I went on, speaking for him as he spoke, "the slave of an Englishman. I am the husband of Mele of the People. I am of her clan, the paint clan. And I do not want to see her people, my people, the Cherokee, trust the English. I will never trust the English. Never. And I intend to fight the English."

My father, a fellow Ulsterman who hated the English the same way, nodded. "I agree with Ian," he said in Cherokee. I do not believe the English will be good to their word. I do not think they will protect Wonaneya and all the other towns of the People."

A revered old woman named Climber spoke up, thrusting a sharp finger at me. "No one sees demons but you. Maybe they play tricks on you. Maybe your mind isn't good. What if you're wrong about this war?"

"I'm not wrong, old mother. I'm telling you what the spirits show me."

"You speak to spirits and trust they are good ones. How are you to know which are good and which are not?"

I shook my head. "There are spirits clinging to the poles of this council house. Soft and bright, sweet souls. Can you see them? I can." People looked up at the ceiling warily, their eyes wide, then shook their heads and traded amused looks. I sighed. "I can only do what my guides tell me. We are all lost in the darkness without their help."

"You go ahead and trust your spirit guides," Climber hissed. "The rest of us have to trust what we see that's real. Are we supposed to listen to you instead of the People's war chiefs? Is this little town of ours supposed to take sides against all the other Cherokee towns and the English too? No! You'll get us all killed!"

Our council put it to a vote, but only to be polite. The decision was no surprise. Some of the younger warriors grumbled. That small faction would follow Ian wherever he wanted to take his personal war against the English. But the majority would not. Wonaneya would fight on the side of the English in a war for the soul of everything we held dear.

We were doomed, either way.

*

I huddled on our bed late in the night, clutching a blanket around me, red-eyed and quietly frantic. Ian sat on a stool by the fireplace with his own blanket around his shoulders, his face grim. He held out his hands in frustration. "Mary, this is making no sense to me. If you see the fecking English losing this war, then why are you so against me fighting them?"

"I know you hate the English. You're an Irishman and so you want to go and fight them no matter why. I understand. But you're a Cherokee now, too. You're my husband. You must not choose sides against your Cherokee family."

"I'm not siding against your folk. I just want to knock off a few fecking Englishmen."

"The Americans will win without your help. No need for you to go to war at all. Stay here with me."

"Mary, hiding from a fight sure the feck isn't my way. Ay, 'tis a pisser if I do and a pisser if I don't. Most of the men in this town are readying to join the damned English and go to killing Americans. But you and me both ken that there's no purchase in that way of doing. The Americans will just take revenge and go to killing every Cherokee in these mountains. I've got a right good bunch of the men here who'll go me to represent the Cherokee on the American side. To fight the American cause."

He thumped his chest. "I'm an American, Mary. And so are you. And that's what the American folk need to know. That at least some of the people of Wonaneya town are not fecking loyalists to the fecking English crown."

He turned my own logic against me. Except for one thing: I knew the prophecy of the pog who came to me in white light.

"You will not be safe," I told Ian hoarsely. "You will not be all right if you leave this place. We're under a protective charm here. The spirit of the Talking Rock has told me. I've seen that spirit, the spirit of the valley, here in our home. It will take care of us. But not if you leave."

"Aw, Mary-girl, where is this talking rock of yours? Have you ever seen it? Show me. My love, isn't it just one of the stories the old people tell around their fires, like your big snake and your little fairy people and so on?"

I sagged. I had never visited the rock except in my dreams. There was nothing like it near our cabin—no rock where a giant snake and a tiny spirit woman gave me counsel. No living, breathing rock that was home to the markings I drew on my amulets. Nothing that hosted the being who spoke to me in white, sparkling light.

But it was as real to me as my own skin, and what hurt me to the bone was realizing that Ian had never done more than humor me. I bounded off the bed and ran to him. "I killed Susannah St. Johns. A demon came out of her body and I banished it. You helped me fight that demon, whether you believe me or not. *I turned you into a panther and you fought a demon alongside me.* You are a soul hunter by trade! But before I banished her she swore her mate would take revenge on us. Ian, we may have a vengeful demon coming after us!"

Ian looked up at me with tender frustration. "Aw, Mary, I love you like my own skin, and I don't fault you for saying whatever it takes to keep me in place. You turned me into a puss cat, did you? Aw, Mary. Sure you did."

"You don't believe in my visions! You don't believe in spirits. Then you don't believe in *me*."

He stood. "That's not a damned bit true and you know it. It's just that I'm thinking sometimes your spirits say what you want them to say, love. You don't want me to join this fight so your spirits come up with fine reasons why I shouldn't. But I promise you, love, 'tis the right thing for me to do. Why, me and the boys'll go kill us a few Englishmen and be home by springtime. You'll see."

"You'll die," I yelled at him. "You'll die if you leave here. And I'll die here without you."

His hard face crumpled. "Love, love, no. Calm yourself." He took me in his arms. I tried to shove him away, but he held on gently until I gave up inside his bear hug. He whispered against my hair. "I'll love you forever, you ken? And I'll never leave you for long or for no good reason. Never."

Pretty words. But the damage was done.

*

Ian threw the last of his gear over the saddle of his horse. "Do not be staying here alone, Mary," he said dully. "Move over to your father's place. I want to think of you safe at the trading post. Would you give me that much?"

I shook my head. All my tears had been shed. I was hard-eyed. "I know where I'm safe. I was safe with my husband here, protected by the spirit of the Talking Rock. But my husband refuses to listen to me. He wants to fight the English. He takes my cousins; he takes the young men who love war, with him, to fight a cause that is already won without his help. I tell you, stay here, with me, and we will all come out all right. We have work to do, capturing demons. Our war is with demons, not with the English. I need your help to fight *that* war."

He rubbed his forehead as if the sound of my voice hurt him. "Maybe I see beyond what you and your spirits see, Mary. I see the future for people, real flesh and blood people, no matter the meddling of banshees and angels."

"You see me waiting for you." My voice broke. "But I will not be here."

He took me in his arms. "Don't lie to me, love. You'll not get shed of me nor me of you. No matter what happens." Tears slid down his face. "And no ken how long it takes, nor how mad you are right now, I'll come home to you. And you'll be waiting, you will."

"Goodbye, forever, " I said hoarsely. The words were permanent and agonized.

"No. You're saying, 'Good day to you, my beloved

husband, and hurry home to me soon.' That's what I hear. Not the other."

He mounted his horse, put his hand to his heart as he looked down at me, then rode away.

13

War raged. Skirmishes and ambushes occurred all through the Carolinas. Sometimes it was army against army, but just as often it was citizen militias, loyalists versus patriots. We heard news of Cherokees allied with the English attacking American settlements; killing and torturing people. And of American militias retaliating. So far the fighting was mostly in the flatlands to the east, but Americans were already attacking some of the lower Cherokee towns in the foothills. Wonaneya, higher in the mountains, was isolated and might escape.

I had not had a message from Ian in months. He and the warriors he led were somewhere in the flatlands, ambushing English troops and loyalist militias. They slipped through the woods to attack quickly then slip away. They had already become famous. Americans even gave them a respectful name. *The Blood Cat Boys.* Father was proud. Aunt Red Bird and Uncle Turtle said there was no shame in Ian's decision to fight the English. But there were people in Wonaneya town who called Ian a traitor and turned their backs to me. I stayed at my cabin and kept to myself.

The being of white light from the Talking Rock came to me often. I think it would have touched me if I let it. It would have fingered me, licked me, let me pretend it was Ian on top of me. Good spirits were often bawdy. Intimacy and comfort included every positive feeling, and they didn't draw distinctions. The being felt my despair. *Believe in your husband's love*, it whispered. *I bring you his love. It is part of what I am.*

Will you tell me if he dies? I asked it.

He will never die, it answered. *Only his body may die. And he will tell you himself, in that case.*

Except for worrying about Ian's part in the war, I had no interest in any of the battles or what the outcome might be. I had my own war to fight. The demons and their lesser allies, the banes, crept through our mountains more than ever. They were drawn to trouble, drawn to horror and the act of dying. They fed off suffering, and encouraged it. I couldn't stop the war, couldn't bring Ian home safe, but I could slaughter the dark spirits who made things worse.

*

There are paths. They follow the mantel of some other world, overlaid on our own, spirit paths, energies, forces that pull and push. The animals and the shamans sense them; sometimes our paths follow the same ways, leading people along with demons and angels. Some of the greatest cities and most terrible battlefields lay at the crossroads of those invisible, irresistible roads.

That summer I set myself alongside a path that followed a ridge above the valley of Wonaneya town. High and windy, nearly treeless in places, capped with rough stone helmets instead of soft earth, the ridge path was a coarse, high, desolate place, perfect for the secret wandering of dark souls.

Every time I stopped one of them, I lessened the terror, the torture, the pain they provoked.

I caught banes by the dozens.

They never expected to meet a soul catcher outright. And so they paraded openly along the path, stinking, grotesque and misshapen—at least, that was how I saw them, but I couldn't say how demons and banes looked to themselves. Maybe they thought they were pretty, and that *we* were the monsters.

"I see you," I said quietly each time, and the captured bane would look up in shock to where I sat on a high rock, a place the being of white light had counseled me to use. An invisible place. "Be gone from this world," I said next, and flashed a hand dramatically.

They shrieked as the wind pulled them apart.

Bigger demons, more powerful ones, like Liver Eater, couldn't be bested so easy. Demons didn't take the paths.

"I see you," I called to a small, green, frog-like bane with nasty teeth. I raised my hand to banish him.

It growled up at me. "Who are you to judge me?"

I froze. Banes didn't usually talk. They were more like

animals. They muttered and chirped, or they made weird sounds, speaking in a language of their own.

This bane complained loudly. "My kind deserves to be here just as much as you. There would be no balance without us. Nothing to inspire people to improve themselves. It's not our fault that human beings are so weak. Bah! Spare me your judgment, and in return I will tell you something important."

I thought of Liver Eater. Maybe my pride had been my undoing. "Maybe I'll spare you. But tell me why I should believe you."

"Oh, no. First, give me your *word* you'll spare me. And then I will tell you about the danger headed straight your way. Whether you believe me or not is your business."

I chewed my tongue. "All right. You have my word. You can go free. What is your news?"

"Your husband is just a few days' ride away. At a white town called Ludaway. He is coming home."

My heart soared. I showed no reaction but desperately wanted to believe him. The bane's yellow teeth bared in a smile. "Unfortunately, a demon has led the English here. Soon all in Wonaneya will die."

As he said those words, grinning, I heard gunshots in the valley below.

*

Wonaneya town was on fire. Smoke and flames rose to the mountains, mingling with the blue mist. Every dome-shaped reed hut in the valley was being destroyed. The People ran in every direction. The council house was ablaze. Bodies were strewn about like straw dolls. Redcoats walked through the town, shooting anyone or anything who did not obey they're orders instantly.

Others of their company raided the summer fields at the edge of town, piling ears of corn onto blankets, striping the beans from the stalks, pointing to mounds of potatoes they would dig up later. Still others rounded up horses, cows, and pigs.

A soul catcher does not command troops of angels. We

cannot call on an army of good beings to attack our enemies, be they human or banes and demons. We work mostly alone, with only our closest confidantes, flesh or spirit, as allies. Why that is so, I did not understand. The Talking Rock told me there many ancient reasons for the way of the spirit world.

My eyes ached from the images coming into them. My body screamed. I watched as a redcoat bayoneted little Squirrel. He fell, blood spurting from his neck. I felt his sweet soul slip past me on the breeze. One day, in another century, I would meet him again.

Father, Aunt Red Bird, Uncle Turtle, where are you? Fury like a thousand fires burned inside me. I heard and felt the rush of banes around me, all of them gloating, running toward my people, my friends, my kin, to feast on their misery. I whirled. A mass of grinning, slurping banes loped and hopped and flew past me, heading for the dying of Wonaneya. This nasty flock could only have been drawn by a very powerful demon.

I singled out as many as I could with the point of a marksman. *I see you. I banish you. I see you. I banish you. I see you. I banish you.* They shrieked and exploded. But I was no match for so many. They leapt at me, slashing. I felt talons gouge bloody stripes on my arms, my legs, my body. A set of sharp teeth sank into one of my ankles. I went down to my knees, saying as calmly as I could even then, *I see you. I banish you.* Over and over. *I see you. I banish you.* Destroying them even as they hobbled me to the ground. A bane's wound is spiritual, not real, yes, but it hurts and it bleeds and even my strong knowledge of the truth couldn't resist the effect. Yes, I could recover from the wounds of banes, but not instantly.

And I couldn't ignore the blow that hit my head. That was the work of a flesh and blood man.

I slid limply to the earth.

The hard, cruel face of a demon looked down at me from a human face.

"I will have my revenge now, bitch," he said.

And he dragged me away.

*

I slumped on my knees outside Father's log house at the trading post. French Stick stood behind me, his copper-brown hand holding one end of the long leather thong tied to my bound hands. French Stick was once a normal man. He came from the overhill towns on the other side of the mountains, where he was known to be fierce and fair war chief. But French Stick had changed in a frightening way since joining the English against the Americans, and now even our own people whispered nervously about him.

My cotton shirt, trailing to my bare thighs, was all I wore. It was bloody and shredded where the banes had clawed me. French Stick had jerked my leather skirt off as I lay, half-conscious, in the woods. He had shoved my legs apart and raped me. Blood stained my thighs.

No wonder. A demon had taken over his body.

"Father," I whispered hoarsely. He lay on the ground, bleeding from the beating the English had given him. Nearby, Aunt Red Bird sat holding Uncle Turtle with his head in her lap. He had been bayoneted in one side. He breathed roughly, grimacing.

The redcoats surrounded us along with French Stick's warriors. The surviving people from town clung to each other inside a circle of muskets. There were only a few dozen terrified old men, women and children still alive. Since most of our warriors had gone to war, we were defenseless.

A shrill English captain paced back and forth, looking down his nose at us. "This town betrayed its oath to the king of England. This peace town betrayed its oath to its own Cherokee brethren, who decreed that all Cherokees would fight on the side of the king."

"Wonaneya sent many a man to fight on the side of the English," my father said, coughing blood. His hands and feet were bound. His eyes were swollen shut.

"But Hagen McMahon, the Blood Cat Boys also come from this Cherokee town."

"Men are free to do what their hearts tell them."

"Men are not free to betray the crown, Mr. McMahon. Not

even you bloody Scots-Irish."

My father spit on his boot. The captain drew back that boot and kicked him in the chest.

"Stop," I said. "What do you want from us?"

"You are the wife of the traitor, Ian Thornton."

"Say nothing else," Red Bird called. A soldier jabbed her in the back with the butt of his musket.

I lifted my head proudly. French Stick's leather thong cut into my wrists. They were raw now, like my vagina. "I am the wife of Ian Thornton, *the patriot.*"

French Stick slapped me in the face. His long, dirty fingernails cut into my nose. Blood flowed. The English captain bent down to look at me. "Tell me where your husband is. I will spare these people—" he gestured toward my family and the remaining townspeople of Wonaneya—"if you do your duty the King of England and tell me where your husband is."

"Tell him no' a damn thing," daughter," Father wheezed.

The captain gestured to French Stick. "Tell your warriors to slit the old man's throat."

French Stick gave the order. One of his men, one of our own Cherokee tribesmen, leapt forward with a long hunting knife ready. He jerked Father's head back by its graying red hair and aimed the blade at his throat.

"Spare him," I gasped.

The captain raised a hand, pausing the execution. "Tell me where your husband is. If you tell me the truth, I'll spare you and yours. Truly."

The bane had said Ian and his men were in Ludaway, a few days' ride away. Maybe the bane was lying. I hoped so. Wincing, I squinted up at the English officer. "What will you do with my husband and his men if you catch them?"

"Arrest them and hold them prisoner. That is all I can guarantee. Once I have them in my custody your family and the other people of this town will be set free."

Without this chance, my father, aunt and uncle, and the rest of Wonaneya would die for sure. My head whirled. *Time.* I was trading hope for time. Ian was smart and strong; the

Cherokee kinsmen with him would never surrender. Was I betraying my husband and my people or saving us all with a desperate play of chance?

"My husband and his men are near the town of Ludaway," I said.

The captain smiled. "Thank you, Mrs. Thornton. Are you telling me the truth?"

I raised my bleeding face. I thought he was honorable, even if French Stick, behind me, was a demon. "You have my word."

"Very good then."

French Stick gestured to his warriors. They slung their muskets and tomahawks over their shoulders and set off through the forest at a lithe trot. The captain straightened, his shoulders back. He turned to his recoated men, then dismissed my father and the rest with a shrug of his hand. "Kill them," he said in a bored tone. "Kill them all."

The warrior who held my father's head stabbed the knife into his throat. Before I could even scream he sliced Father's neck from ear to ear. Blood spurted. Father's beard became a sopping crimson sponge. His eyes went blank.

I met Aunt Bird's despairing eyes just before the warriors and redcoats slammed their tomahawks and bayonets into her body and Uncle Turtle's. The people of Wonaneya screamed as the soldiers fired into their midst. The warriors set about hacking the scalps off the fallen. Our people were killing their own tribesmen and mutilating them.

I gagged. Betrayal was an acid in my throat. I watched my father die, his eyes staring at me. I watched my aunt and uncle die; I watched the slaughter of my townspeople. I blamed myself. I thought I would die too, at any moment, and I didn't care. But Ian would survive. *Ian will not be caught. They will never catch him. I have not doomed my husband the way I just doomed my family and my town.*

Two redcoats headed toward me, bayonets raised. French Stick stepped in front of me. "The woman is mine. That was the bargain I made for leading you here."

The captain raised a hand. His men backed away. He nodded to French Stick. "Do what you will with her."

French Stick took me by my bound hands and dragged me to a small barn near the trading post. For the last time I looked back at my father's blood-soaked yard.

*

My boon and angels fought for me. Fox and Owl, the Small People, and others—they surrounded me as I lay naked, tied between two posts in the middle of the small, log shed where French Stick, the man and the demon, his nameless owner, tortured me. My good spirits tried to ease the pain, the humiliation, the terror. They fogged my brain so I drifted away at times; they battled the banes who gnawed and spit and tried to invade my most private places. But they could not stop the demon.

French Stick sat patiently on a pile of blankets near the barn's open door. He stroked long strands of black hair he'd cut off my head, carelessly taking bits of my scalp with it. He wove some of the bloody hair into a small mat and admired it. Other strands he braided into his own hair, which hung from a narrow swath off the crown of his plucked head. He attached my earrings to his own pierced ears. He rubbed my blood into his bare chest and licked it off his knife. He had carved long lines down my breasts, my arms, my legs.

Just outside the barn door, water bubbled in a small iron pot on a fire he tended. Small pieces of my skin, cooking in that water, gave off a sickening, meaty aroma. He dipped a tin cup into the thin stew of my flesh and drank it as he watched me, his black eyes satisfied. I knew I was ruined, that if I lived there would never be anything pretty about me again. I never wanted Ian to see what was left of me.

Ian. My only remaining desire? That he should survive. That he and his men would not be caught in Ludaway by the Redcoats and Cherokee warriors. I prayed that the terrible, grinning bane who'd told me where Ian was, had lied.

In the dark, fire lit shadows of one endless night, French Stick taunted me about Ian's fate. He stood over me, his booted feet on either side of my bloody hips, and he untied the front of his britches, pulled out his penis, and pissed on me, my face, my wounds. My boons crowded closer, sealing my mind against the stinging pain. But nothing could take my eyes off French Stick. He wanted me to watch him.

He squatted over me, smiling. "My men will make him scream," he whispered. French Stick spoke in terrible detail about the horrors a Cherokee warrior could perform on a captured enemy, all the more real because I'd seen Cherokee turn on their own people in Wonaneya. I refused to let myself think of Ian being carved and punctured and burned and broken. My boons drove the images from my mind. Fox and the other fighting spirits crouched and snarled, snapping at the banes that watched both French Stick and me with glowing, hungry, red eyes.

"Demon, I . . . banish . . . you," I murmured through lips so swollen I could barely make a sound.

French Stick threw back his head and howled with laughter. His eyes gleaming, he huddled close over me, casually circling the tip of his knife along the tops of my mutilated breasts. "You are so weak you can't even banish the banes now. You're no match for me, soul catcher," he sneered. "You cannot see me. I'm safe inside this human form. Your spirits are weaklings who barely keep my banes away. They cannot stop me. You cannot stop me. Your husband cannot stop me. You cannot deceive and murder this body of mine, as you did with my *Other.*"

I stared up at him, my vision blurry. My eyes cleared just enough to see the strangest emotion on his hard, hawk-nosed face. *Grief.* He tilted his cruel expression closer to me. The firelight glowed on his vicious, glimmering eyes. *Tears.* "You think only your kind knows love, soul catcher? You think this world and all the others belong to only *your* kind, only *your* idea of good and evil, only *your* notion of heaven?"

I couldn't form an answer with my swollen tongue, and he wasn't waiting for it anyway. He hunched down so that his face was only inches from mine. He sliced the tip of his knife along the front of my ear. A part of me felt my skin splitting, but I no longer absorbed the pain. His eyes bored into me. "You and your soul hunter showed no mercy to *her*. So you will get no mercy from *me*."

Liver Eater. His *Other*. His . . . love. His . . . soul mate? I had never imagined demons having soul mates. But even if they did . . . my mouth moved sluggishly. My lips parted just enough to push out a few words. "Liver Eater showed no mercy for my people. I saved others by banishing her. She . . . belongs . . . in the dark lands of Hell."

He uttered a furious, growling sound no human could make. His face changed, shifted, enlarged. His coppery Cherokee skin bled into thick, greasy, gray flesh, pockmarked and sprouting stiff hairs. His hawked nose turned into a heavy snout, and his human teeth into long, yellow tusks.

He was a pig-faced demon.

"I have a taste for your ugly tongue," he said. He rammed one hand inside my mouth and pinched my tongue between his fingers. He tugged it outside my mouth. He posed his knife to slice it free.

Suddenly his banes shrieked in terror. An ax came down hard, cutting through the mush and skin of bane flesh, spewing bane gore into the air, then sinking into the bloody straw and clay floor with a bone-chopping thud. Pig Face vanished inside French Stick's body again. He leapt to his feet, looking around wildly, his knife ready. The ax came down again and again and again. All the banes were screaming and running now. I couldn't see my rescuer; I only heard the *swoosh* of his ax and the crunch of its thick blade.

French Stick backed away from me. The sound of the phantom ax faded away. I heard the banes mewling in fear and pain, but they kept their distance from me, and so did French Stick.

His terrible human face was tight with alarm, but slowly he began to smile. Then he threw back his head and laughed, a guttural, grunting noise lifting into the fire light. Finally he looked down at me with an ugly grin. "Your soul hunter can only threaten the banes, not *me*. I'm a flesh-and-blood man, and he is only a ghost. But I will let him enjoy his small victory. You can keep your tongue. For now."

He laughed again as he returned to his blankets and stretched out happily. "You know what this means, don't you, soul catcher? Your husband's ghost is here." He smiled as he turned on his side to watch me suffer. *"Because he has left this life."*

I knew that was true.

Ian, I moaned inside. Ian was dead.

*

The next morning, French Stick's men delivered Ian's ruined body to the trading post. They dumped it beside me, on the barn floor.

My vision was cloudy. A blessing. But I could see what they'd done to him. They had tortured him to pieces before he took his last breath; the bloody corpse that lay beside me had been scalped and gutted. His body was so close to mine I could touch him by unfurling the fingers of one bound hand. I stroked the cold skin of his arm.

I bled inside. I would never forget, deep in my soul, the sight of his body, and how I had betrayed him to the enemy. French Stick, who I now knew as Pig Face, squatted at our feet, grinning. "He died screaming," French Stick said.

That's a lie, Bird Woman whispered to me. She sat by my head, stroking my face. *Our kind helped him to stay strong. He wanted you to be proud of him.*

My heart, the heart of my soul, broke open. I had told them where to find him. How could he ever forgive me? And I had turned the Pig Faced demon's vengeance on us by banishing his Other; my pride had never considered showing a demon any mercy or compromise. I had not believed her threats.

Every terrible thing that had happened to Wonaneya Town, to my family, and to Ian, *was my fault*.

French Stick bent over me. "In every life from now on, I will find you. And I will find *him* when he searches for you. I will destroy you both and everyone you love. From now on, you understand?" He spat on Ian's corpse, then kicked me. "I will track you down. I will track down your spirit guides too. I will kill them. And you. And him. Over and over. Until even your souls give up. In every life, you will suffer. And he *will* suffer again, because of you."

The demon walked outside and began stoking his cooking fire in the morning sunshine. "Now I will eat your tongue," he called. "After that, I will eat your heart."

I could still cry. Tears slid down the sides of my face. Not for myself, but for Ian. *I need to die, I need to go,* I prayed. *Bird Woman. Uktena. Help me.*

Uktena curled gently around my mind. Bird Woman stroked my face. *We don't have the power to free a soul from this life. But the Talking Rock does.*

The white light crept over me and inside me. *I am not strong here,* it whispered. *I am too far away from my place. I would have protected you and your soul hunter if you'd only stayed close to me.*

I know, Talking Rock. But can you help me leave this life now?

Yes. The white light warmed me. I felt it squeezing my heart. *Tell your heart to stop beating, Mele. It is tired. It will listen.*

Talking Rock, make me a promise. Hide my soul from Ian's soul. I don't ever want him to be hurt by my choices again. If we meet in other lives, don't let me remember him. Make it hard for him to find me. If he can't find me, maybe the demon can't find him. Or the others we love. Promise.

Her light filled my heart. *I promise, Mary. I will hide you from him until you feel strong enough to fight this demon with Ian by your side again.*

Should I have shown his Other the mercy she demanded? Did I bring this horror upon us through a cruel act of my own?

Demons are not redeemed by mercy. Never forget that. Now rest, Mary. You have other lives to live.

I stretched my fingers along Ian's cold arm. I touched the body I had loved, dying inside quickly, leaving that life forever, leaving *him* forever, for his sake.

My heartbeat faded away. My vision dimmed, and I saw

nothing else through my living eyes.

I lifted myself from my corpse and stood, whole and unhurt in my spirit form. I looked down at mine and Ian's damaged bodies with a grief I thought no ghost could feel. I watched as French Stick, frowning, stopped arranging logs in the flames under his stew pot. He walked over to my corpse, studied my blank eyes and unmoving chest, then howled with frustration. Around him, the banes growled and gnashed their teeth.

"Bitch," he hissed, looking around the dimly lit barn. "Where are you? I know you're still here, watching. Look what I'll do to what's left of you and your Other. He is a coward. His soul has deserted yours." He went to his blankets and came back with a tomahawk. "Watch me, soul catcher, while I chop his body and yours to pieces and hang the pieces over my fire to cook."

He raised his lethal ax over our bodies. Something heavy whistled through the barn's wide entrance in a swirl of wood and steel. French Stick staggered from the impact. His back arched, his head craned back. Blood spewed from his mouth. His eyes opened wide. His tomahawk dropped to the bloody floor. He sank to his knees. I saw that an ax—a corporeal ax, not the spirit-kind that had struck the banes—stuck out like a strange wooden arm from between his shoulder blades. Blood gushed down his sides and hips.

Into the barn ran a red coated British soldier. He staggered from exhaustion. His tri-corner hat was gone; his uniform was dirty and streaked with grime. But he was young and muscular, with shaggy brown hair falling out of its tie.

His eyes went to the mutilated corpses, and his face contorted first with anguish, then with rage. His gaze shifted to the kneeling, dying body of French Stick. He pulled the ax from French Stick's spine then circled him, facing him, raising the ax again.

The body of French Stick looked up at him as the life faded from its eyes. Slowly, the demon inside French Stick pulled the corpse's bloody mouth into a smiling grimace.

"She tasted good," a voice gurgled inside its bloody throat.

The red-coated stranger uttered a shriek of fury and swung the ax like a scythe.

He hacked French Stick's head from his body.

The head, its long black tail of hair flying, thudded against the barn's log wall and fell to the dirt floor. Bright-red blood boiled from the headless neck. French Stick's body collapsed sideways, twitching.

The soldier stood over it with his ax posed to strike again. He didn't see the shadow rising from French Stick's carcass, a large, hideous form in the dappled morning light. The pig-faced demon, freed from the human body it had occupied.

The demon lurched free of its latest form and balanced his massive, skull-gray body on short, knotty legs. His small, round eyes gleamed crimson. He bared long tusks and roared at me. The guttural sound filled the barn.

"You cannot harm me in this realm, Soul Catcher. You are no more than a wisp of putrid air."

I lifted a hand in warning. "But neither can you harm me, Demon." My boons and angles gathered around me, along with the newly dead—my father, Red Bird, Turtle, Cera. The being from the Talking Rock rose in a white glow around us all, facing Pig Face. "And you are out-numbered."

The red-coated soldier, a living being, did not hear or see any of us. The soldier dropped his ax and staggered to my body. He stood looking down at it with his hands clenched; he shivered violently and uttered a sob. His devotion was a mystery to me. I wanted to soothe him, but also to shoo him away.

Finding Ian, that is my only interest.

Pig Face snarled at the spirits massing against him, but he began backing away. "Remember what I said, Soul Catcher. I will find you in every new life. I will find *him* too—" the demon cast a clawed hand toward Ian's body—"and I will make you both suffer, and I will make you both die. And in the end, my soul will live on, and yours will give up. It is *you* who will be banished from this world forever. Not me."

He kept laughing as he faded away.

I stood alone in the barn with the mysterious, tormented redcoat. He dropped to his knees beside my body. Sobs wracked him. He tore at the thongs that tied me down. When my body was free of them, he curved his arms underneath my body and lifted it to his chest. He bent his head to my bloody skull and rocked me as he continued to cry.

The world of Mary and Ian Thornton was becoming too vague for my understanding. Who was this stranger?

The white light whispered gently, *You are beginning to forget. Just as you wanted.*

I caught my breath. *Not yet, let me see. Who is he?*

The soldier tilted my head back and stroked my dead face with a shaking hand. Suddenly I saw him as he was, not as the body his soul had taken after his death.

"Ah, Mary, Mary," Ian groaned. "I let this happen to you."

Ian.

After *his* body died, his soul had taken a stranger's body. Using that body, he had rushed here to save me.

Ian cradled my body tighter against him and held my head to his shoulder. The deep, racking sounds of his despair grew dimmer even as I strained to listen. *Not yet,* I told the white light, who was tugging at me.

The Talking Rock sighed. It left me alone to watch as Ian, his eyes now dull and staring, wrapped my body, and then his, in French Stick's blankets. He found a horse wandering nearby and used it to drag our corpses on a sling he made from rope and tree branches. I followed as he led the horse down a path into the secluded cove, where our cabin stood.

He slung his red soldier's coat off with a groan of disgust, then took a spade from our little barn and dug a single large grave in a small meadow that fronted our home. By the time he finished he nearly collapsed from grief and exhaustion. The sun was setting.

He dragged his own body into the grave with no ceremony, then fell to his knees beside mine and gathered it in his arms again. He was beyond tears, now, just gently rocking my body and groaning. He laid it in the grave alongside his own. Then he sat by the open hole a long time, his head slumped on his chest, before he could bring himself to take the shovel in hand and fill the grave. When the dirt was mounded he covered the pile with dozens of large rocks from a stash Ian and I had gathered to build the foundation of our cabin.

He made a cairn over the grave.

Long shadows crept through the mountains. The sun splayed gold and blue rays through creamy clouds above the horizon.

Everything was so quiet.

I stood beside him, crying, telling Ian's soul goodbye forever, promising him that staying apart was the only way we might survive Pig Face's eternal revenge.

He couldn't hear me.

He pulled a small, sharp knife from his British solder's britches, stabbed it into his wrist, and sliced upwards.

"Ian, no," I moaned.

Blood poured from his gashed arm. He mutilated the other wrist the same way.

He sank to his knees, spurting blood, then spread himself face down on the stones of our grave, as if blanketing me for the night.

The blood in his new body stained the rocks. He shut his eyes.

He is doing a very unwise thing, the Talking Rock told me. *He will return to being a soul hunter now, but with no soul catcher to anchor him. He will spend all his lives hunting for you. He will be a lost soul. Are you sure you want to hide your soul from him?*

More tears slid down my face. "Yes. It's safer for him, that way. I'm going, now. Make me forget him, now."

"So be it," the light said gently.

As my memory of that life, and of Ian, faded with the sunset, my last glimpse was of his soul forming in the mists by the cairn. He was tall and strong, just as in life, his long, dark hair catching a slip of the evening wind, his head lifted high, his loving blue eyes already searching for me.

But in that moment, that turning point in our many lives, I frowned lightly and floated upward on the same evening breeze, thinking, *That ghost looks so urgent. I wonder who he's looking for? I wonder who he is?*

And then I was gone.

14

The bright morning sun stabbed my eyes. I lurched upright in the grassy clearing where Ian and I had sat inside Crow Walker's mystical shanty. I heard Ian gagging nearby.

Our motorcycle was still parked under a tree—one little sign of reality—but now there was no shanty, no booger masks, no Crow Walker. My t-shirt and jeans were drenched with sweat and dew.

I pitched forward on all fours as I vomited.

It's hard to puke, sob and punch a fist into the ground all at the same time, but I managed the trifecta. A couple of feet from me, Ian was doing the same thing.

He crawled to me. "Mary-Livia." His voice was a hoarse, ripped-out growl. I shoved myself away from the watery bile I'd spewed on the meadow grass then continued slamming the ground with one fist. I wanted to eliminate the excruciating *feel* of what I'd seen, to channel it through my fist and into the earth. I wanted to forget how Ian and I and everyone we'd loved had died, and why.

"Stop it, you hear, Mary-Livia?" Ian shouted raggedly.

I kept pounding the grassy soil. "What your body looked like . . . what he did to you . . . and me . . . *and to everyone we loved.*"

Ian wrestled me down. He pressed himself to my back then snared my scratched and bleeding fist in one hand and trapped it against the ground. His chest heaved against my shoulder blades.

"I heard what the Talking Rock told you, Mary-Livia. You did the right thing by banishing the Other. 'Twas not your fault that Pig Face came lookin' for us. 'Twas *me* who had too much pride. Me who wouldn't listen to your warnings. I was all about fighting the fecking English no matter what you begged of me, and *that's* what brought the feckers there to slaughter everyone."

I shook my head. "If I'd just let Liver Eater go . . . none of it would have happened. I'm the reason he came there. He wanted revenge on me for killing his . . . mate. I'm the reason everyone died. I'm the reason they ambushed and tortured you. Ian, they cut off . . . "

"No need to remind me, love. I was there." Ian shook me gently. "Mary-Livia, for godssake, are you blind? 'Twas *you* who saved Wonaneya from the pox. That she-demon would've put the whole village in the grave if you hadn't banished her. Because of you the people lived."

"Lived? Just long enough to be massacred by the English."

I twisted onto my back, staring up at him beneath the weight of Greg Lindholm's body. "Pig Face has tracked me down in every life I've lived since then, and every time you've found me he's killed me and you, Gigi, Dante, Sarah, Charles" I struggled. "Let me go, please, Ian. Please. You need to get as far away from me as you can. "

"No. Fecking *no*. Enough, Mary-Livia. Enough." He threw one long leg over mine when I tried to kick. We looked at each other tearfully, face to face, dirty and damp and filled with the memory of torture and grief and regret.

"You *listen* to me," he said through gritted teeth. "I left you to be killed by that bastard once, and I'll *n'er* fecking do it again, you ken? *Never.* That was my fate, too. I'll n'er get over the sight of what he did to you. N'er, not in this life, not in a thousand more lives. I'll n'er stop until you and me bring the bastard down. We've got a *chance* this time, love. We've got to believe that *this* time we'll beat him."

"You'll always be sacrificed if you try to help me."

"Then so be it. I'd ruther stay a soul hunter, fightin' by your side, dyin', havin' to find you over and over again, than losin' you forever."

My hands unfurled. I cupped them around his jaw. It was still hard for me to touch Lindholm's face. I kept my attention on its gray eyes, looking behind them, looking inside them, at Ian.

"All right," I lied, dropping my voice to a soft promise.

"You win." I stroked the short brown beard that now fully covered Lindholm's lower face. "Let's go back to the casino. Under the protection of the casino pog. Get some rest. Try to sleep. Try to forget what we've seen, if only for a night. Let's find out if we've still got the mojo to love each other like there's no tomorrow."

I tried to sound seductive. Not an easy thing to do when you're shivering and smell like puke. If I could distract him, I'd think of a way to disappear. I'd lure Pig Face away from him. I'd be a decoy.

Ian studied me intently. For a split second an achingly tender look filled Lindholm's gray eyes. Then he jabbed his free hand between his thighs and mine. I bucked and yelled, but he wiggled his fingers inside the front pockets of my jeans and plucked out the motorcycle's ignition key.

He held it where I could see. "I've come to understand that the motor thing won't roll without this magic key, eh?"

"Goddammit, Ian." My voice cracked.

"Ay, damn me all you want." Tears glittered in his eyes. "But I'll truss you up like a wild goat if that's what it takes to keep you with me."

Exhaustion, frustration, fear, love. I turned my face away and shut my eyes. He bent his head to mine. I still held his face between my hands, giving into the need to touch him.

You must come with us now, a deep voice said. *The Talking Rock sent us to bring you.*

Yes, hurry, it's a long ride to Wonaneya, a second voice added.

We sprang to our feet.

Two horses, saddled and waiting—and talking—stood at the forest's edge.

*

"Talking animals shouldn't surprise me," I said wearily as I clung to a western saddle. My tall bay mare climbed a narrow mountain path through the forest without me guiding her. She didn't even wear a bridle. "After all, the Talking Rock showed me how to turn you into a panther."

Ian's big gray horse had no bridle or reins either, but Ian

didn't hold onto the saddle horn like a rookie, the way I did. He rode with his hands resting comfortably on his thighs. His axes clicked gently in the backpack he'd hung from the saddle horn. "Speaking of which," he went on, watching the trail take us higher into the mountains and closer to more no-doubt sickening secrets of the life we'd lived together. "Next time you're in need of my help, could you not turn me into a big fecking puss cat, Mary-Livia?"

Except for the fear strangling my throat, I might have laughed.

*

Ian and I stood on a knoll high in the forest, looking down at creek bottoms now filled with trees more than two centuries old. "We were right there, just like yesterday," Ian said quietly. "But now it's no more'n a dream."

The site of the village that had been Wonaneya was still beautiful, but so heartbreaking. Only Ian and I knew that a community of human beings had once lived in this cove along a mountain creek near an Ulsterman's trading post. This forgotten Cherokee town had been filled with families, children, laughter. People had planted corn and beans in the creek bottoms, they'd made love and played stickball games and worshipped and gossiped and dreamed in a place that had been a safe little paradise with the high blue mountains looking down on it.

And then they had all been murdered.

Nothing was left. It was if the whole town—along with Ian and Mary Thornton—had never existed. Mother Nature is one tight dominatrix. She cleans up the messes we leave behind.

"It's as if there were never any bloodstains," I said hoarsely. "No memorial to the lives that were sacrificed here. No justice."

No justice.

A shiver went through me. Strange energy. I didn't recognize the emotion immediately. I curled my hands in fists, then unfurled them and held them up, trembling, studying them. They had a soft white aura.

I am a Soul Catcher. I am the only one capable of bringing justice here. I can fight the evil that continues to massacre the innocent of this world.

Righteous. For the first time in my life, I felt . . . *righteous.*

I whirled toward Ian. "The Talking Rock brought us here for a reason, but it's up to us to figure it out. We need—"I paused, frowning, searching my intuitions, my rusty knowledge of the spirit world . . . the word *markers* rose in my mind—"we need to connect with the past. Help me. There have to be remnants of the trading post. A rock foundation, a fireplace hearth."

Ian's eyes gleamed. "Ay, that's a notion!" He swept the terrain with a frontiersman's eye for details. "Down the way, yon. That little ridge. As I recall it, that was the lay of the land."

He strode down the knoll with me trotting after him. The land flowed into a wooded plateau. When I squinted through the trees I glimpsed the creek valley below. Ian pivoted, arms out, assessing the site. "Picture a clearing, with a wagon road yon—" he pointed—"so's there was a view of all visitors from the valley."

I turned in a slow circle as well, trying not to cringe as I relived the sad scenes of our past life. "There!" I jabbed a hand toward a granite outcropping, now nearly submerged in the roots of tall trees. "Mary liked sitting on that rock ledge. When Ian first came to the post, she would sneak up to the ledge and watch him work below, at the forge."

"Well, well," the modern Ian said jauntily. "That's a bit of flattery Mary never shared with me."

We hurried to the spot, weaving among the trunks of trees, stumbling over rooted and jumbled terrain that could easily hide the submerged foundations of the post. When I reached the rock I flattened my palms on its cool, mossy face. "Is there a pog here?" I asked softly. I shut my eyes. "I have an image of a sweet, mossy face with eyes flecked with mica. Eyes like gold."

A voice rumbled in my mind. *Hello, Mele. You are always so gracious. How long has it been?*

Over two hundred years, I'm afraid.

Just a short spell, then.

Clearly, rock pogs have a different concept of time.

I stroked the rock's soft coat of moss. *We're trying to find some of your fellow rocks. The small ones that were used to build the foundations of the buildings here. Can you help?*

Yes, Mele. But . . . if you're hoping to find any other old friends here . . . the boons, I mean . . . I don't know if they'll show themselves. They went into hiding after that terrible Pig Faced demon was here. He put a shadow on this place. It draws banes now. Lots of them. I'm not afraid. Rock pogs don't fear much of anything. But the boons have battled so many wicked banes since then. They don't trust strangers anymore.

I was silent, my heart twisting.

Behind me, Ian said, "I can make out enough of what the pog's sayin' to you. I tell you, Mary-Livia, a Soul Catcher's work is no' just about protecting the souls of the flesh world, but the souls of other realms, too."

I nodded, and took a deep breath. *I'm here to redeem my mistakes,* I told the pog. *Ian and I . . .we're here to make this place safe again. We'll earn the trust of the boons here.*

Well, Mele. Let's get started then.

The rock pog reeled off directions, speaking like an antique compass come to life. Ian stepped off the distances, knelt, pulled one of his axes from his back pack, and used it to chop the soil. Dark loam and bits of frayed roots arched into the air. I rushed over, knelt beside him, and scraped the debris aside.

A foot beneath the surface, his ax hit stone. He laid the ax aside, and we traded a breathless look. Slowly, we both reached down into the earth, our fingertips stretching out. We touched a large, flat surface.

Warmth zoomed up my hand and arm, along with memories of kind flames, comfort, family, food. *Us.* When I looked at Ian again his eyes were half-shut, savoring the memory too. "'Tis the hearth of the main room," he said. "On a cold fall night in front of this hearth, warm and happy, whilst all others in the family slept or pretended to sleep, you kissed me for the ver' first time, Mary-Livia. Do you ken? Do you remember?"

"Yes," I admitted. "It was wonderful."

Branches snapped. Limbs rattled. It sounded as if the forest had come alive with creatures descending on us from all angles. We shot to our feet, Ian grabbing his axe. I pulled my knife.

"I see a world o' shadows in the trees," Ian said. "I'm thinkin' they're boons, but it worries me that they're not showin' themselves, even to *you*."

"They're afraid of us." I scanned the trees. I glimpsed soft, wide eyes, fearfully twitching ears, and snuffling noses. They resembled ordinary animals but . . . not quite. Some of the faces were as small as a mouse's. Others . . . larger than the biggest bear.

"What kind of demons are you?" a growling voice called out loudly. "You've got no business here, digging in this sacred ground, claiming the dead's memories for your own. Drop your disguises, demons."

"We're not demons. We're . . . Mele and E-o-nah."

My claim raised a loud murmur of astonishment from the watchers. But the growling voice accused, "*Lies.* Mele and E-o-nah were banished by the Pig-Faced demon. They can never return."

Ian snorted. "Did I hear that whisper right? The little fecker's callin' us liars? Banished, were we?" Without waiting for me to confirm it, he shook his ax at the assembly. "There was no banishin' done of me nor Mary that day or any t'other! You've been fed a bowl of gumption by the connivin' banes!"

"Oh?" the voice retorted. "If Mele and E-o-nah weren't banished, why did they not return before now, to help us reclaim this territory? Mele and E-o-nah would never desert us. So, the only answer is that they were banished somehow."

I held up a hand. "Listen, please. I've been . . . in hiding. And E-o-nah has been searching for me."

Another round of astonished murmurs, this time sounding even more distrustful. "Mele the Soul Catcher would never hide!" the growling voice roared. A massive paw with long, gleaming claws appeared in the air. It swiped at us in warning. "Prepare to fight us, you lying demons!"

Ian raised his axe higher. I clamped a hand over his. "I won't fight them. They have a right to be distrustful. I've lost their respect."

This brought more muttering from the throng, and I sensed a little softening. "Look at the demon's arm," a squeaky voice called out. "It has the Soul Catcher's symbols on it."

I quickly held my arm high, so all could view the tattooed symbols on my wrist.

That brought lots more twitters and rumbles.

"It could be a trick," the growling voice said.

"I, for one, am won over," a new voice countered.

"I as well," another added.

A large gray fox stepped into view. Larger than any real fox, and more silver than gray. Above him, on the branch of a maple tree, sat a tiny owl. The owl was pure white, with green eyes. *Welcome home,* Soul Catcher, the owl said in a feminine voice. *Whatever your reasons for hiding, we will give you a chance to prove yourself.*

Welcome, the fox added. *Yes.*

Behind them, the other boons gasped and grumbled.

"Thank you, Fox, thank you, Owl. I have a request. Will you show us where the barn stood?"

Ian scowled at me. "No, no. Don't let the sadness get all over you again. Let's move on from this spot, Mary-Livia. Let's not stand here mourning what's done and gone."

But I couldn't help myself. My skin crawled. I looked at Owl and Fox. "Show me where the barn was. Where I . . . where Mele died. Where Ian came back as the redcoat and killed French Stick."

"Aw, feck, no," Ian groaned. "Let's not wallow in it."

I turned to him. "That's where the banes *celebrate.* That's their power point."

Owl and Fox traded dark looks. *It's a cursed spot,* Fox said.

Ian looked around grimly. "Mary-Livia, if there are banes about, then we're not going looking for them."

"Do you want them to *own* the site where we suffered? Do you want their fucking monument to the destruction of Wonaneya to go unchallenged? Do you want these boons to always feel disenfranchised because we didn't confront the banes here?"

He stared at me with his chin up. "Now you're fecking with my pride."

My stomach churned as we trailed Fox and Owl through the forest, with dozens of suspicious boons following closely. Ian carried his ax in one hand, his grip tight. A slithering chill began to run up my spine as we got closer to the site of the barn. I began to feel naked and helpless, terrified and ruined. The scent of my own blood—and the image of Ian's desecrated body laying next to mine—began to fog my brain.

This is the place, Fox said sadly, halting in a small clearing where the trees wouldn't grow.

Owl perched in a nearby tree. *If you scrape away the leaves, the soil is gray. Dead. When banes love a spot, they ruin even the earth there.*

I stumbled. Ian caught me by one arm. His face was pale, but mine must have been worse. "Got your wits about you?" he asked gently.

I nodded shakily. A low, evil cackle began to fill my ears. I jumped. "Do you hear that?"

"Afraid so, Mary-Livia."

Leave this spot, Fox said. *There are banes here right now.*

Ian stepped in front of me, his ax raised. In front of us, on the dead soil at the center of the barn where I had died, where Ian's corpse had been thrown down next to me, and where Pig Face had emerged after the redcoat hacked French Stick's head off, misty forms began to grow.

Nahjee, who had been silent since we left Asheville, suddenly spoke. *Remember who you are. Not what you were.*

Slowly, to my horror, two human images formed. Bloody, mutilated, naked. Intestines hung from the one who'd been gutted. The skinned sections of the other's breasts and stomach dripped watery red fluid. Their eyes opened wide, staring and begging. They held out their hands to us.

Mary. And Ian.

Us.

"Help us," Mary groaned, her hand clawing at me, missing several fingers. "Come back with us and change the past for us and the future for yourselves. You can earn forgiveness for your mistakes."

The gutted and emasculated male corpse stretched the fingerless stump of his fist toward Ian. "'Tis true," the thing rasped in a perfect imitation of Ian's voice. "Do no' condemn us to this fate. Do not put me through what they did to me with my legs spread, I'm beggin' you."

Ian, the living one, gagged. I dragged him by one arm and he staggered back from those hands, *our* spectral hands. I couldn't speak, couldn't form words. Ian trembled, and so did I.

Don't be persuaded! They are banes, Nahjee whispered. *Do not be fooled by your horror and sympathy for the faces they wear.*

But we were hypnotized.

Tabby, the far quieter of my two amulets, curled her glass form against my throat. *If you let them come closer they'll claw you. They want to shed your blood on the ground where you died in another life. If you let them do that, this place will remain cursed forever.*

"If you try to draw blood," I told the ghostly corpses, "I'll banish you."

"How could you betray us this way!" Mary cried. Tears slid down her bloody face. One hand drifted sadly to her raw head, where French Stick had scalped off the long, black hair. "Don't let this happen to me again, Livia. You can step back through time and change it. Please, Livia. I'm not a bane. I'm *you.* Just like Amabeth in the mirror. Only this time, you can *stop* what's happening. You can save me—and Ian—from being tortured like this."

I was ripped apart by the fucking helpless wish to do that, to step back through time and alter everything that had condemned me and Ian to horrible deaths then—and lifetimes of being stalked by Pig Face ever since.

This is a test, Sister, a voice said. *And you won't fail it. I have never lost faith in you.*

I looked around wildly. Alex? Speaking to me, after all these years?

My baby brother said nothing else. He sounded far away, as if speaking through thick walls.

Ian looked at me over one shoulder, his face, Lindholm's face, carved in agony. "I can't say what's best to do, Mary-Livia." His voice broke. "Are they banes or boons? Or are they the ghosts of ourselves?"

The two spectral forms stepped closer, hands still out. "Have mercy, love," Ian's mutilated corpse said to me. "Trust me. Believe in me. I'm not a bane. I'm begging you for forgiveness."

"Ian, save me," the female corpse begged.

Ian drew his ax back. "Mary-Livia, the thought of sinking this ax into the body of your body as I ken it, is near more than I can manage."

Ian's corpse looked at me with blue eyes that tore my heart out. "Livia," it said tenderly. "I'd give my life again to have you trust me. Don't kill me once more."

"Don't hurt me," Mary cried, her disfigured hands grasping at Ian's upraised ax. In another second her bloody fingers would claw his forearm.

I shuddered. Nahjee and Tabitha curled furiously on my skin.

Suddenly I knew the truth.

Ian is standing beside me. Not there. Here. If I don't believe in the here and now, I can't believe in the future. And I can't let these monsters harm him.

"You fucking liars," I said to the corpses.

The dead Ian and dead Mary staggered back from us, shrieking.

"I see you. I damn you, you stinking banes" I yelled hoarsely. "I banish you."

They writhed. They oozed from their human forms into the nasty, furred, scaled, stinking forms of two banes. They hissed at us in abject defiance.

Then they exploded in inky tendrils of dark, fetid energy.

My legs collapsed. Ian caught me by one arm and helped me sit down. He squatted beside me, his jaw working, his teeth clamped, tears in his eyes. We huddled there, clutching each other, for a long time.

"How could you be so sure they were banes?" he asked.

"She begged you not to hurt her." My throat worked. "If she were really me, she'd never say that. She'd know you could never hurt her."

He bent his head to mine.

Fox settled next to us. Owl perched on his silver back.

Fox raised his majestic silver head to the watching boons.

The Soul Catcher and the Soul Hunter have returned.

Silence. Would the boons accept the decree?

We have seen the evidence, Owl proclaimed.

The growling voice of the spirit bear said solemnly. *It is proven. All hail them.*

As Ian and I held each other, the souls around us cheered.

*

I sensed the white light even before it surrounded us. We had followed Fox and Owl through old-growth forest, the huge trees towering over our heads, to the home of the Talking Rock, the site of the cabin we'd built with our own hands.

"The color of the air is changing," I said to Ian. "She's here. The Talking Rock. The white light."

He halted, stopping me with an outstretched arm. "I can no' see her as you can. Are you sure she's the one?"

"Yes."

Mother, Nahjee whispered happily. The uktena who lives here with the Rock, *she is my mother in spirit. Mine and Tabitha's. The serpent spirit is one of the most ancient.*

My pendants curled together in shared happiness.

The light grew stronger, brightening the trees, glowing, pulsing, sparkling. There was a soothing quality, like lotion. "Can you feel her on your skin?" I asked Ian, turning my face up. "She's warm."

"She's all about the touching and the feeling, ay," he said,

too tired to sound pleased about a groping light. He scrutinized
the silver-white mist closing around us.

"You still don't believe in her."

"I'm not sure I ken to her reasons for doing what she does.
Seems a mite suited to her own whims. " The light swirled
around his legs and mine, massaged our thighs, gave a quick
kiss to the in-betweens and moved up our bodies. "She's
putting us under a spell, Mary-Livia."

I couldn't deny that. The light nuzzled me through my bra
and t-shirt. My knees nearly buckled.

"She's licking my neck," Ian said.

Fox, with Owl perching on his head, sat down by our feet.
*Don't worry. You're safe with her. There's nothing to fear when you're
inside her light. She's always provided a sanctuary here for you and—*

She's part of what you are, Owl put in. *You've come back to the
Talking Rock many times in many lives when you needed to rest. Soul
catchers and soul hunters have so few refuges.*

I was going to tell them all that myself, Fox said, annoyed.

Owl bent forward and tweaked his silver fur with her tiny,
hooked beak. *I know, darling. Sorry.*

"Are you an old married couple?" Ian asked them.

Oh, yes, Owl answered. *We've been soul mates for ages. We bicker
because we care.*

Like the two of you, Fox added, looking up at us solemnly.

The mist stroked our faces, entered our lungs, ballooned
our veins. The Talking Rock puffed a sweet high through our
bodies, stretching out the coiled muscles, dropping a veil
between us and the horrors we'd seen in our journey back to
her. The images were still there, but they hurt less than before.
Ian's shoulders relaxed. He let the ax rest by his leg.

Her soft, crooning, female voice spoke in our minds. *I'm so
glad you've come home. So glad you're ready to be together again.*

Are we ready? I asked her, swaying a little. *Can you promise us
we'll survive this time?*

You always survive.

Talking Rock, you know what I mean.

I promise you this: If you learn the right lesson this time, if you understand what's truly important, your souls will never fight these battles separately again.

"Could you be more specific, mum?" Ian said aloud, frowning. "I'd just as soon not see Mary-Livia nor myself lose any tender parts again."

Laughter. She had the softest yet heartiest laugh. It faded gently to a low, happy sigh. *I've missed seeing you together. You bring out the best in each other, believe it or not. Come along now.*

The forest transformed around us. Now we stood on a new path looking downhill into a creek glen. The scent and sound of trickling water filled my brain.

Ian followed me down the path. I felt as if I were floating. Maybe everything would start to make sense. The light shimmered around us, rubbing like a cat, sending a slow, throbbing heat through my body but also warming my mind, whispering, *Rest. Rest, now.*

We reached the same large fallen log I'd climbed over in my dream, butting up against the side of boulder that towered above our heads. I stopped and Ian stopped close behind me. I could feel the heat and the shimmer connecting us.

"Mary-Livia," he said gruffly. "Will you at least give me a look?"

"This is happening too fast."

"Do you not ken?" Ian went on. "Madam Rock wants us to make a grab for one another. She's trying to give us back the gift we once held dear. But you've naught to fear. That's all I'm telling you. I'll n'er lay a hand on you if you're feared of me."

She's not afraid of you, the light answered. *She's afraid of herself. Afraid of losing you again. Of being alone again.*

I climbed over the downed tree with Ian close behind me. We dropped to our feet on a wide shelf of rock. Water bubbled from a deep spring into the wide, dark pool at the rock's base. A tiny creek drained it over rounded rocks covered in dark green moss, just like in my vision. "I've always loved this place," I whispered. "I know that much."

Ian took a deep breath. "A bit of paradise. So this was where you always came on your rambles." The despair in his voice swiveled my attention to him. "When I was courting you, Mary-Livia, I used to wonder where you went for so long at times. You said you were just needing to wander free. I wish you could've told me about this place. And I wish I could've opened my eyes and understood." His expression fell. "Because there I was, praying that you didn't have another man."

She had no other man, the light reported. *She was always here, asking advice about you and you alone. Uktena and Bird Woman counseled her not to marry you but she couldn't resist. They didn't realize you were a soul hunter because you weren't ready to admit it to yourself in that life. So they underestimated your devotion.*

Ian looked at me with a mix of new warmth and annoyance. I conceded with a duck of my head. "Okay. She knows the skinny. It must be true."

Each soul is responsible for its own deeds, good or bad. Each soul chooses its path, its lessons, its sacrifices. But demons are the essence of every destructive impulse, and the dark side of human nature is influenced by them, just as the bright side is encouraged by the angels of our better nature. Demons absorb power with each victory. They relish destruction. The demon who stalks you, the one you call Pig Face, has been about in the world for a long, long time, and he has provoked terror and misery far and wide. If you don't stop him soon, he will become too powerful to be conquered by you at all. Wars, plagues, massacres—those are the consequences when demons gain so much strength.

Ian shook his head. "I mean no disrespect, mum, but the fecker wasn't even powerful enough to keep me from taking this body from him."

You have the strength of your love for Livia on your side. The bond between you two makes you far stronger than either of you alone. Your demon knows that. He has always feared the time when you would find each other again, a time when Livia would remember you, finally, and accept the fate you have together.

I shivered. "How can we save the world from Pig Face if we can't even keep each other alive?"

You don't have to be alive to be together. Never confuse the eternal soul with the temporary body.

The rock's broad, granite face began filling with symbols.

Lines of symbols. The pictograph writing—the same as the symbols tattooed on me, and that had appeared on Ian's ax heads. They *covered* the rock, not so much carved as embossed on it, their color like fire, rising and shifting, moving, as if the secret language they spoke was alive in the rock. Most of the lines only glimmered for a second then disappeared. I squinted. It was as if my eyes weren't trained to see them yet.

Slowly, all but three short lines disappeared. Those three glowed a soft gold against the silver stone.

The first is knowledge you had as Mary, the Talking Rock said. That line faded and vanished. *The second is the knowledge you've gained in all the lives since then. This is where you are in your wisdom right now.*

I raised my trembling arm. "Those are the symbols I wear."

Yes. The second line disappeared. Only one line was left. *This is what you and Ian are learning and are about to learn. But in order to progress, you must accept who you are. You must be together, fully and completely. You must merge.*

I scrutinized the remaining line intently, trying to memorize it. The symbols gave off a too-bright, effervescent sheen that merged with the white light itself. Ian and I shaded our eyes and looked away. The light began to dim around us. The scene shifted, faded, transformed. We stood on the rock ledge in the middle of a world that began to melt and surge around us.

Ian and I closed ranks, him throwing an arm around me and me grabbing him around the waist.

With a soft whoosh of energy, we were back in the real world, or at least some part of it. We stood in a shadowy clearing surrounded by trees. It was almost sunset. The huge hummocks of blue-green mountains rose in the distance. A silver-blue mist filled their hollows and the sky above them was red and gold. The air smelled perfect, sweet, cool, full of a ripe, spring night to come.

We turned around slowly. We stood at the base of a gentle slope.

At the top of it, sheltered by oaks, was the log cabin Mary

and Ian had built.

Home.

Cold prickles spread over me. "It looks . . . not old. It should be gone, like everything else, or at least just a pile of rotting logs."

I've kept it safe for you, the white light said gently. *It stands here as it was the day Mary walked out the door the last time, the day she went to the ridge to battle the banes and was captured by the demon. It is no illusion. I have hidden it from the outside world and protected it. And now it's waiting for the two of you to share a night inside its arms again.*

The light kissed me, slowly, on the mouth, and in less than a platonic way. When I looked at Ian, whose eyes were half-shut and his mouth parted, it was clear she was kissing him, too. Then she was gone.

We walked slowly up the slope. My stomach twisted. "Look. That low pile of stones among the trees over there. The hummock of rocks covered in vines. Is that our . . . oh, God, it is—"

"Just a grave," he said hoarsely. "Naught left it in but dust."

My eyes stung. "I guess only the cabin has a protective charm over it. Because out here we had a little barn, and a chicken coop, and a split-rail fence around a little garden. I saw all that in Crow Walker's visions. But it's all gone now. And . . . so are we."

"Our bodies are gone, not our souls." But he sounded upset. We hurried past. I couldn't make myself look toward the grave again.

15

We ate unleavened cornbread older than the Constitution. The golden, fried hoecakes were still fresh and crunchy in a covered iron pot on the hearth in the cabin's main room, just where Mary had left them. We drank creamy milk she'd stored in a crockery urn; milk from a cow that had lived out its life when the flag had only thirteen stars.

We sat across from each other on woven cane chairs at a rough wooden table the other Ian had built. This Ian rubbed his fingertips over the smooth tops of iron nails the other Ian had made at the forge. I examined a beautiful table runner woven of pine needles. "I bet Mary made this. She was probably an artist. Like me. Or I'm like her. I think of her as somebody else. And I miss her like she was my best friend. Go figure. But she's right here." I touched my chest. "Right?"

"Ay," Ian said quietly. "I know she's in there somewhere, just like you can see him in me at times, I hope."

We looked at each other over a flickering oil lamp, sharing a deep pit of longing to be comfortable together as Mary and Ian, the people who'd never gotten to grow old in this sweet little place, the people we'd been.

"We've eaten a meal we left for ourselves," I rasped. "I think we're on the verge of a paradox."

"And what would that be meaning?"

"A *then* and a *now* that can't possibly be connected, but they are."

I looked around. The cabin was full of dark shadows, but it still felt cozy. Safe. We sat inside the lamp's small pool of light like we were floating in a new universe. "Maybe this isn't real, Ian. Maybe we're dead."

He laughed. "Now you're fecking with my head a bit too much. No. We're alive, Mary-Livia." His humor faded to a somber smile. "And we've got to *merge*. Madame Rock said so."

I stood, agitated already. "I'm not sure I'm ready."

Ian stood too, scowling. "God's balls, woman. It's not the poking and the humping that Madame Rock is talking about. It's the *giving*."

"I don't know how to *give*. Everything and everyone I love has always been *taken* from me. I've been alone too long. And I still think I should fight this fight *alone*."

He thrust out his jaw. "Well, that's all moot, isn't it? You're stuck with me, Mary-Livia. Now, look. If it's just a ceremony with no heart you're after, let's head over yon right now—" he jerked his hand at the bedroom across the dog-trot hallway outside—"but I'll be damned if I'll settle for you just laying there staring at Lindholm's face and gritting your teeth 'til it's over."

Wounded and grim, he picked up his backpack and headed for the door to the hall. The axes clinked dully.

I blocked his way, furious. "Do you think I'd be that cold?"

He glared down at me. "You're changing the subject. Do you want to feck me or not? You just don't want to feck me. Admit it."

I grabbed the tail of my t-shirt and dragged it over my head. I reached behind me to snatch off my thin black bra. Ian grabbed me without a word, picked me up around the waist, shoved open the door, dragged me across the open hall, shoved the door to the bedroom open, then toted me inside, kicked the door shut, and set me down hard in a rocking chair by the fire place.

It was dark. No fire. No lamp. Just a soft glow of moonlight through the wavy glass windows of which Mary and Ian had been so proud. He dropped to his heels in front of me, holding me in the chair with both hands pinning my wrists to its arms. "Do you give a damn that I have feelings too, and that I'd treat you tenderly if you just gave me half a chance?"

"Of course I care—"

A fire whooshed to life beside us.

We jumped.

In Mary and Ian Thornton's fireplace, on logs Mary had placed there herself before leaving her home for what would turn out to be the last time in her life, a cheerful little fire started itself.

"This isn't the Talking Rock at work," I said in a low voice.

Ian nodded slowly. "'Tis my Mary herself. *Mary.*" His voice rose gently. "Love," he called. He searched the shadowy room for any glimpse of her. The room was simple, with just the fireplace, a low bedstead covered in woven blankets, and the rocking chairs. "Mary? Would you have a talk with yourself, I mean with this one here, for me?" His eyes gleamed with tears. "Mary. Speak to *me*, at least, m'love."

No answer. He sat back on his heels, his head bowed.

I looked at him sadly. *He loves her. That me. Not this me. Not that I blame him.*

She did not answer him, or me.

After a moment, he settled on a stool by the hearth, his face carved with disappointment.

I choked back my own emotions and said as casually as I could, "I suddenly understand something. We're not the same people we were then. We can't be. Every life changes us. Not just what we look like, but what we know and expect. You . . . don't have to love me in this life. It's all right. I don't mind being a substitute for her."

A lie, but I managed to sound sincere.

He scowled at me. "What you're really sayin' is that I should no' expect you to love *me* now, because you're still in love with the man I was. You do no' see how you look at me sometimes still, Livia. It hurts. You're doin' it even now."

True. I was staring at Lindholm's bearded face and gray eyes, his dark hair shagging over his ears and forehead. Through the open collar of his shirt I saw short, wavy hair where Lindholm's chest had been shaved and smooth. Ian looked less like Lindholm every day. And the expression in his eyes had transformed him from the beginning. But the rest of him was still not Ian.

I said hoarsely, "Maybe we're *both* in love with the past."

He scowled harder, then looked from the fire to the bed to me. "If you'd rather not look at me I could put a sack over my head. Or I could put a sack over yours. But I like looking at your face, Mary-Livia."

I craned my head. Everything was a challenge. "Why?"

"Those grand green eyes, that little sideways crook to your nose, the way your long hair swoops across your forehead, and how your lips press together when you're mad . . . seen a lot of *that* look, I have . . . "

"You don't have to flatter me."

"And you do no' have to pretend it matters to you, one way or t'other, what I think."

But it *did* matter. I sat back in the rocking chair, pulling a blanket around me.

He hunched toward me. "Just tell me that deep inside you, you wish you could open up and have the feeling for me."

"I do. I wish. But it's not that simple."

His face brightened. "Oh, yes it is. Let's get back to discussing how much I like looking at you."

I gestured at my scarred feet and tattooed arms, then at the row of studs marching up the sides of my ears. "This isn't how Mele looked."

He leaned closer, his elbows on his knees. The firelight carved Lindholm's face in half-shadow, half-light. I desperately scrutinized it for hints of the black-haired Irish frontiersman inside. Ian frowned dramatically, cocking his head to study me from more than one angle. I huddled deeper inside my blanket. "You've got *arms* and ears on either side of your hypnotizing breasts?" Ian asked slyly. "I have not noticed." He leaned closer, peering at the blanket as if seeing through it. "Ock. There they are. Well, you do! Arms and ears and bosoms. Glory be."

A strange sensation bubbled in my throat. *A laugh*. I smothered it. "Just tell me the truth. Do you wish I looked like Mary?"

He pushed his stool between my feet, splaying his legs on either side of my knees. He frowned at me. "Did I not point a hard cock at you that first day, when I stood naked at Sarah and Charles' place?"

"Cocks point at anything warm."

"Have I not made it clear I've wanted to touch you every moment since?"

"Men like to fuck."

"Ah, there she is right now, such a gentle soul, and such a sweet way with words."

"Ian."

"Do I like you? O' *course* I like you. More'n you like *me*. Besides, you were n'er a sweet little daisy. I'd be disappointed with you if you changed. Mary once threatened to clang me with a cooking pot. In fact, I have a clear memory of her throwing one at me."

"Really?"

"Ay. And, no doubt, whatever her beef, I deserved it."

I slid to the edge of the chair. "Look, I know we need to bond on a deeper level. So let's just . . . get on with it, okay?"

"Now, now. I know you're raging to have me, but I'm not the kind of man who fecks at the drop of a hint, you ken? I have to work my way up to the moment."

He leaned down, took my left foot, and lifted it to his thigh. He unlaced my left hiking boot. Strange, how his hands in that simple act, undressing me by way of my shoe, made me want him a little. He set the shoe aside, slid his fingers up my ankle, hooked them in my heavy gray sock, then curled the sock down. He stripped my foot as if the sock were a silk thong sliding from between my labia. "Ah, Livia," he whispered, cupping my bare foot in his hands. He stroked his fingers over the coarse pink scar tissue. "Ah, Livia," he said again, sadly. "Your poor feet. Do they hurt?"

He called me Livia. Not Mary-Livia. Livia. *My* name. A heady moment.

"Not anymore," I said.

He took off the other shoe and sock then sat with both of my bare feet on his thighs. I could feel the thick muscles of his legs flexing under my heels. I resisted an urge to curl my toes.

He stroked my scarred skin. "Do you like having your feet rubbed?"

"I don't know. No one's ever done that before."

"Well, now's the time." He massaged my feet, my ankles, and worked his hands inside my jeans to rub my calf muscles. It felt good. I relaxed, but only from the knees down. I flinched when he slid his hands higher.

He looked at me as if I'd stomped his heart. I eased my foot from his grip. "I'm sorry," I said hoarsely. "This isn't going to work for me. Too much time to think about the wrong things."

He blew out a long breath and scrubbed his hand over his hair. "You know, maybe we *should* just strip down and get it over with. You shut your eyes and I'll be as fast as I can. Maybe more good will come out of the coupling than we know. Maybe all we have to do is make the effort?" He looked up into the darkness of the room. "Whoever's judging us, listen up, you ken? Give us some scores for trying, all right?"

I nodded and stood up, easing away from him with what I hoped was a casual step or two. Didn't work. His mouth flattened. "No need to run, Livia. I'll not try to corner you."

"I'm going to take off my clothes and get under the covers of the bed. Then you take off your clothes and get in bed with me. I won't try to avoid you and I won't try to make you feel unwanted."

"When you put it that way I can no' resist," he deadpanned.

I turned my back, stood by the bed, undressed but left my bra in place—how stupid, but I was suddenly shy. Then I pulled back the half-dozen thin blankets that Mary had left on the narrow, double bedstead and climbed in quickly, covering myself.

The sheets were a soft gray, some kind of coarse, hand-woven cotton—fancy stuff for the 1700's, probably because Mary's father could get the goods from traders passing through the mountains. So his beloved oldest daughter and his beloved son-in-law would have fancy woven sheets from the fine port cities of Charleston or even up north, Philadelphia, for their cabin in the wild woods.

I touched the sheets gently, flattening my hand on the cool surface, trembling, then turned on my side, facing the log wall. Behind me I heard the fire crackle as Ian stoked it, and I felt Ian's gaze on me like a worried laser. His heavy boots, the ones I'd called his urban lumberjack look, made slow, somber sounds as he crossed the plank floor. The skin along my bare spine puckered.

"Aw right, Mary-Livia," Ian said behind me, his voice tired. "I'm shucking off and climbing in."

"No problem," I lied. I sounded hollow. "Do me a favor. Could you just call me Livia?"

"Ay. Sorry." He sat down to undress with his back to me, his hard ass brushing mine, his weight tilting the thin feather mattress downhill toward him. I clutched the bottom sheet, holding myself in place. His boots scudded as he tumbled them to the floor. The whole bed shook with his slightest move. I heard the zipper on the fly of his khakis. He stood. I heard the soft rustle of the pants, and no doubt his briefs, heading south.

The bed shook again as he turned to face it, bumping it with his bare knee. "Sorry," he said.

"No problem."

I started shaking when he lifted the covers on his side. He sat down quickly and slid his legs under the blankets and sheet, and suddenly there he was, taking up more than half of the bed, Lindholm's brawny, six-foot-plus body instantly crowding me. He lay on his back, one thick forearm plowing a furrow between my shoulder blades, his naked thigh pressing into my naked ass. He still wore his shirt, just like I still wore my bra, but the rest of us was skin-to-skin.

"Livia," he said in a miserable tone. "Stop your quivering. I'm not just going to pounce on you, all right?"

I turned to lie on my back too. I stared up at the plank ceiling, watching the shadows from the fire. "Don't worry about me. I'm not stupid about sex. I haven't been a virgin for a long time. I'm not Mary."

"Mary was no stranger to men by the time I came along."

"Really?" I twisted my head just enough to look at him. "I

thought things were stricter for women back then."

"No. About like now. Everyone pretended to be saints whilst merrily sinnin'. Besides, her mam's people weren't sticklers for chastity. The women didna bow to the menfolk. They didna live under the men's thumbs. Or under their cocks, neither."

"I'm impressed."

"She gave up the chance to marry a chief's son in a town further up the mountains. I saw the fecker naked at a stick ball ceremony once. Hung like a fecking horse. But I won her away from him. I took great pride in that."

"I bet it wasn't much of a contest after she met *you*."

He twisted his head a little to look at me. "Ah. Now tell me, why would you think a homeless blacksmith wandering the Cherokee lands with naught but a mule and an anvil would be such a catch? Not that I'm fishing for praise, you understand. Just curious."

"She saw your good heart, your sense of fair play, your endless courage and loyalty. She knew you were special."

That was all it took. "Livia," he groaned. He turned toward me quickly. Under the covers, his right hand slid over my bare stomach. His fingers splayed on my skin.

Lindholm's fingers.

I made a startled sound, not a welcoming one. My stomach muscles pulled back from his touch, leaving his hand in thin air. At the same time I felt his hard cock poke my outer thigh. I shifted away from it. He pulled his hand back. "Damned hand," he said gruffly. "Has a mind of its own."

Our sweet intimacy was now just a dull chill. I hated my reactions, but I couldn't stop them. "No more talking," I told him wearily. "Just come here."

"All right." The words dripped defeat. He sat up then got to his knees, taking the blankets with him. The room's warm, pine-scented air hit my bare stomach and crotch. I clenched my fists by my sides.

I stared at the ceiling rather than look at Ian, no, Lindholm, no Pig Face, no, *Ian, Ian, it's Ian!* kneeling beside me with his hard-on at full mast. "I'll move to the center of the mattress," I announced. I sidled to the bed's middle.

"Ay, a good plan. Pull up your leg, please, and let me betwixt your knees." I bent my right knee to let him past. "I'm putting a hand of each of your knees, all right?" he asked brusquely.

"No problem."

"Do me a favor, Livia. Stop saying that."

"No . . . okay."

He clamped a hand gently on my right knee, then my left, and eased them apart as he moved in for the kill. That's how I thought of it.

"Livia, I know you do no' want me rubbing your bits nor coaxing you with a finger, so you best tell me. Are you wet at all?"

"It doesn't matter."

"Goddammit, Livia. It matters to *me*."

"All right, I'm dead dry inside. But I don't care. Just rub some spit on yourself and stick it in slowly. I'll loosen up."

Still staring at the ceiling, I heard his huge, unhappy sigh. "So be it." I heard him spit into one hand.

Then I felt a large hand slowly, gently clasp the top of my left shoulder.

It wasn't his.

I jerked my gaze from the ceiling and searched my side of the bed wildly. Nothing. No stranger had sneaked into the room. Yet the sensation was still there. A hand, a man's hand, thick-fingered and rough-skinned, gently grasping the spot where my arm joined my body. The fingers flexed. The thumb rubbed a small circle on the tender skin just below my left collarbone.

"There's a hand on my shoulder," I told Ian in a low tone. "And it's not mine. And it's not yours."

Ian instantly snatched me to his chest, wrapping his arms around me and twisting his body to shield me from the invisible visitor. The hand trailed away. I twisted my head to look over the muscled hummock of Ian's shoulder. We both searched the darkness beside us.

"Who's there?" Ian demanded. "Speak your name, boon or bane or ghost or whatever you may be. Who are you?"

A form began to grow in the darkness. It didn't fully fill in; it was translucent, but still vivid. A man's shape, tall and lean. Dressed in a thigh-length pale shirt with blousy sleeves, open down the front, and leather britches. The visitor had long, dark hair and eyes I would always remember. They showed blue, even in the shadows.

Ian repeated grimly, not seeing him as well as I did, "Who the hell are you?"

The ghost looked at Ian with a proud nod of his head, as if not the least bit surprised that he was giving himself hell for invading our privacy.

"'Tis yourself you're looking at," he answered. "I'm you."

The air seemed to glow around him. My heart caught in my throat. *Ian.* And yet he wasn't Ian. He was the previous Ian, just as Mary and Amabeth and Maratile weren't me, just different facets on the same diamond of the soul we shared. But he *was* the image of Ian's soul, the one I'd painted back at my studio, and that soul was inside Lindholm's body. All I had to do was quit seeing the many different shells that encased it.

In the meantime, the current Ian went silent, switching his frown from his ghost image to me and back again. His ghost looked at me possessively. My skin warmed. A flush of strange arousal began to burn in my nipples and between my legs. I lay there, naked except for the bra, being looked at by two men. One dead. One alive. Both Ian.

The living Ian released me slowly, then uncurled his long legs and sat down between my knees, casually draping the end of his shirt over his still-hard cock. His throat worked. "I can no' blame Livia for hating this body of mine," he told his other self. "I want her to feel how much I love her. I want her to love me back, what she can see of me, the me that looks like yourself. Can you help us with that?"

The ghost nodded. "Ay." He looked at me tenderly. "You're not my Mary on the outside. I don't see her when I look at you. But I know she's there. And I want so bad to touch her again."

"How can you . . . you're not flesh. How does that work?"

"It's the *wanting*, Livia Belane. It's me touching you in spirit, and you feeling it as if my hands were on your soul."

I looked from Ian's ghost to Ian. His eyes were sad but resigned. I shook my head. "You don't have to do this for me. I don't want to treat you like a substitute."

"You need to be with him, Livia. And it's me, all the same."

"No. It's not."

Ian began to push himself off the side of the bed. "I'll go out in the hall. Give you and . . . myself . . . some privacy."

"No." I grabbed his hand. "This isn't an orgy. It's a . . . I don't know what it is. But you're part of it, and I don't want you to go."

The pleased expression on his face, the warmth in his eyes, was not Lindholm, it was Ian. For just a second his eyes turned from gray to blue. My breath churned. "I *do* see you inside that body," I whispered. I turned to the ghost. "I see the same man in both of you."

The ghost stretched out a hand. The backs of his fingers brushed my bare shoulder, then stroked lightly down the length of my arm. They left a heated sensation. My back arched.

The living Ian touched me, too. My eyes met his. The blue in them grew brighter. I couldn't look away. He slowly reached beneath me and unsnapped my bra. It hung loosely on my shoulders, still covering my breasts, but just barely. Ian drew a finger down my throat and into my cleavage. He hooked his fingertip into the centerpiece of the bra, then tugged just so.

The bra slid gracefully down my arms. The ghost trailed his fingers back up my arm then curved them under my hair. When his fingertips massaged the base of my neck I thought my spine would collapse.

I twined my fingers through Ian's. *We're in this together.* He nodded as if I'd said it out loud. We looked at his ghost.

"Go ahead," the living Ian said. "She and I want to be one

with you and Mary."

The ghost eased closer, sitting beside me with his long thigh drawn up, his knee pressing gently into my bare hip. He drew his hand up the side of my face, outlining my cheekbones, my brows and my nose with the callused tip of his forefinger. He touched my lips, scrubbing them, making them swell. When I inhaled sharply he slid the tip of his finger inside my mouth. I sucked it.

"That's my Mary," the ghost whispered, his voice, Ian's voice, deep and aroused.

The living Ian's hand tightened around mine. His thumb rubbed a slow circle in my palm. Both Ians were good at that, the thumb caress. The ghost withdrew his finger. Whether real or an illusion, it was wet from my mouth. He stroked the moisture over my lips.

His fingers trailed down the tip of my chin, then the center of my throat. He splayed his fingers over my neck, making a wide swath of rising heat as his flattened his hand on the swell of my breasts. His hand stopped over my heart, rising and falling with my fast breaths. Then he turned his hand over and stroked the backs of his fingers down the center of my left breast. He curved his hand under it then closed his thumb and forefinger around the nipple, squeezing carefully.

Again my back arched.

I felt the imaginary heat of his face and body as he bent over me. His mouth surrounded the nipple of my other breast. He sucked, moving the tip of his tongue over the nipple. I was writhing on the bed now, and I squeezed Ian's hand hard. "That's a girl, Livia," he urged in a low, sodden voice.

The ghost continued to suck my nipple as his hand moved down my stomach. He smoothed it over one thigh, inside and out, slowly, then back up to my stomach, then down the other thigh. Then he slid his hand deep between my thighs and stroked upward with the coarse tips of his fingers. Fire. A surge of damp electricity spread through my belly. Everything relaxed. I was throbbing. I shut my eyes.

"I'm going into you now, Mary," the ghost said against my

nipple. He raised his head to my throat, kissing the side of my neck, sucking the skin between his lips. His hand, between my legs, unfurled its long middle finger against the mouth of my vagina. He circled that opening, massaging. I felt my silky juice spreading everywhere. His finger made a wet sound in the soaked folds of skin. He slid his finger inside me.

My hips came off the bed. He slipped a second finger inside me, slowly thrusting. I was now gripping Ian's hand so hard my knuckles ached. His ghost kept moving his fingers inside me as he kissed a line down my body. When he reached my thighs he pulled his fingers out of me, spread my folds wide, and nuzzled his tongue inside me.

I came, groaning. I'd never had an orgasm like it before in my life. The squeeze and lift of pleasure, the transforming moment when *something* important and profound felt almost within reach, the sheer release of core energy that made every inch of my body aware of being alive.

"Livia," Ian groaned, "look at me, love."

I opened my eyes. He was over me, kneeling between my legs again, still holding my hand on one side but sliding his other hand up under my ass to tilt my pelvis up to his cock. As I stared at him in wonder his Lindholm eyes turned Ian-blue and the glow of his own ghost surrounded him. I watched as the image of the long-dead Ian merged with the body he lived in now. He *was* Ian, fully, no matter who he looked like in this life.

"Now I see you," I whispered.

He smiled and groaned as I pulled him inside me.

*

And the most amazing thing was, Ian's eyes stayed blue.

"You've changed," I told him in the first pink light of dawn, as I sat on top of him.

He smiled up at me, his face flushed, his blue eyes heavy-lidded, his beard still wet from an earlier encounter with my thighs. "Have I, love? I think that's just your fancy talking."

"I don't care if it's an illusion. I like it."

He raised his hands to my face, cupped it between them,

and stroked my long hair back in shaggy, damp clumps. "Livia Belane, I find you so fecking beautiful you make my heart ache. From the first moment I saw you at the jail, fully and completely and no longer through a mist of the other worlds, from that very moment I was taken with you. It took me awhile to make peace with it."

"To make peace with it?"

"I felt like I was two-timing Mary. Even though you're her."

"I'm jealous of her. Even though she's me."

"Ock. I was jealous of my own ghost earlier this night."

"I'm sorry."

"But watching you come off the bed for him, for my own self, ghost or not, was a grand sight." His body twitched at the thought. I pressed myself down on him.

Ian made a low sound in his throat. He stroked his hands down my shoulders. "I was a little worried you wouldna ever get past the loathin' of Lindholm's body."

"Only about a half-dozen fecking times," I intoned, trying to mimic his brogue.

He grinned. "Ay. I've got no worries now."

I slid down beside him, and we arranged Mary and Ian's covers over ourselves. We spooned, his arms around me from behind, holding me tight. I tucked my hands inside his. It was impossibly sweet and tender and intimate. I didn't want to think about our future. *Ever*. Didn't want to wonder when and where Pig Face would find us and what would happen then.

We slept.

*

We sat outside on the cabin's stone steps, trying to get back to reality such as we knew it.

Ian looked at me. Time had run out. Or the time had come. *Time to go back to Asheville*, we agreed.

Two sets of hooves rustled in the loam at the forest's edge. We looked over to find our familiar boons waiting.

"We're ready to take you," the horses said.

16

By mid-afternoon we reached the site of Crow Walker's shanty on the Cherokee reservation, where we'd left the big cycle. It was speckled with spring pollen but otherwise untouched; we were too far off even a back road for any wandering hikers or local residents to find it.

We stood in the meadow wearily, fiddling with the helmets, watching the horses disappear into the woods. Really disappear. They ambled a few yards back up the narrow deer trail then evaporated.

"I've gotten used to a lot of strange shit," I said dully. "That didn't even make me blink."

"Ay." Ian's face was grim. We both glanced at the grassy clearing where we'd looked into Crow Walker's memory pool. "Feels like we've lived a lot of years in just the past couple of days."

"Ay," I mimicked gently.

He brightened as he gazed at me. "Some of that living was very, very good, love." He couldn't resist a jaunty smile.

I looked up at him quietly. Those blue eyes. "I'm more worried than before. You've given me something to look forward to. I don't want to lose it."

He took even that small confession as a big victory. He wagged a finger at me. "Now look what you've done. Even with the fate of all that's hanging over our heads, you've made me go and kiss you."

He dropped his helmet, quickly cupped my face between his hands and kissed me. His tongue was sweet on mine; his beard tickled. I gently bit his lower lip as he drew back to let me breathe. He bent his forehead to mine, chuckling darkly. We were both scared and worried and trying not to show it. "Livia, are you trying to put your mark on me?"

"Maybe," I whispered.

"Could you just do it with words? Could you just say so?"

Three words I never thought I'd speak out loud to him or anyone else crept up my throat. *I love you.* He wanted to hear it. He needed to hear it. I needed to say it. I swallowed hard, trying to give the words room to pass. Dammit, I'd get them out, no matter how long it took.

Suddenly, shrieks filled the sky above us and large things with heavy paws rushed our way through the forest.

*

I picked off as many banes as I could while Ian burst others into dark flecks with his axes. A multitude of boons appeared to fight on our side. They came in the shape of birds mostly, similar to the big hawk I'd seen at the studio that day. But there were stark white bears too, and a huge buck deer with blood-red antlers, and other boons that took no shape I can easily describe—glittering, winged and clawed, ferocious.

Right makes might. Boons don't have to be sweet little angels, I realized then.

But in the end the banes overwhelmed us. Slapping, clawing, pinning us down. One of them puffed something into my eyes, and everything went black.

"I'm blind," I called to Ian. "I can't see to banish them!"

"Do no' give up," he ordered.

They trussed us with ice-cold ropes of some kind. We were bound hands to feet. They dragged us away.

*

We lay in a small cave somewhere. Dark, moldy, damp. I didn't have to see it to feel it. Ian, whose eyes they'd left alone since he couldn't banish them on sight, tried to talk to me in between banes shoving him to keep quiet. "We're no' far from the cycle. I can see the cave opening just up yon. We can get out of this, Livia."

The banes cackled. At least one of them could talk. It hunched beside me, lightly slapping my face with a scaled, claw-like hand. "Escape," it hissed, chuckling. "There is no escape this time, soul catcher. You can't see us, so we're safe from you. All we have to do is keep you here until our master comes. He's on his way. He's found another strong body to use. When he gets here, he'll do much worse to you than you can ever imagine. Much, much worse than he did the last time. He'll make you listen to your man scream and beg. And then he'll cut you to pieces, little by little, just like before, only slower."

"Do no' answer him, Livia," Ian called. "Ignore the bastard."

Of course I couldn't keep my mouth shut. "I'm going to pop you like a fucking water balloon," I said to the bane. "And all your fucking ugly little friends, too."

The bane growled. He pinched my jaw open and jabbed his knuckles deep into my mouth. "Try to talk some more, soul catcher."

I strangled and kicked. I heard Ian struggling, cursing the banes who leapt on him and held him down. The bane's foul knuckle made me gag. He unfurled a claw and poked my tongue. I tasted blood.

I yelled an order inside myself. *I'm a Soul Catcher. I want to see these banes.*

My vision returned. I saw the nasty fucker squatting over me, saw his red eyes and the hump of his scaled wrist protruding from my mouth. I couldn't get the words out but I formed them in my throat.

I see you. Die, you fecker.

He jerked his hand out of my mouth. His red eyes went wide. He screamed.

He exploded.

The other banes went ape shit.

I rolled upright, watching them scatter. Ian lay on the cave floor, scratched and scraped but watching me with a smile growing on his face. A small bane squatted on his belly with its claw posed over his groin. It stared at me in alarm.

"His body belongs to me," I said. "*Feck* off."

It exploded.

I whipped toward the others, who were running for the arch of light at the cave's opening. "You can't run fast enough," I yelled. "I see you. I banish you. All of you, you feckers."

A dozen banes exploded at once.

Silence. Stillness. My chest heaving, I scooted toward Ian. He managed to sit up. Our hands were still tied to our feet. The cord was very real and very tight. Ian jerked at the binding. "Ock. It just gets tighter."

I jerked at mine. Tighter, yes. Fuck. We'd offed the banes but we'd still be laying here helpless when Pig Face showed up.

I saw a flash of movement from the corner of one eye.

A small bane, no bigger than a rat, was trying to creep away.

"Stop right there if you don't want your ass turned inside out," I said. It shrieked and hunched down, quivering.

Demons don't respond to mercy. And neither do banes.

But mercy can be traded for help.

"I'll spare you if you set us free. You have my word."

The little bane leapt to work. It gnawed Ian's bonds in two first, then quickly chewed through mine. Ian vaulted up, grabbed me under the arms and hoisted me to my feet. The rat-like bane scurried away.

"He'll tell Pig Face what happened," Ian said. His eyes widened. He looked around quickly. "My axes!"

We ran outside and searched the area of the fight. Ian found his empty backpack. But no axes. His shoulders slumped. "The feckers stole them."

I swallowed my fear and said cheerfully, "We'll find you a new ax. Even it's just an ordinary one, it's better than nothing."

He feigned a smile. "Ay, 'twill be all right. I'll feel fine soon as I get a weapon in my hand."

We ran to the bike.

*

When we reached the outskirts of the city I steered the cycle off the main drag and took a maze of isolated two-lanes. At a mom n' pop convenience store I turned in and parked. "I'm going to call the gallery. I have to take the risk. I'm worried about everyone."

"Ay, I'd like to hear that all are well. If they stayed in the gallery under Sheba's protection they should be fine."

Ian followed me inside. Pay phones are rare as these days, but the old man at the counter pointed us to a scruffy unit in a corner between the donut racks and the soft-core porn.

I punched the gallery's main number. No answer. I tried the phone in Charles' pottery studio. Nothing. I didn't risk leaving a message on the answering machine. As I hung up the phone I looked at Ian worriedly. "They'd answer if they were there. This scares me, Ian."

His face grim, he nodded.

Tap, tap, tap. The sound of a knuckle rapping on thick glass. *Tap, tap, tap.* We looked around quickly. The ATM machine was located on the other side of the porn rack.

Leonidas's angular face looked out at us. He rapped his knuckle on the glass again. Ian and I crowded up to the screen. *Hi,* I mouthed. I assumed he could see us. Leo drew his finger tip in a horizontal line on his side of the screen. Words sprang up.

Trouble. Dante left the gallery last night to pick up groceries but came back acting odd. Left again this morning. Everyone's worried. Went looking for him downtown. Sheba and I think it's a trap.

I wasn't sure how to communicate. Finally I put my finger on the screen and drew invisible words on the glass. *We're going downtown to find them.*

Leo scowled then drew another line with his finger. *Dangerous. I'll alert some friends. I'm putting the word out that a true soul catcher is joining the game. I never doubted you. Not much, anyway.*

I replied, *Yeah, sure.*

He shrugged but smiled. The screen returned to normal.

"That damned ATM ain't working right today," the old man said as we left. "Must have got a bug in it."

"A big one," I agreed.

*

We heard the drums even through our helmets. Asheville throbs with rhythm at Pritchard Park on Friday afternoons from spring to fall. On a good night there are several dozen musicians of every race, sex, age and creed, seated or standing in a semi-circle on the wide steps of the park's small amphitheatre. The energy is incredible: a mind-hooking, rhythmic boom and clatter as sweaty people pound waist-high *djembes* and big *congas*, women in dreads shake gourd rattles, rednecks whack cow bells and kids paddle their little bongos or beat an occasional snare drum.

Crowds of old hippies, dopers, young slackers, bums and white bread citizenry gather to listen and dance in one big, excited stew of community jiggyness.

Ian and I parked the bike in a nearby alley. The pulse of the drums pounded our ears. We stepped onto a sidewalk, furtively studying the strolling downtowners for anyone trying to hide claws, wings and fangs. Asheville's most venerable office buildings towered over us.

A steel door opened slowly. Service entrance. We side-stepped it, expecting an after-work secretary or sales rep to pop out. But there was no one there. I glanced into the dark interior and saw two large, silver eyes looking back. They blinked. No face. No body. Just a pair of eyes floating in the dim light. *I'd heard there was a soul catcher and a soul hunter patrolling the city,* a voice said, *but I could barely hope it was true. Soul hunter, I've been told you need an ax to use? I can open the emergency fire box for you.*

I put a hand to my heart in thanks. So did Ian.

With the red *Asheville Fire Department* ax tucked blade-down in Ian's backpack, we walked up the sidewalk to Pritchard Park. The crowd numbered at least two hundred, filling the tiny downtown green space with a clapping, gyrating street party. Asheville police officers supervised the event casually, chatting with the street people, chilling.

"Oh, feck," I said in a small, anguished voice. The officers were a problem, but they weren't the main reason my blood congealed.

"Ay, dammit," Ian whispered.

Gigi, Sarah and Charles stood stiffly, huddling close together, under the park's main tree. Trapped. Pale. They looked like they'd been roughed up. At least two-dozen banes surrounded them. The banes squatted around them like weird monkeys or hung from the tree limbs over them. Some even hunkered by their feet, clutching their ankles so they couldn't try to run.

"We have to get closer before we make a move," I whispered. "And don't pull out your ax unless I need help. It's hard to explain an ax-wielding man to the Asheville PD."

"Ay."

"Those officers are watching *everyone*. If they recognize you or me from Detective Beaumont's alerts . . . "

"Illusions," a voice sang out. "Get your fresh, hot illusions right here."

We looked over. A young, tattooed street preacher, standing atop a low plywood box, waved us closer, using his Bible like a scoop. The slightest glow surrounded his earnest boon face and clean-cut boon outfit—rumpled khakis and a tie-dyed *Jesus Saves* t-shirt.

"What would you be suggesting?" Ian asked him solemnly.

The boon waved the Bible over Ian. "And the Lord said, let the soul hunter look like a little blond man in knee shorts. With an overbite."

"Oh, feck," Ian said.

The boon swooped his Bible over me. "And the Lord said, let the soul catcher look like an obese grandmother in a sundress that shows the big moles on her arms."

"Oh, fuck," I said.

"And the Lord said, let the soul hunter's ax look like an umbrella."

Ian scowled. "Do no' be messing with my weapon."

"Chill out," I told Ian. To the boon I said, "It's still an ax under the illusion, right?"

"The Lord says yes, it's still an ax."

"Hallelujah, brother."

The boon nodded to us. "Go ye and confront the devil on our terms, not his." He lifted his arms and his Bible to the sky and shouted, "Because the Lord told his disciples, Heal the sick, cleanse the leper, raise the dead and *cast out the demons.*"

We walked on. "Am I waddling?" I asked. "Do my moles

have hair growing out of them?"

"Only a few short sprigs. And as for me?"

"I don't mind the buck teeth so much. But your scrawny knees really suck."

He grunted his amusement then reached over his shoulder, grasped the ax handle sticking up from his backpack and pulled out an umbrella. "This makes me a wee bit worried."

"Ay," I admitted.

We made our way through the crowd in the park. Gigi, Sarah and Charles looked stoic but tormented. A bane slithered its clawed hand inside Sarah's peasant skirt, and when she kicked at it another bane pinched her hard on the arm. All of this happening in the middle of a crowded event where regular people saw only three twitchy, unhappy looking adults huddled under the tree.

Gigi snatched one of her potion vials from a front pocket of her overalls. Banes grabbed for it but she popped the lid off and flung one of her herbal powders at them. Two banes screeched and fell to the ground, rubbing their eyes, but others grabbed her around the waist and legs then shoved her against the tree trunk. A third one reached down from a limb and slapped her in the head. When Charles lunged at them two large banes grabbed him around the throat while Sarah punched them uselessly.

My heart twisted. At the same time a raw new feeling rose up inside me. It was time to do my job: To protect the innocent of this world from the sleaze balls of the other ones.

"Let's rock n' roll," I told Ian.

"Meaning?"

"Attack the banes."

"Ah! Ay."

There we went; a roly-poly grandma sprinkled with moles the size of prunes and an anemic blond guy with rabbit teeth, carrying a fucking umbrella.

Gigi and the others, unsuspecting, looked at us askance as we reached them. "Folks, you probably don't want to join us under this tree," Charles said politely. "We're dealing with some personal . . . some personal demons at the moment."

"Oh, I dunno," I drawled. "Looks more like to me that y'all got yourselves a nasty infestation of ectoplasmic yard apes."

Ian jabbed a bane with the tip of his ax slash umbrella. "Let go of my friends, you filthy fecker."

"Ian and Livia!" Gigi squealed.

Two dozen banes, hunched on the ground or hanging from tree limbs, whirled toward us with startled red eyes. Their jowls and beaks and muzzles and lipless holes parted in shock.

I drew a bead on the tree division first. "I see you," I said. "I banish you."

The tree filled with dark sparkles as every one of them burst apart.

The ground division scattered like terrified squirrels. Ian chopped two to sparkling pieces and hit a third with an agile toss of the illusionary umbrella. I waddled after the rest, pointing and pronouncing. "You're gone. Fuck you, too. Go to hell. You, too. Bye, fucker. Feeling lucky, punk? Don't. Yeah, that'll do pig, that'll do. Here's looking at you, bane. Hey, Rosebud, say hello to Kane. Howdy, bane-bro. Squeal like a pig, would ya? And you? Fuck *you* up the ass. Because *nobody* puts Baby in a corner."

Quoting old movie lines made me giddy with small victories and stupid with overconfidence. The surviving banes escaped into alleys between the restaurants and shops.

I could have enjoyed my creativity if I weren't terrified that Pig Face lurked around a corner somewhere. And where was Dante?

"Livia," Ian called. He grabbed me by one arm.

"Livia?" Gigi cried. She and the others crowded around Ian and me. "Is it really you guys?"

Sarah stared at me, then Ian. "The boon who disguised you two certainly has a sense of humor."

Charles hugged me then clapped a hand on Ian's shoulder. "Come on. People are staring. All they saw was our little group making a lot of strange motions at thin air."

"And Livia wandering through the bushes pointing and muttering," Gigi added.

I raised anguished eyes to theirs. "Where's Dante?"

"We don't know," Sarah admitted.

The five of us hurried down Patton Avenue, turned right and walked quickly. A few minutes later we darted into the privacy of a big parking deck. There were only a few cars on our level, and no other people around. "We'll go back to the gallery and get a plan together," Sarah ordered, huffing as she dragged Gigi by one hand and me by the other.

I looked over at Ian. The illusion had worn off. He was back to normal—big, brawny, bearded. "Thank God, it's you again," I said hoarsely.

His newly blue eyes lit up. "'Tis good to see your old self again too, love."

The others cast curious looks at us. Gigi burbled, "Livia and Ian *bonded* while they were gone! I'm so happy!" She pressed a hand to the heart of her black overalls with pink trim.

A dark figure stepped from behind Charles and Sarah's van. We all halted.

"Dante?" I whispered. His black t-shirt was smeared with grass stains and a dark mystery blotch on one shoulder. His dark chinos also had stains and a tear in one knee. The ebony sheen of his face showed a red scrape on one swollen cheekbone.

Gigi rushed forward. "Are you all right?"

He took her in his arms. "You bet, sweetheart. Just chasing Pig Face all over Asheville, that's all."

Sarah and Charles frowned at him. "Where have you been?" Charles asked.

"I didn't want to worry you all. Last night at the store I earjacked a couple of banes whispering about Pig Face. I've been tracking him."

Charles frowned harder. "I want to hear the details, but let's go back to the gallery first, where it's safe." He pointed at an old, oversized, Econovan with a magnetic sign on the driver's door that said *Ablehorn Folk Art Gallery. Outsider Art For*

The Insider Soul.

Dante sighed. "I didn't want any of you to come looking for me. I was trying to take care of Pig Face by myself."

Dante, who preached teamwork, had become a loner, suddenly?

An icy glove closed around me.

I was not the rookie who'd said goodbye to him when Ian and I headed to the mountains. My perceptions were stronger, my instincts more practiced. I had traveled to the dark side of my past and returned with a far keener sense of trouble.

I looked at Dante and knew he was lying.

Ian stiffened beside me. We traded a careful glance. Yes, he suspected trouble, too.

"But you've always preached *teamwork* to me," I said, frowning. "You can't take down a demon by yourself."

Dante's dark eyes flashed. "Sweetheart, we all have our *mission* in life. Don't question mine." That sounded curt by Dante's laidback standards. As if he realized he was being a douche, his face softened. "Look, your situation is personal to me, all right? I can't play it safe."

I stepped closer. "I know the truth, now. You were my father in the seventeen hundreds. And you were my dad in this life, when I was a kid. You've probably been my dad in a lot of lives, always fighting for me, always willing to die for me—and for Gigi, and Sarah and Charles, and Ian. The demon who stole my mother's identity pushed you off a cliff at Ludaway Ridge when I was ten years old. I thought I'd never see you again. But you found a way to come back into my life when I needed you most. You've been trying to take care of me here in Asheville the past few years. *Are you still my dad?*"

"Yes," he said softly. "I'm dedicated to tracking you down in *every* life." He had one arm around Gigi. He opened the other to me.

"No time for hugs," Ian said quickly.

"Just a quick one." *He's got Gigi.*

I felt Ian's ax hand twitch as he touched my arm. *Take care.*

I slid into Dante's embrace and pressed my face to his

shoulder. I shut my eyes and searched every sensation.

The stink of evil rose in my brain.

Get away from him, Nahjee whispered.

I can't desert Gigi.

Tabitha added a shrill warning. *He will kill you both.*

Dante kissed Gigi's head. She smiled up at him, completely fooled. Then he kissed the crown of my head, almost as if he were *tasting* me. He smiled at the group. "Follow me into the stairwell over there. We need to discuss a plan for confronting Pig Face. I agree that standing out here in the parking rows isn't a good idea. Let's get some privacy."

"No," Ian said. His hand went over his back and gripped his ax handle. *Asheville FD* was stamped on the handle's butt.

Dante studied that emblem, his eyes gleaming. "What happened to your anointed blades?"

"I think you ken what happened to 'em, you fecker." Ian pulled the fire ax from his pack, positioning it with lethal grace, his legs shifting into a power stance." Let go of Livia and Gigi, or I'll split you like kindling wood."

Charles and Sarah, who had been staring at the scene in growing alarm, gasped as the truth sank in. "Let them go," Sarah ordered. "If there's anything left of Dante in that body, I'm talking to him. Dante, listen to us."

"Honey, Dante's gone," Charles said hoarsely. "I can sense it now. He's not there."

The thick arms of Dante's body tightened into a strangle hold around mine and Gigi's necks. He glared at Ian. "Throw that puny ax, Soul Hunter, and I'll crush their throats."

Gigi's expression collapsed into horror. She struggled and rasped out, "Livia, how could I have been so stupid . . . "

"Let her go," I ordered, strangling, coughing. "You've got me. That's enough."

Pig Face laughed loudly. "I intend to kill *all* of you."

He backed toward the stairwell, dragging Gigi and me, squeezing harder every time we struggled. Gigi's eyes rolled back. Stars flitted across my vision. As my sight dimmed I saw Ian closing in on us, his face carved in rage and frustration, the ax raised but frozen.

Sarah started for the van.

"Stop, bitch, or I'll kill them," Pig Face warned again. "Don't bother getting a gun."

Ian called over his shoulder to Sarah and Charles, "He means to trap us all on the stairs. Keep back, I'll go. Just me."

Pig Face sneered. "You don't make the rules, Soul Hunter. You never have."

A huge, flying bane materialized in and caught Ian's ax with pronged feet. Ian wrestled him.

I tried to raise an arm and to call out a banishment.

Pig Face choked off my air. He continued dragging Gigi and me into the stairwell. Sarah and Charles followed us doggedly.

They'll all die for me. Just like always.

The bane jerked Ian's ax free then sailed out of the parking deck with the ax in his grip.

Ian leaped down the steps behind Sarah and Charles. Another bane suddenly blocked their way. A big one, ten feet tall, a furred *Sasquatch* with a head like an alligator. It bellowed.

I waved my weakening hands. Beside me, Gigi was already slumping, her face going blue. *Be gone, I* gasped through numb lips.

The bane exploded, but was instantly replaced by another bane, larger, looming over Ian and the Ablehorns.

On the landing below us, howls of hungry glee arose. More banes, heading our way.

"Poor Livia," Pig Face said to me, kissing my forehead again. "After the others are dead I'll take you some place private. You always die after such slow and interesting tortures. I look forward to watching."

I could hear Nahjee and Tabitha trying to pierce the fog in my brain, to keep me conscious, but it wasn't their guidance I needed now.

It was my own.

Through all the past lives, the mistakes, the unending stubbornness to go it alone, came a surrendering and a new understanding. Asking for help in a desperate situation was merely obvious and convenient, not a sign of true wisdom, and would never save us. But welcoming our friends to the fight, and embracing them as partners, would. They were part of me. Facets of my soul.

Come here, my friends, I am you, and you are me.

Immediately a rush of energy filled the space. A shimmering, flowing shadow formed on the landing below ours. There was a rustling of wings, a settling of robes. The angel from the art museum. Light flashed. Shrieks and howls mingled with the clatter of claws running on concrete and steel. Ian leapt at the bane.

Boons and banes filled the stairwell, in battle.

Even Pig Face couldn't command the situation, at least not instantly. Ian reached him and slammed a fist into Dante's face. The blow drove Dante's body backwards. Boons pried at his arms. I slipped free of him then pulled Gigi out of his grip, while Ian continued to pummel the dark, bloodied face that snarled at him.

A roar came from that thing's throat.

Pig Face lunged at us.

Boons suddenly blocked his way—as long as he was in Dante's body he could not escape them easily. But he would take control in another minute. His banes were ripping at us, trying to reach past a shield the angel made, to tear us apart.

"Run back to the deck," Charles shouted.

He dragged Gigi up the steps while Ian hoisted me over one shoulder and pulled Sarah after him.

We staggered out of the stairwell, back into the parking deck.

A late-model SUV roared toward us, but struck a smaller car and careened into a concrete pillar. Ian set me down and pointed. "To work, my love. That bane has to go."

I took a quick breath as the oozing creature in the SUV slithered inside the driver's seat of a large truck.

"I see you, be fucking gone," I yelled hoarsely.

He burst into slimy bits.

But Sarah, Charles and Gigi were cornered on the other side of the crashed SUV, and more banes were heading their way.

I spread my arms and shouted, *"Burn them all!"*

The entire deck filled with the vaporizing energy.

The angel floated toward Ian and me. *Go now. You'll have a short time before more banes arrive and the demon frees himself. This is your battle, soul catcher, and yours, soul hunter. I'll escort the others to safety.* She smiled. *I'll take them to the Woolworth pog.*

"Thank you, Angel."

I'm honored, Soul Catcher. You are now fully vested and have gained the wisdom necessary to follow your destiny, though your choices will never be easy. Now go.

"Don't worry about Ian and me," I yelled to Gigi, Sarah and Charles. "Go to Woolworth's. The angel will help you get there, and the Woolworth pog will take care of you."

They nodded and waved.

Ian and I ran to the gallery's van.

We dodged the sudden *whump* of a giant bane's fist as we dived into the front seats. I cranked the engine while banes beat against the windows. We peeled rubber onto a street.

No one but us saw the banes clinging to the van's hood, or the sprays of inky fluid and flashes of light as they exploded at my command.

We careened up College Street and headed out of downtown, toward the river district and the safety of Sheba's protection at the gallery.

17

We didn't make it. Too many banes, too many detours to avoid ramming the Friday evening traffic, a constant battle. We ended up near my studio, not the gallery.

A huge, flying bane broadsided the van as I drove wildly down the weedy, deserted industrial lane beside the Swannanoa's bank.

The van plunged down the embankment. A tree stopped it.

Ian reached under the van's front seat and pulled out the pistol Charles always kept there. "Run for it, Livia. I'll cover you. No arguments now. Do your banishin' work, while I follow. That's my job, you ken?"

We stumbled down the bank, with me yelling at banes on all sides. It was a war zone; the earth with concussions as they exploded.

"Watch out," Ian yelled, pulling me aside as a bane ambushed us from behind a junked car. The bane slapped him with a clawed foot.

"Die, fucker," I yelled, and it vanished. But it left a triple stripe of gashes across the left side of Ian's jaw. We staggered to the river and slid into the water. Even though the Swannanoa is just a big creek, maybe twenty long steps across, I didn't know how we'd make it through the waist-deep depths with a small army of banes after us.

Come to me, friends. I am you and you are me.

A huge, gray, snake-like boon rose from the river. An uktena.

The Swannanoa uktena coiled around Ian and me, lifted us, and carried us across the river. It set us down atop a sandy bank behind the Harken Bible building.

Thank you, I said.

An honor, soul catcher.

Suddenly, everything was quiet. We were alone. Our chests heaving, Ian and I looked at each other numbly. I gestured toward a side door in the building's ground floor, near the huge garage door I used when I parked my truck inside the building. "I have an emergency key buried outside."

I ran to the rusty, fifty-gallon drum where I burned my demon canvases. I fell to my knees and began digging in the charred dirt at the drum's base. My breath rattled in my chest. Ian took us a guard spot beside me. Blood dripped from his jaw. As soon as I had a moment, I'd heal the bane wound.

"What the feck is that noise?" Ian asked suddenly. We heard a loud rumble coming up the service road in front of the building. Massive wheels, a big-ass engine. Something so large it moved slowly. But not slowly enough.

Ian ran to a corner of the shop and craned his head to look. He bolted back to me. "Up. 'Tis Pig Face. *Run.*"

The roar grew louder. The ground trembled. It was hard to talk over the sound. I stabbed a hand under the steel drum and pulled out a plastic baggie with the key in it. "Got it!"

We scrambled toward the door.

Too late. The enormous scoop of a bulldozer clipped the building's corner. Shards of brick and aged mortar sprayed the air. We stared up into the dirty yellow cab of a huge machine. The dark, intense face that had belonged to Dante now gazed down at us through the dozer's mud-flecked windshield with a bored expression. Pig Face revved the giant engine and pivoted the scoop so its lethal scraping edge was aimed at our bodies. Ian raised the semi-automatic pistol and fired repeatedly.

Bullets ricocheted off the cab and shattered the windshield, but Pig Face had already ducked behind the console.

And the bulldozer kept coming.

He isn't afraid of us at all, I thought frantically.

Ian shoved me toward the door then stepped between me and the oncoming blade as I jammed the key into the lock. The stink of diesel and the roar of the engine wiped out every other sensation. I felt the lock turn, slammed my shoulder into the door, and it swung inward.

Ian pushed me through.

The dozer rammed the doorway. One end of the scoop

caught Ian under his left arm, pinching the outer wall of his torso against the door jamb. He groaned and wrenched himself backward.

The skin along his ribcage ripped. He fell inside the doorway with me grabbing him, holding on from behind, breaking his fall. He landed on me. A giant fist knocked all the air from my lungs. His shirt tore down one side. Blood immediately spread down his side and onto me.

The building groaned as Pig Face pressed the dozer's full weight and power into it, but the wall wouldn't give. Not yet, anyway. He jerked the levers. The dozer began backing away. Readying for another full-speed run.

I staggered to my feet, grabbed the door, slammed it shut and turned the deadbolt. As if that would save us. "Ian!"

Oh my God. His blood was everywhere. I could see an open wound bigger than my hand on his side just below the ribs. But if I didn't get him on his feet and upstairs, Pig Face would knock the wall down on top of us. I snatched the pistol off the blood-stained concrete floor then grabbed Ian's hand. I pulled hard. "Come on," I begged. "Get up. Move!"

I would never forget that moment. His face bloody from the bane's scratch, his torso turning crimson, his blue eyes stark with pain, he still managed a cocky smile. "Always orderin' me about," he said, his voice strained.

He grimaced as I helped him get to his knees, swaying. Outside, the bulldozer's engine bellowed as it rushed the wall again.

"Walk, Ian, walk!"

He staggered to his feet. I snugged myself underneath his good arm, wedging my shoulder under his armpit, trying to brace him. We made our way slowly toward the wooden stairs that led to my loft.

The dozer rammed the wall again.

Chunks of mortar sprayed us. Dust fell in a thick cloud. Bits of brick and splintered wood fell from the thick joists of the floor above us. But the wall didn't give. Didn't even buckle.

"Building . . . won't collapse . . . " I gasped as we worked our way up one step at a time. "Fucker... can't knock down... Harken Bible. All we... have to do... is get upstairs. Safe!"

I tried to ignore the blood soaking the left side of Ian's torso and making a growing stain down the left side of his khakis all the way to his knee. I wouldn't let him bleed to death. Goddammit, I had the power to heal him, didn't I?

We made it to the top. I could hear the dozer revving up again. I got Ian almost all the way across the wide floor, planning to settle him on my small bed, but just before we reached it his knees buckled. We collapsed on the floor with me cushioning his head and shoulders. He lay there with me pillowing him, hugging him desperately. He drew deep breaths.

"I can heal you," I promised. I placed a shaking hand on his clawed face. "This is just a bane wound. A fucking illusion. I order it to go away!"

When I lifted my bloody palm, his face was healed. "Yes!" I helped him stretch out—his eyes were squinted shut with pain—and then I knelt beside him quickly, pressing my hands on the horrible wound in his side. "All right, now, go away, you fucking hole, heal now, stop bleeding—" my voice was raw—"I'm a soul catcher, I order this wound to heal itself—"

"Love," Ian said gently, weakly. "'Tis not a bane wound. 'Tis a real one. And you can no' heal it."

I knew that all along, but I refused to admit it.

"Yes, I can. I fucking can! I didn't get you up here to let you bleed to death—"

Pig Face rammed the building again. Not the wall this time. The big garage door, instead. The door was built of massive timbers with steel braces, but it couldn't withstand the full force of a bulldozer. The timbers made low, screaming sounds, wooden shrieks as their fibers tore and the rivets in their steel frame began to rip free.

"Love," Ian rebuked, as I continued to press on his wound. "Stop."

"I will not... give up," I said in a high, gritted voice, keening, furious, terrified that Ian was leaving me.

He reached across with his good arm and put that hand over mine. Held still, I shivered. When I looked at him the quiet resignation in his eyes tore me apart. "Livia, the fecker's going to tear down that big door in another pass or two. He's coming up here to kill us both."

"I've got the gun—" Suddenly the studio's tall windows filled with shadows. Hideous, winged banes attacked the glass, clawing, shrieking, slamming their beaks and tusks into the panes and the steel frames. "I see you, I banish you," I screamed at them, and they blew apart, but others took their places.

Ian's hand clamped hard on mine. "They're empowered by himself, by him being here with murderous intent. They'll get in, Livia. When he breaks the door they'll come with him. You won't be able to shoot him quick enough to fend off him and them as well. And even if you can kill his body quick you'd only be releasing his true self. He'll be on you before you can get through the ritual of banishment. It takes a bit of time to banish a demon. A thorough job. You'll need help."

"I'll call for Sheba—" I threw my head back and yelled—"Sheba! We need you here!"

"They can't stop him now, love. He's too powerful." He groaned. "Livia. I can fight him and give you the chance you need. But not like this. Not in this wounded body."

I hunched over him. "What are you saying? No. *No.*"

"Have you come to believe so little about the way of souls? You know it's not worth fighting to keep a soul stuck in a bit of ruined flesh. You know it's no' the end."

The dozer slammed the door again. The timbers tore apart. The whole building shook. All it would take was one more run at those failing supports, and Pig Face could walk through.

"Livia. Take the gun. Do no' think about it. When the fecking bastard comes up the stairs, kill him quick too. Then you and me will go at him together. 'Tis the only way."

I put my forehead against his chest. I kissed the spot over his heart. When I lifted my head I gazed into his blue eyes. "I love you. I always have, I always will. No matter what you look like, no matter who you are on the outside. *Always*."

He smiled so broadly it broke my heart even more. "I love you too. Now, then, forever." His smile faded. "Go on, now, m'love. Do no' hesitate."

I reached beside us and picked up the pistol.

I knelt over Ian, straddling him. His blood stained my knees. I put both hands on the shaking gun to steady my aim. My tears fell on his blood-stained face. He managed one more smile. "Now, that's a sight I'll remember to death and back," he whispered. "You crying o'r me." He clamped his hand atop mine. As always, we shared the choices, the pain, the passage.

"See you later," I said hoarsely. I pulled the trigger.

His body convulsed between my legs. It was as if he came inside me one more time. Death and sex. No. *Death and love*. I loved him. I loved him so much. And I'd killed him.

I laid the gun down and bent over him, taking his face between my hands, crying, stroking the shaggy, dark-brown hair, the blood-smeared beard. He looked up at me and never looked away. I tracked every second as the life of his body faded. As the light went out of his eyes.

As the blue in them returned to gray.

At that moment I didn't care whether souls lived forever. I didn't believe I'd ever see him again. *I can't live like this*, I thought. *I want to go wherever he goes. It'll be easy.*

I picked up the pistol and lifted it toward my head.

"I'll ne'r forgive you if you pull that trigger," Ian said.

I twisted toward his voice. He stood a few feet away. No wounds, no blood. He was whole again, and strong.

And he carried one of his prized, handmade axes.

I lurched to my feet. "Ian—"

The dozer plowed through the garage door. Timbers crashed. The stink of diesel fumes rose up the stairwell. The engine went quiet.

"He's here," Ian said. "He knows I'm dead. He thinks I'm gone. And he's thinking you're easy pickings." Ian lifted the ax. "This is the same as me. It exists in a separate world, not this realm of yours. It's no good against Dante's mortal body. But it'll be plenty good once you roust Pig Face from Dante's form."

We heard the soft, sinister thud of footsteps on the stairs. I dropped to a squat and pretended to sob. I tucked the pistol behind me.

"No point in sounding pitiful, Soul Catcher," Pig Face called, his voice a hollow and harsh mimic of Dante's rich tones. "I don't deal in mercy."

"Ian's dead," I moaned. "Isn't that enough for you? Can't you just leave us alone?"

"The way you left my Other alone?"

"She was a murderer. She was evil. If I'd let her go, she'd have destroyed many other innocent souls. I understand that, now. I wasn't wrong to banish her." I groaned loudly again. "If you kill me, I'll just come back. Can't we agree to a truce?"

Pig Face laughed. "No. I enjoy killing you and the people you love. After I kill you this time I'll fuck your body and *his* too. A little treat I give myself."

The demon stepped off the top of the staircase and looked down at me as I squatted across the big room from him, beside Ian's bloody, ravaged body.

His mouth curled. "I expected a little more challenge from you. But you've weakened in every life since Wonaneya, a little more each time. Before long you'll be so gutless and cowed that you won't bother to come back at all. And *that's* when I'll say I've conquered you. *That's* when I'll bow my head to the memory of my Other and tell her I've avenged her." You think only banes and demons can be banished from this world. But your kind and your allies can be banished, too. That's just one of the *many* things you don't know about the way things work."

He held out a hand. "You can't escape. Come here."

I sighed deeply. I stood, head bowed, shoulders slumped.

Then I brought the pistol up swiftly, clamped my other hand to it for a steady aim—just as Dante had taught me to do in his weapons classes—and stared down the barrel at Dante's dark eyes and handsome features. For one second, the gun trembled in my hand. *Dante.*

Then I remembered I was looking at nothing but the shell around Pig Face.

"How about a quick bullet between your fucking eyes?" I said.

I shot him in the forehead.

He dropped. He twitched. His body went limp. I walked toward him slowly, the gun still posed. I didn't trust the pool of dark blood spreading on the gray, weathered floor beneath his head.

Ian's spirit stepped in front of me. "My turn, Livia. Back away. Get ready to speak your words."

A bloody green mist began to glow over Dante's body.

I halted. I backed up. I lowered the gun.

It wasn't going to be useful anymore.

I kept backing up until I could lay the pistol on one of my art-supply cabinets. Ian turned to watch Dante's body. I couldn't take my eyes off the horror. The seeping green mist quickly formed a sight I'd hoped I'd never see again in this life or any other: Pig Face's hulking, grotesque self.

I fumbled inside the cabinet's open shelves, pulled out a large sketch pad, and flipped it open. Maybe I didn't need real paper, a canvas, paint, nothing. Mary had shown me it was all about the ritual, not the actual drawing. But this fucker had come into my life, this life, in my art.

And I wanted him to leave the same way.

Pig Face rose to his full height, towering over Ian by a good two feet. Ian raised his ax in warning. Pig Face gnashed his tusked jaw and flexed his powerful arms. His legs were thin and short but not weak-looking. He balanced on large feet—splayed like paws, with long, knotty claws that matched the claws on his large hands. His dick swung gracefully in the air, always stiff. He glared at Ian but flicked a hyper-alert look toward me.

I lunged forward, dropped to my knees by the crimson pool from Ian's body, and placed the sketchpad on the floor.

I swiped my hand in Ian's blood. Staring at Pig Face, I called loudly, "I see your eyes." I smeared my bloody fingers across the bright white art paper in front of me. "I capture your eyes."

Pig Face charged.

Ian brought the ax down. It sank to the hilt in Pig Face's chest. What harm a spiritual ax can do to a demon is hard to say, but it seemed to do plenty. He uttered a bone-chilling growl and slammed a paw into Ian. Ian held onto the ax handle and jerked it. Still holding on, he and the ax sailed sideways and plowed into a stack of large canvases against one wall.

Pig Face leapt at me.

"I see your mouth, I capture your mouth," I yelled, my hand moving swiftly. More blood on the paper. "I see your head. I capture your head!"

He was nearly on me when Ian sank the ax into his back. Pig Face whirled, giving a shriek of sheer rage and pain. This time Ian levered the ax free and struck again as Pig Face pivoted once more toward me.

"I see your arms, I capture your arms!"

The ax sank into Pig Face's left shoulder.

That arm fell to the floor. Fluid, a cold silver color, sprayed in all directions. The arm twitched and crept toward me on its own.

"I see your chest, I capture your chest!" My hand moved feverishly on the blood-stained paper.

Pig Face had no choice but to whirl toward Ian again or lose his other arm. He grabbed the ax blade as Ian swung it. Ian held on. A violent tug-of-war erupted. They crashed into chairs, broke framed canvases, scattered jars of paint.

"I see your legs, I capture your legs!" I shouted. "I see your feet. I capture your feet!"

Almost done. Only one more part to name.

Pig Face released the ax. Ian was caught off balance and tumbled backwards. Pig Face swung toward me, his tusks bared, his good arm rising in a fist. His disembodied arm reached my sketchpad. Its paw splayed out; it dug its claws into the bloody paper. I pounded the paw with my fist.

Pig Face lunged at me one last time.

I looked up into his furious, evil face. Then I looked at the part of him I hated most. "I see your dick," I said. "I capture your dick."

I put my bloody hand on the bloody paper.

His lost arm withered and shrank back.

Ian brought his ax down into the center of Pig Face's hunched spine.

The demon collapsed slowly to the floor in front of me, close enough for me to feel his breath.

He breathed.

He was alive. In some way. As alive as me. A living being. I never expected that.

I looked over him at Ian, who stood there strong and alive . . . but not. Not really. My heart began to rip apart as I realized he was already less vivid; he was fading, along with Pig Face.

"Ian," I rasped.

"I'm making sure he goes where he's meant to go, love. I'm a soul hunter. I'll track him out the door of this world."

"Don't leave."

"I have to, love."

Pig Face laughed. His bloodshot red eyes, their round black irises going wider, stared straight into mine. Weakening, he slumped, holding himself up just barely with his arm. His eyes glittered. The hatred poured out. "You'll be with him again. No one's banished *your* Other. Not yet."

"You murdered my family. Any misery that came to you and your Other is misery you brought on yourselves."

"Ah, soul catcher! I have done more damage to you and yours than you know." He wheezed. "And there are others who will come now. Demons like me, and even stronger. You will never have any peace. Neither you nor yours."

"I'll take my chances." I held up the bloody paper. Just smears, yes, but as I turned it to the light they shifted and formed his image. I put a hand on either side. I ripped the paper down the center and said the words that had been born with me.

"I paint you. I trap you. I burn you."

Pig Face sank into the floor. His eyes stared at me with stark hatred until their last, faded glimmer.

And then, nothing.

So that was how it finished. One demon's reign had ended. Two-hundred and thirty-some years of existential stalking, revenge, loneliness, hiding, death, suffering and more death, and it all came down to this: The vapor of a creature I'd named Pig Face now withered into thin air, hovered over boards where the holy mysteries of Bibles had been printed and stitched and bound, and then, he vanished.

The air snapped his essence apart. He went . . . somewhere. *Dear Heavenly father-mother-whatever-you-are, please make it true that he can never come back here.*

Gone. Done. Finished.

I looked up at Ian proudly.

I froze.

He was gone, too.

I was alone, just alone, sitting at the feet of Lindholm's body.

I turned my face slowly, so slowly, toward that body, and I looked at it. At the bloody, torn chest, the splayed hands, the staring, dead eyes.

"Ian," I moaned. Then, louder, rocking. "*Ian.*" Then a groan that turned into a hoarse yell. "*Ian!*" I sank my head into my hands and cried like I hadn't for years, like never before in my life.

The air simmered and glistened. Suddenly I went to an unfamiliar place, standing in the anteroom of an intimately lit ballroom, looking down at an elaborate marble floor, seeing the pointy toes of my own black stilettos. And then up at myself I looked in a large, gilt-edged mirror, and I was dressed in a short black dress—elegant, long-sleeved; for once I wasn't about the tattoos and their symbolism, no, I was just a plain, happy girl. Just a pretty woman in spiked heels and a little black dress, with my black hair piled up on my head and a pair of little diamonds in my ear lobes.

"Ay, love, you're as beautiful as I expected," Ian said gruffly, behind me. I pivoted and there he stood, the Lindholm edition, but that didn't matter anymore, I looked up into his blue eyes and saw Ian. I would always see Ian in other men's faces, whatever and whomever he chose to be. He was dressed in a tux, by god, a tuxedo, and that should have been so corny and obvious and white bread but it was . . . sweet, yes, I *loved* looking at him in that tux. This was a fantasy of normal life come true, his gift to me, and I loved it and I loved him.

He held out a hand, and I took it, and he drew me to him, and we put our arms around each other just like they do in the movies. Somewhere an orchestra played something slow and romantic. And we danced a slow dance.

I put my head on his chest and felt the slow, steady pulse of his heart, a rhythm that would survive every life. "You'll not be worryin' too much," he whispered, ordering and cajoling.

"I'll not be worryin' too much," I agreed. "If you'll hurry back."

He laughed. "I will, love." He kissed me.

Then he was gone. I sat on the floor beside his body again, smeared with his blood, dazed. Gigi, Sarah and Charles rushed up the loft stairs. They gasped at the bloody carnage of Dante's and Lindholm's corpses, then hurried over to me and squatted around me, gazing sadly at me, worrying.

"I'm so sorry, Livia." Gigi stroked my arm. "Ian's gone."

I looked at her calmly. "No. Just dead."

She searched my face, saw that I really was at peace with Ian's passage, and smiled through her tears. She, Sarah and Charles hugged me and each other. We managed some kind of laugh. At least, they did. I was a believer now, sure—death is nothing, everyone comes back—but I wasn't quite *there* yet, not enough to laugh about losing Ian's mortal coil.

I held his cold hand, and stroked it gently.

18

Detective Sam Lee Beaumont didn't seem to mind the smell of dried blood. Even a haz-mat team couldn't fix the odor of the old Harken Bible building. The garage door was in shreds, and the downstairs wall on that side needed reinforcing. So I was vacating the Bible shop for now. Too many demon memories and no good memories of Ian there.

Beaumont stood like a southern-fried Buddha in the middle of my studio's stained floor, hands on stocky hips. He wore ugly-ass, laced-up, orthopedic shoes with his slacks, dress shirt and striped tie. "My feet hurt," he said. "I'm not used to these feet yet." He kept making that kind of odd, off-hand remark.

I stared at him from my interrogation spot astride a folding chair. He arched a brown brow over his half-Vietnamese eyes. The mountain-man part of him drawled, "You think I'm a lard-ass, don't you? That my feet wouldn't hurt if I lost fifty pounds."

"Seventy," I said.

"Now see here, I'm fixing this mess for you. Calling you the 'poor little innocent crazy girl' who was coerced by Lindholm. Putting a smack-down on what happened here. Tweaking the forensics. Who shot who, and why. You're gonna need me on your side, girl. Not just for this mess but all the other messes you'll get into *next*. So don't you disrespect me. Not much, anyway. I won't hear it, you hear?"

"Why are you covering for me? What do you want?"

"I just want peace and quiet in my city. And a membership at that gym Mr. Fusion left you and that little pink-haired girl. I plan to work out. Get in shape. I don't like being kicked in the face by girls on their first day of kickboxing class. It's embarrassing. Don't kick me in the chops again, White Lightning. All right?"

I stood slowly. Gigi, who'd been hiding in the bathroom

pretending I was being interrogated alone, popped out. Beaumont arched a brow at her. "I knew you were in there. I can always smell that cinnamon potion you wear. I love it, you know."

Gigi and I traded a look then stared at him tearfully. "Dante?" Gigi whispered.

"Daddy?" I asked.

Our soul-father smiled.

*

I buried Lindholm's body in a suburban Asheville cemetery with the blue mist of distant mountains as guardians and a soaring sky for a cathedral. I buried his body gently, with honor. We had a lot of history, me and that chunk of earthly flesh. Part of Ian was imprinted on him, if nothing but a shadow of the spirit. That body died to protect me.

I'm not fond of modern cemeteries, the art museum angel said pensively, hovering beside me. *No headstones. They seem so lifeless.*

Since she was based on a famous piece of cemetery statuary, maybe she had a bone to pick with the new-fangled ways. She went silent as I wiped my swollen eyes. I knelt by the plain, sodded rectangle, pulled back a small chunk of grass, and dropped a handful of paper ashes underneath.

A note from me to Lindholm's body. To the aspect of that body I'd come to love. Personal.

"Done," I said gruffly, and got to my feet. I looked up at the angel. Her color cycled from a basic bronze to the light pastels I'd given her in my sketches. I'd offered to paint her in lavender and gold sometime. She said she'd like that.

Look, she said, and pointed. *You have visitors.*

I swiveled worried eyes across a mown green lawn dotted with grave plaques and flower vases. What I saw nearly made my knees shake.

Greg Lindholm. He stood there, only a couple dozen feet from me. Vivid. Real as real. Gray eyes, clean-shaven, in a Minnesota Vikings football jersey, khakis, and running shoes. And beside him stood his pleasant-looking wife, and between her and him, holding each of their hands, was their cute little boy.

"I want you to meet my wife and son," Greg Lindholm said. "I want you to know I didn't hurt them. I never abused my wife. They died in the highway accident, just like you read on the Internet. I'm sorry I let the demon talk me out of my body. I just wanted to be with my wife and son again. I'm sorry he used my body to hurt you."

I took a few seconds to wrap my mind around all that. What could I say in front of his wife? That Ian had redeemed Lindholm's body and then some? The angel leaned close. *A simple 'Thank you' will do,* she whispered.

"I'm glad to meet you," I told Lindholm sincerely. "Do you like where I buried your corpse?"

Shit. I had no social skills.

Greg Lindholm smiled and shrugged. "Sure. It's just a body. I don't miss it. Well, I'd better say goodbye now. My family and I have a new life to start."

As he, his wife and son began to fade, I called out, "Where are you going? Any idea?"

The wife smiled. "Florida. I'm tired of Minnesota. Too much snow and ice on the highways."

And then they were gone.

A little shaken, I looked up at the angel. "I'm glad to find out he's a nice guy." She nodded. I studied Lindholm's grave with a new sense of peace. "I hope Ian knows about this."

My left wrist began to feel warm. The sensation was startling, not painful, but weird. A band of heat stretched around my wrist, following the symbols tattooed there, the mysterious line of hieroglyphs from the Talking Rock. They glowed. I hyperventilated a little, holding my arm out from me as if it might catch fire and take the rest of me up in flames with it.

Golden light gushed from the tattoo. I shielded my eyes. The glow vanished, my arm cooled to normal, and I stared at my wrist.

The old tattoo was gone. In its place was the new line of symbols. I felt dizzy. "Does this mean I've graduated from

'Gandalf the Grey' to 'Gandalf the White?'"

Yes, the angel said, putting a bronze hand on my shoulder. *Congratulations, Soul Catcher.*

*

Gigi and I ran Dante's nightclub together, and we moved into the gallery to be near Sarah and Charles. A family. Beaumont visited a lot, though he always called it official business. He was losing weight, shaping up. He took kickboxing classes at the gym.

Gigi and I renovated the attic, turning it into a multi-room apartment for us to share. We hung the big scrying mirror on a wall but saw nothing in it but ourselves. Dolly and Amabeth had moved on. A good sign, I thought. Sarah, Gigi and Charles felt they were at peace now. Maybe *all* our past selves had scored a big win when Ian and I offed Pig Face.

I hoped. At least for now.

I dreamed of Ian, ordinary dreams, nothing that hinted he was really there, psychically touching me with his lips and hands and cock. I was disappointed in the lack of contact. I mourned for him. I missed him. I was pissed at him. I talked to him out loud all the time, but heard nothing in response. Sarah told me souls can't always stay in touch. It's not like they have a wireless connection.

"His soul is interviewing other souls who want to vacate their living bodies' premises," she said casually, like it was no big deal, as we hung new landscapes of mine in the gallery. "It takes time. I'm sure he wants to pick a body that you'll be really hot for."

"One that's breathing and has all its teeth will do," I grunted. A lie. I was nervous about the body issue. I'm a one-body kind of woman.

I stayed busy, painting. My mountain scenes were more mysterious than ever. There were places near the Talking Rock I'd never seen except in visions. I think the rock, that being of white light, was sending me messages. More to do, more to learn, more to overcome. See Rock City.

Not until I get Ian back, I told Her Rockness. I was dealing, bartering. *No Ian backee, no soul catchee.*

But I lied.

I chewed my Spam-on-healthy-whole-grain-bread as I watched a little blonde boy sidle up to the chain link gate on a day care's playground in west Asheville. The gate wasn't locked right. Across the street was an open manhole cover.

The child fiddled with the gate's fastener. He flipped it open. In five minutes the kids would come outside to play. One or two would find the unlocked gate, and beyond it, when they fell into the manhole, they'd find the city sewer waiting for them—and worse—in the stinking darkness below ground.

I tossed the crusts of my sandwich bread to the pigeons, then ambled over to blondie, waiting with my hands in the front pockets of my low-rider camos. It was a hot August day. The little boy looked up at me, startled, realized what I was, and froze.

His sweaty blonde hair became a mat of putrid coils. The sweet eyes turned red. The blushing face and pink mouth grew fur and extra nose holes.

Just visiting the children," the bane grunted. "Planning to play hide and seek. No harm intended."

I bent down to him. "Peek a fucking boo," I said.

He exploded.

All in a day's work, now.

*

As autumn arrived I grew so lonely for Ian I couldn't be still. I roamed the streets constantly. I spent my time banishing banes and meeting more of the local boons—who treated me like a swell new sheriff who'd come to clean up the territory. I stepped inside many dark, uncertain doors to introduce myself to curious pogs.

Word spread. I was the real deal. A Soul Catcher beyond Fearless.

Unforgiving.

The city resonated with souls of many kinds, some living inside flesh, some inside steel, wood, rock or thin air, greedy for sex, power, money, fame; good and bad, fighting for dominance of our world.

Me? And Ian? We would always be stationed at the edge of this spiritual frontier, trying to keep the peace. Our legend was now established.

We knew the enemy. And the enemy knew us.

Bring it on, hellions.

*

Ian had been gone for over five months now. I ached for his touch, his voice. October clouded the air with frost and early sunsets. Something began to whisper to me. Portents, energies, time to get back in the groove, demons might start prowling. "They're like tomcats," Charles told me. "Always looking to stake their claim on unguarded territory."

Great. Pig Face wasn't around to spray the furniture anymore, so some new demon would confiscate his digs. I woke up one chilly morning not in my big attic bedroom but in a corner of the gallery where I painted. I sat up in the dawn light, aching from hours spent passed out on the floor, smeared with paint.

"Oh, fuck, oh, no," I whispered, afraid to raise my eyes to the big canvas propped across from me.

No, no, it's all right, Sheba whispered. She often snuggled with me, helping me relax.

Yes, all is well, Tabitha and Nahjee agreed.

Mary and Ian looked down at me. Together. They stood outside their cabin at Talking Rock, his arms around her from behind, her hands and his on her big, pregnant belly. They smiled at me.

Together. They had each other again, and they had a baby on the way. They'd have their version of a life now, a parallel family. I probably wouldn't see them again. We all have our own cake-layers of lives to lead.

Mary had written me a message on the floor, in sweet blue acrylic.

It's time for you and your Ian to start over again, Livia.

*

It was a dark and stormy November day. I sat in the gallery

window seat, knotting and unknotting my hands, watching gusts of wind maul the trees along the French Broad. The last of the red and gold autumn leaves burst out of the treetops like confetti.

Something big was in the air.

When the gallery's portable phone rang I stared at it with a racing heart and a bone-dry mouth. I'd propped it on the window sill beside me. Nahjee and Tabitha wiggled happily against my throat. *Answer,* they chimed. *Answer it!*

Hand shaking, I picked up the receiver and punched the button. I put the phone to my ear. "It took you five months to find a new body? Dante nabbed Detective Beaumont's flabby ass in less than three days."

Ian laughed, the melody long, deep and happy.

His voice, though channeled through a new throat, melted me as always. His attitude was the same. That and the blue eyes would always be with him. His laugh drugged me. I felt high. I shut my eyes. I inhaled him. I got off on him. When he finished laughing I said hoarsely, "Laugh some more. Just a little to the right. And faster."

"I best not, love. It looks a wee bit strange, considering the circumstances."

I climbed off the window seat. "What circumstances?"

"I'm in prison, love."

"Where?"

"They tell me this is the city of Raleigh. Not too far a drive from you, or so I ken."

"What's your name?"

"Alvarez. John." He said as if reading it off a patch on his prison coveralls. "I'm a fine-looking criminal,, if I do say so myself. This Alvarez, he killed some people, they say. You know, love, the soul can no' be depended on to pick what the spirit tells it to pick, but it looks like my soul did a right good job of finding you a big-cocked—"

"He's a *murderer?*"

"Well, ay. But he's not *all* bad. He's got some tattoos I think you'll like—"

"Ian, what's the name of the prison?"

"Ock. 'Tis 'Central.' Central Prison, I think."

My blood chilled. "Ian, that's where the state of North Carolina keeps men who are on death row."

Silence. Then, with a certain grim embarrassment, "Ay."

"Are *you* on Death Row?"

"Ay. But 'tis not all that bad a place—"

"Is your case on appeal? You're not close to an execution date are you? *Are you?*"

Silence. Then, "How would you be defining 'close?'"

"*Ian.*"

"We've got a full five days to figure this out, love. No problem, right?"

Silence. Mine, this time. He was on death row. He had five days to live. Five days for me to spring a convicted killer out of the state pen. And then what?

It's just another life to lead, Nahjee whispered. Tabitha giggled.

Sheba added, *Go and see where it takes your souls this time.*

True. He was alive. Again. Nothing else mattered.

"I'm leaving right now for Raleigh," I said. "I love you. No problem, nope."

He whooped. "Is this Livia Belane Thornton I'm speaking with? Or have the boons taken her and put a kind-hearted woman in her place?"

I heard the joy in his voice. The relief. The devotion.

I was already heading for the door, reaching for my tote bag, grabbing a coat. "Oh, don't get cocky. I'm going to kick your *arse* as soon as I get there."

"Now *that*," he said cheerfully—my old man in a new body, the love of my many lives, the man I would die to keep, and who had died to keep me, repeatedly—"is a woman worth coming back to life for."

"See you soon," I promised.

"Always," he answered.

I smiled as I headed his way.

THE END

Coming in 2010

Soul Hunter
Book 2, The Outsider Series

Livia finds herself struggling to adjust to another new incarnation of Ian, this one doomed to be executed for heinous crimes. At the same time, she and Ian must battle the rising threat of a powerful new demon *and* the arrival of a Soul Hunter who has competed with Ian for Livia's love over many centuries.

Also From Bell Bridge Books
Once Bitten
Kalayna Price
Book One, The Haven Series
Trade Paperback
Available at all online booksellers and bookstores everywhere
Kindle Edition at Fictionwise.com
A top ten ebook bestseller!

"Urban fantasy readers who enjoy the works of Kelly Armstrong and V.K. Forrest will have a great time reading this exhilarating story."
-- Amazon.com Top Reviewer Harriet Klausner

Dead cats don't cry. Kita Nekai finds that out the hard way. For the past five years, Kita, a shapeshifter, has faded into the background of the human world, but when a rogue shifter begins littering the city of Haven with bodies, Kita becomes a suspect. Hunters are after her. She barely avoids being plucked off the street, and owes the near miss to the fact her second form is a five pound kitten—an unexpected size considering she's descended from lions and tigers. As the night wears on and she is unable to skip town, her luck runs out and she is forced into a confrontation she can't win. Rescue arrives in the form of vampire Nathanial Deaton, and Kita soon wishes it hadn't.

Nathanial accidentally turns her into a vampire like himself, robbing her of the ability to shape-shift. Kita thinks her life has hit rock-bottom, but then a vigilante underworld magistrate accuses her of creating and setting loose the murderous rogue who is tormenting the city. To avoid an instant death sentence and to clear her name, Kita and Nathanial agree to hunt down and deliver the rogue.

Excerpt

In the last ten minutes I'd gone from miserable to totally
screwed.

An hour ago I'd thought a city named Haven would be
good luck. Now I wondered who it was supposed to be a
haven for—polar bears and penguins? Next time I snuck
aboard a train, I would remember to check whether it was
headed north or south. The snow-laden streets were the
miserable bit; "screwed" began two blocks back when I picked
up the scent of something never meant to exist in the human
world. Well, a something other than me.

A woman cut a beeline through my path, her attention on a
curbing taxi. I stopped, the man behind me didn't. He
shouldered by with a grunt, his briefcase slamming into my
thigh. I scowled after him but he didn't look back, let alone
apologize.

I hated crowds. Any one of the bundled-up people
trudging down the street could be hunting me. Of course, that
same anonymity protected me. Shivering inside my over-large
coat, I resisted the urge to glance over my shoulder as I
matched pace with the pedestrian traffic. Remaining
inconspicuous was key.

A "do not walk" sign flashed, and the crowd stopped on
the corner of 5th and Harden. Horns blared and drivers
shouted, but despite the green light, there wasn't much room
for the cars to move. Some of the more impatient foot traffic
wove through the vehicles, earning a one-fingered wave from a
cabbie as another car slid into the space that opened in front of
him. I debated crossing but decided keeping a low profile
among the suits on the corner was safer. Shifting my weight
from foot to foot, I held my breath as a city bus covered us in
a dirty cloud of exhaust.

A hand landed on my shoulder.

"Kita Nekai," a deep voice whispered. "Come with me."

I froze, unable to turn for fear any movement would betray me into running. *Breathe.* I needed to breathe, an impossible task around the lump in my throat. My first gasp of air brought the hunter's scent to me, and the skin along my spine prickled in a response more primal than fear. *Damn Wolf.* The blood rushing through my ears drowned out the street sounds so the crowd moved silently, in slow-motion.

The fingers digging into my shoulder tightened, and my eyes darted to them. The manicured nails and white cuff peeking out under his brown coat sleeve marked the hunter as a suit. He'd blend in nicely with this crowd.

"Let go of me." I didn't bother whispering, and the woman beside me coughed as she glanced at us.

A half turn put me eye level with the hunter's red silk tie. I grabbed his wrist, a weak illusion that I was the one doing the restraining, and cleared my throat.

"Thief! Pickpocket! He stole my purse!"

People turned, their eyes taking in the hunter's pinstriped suit and my Salvation Army duster. The suits closest to us shuffled further away, casting leery glances from the corners of their eyes. But they watched. They all watched us, and the hunter couldn't just drag me off the street with so many human witnesses. I saw that realization burn across his amber eyes.

The light changed, and the crowd surged forward, filling the small gap that had opened when I created my scene. The hunter clung to my shoulder, but the push of bodies dislodged his hand, and I let myself be carried away. The businessmen in tailored suits and women in pumps towered over me. I never thought I'd be grateful for being short, but with any luck, that would hid me from the hunter's view—if only I could cover my scent that easily.

The crowd flowed down a set of cement stairs to the subway. The voices of hundreds of commuters bounced off the underground walls, a symphony of impatience accented by flickering florescent tubes. As they pushed into lines in front of the turnstiles, I realized the flaw in this plan: money, or really, my lack thereof.

Okay, no time to panic.

A weathered sign advertising public restrooms hung on my side of the turnstile and I hurried through the door. The hunter wasn't likely polite enough to obey the little girls sign, but I was willing to bet the line of women waiting inside would give him pause.

I bypassed the line, ducking inside the first open stall and locking the thin door against the angry murmurs of protest. The cramped space boasted dingy walls covered in scrawled insults and just enough room to stand in front of a rust-rimmed toilet. *What a lovely hiding place.* The need to pace itched my heels, and I rocked back and forth on my toes, hugging my arms around my chest.

Someone pounded on my door.

"Stall's taken."

"Hurry up," an agitated, but clearly female, voice said.

I ignored her. There were two other stalls she could use.

I rocked on my heels again. I needed a plan. The bladder-heavy humans aside, if I tried to wait-out the hunter, the after-work crowd would thin, and I needed human observers to protect me. The bathroom had only one door, and if the hunter saw me enter, all he had to do was watch for me to exit. Of course, if I could slip out without him recognizing me...

How much did he know about me? He knew my name and clan, but did he know anything else? It was a chance I had to take.

Balancing on the toilet seat, I tucked my knees to my chest so I wasn't visible under the stall walls. Around me, agitated voices complained about everything from the wait to the grey weather. I closed my eyes and tuned them out. I needed to center myself. Mentally I stroked the coiled energy inside me. It boiled. Spread. I anticipated the pain but still drew a ragged breath as the energy burst to the surface.

A sharp sting shot down my back, and the skin split open. My clothes vanished. A whimper trembled in my throat and I choked it back, but it escaped as my skin slipped off and reversed itself. My joints popped loudly as they reformed.

Someone banged on my door again. Could they hear the fleshy sound of my muscles and organs rearranging? I hoped they were just impatient. Then I passed into the seconds of the change in which I had no awareness of my surroundings.

My skin sealed around my body again, and the dingy stall snapped back into focus. My right foot slipped, and I fell up to my hips into the toilet bowl. Hissing, I scrambled over the seat and landed with a wet plop on the tiled floor.

Great, now I resembled a half drowned rat.

Twitching my tail, I shook my back legs and tried to dislodge as much of the water as possible. I only accomplished further soaking the gritty tile. My back paw slipped, leaving grey streaks in its wake across the brown tile.

Disgusting.

I craned my neck, then hesitated. Did I really want to give my fur a quick bath? That was toilet water. It was better for it to be on my fur than my tongue, right? I struggled with that thought a moment, my instincts demanding the offensive substance be removed.

"Anybody in there?" Someone shook the stall door.

My attention snapped back to more important matters— time was of the essence, a bath would have to wait. I was taking a risk by shapeshifting into my second form. If the hunter found me, I wouldn't be able to defend myself, and no one would question him chasing down a cat. But, I had to get out of this subway station.

A child pointed as I crawled under the bathroom stall.

"Look Mommy, a calico!"

I sauntered closer to the girl, staying just out of reach— children had the tendency to pull tails.

"Stay away from it," her mother said, jerking the child back. "It might be rabid."

My lips curled to hiss at the insult, but I curbed the desire. Hostility wouldn't get me anywhere.

Purring, I wound around the legs of the next lady in line. She pressed a tissue to her nose and backed away. Great.

Who was my most likely ticket out? My gaze landed on a woman washing her hands. She'd been shopping and several large department store bags stood staunchly at her feet. Slinking over, I dove into a fancy white bag and curled up beside a hat box.

The sink turned off, and I repositioned myself as she claimed her belongings and bustled out of the bathroom. The bag swung in her grip, propelling me into something hard. The turnstile was a nightmare as she pushed through it, and one of the packages squeezed all the air out of me. I thought the worst must be over as the bags swung free again, but the swaying made my stomach threaten to rebel.

No, I won't be sick. I refuse to.

I got sick all over her hatbox.

Shaking, I eased away from the box. The swish of the train doors opening initiated another barrage of attacks as people pushed their way into the car. The train lurched into motion, but the movement of the bag settled.

I peeked out, and found myself at eye-level with a startled brunette. She screamed, dumping the contents of her lap to the floor. I guess the cat was out of the bag—well, not yet, but I needed to be. Dashing through a forest of legs, I hid under the seat of a man in mud-caked construction boots.

From the limited shelter, I sniffed the recycled train-car air. Not a hint of the hunter's scent.

Thank the moon.

In the past five years I'd caught a hunter's scent maybe half a dozen times. Most cities had at least one stationed somewhere in the social structure to watch for rogues and strays, but I'd never before had any reason to believe they were hunting me specifically. They obviously were now.

Closing my eyes, I mentally touched the tight coil inside me. It would be awhile before I could return to human form. Well, chances were good that the station where I ended up would be far from the hunter. Tucking my tail around my body, I resigned myself to a long ride.

More Fantasy From Leigh Bridger
Writing as Deborah Smith

Alice At Heart
Deborah Smith
Trade Paperback 14.95
www.bellebooks.com
Order at Amazon.com or wherever books are sold
Ebook at Fictionwise.com
Audiobook read by the author
at Audible.com, iTunes, Amazon.com

Get ready for a new take on mermaid mythology. In Alice At Heart, modern, southern-belle mermaids and their mermen lead glamorous lives on the Georgia coast. The legendary Bonavendier sisters discover their long-lost half-sister, Alice, languishing far from the ocean. They lure her to their island and transform her into a confident mer diva.

Excerpt

1

This morning I stood naked beside the icy waters of Lake Riley, high in the Appalachians of north Georgia, above the fall line where the tame Atlanta winters end and the freezing wild mountain winters begin. A mile away, in my dead mother's hometown, Riley, people were just breaking the ice on their gravel roads and barnyards and church lots and sidewalks, stomping the mountain bedrock before little stores with mom-and-pop names, most of which belong to heavy-footed Rileys. But there I was, alone as always, Odd Alice, the daughter of a reckless young mother and an unknown father who passed along some very strange traits. I had slipped out to the lake from my secluded cabin for my morning swim, stripping off my dowdy denim, doing the impossible.

It is February, with a high of about twenty-five degrees, and the lake has an apron of ice like the white iris on a dark eye, narrowing my peculiar view of the deep world beneath. Not that that scares me. The water is the only element in my life I never fear. I stood there in the cold dawn as usual, not even shivering.

As I stretched and filled my body with frigid air, I looked out over the icy mountain world and heard a thin trickle of sound stroking the frosty branches of tall fir trees so far around a bend in the lake my ears shouldn't be able to recognize it if I were like anyone else. The sound was a child screaming. And then I heard a splash.

I may be a freak or a monster—some unnatural quirk of nature too odd for normal people to accept or for anyone to love— but I couldn't let a child drown just to keep my secrets. So there I went, into the cold, safe water, deep into the heart of the lake, faster than anyone imagines a person can swim, fluting the currents with the iridescent webbing between my bare toes, able to go farther, deeper, quicker, and for much, much longer in that netherworld than any human being possibly can.

We are all bodies of water, guarding the mystery of our depths, but some of us have more to guard than others. I've never known quite who I am, but worse than that, I've never known quite *what* I am.

And after today, I won't be the only person asking that question.

*

Griffin Randolph fought panic in deep water. In the vast, dark ocean off the coast of a Spanish fishing village, he touched one hand to a small tattoo on his left forearm, where a naked woman held a dolphin in her arms. *Now I'll find out which one owns my soul.*

As a scuba tank hissed its last minutes of oxygen into his lungs, he once again aimed a cutting torch at the shelving that had collapsed around the legs of his nervous diver, an Italian nicknamed Riz. Griffin and the diver were deep inside the cavernous hold of a sunken American cargo ship named the *Excalibur*. During World War II, the *Excalibur* had ferried ammunition to allied warships off the coast of North Africa until a German submarine torpedoed it. Alongside Griffin and the trapped diver were stacked hundreds of gunnery shells, each as thick as a man's forearm, all nearly a half-century old, threatening to tumble to the bottom of the ship's hull.

No problemo, Griffin's head diver, Enrique, had proclaimed when they first surveyed the ammunition. Old and wet. *Not going to cause us any trouble*. Griffin had agreed until he surveyed the dive on this last day and the storage shelving collapsed on Riz. As the crew worked methodically to free him, Griffin discreetly picked up one of the precariously balanced shells.

The old missile spoke to him, just as he feared it would.

Death.

The sensation—which he often felt in the water, but never revealed to anyone— was like hearing a silent song, or *feeling* a song, the vibrations of sound waves or the tingle of static electricity, only multiplied and softened. In every instance where some object spoke to him, Griffin felt an almost orgasmic shiver, the stroking of an unseen and dangerous hand. Along with that sensation always came knowledge. And this time that knowledge made Griffin's blood freeze.

This shell, or one of its brethren, would kill them all.

Riz's dazed eyes begged him to hurry. The rest of Griffin's six-man team huddled on the surface aboard the deck of the *Sea She*, Griffin's massive boat, whose high-tech, state-of-the-art computers and dredges and sonar and satellite tracking systems had helped locate some of the world's most famous undersea treasure wrecks. *Absolutely goddamned worthless for saving a man's life*, Griffin admitted.

He strained to see through the fierce light spewing from his cutting torch in the dark Mediterranean water. The torch finally burned through a thick steel cable, and he began prying the tangled shelving apart with hands too large and brutal for the bourbon-and-magnolias Southern aristocracy that had birthed him amid the wealth of coastal Georgia thirty-nine years earlier.

Riz kicked and struggled. Griffin's muscles burned as he strained to separate the shelving, his gaze always going back to the shells, hundreds of them, ready to fall. All it would take was the right one, just one. Finally, he eased Riz free. The diver's face relaxed into smiling eyes. Griffin squeezed his shoulder, tugged on the guideline attached to a harness, and instantly Riz began to fly upwards through the water, pulled by a powerful electric wench. The shelving shuddered and gave a soft, wrenching groan. A half-century after men had died inside its steel sanctuary, the *Excalibur* would close like a flower over what remained.

Griffin eased out of the tomblike hull, *feeling* the ship's sinister memories, the hum of its ghosts inside him, the hum of his own ghosts, too. The *Excalibur* was just waiting for him to move. No, it wasn't the ship waiting. It was the ocean. Always waiting for him to make one *wrong* move.

Test me, Griffin told the invisible forces. He surged upward, exiting the hull with a speed and grace that always astonished people when they saw him swim, even when he was hampered by scuba gear. He shrugged off his tank, spit out the mouthpiece, then ripped the mask from his eyes. He propelled himself toward the light, dozens of feet above him.

In the depths of the *Excalibur*, one shell tumbled from the shelving. It pirouetted downward through the dark water, almost beautiful in its heavy grace. It struck the hull's bottom with a muted clang, its voice the last ringing of any bell for the lost ship.

And it exploded.

The world erupted in billowing, churning chaos. Griffin felt a giant hand slap him from below, then sweep around him, squeezing him between invisible forces. The ocean, which had always been a living monster to him, pressed him in its jaws. Pain shot through his body; his eardrums ruptured. His wet suit tore and then his skin as fragments of the *Excalibur*'s hull sliced him. The explosive concussion slammed into his brain. He went limp and floated, filling the water with his blood.

He opened his eyes, dreaming of death.

You have life inside you that you've never used. Breathe. A voice. Feminine, quiet, strong. She hummed a rhythmic song to him, a stunning vibration of emotion that made the deadly shell pale in comparison.

Griffin struggled. *Can't. No one can. Can't breathe.*

You can. Try.

He fed on her passion and suddenly his lungs expanded, he expelled the water from his throat, and somehow, life bloomed into blood-red oxygen inside him. The mystery, the knowledge of a miracle, increased with the darkening of his brain, softened only by the stranger's unbelievable voice.

Who are you?

Just Alice.

She was gone. He made himself remember, as darkness surrounded him fully, that he was breathing because of an extraordinary illusion named Alice, singing to him beneath the bloody water.

*

I've never had a vision before and never wanted to. But there he was, vivid in my mind's eye, floating in front of me as if he really existed. He was clothed in a diver's wet suit, torn and bloody. His dark eyes, half-open and dreaming of death, were set in a handsome, determined face. He gagged and fought. I felt his pain, his fear, his confusion. Yet I knew he could live if he wanted to. *You have breath inside you that you've never used*, I sang to him. *Breathe.*

He looked straight at me, and a kind of wonder appeared on his face, infusing him. He understood. *Who are you?*

Just Alice.

And amazingly, he smiled.

I blinked and he was gone. I was alone again in the freezing, black water at the bottom of the Lake Riley dam. Then my hand closed around a little girl's soft arm. By the time I reached her, she had sunk, unconscious, into a grotesque underwater landscape of junked cars and appliances and huge, tickling catfish. The temperature slowed her heart and respiration, making her as quiet as a hibernating animal, prolonging her life, saving her from any serious, permanent effects.

She did not know she was drowning, I think. I carried her to the shallows. Her parents screamed when they saw us. Two local paramedics and several of our county sheriff's deputies began yelling.

At me.

"I found her—" I started nervously, but then they were all over me. The men snatched the child away and threw a blanket around her as I huddled in the lake with my arms crossed over my breasts. Then they dragged me out and covered me, too.

"What the hell were you doing out here, Alice?" yelled one of the deputies, a Riley cousin of mine.

How could I possibly explain? I lay there on the ground, hugging the blanket over me, and said nothing. In the water, I came alive. On land, I tried very hard to be invisible.

At the moment, I wished I were dead.

DEC 23 2009

LaVergne, TN USA
14 October 2009
160808LV00001B/1/P